INDULGE YOURSELF IN THE NOVELS
OF JULIE ANNE LONG

WAYS TO BE WICKED

"4 stars! Readers yearning for a light-hearted, fun,
fast Regency romp with a cast of delightful characters (including a rakish hero) need look no further.
Sit back and enjoy this confection that makes you
laugh and feel good."

—*Romantic Times BOOKclub Magazine*

"Wonderful . . . a great book . . . engaging and keeps
you quickly turning pages."

—TheRomanceReadersConnection.com

"A complex story well worth the read!"

—NovelTalk.com

"Fascinating . . . a fun Regency romance."

—*Midwest Book Review*

more . . .

BEAUTY AND THE SPY

"4 ½ stars! There's enough action, romance, passion, wit, and historical details in Long's latest to have readers sighing with delight."
> —*Romantic Times BOOKclub Magazine*

"A delightful historical tale."
> —*Baryon Magazine*

"Very good."
> —*Aptos Times*

"Lovely historical romance with the perfect blend of mystery . . . kept me engaged from the beginning . . . Ms. Long has created an excellent blend of mystery and romance that's perfect reading."
> —FreshFiction.com

TO LOVE A THIEF

more . . .

"Compelling and highly entertaining . . . *To Love a Thief* is extremely well written, fast-paced, and entirely enjoyable."

—RoadtoRomance.com

"Lily is a wonderful heroine, and *To Love a Thief* is a fun read."

—Bookloons.com

"An excellent historical novel . . . the relationship between Lily and Gideon is the very substance of every young woman's romantic dreams."

—RomanceJunkies.com

THE RUNAWAY DUKE

"A delightful debut novel—full of wit, action, passion, and romance."

—Mary Balogh, *New York Times* bestselling author

"Wonderful and charming . . . at the top of my list for best romance of the year . . . It is a delight in every way."

—LikesBooks.com

ALSO BY
JULIE ANNE LONG

Ways to Be Wicked

Beauty and the Spy

To Love a Thief

The Runaway Duke

THE
Secret
TO
Seduction

Julie Anne Long

WARNER
FOREVER

NEW YORK   BOSTON

Copyright © 2007 by Julie Anne Long
All rights reserved. Except as permitted under the U.S. Copyright Act of 1976, no part of this publication may be reproduced, distributed, or transmitted in any form or by any means, or stored in a database or retrieval system, without the prior written permission of the publisher.

Warner Forever is an imprint of Warner Books.

Warner Forever is a trademark of Time Warner Inc. or an affiliate company. Used under license by Hachette Book Group, which is not affiliated with Time Warner Inc.

Cover design by Diane Luger
Book design by Stratford Publishing Services

Warner Forever
Hachette Book Group USA
237 Park Avenue
New York, NY 10169
Visit our Web site at www.HachetteBookGroupUSA.com.

Printed in the United States of America

First Printing: May 2007

10 9 8 7 6 5 4 3 2 1

To the warmest, most wonderful, most enthusiastic readers an author could hope for. I'm outrageously lucky to have you, and I promise to do my utmost to continue writing stories you simply can't put down.

ACKNOWLEDGMENTS

My gratitude to my splendid editor, Melanie Murray; to my remarkable agent, Steve Axelrod; and to the stalwarts who know me *oh* so well but love me anyway, in particular Ken, Karen, Melisa, and Kevin.

THE Secret TO Seduction

CHAPTER ONE

IN THE WINTER of 1820, Sabrina Fairleigh, daughter of the Vicar of Tinbury, discovered that her future happiness rested entirely in the hands of a libertine.

Or, rather, not just *a* libertine.

The Libertine.

This was how the Earl of Rawden signed his poetry, poetry that scandalized, enthralled, and allegedly caused women of all ages and ranks to cast off their dignity and trail him like hounds on the scent of a hare: *The Libertine*. It was the sobriquet by which he was known throughout all of England, and his reputation was in fact such that word of it had managed to waft, like opium-and-incense-scented smoke, all the way to the tiny, tucked-away town of Tinbury, Derbyshire—where the air, incidentally, had never been scented by anything more controversial than roast lamb, or maybe once or twice a cigar, and where life was as sedate, predictable, and pleasing as a minuet. The gentle green hills surrounding the vicarage, not to mention the Vicar of Tinbury himself, seemed to prevent local passions from becoming unduly inflamed. No one in Tinbury seemed in danger of writing sensual poetry.

But neither the gentle hills nor the vicar had been able to prevent the quietly determined Sabrina Fairleigh from forming a—well, "attachment" was the word she carefully used in her own mind, though no such word had been spoken aloud by anyone—to her father's handsome curate of less than a year, Mr. Geoffrey Gillray. It was the fault of the shock of hair that dropped down over Geoffrey's brow: sometimes when her father allowed Geoffrey to give the sermon, he gave his head an absent toss, sending the hair flying rakishly. Sabrina had wanted to brush it away from his eyes for him. She'd never before had such thoughts about a man, and they made her blush.

And one day Geoffrey had looked up to see her watching him. She'd blushed again, of course, for she was certain he could read her thoughts in her eyes.

He'd smiled.

Later, he had invited her for a walk in the spring air. And in fits and starts, amid the smell of warm grass and blooming trees, they'd begun to know each other.

And then, the following day, he'd invited her for another walk.

Little by little, the walks had become a habit between them. Sabrina told him about the miniature of her mother, and her memories of long ago. And after she'd confided to Geoffrey her special dream of being a missionary in a faraway land, such as India or Africa, she'd believed afresh in miracles.

For the handsome curate, professing astonishment, confessed he shared this *very* same dream.

But it was perhaps evidence of the Creator's sense of humor that Geoffrey, the quiet curate, and The Libertine, the Earl of Rawden, were cousins. Geoffrey had confided to Sabrina his hope that his wealthy cousin would help to finance this grand missionary dream, and he would be attending his cousin's house party at La Montagne, the grandest home in all the Midlands, this week, to make his petition.

She didn't doubt that Geoffrey—as she now called him, rather boldly she thought, and never in front of her father—with his lean, elegant face and long, slender body and penetrating, dark eyes, could be related to an earl. He, in fact, could have *been* an earl, she decided, though she hadn't the faintest idea what one looked like, as Tinbury featured only a squire or two, and one was Lady Mary Capstraw's husband, and the other Mary's father.

And now, due to the machinations of her friend Lady Mary Capstraw, who, like all married women, conspired to get every unmarried woman into the state of matrimony, Sabrina sat in a carriage hurtling toward La Montagne.

Geoffrey was going to be very surprised to see her.

It had been Mary's idea. Her husband, Lord Paul Capstraw, had been visiting his uncle in Appleton, a town in the Midlands. La Montagne was situated almost precisely between Tinbury and Paul's uncle. Mary had written to Paul, Paul had written to the Earl of Rawden, and the earl had invited the couple to reunite at La Montagne, from which they would go on to visit more relatives. For Mary was a social creature, seldom at home in Tinbury for more than a fortnight, and she dragged her cheerful husband about on seemingly endless rounds of visits to friends and relatives like the tail on a kite.

Legend had it that Mary's husband had scarcely said a word since he'd been married. Certainly he'd hardly said more than two words to Sabrina ever; he communicated primarily in bows and smiles. Sabrina half suspected that he'd married Mary in order to relieve himself of the need to talk. Mary—golden-haired, blue-eyed Mary, her face round as a moon and always animated—seemed to only stop talking in order to sleep.

But Mary was sleeping now on the carriage seat across from Sabrina, mouth slightly parted, snoring softly.

Mary, Sabrina decided, was cleverer than she had given her credit for, at least when it came to the business of acquiring husbands: for Mary had invited Sabrina along to La Montagne as a companion, as what married woman travels alone? And though Sabrina was accustomed to being the clever one, she felt rather at sea in the business of romance, and was grateful to Mary for a bit of a steer. She'd never been to a house party, but many an engagement had been secured at them, or so Mary assured her.

It was perhaps the most daring thing Sabrina had ever done, this dash to La Montagne, as her father had simply been told she was paying a visit to Mary. It wasn't at all *strictly* a lie, of course. And surely her father would forgive her—that is, if he ever found out—should she secure an engagement to Geoffrey. Sabrina was all but positive that the young curate would offer for her the moment he knew precisely *what* it was he had to offer her.

But the idea of the Earl of Rawden—*The Libertine,* for heaven's sake—with his duels and his mistress and his poetry that caused such a tumult in the hearts of women . . . well, it all sounded so very *impractical.* How dreadfully uncomfortable and inconvenient it must be to be slave to such passions, such untidy emotions. She wondered whether the wear of his life would show on his face, or on his body; surely debauchery would take its toll.

She decided, quite peacefully, that rather than being intimidated or scandalized, she would feel compassion for the earl.

Sabrina peered out the window of the carriage. Mrs. Dewberry, a poor elderly woman confined to her home in Tinbury whom Sabrina visited at least once every week, would have called the early snowfall an omen, and Sabrina was inclined to believe her. Then again, everything—the shapes of clouds, the spots on sows, the calls of birds—had begun to feel like an omen to her now that she was very likely on the brink of marriage and the rest of her life.

But only little patches of snow remained, scattered across the green like abandoned lacy handkerchiefs. The wan early sunlight was gaining in strength, and the bare birch trees crowding the sides of the road shone nearly metallic in it, making Sabrina blink as they flew past in the carriage. She wondered, idly, why trees didn't become woolly in winter, like cats and cattle, but instead dropped all of their leaves and went bare.

She smiled to herself and tucked her chin into her muffler. It was the sort of thought she had grown accustomed to keeping to herself, and it was because of the furrow that ran the width of Vicar Fairleigh's forehead. It had been dug there, no doubt, by decades of pious thoughts and an endless stream of little concerns—his parishioners, his next sermon, how he was going to feed his children—and every time Sabrina said fanciful things, or played a hymn on the pianoforte with an excess of feeling, his eyebrows dove, that furrow became a veritable trench, and his gaze became decidedly wary, as though it were only a matter of time before she sprouted wings like a fairy and flew out the window.

So she'd learned to lock such thoughts away in her mind, much the way she'd locked away her other treasures: the small rock she'd found with the imprint of a leaf, the needle she'd first used when she'd learned to sew, and of course the miniature of her mother, a face so like her own.

She knew that Vicar Fairleigh worried just a little bit more about her, had always been just a little more watchful of her than he was of his other children, two boys much older than she, as though he was prepared for her to do . . . something. She knew not what. Something disquieting, no doubt. Possibly because by the age of thirteen she'd gone and done the unthinkable and become what could only be described as . . . Well, "pretty" was the word everyone in Tinbury used, but they used it gingerly, for it seemed unlikely—unnecessary, really—for a vicar's daughter to be pretty. She was fine-boned and creamy-skinned, with rich dark hair that fell in loose spirals to nearly her waist when she brushed it out at night. And then there were her eyes: large with a hint of a tilt to them, green as spring. In truth, the word "pretty" was very nearly a lie. Where Sabrina Fairleigh was concerned, the word "beautiful" begged consideration.

Certainly, as Sabrina grew older, it became clear that many of the male members of the congregation had ceased pretending to listen to the sermons and were instead admiring the vicar's daughter, and all of this was rather inconvenient for the vicar.

And of course no one in Tinbury was surprised when it became clear the handsome curate had eyes only for

Sabrina. Sabrina rather suspected her poor father wouldn't mind at all seeing her safely married off, happily pursuing work for the poor on some other continent.

She peered out the coach window once more as the horses and carriage decisively took a curve in the drive. Here, suddenly, the trees grew more snugly together, evenly spaced and rigorously groomed and each equally as tall as the next, as though here the owner of the property had decided to show nature precisely who was in charge.

Her heartbeat accelerated. She knew that as the end of their journey approached, very likely, so did the beginning of the rest of her life.

She nudged her friend with the toe of her boot.

Mary opened an eye. "Mmm?"

"Mrs. Dewberry said the squirrels were gathering more nuts this year, and the bark was thicker on the north side of the trees."

Mary opened the other eye and stared at Sabrina blankly.

"Winter," Sabrina explained impatiently. "She said it would be both early and hard this year because of the squirrels and the bark."

Mary stretched. "Oh, the snow has scarcely stuck to the ground," she scoffed cheerfully. "Winter might be early, perhaps, but I daresay this little dusting means nothing at all."

Sabrina said nothing.

Mary sighed. "I know what you're thinking, but it's not an omen, Sabrina. All will go according to our plan. You and Geoffrey are meant for each other. You'll see."

And as she was awake, like a bird, Mary began to chatter.

But moments later, when La Montagne came into view through the carriage windows, even Mary went quiet.

The two of them gaped.

It was less a house than a . . . than a . . . *range*. It dominated the landscape the way she imagined the Alps must. An edifice of tawny stone, easily four times as long as it was tall, row upon row of windows staring down like indifferent, aristocratic eyes. As they drew closer, Sabrina could see that the vast cobblestoned courtyard featured a large marble fountain: the Three Graces seemed to compete with one another to hold up a single urn, from which water would no doubt shoot up during warmer months. One of the Graces was losing a glossy marble breast from her toga. Sabrina quickly averted her eyes from it.

It occurred to her that this was both a magnificent and stunningly . . . *arrogant* house. Who on earth would feel entitled to such a dwelling, or could live here without feeling dwarfed by it?

In silence, Sabrina and Mary allowed themselves to be helped from the carriage by a swarm of footmen, and watched as their trunks were deftly ferried up rows of marble steps into the house.

It was then that Sabrina glanced to the left of the entrance and saw, on the snow-dusted green surrounding the courtyard, a man and woman standing close together. Something about their postures, the tension and intimacy of them, riveted Sabrina's gaze.

The man was very tall, and his greatcoat hung in graceful folds from his shoulders to his ankles—the way it fit him told her this was her first glimpse of truly fine clothing. His hair was dark, straight, gleaming with nearly a blue sheen; his head was lowered as though he was listening intently to whatever the woman was saying. The woman wore a scarlet pelisse, the furred collar of it cradling her delicate chin, and her hair was fair, bright as a coin in the sun. Her shoulders sloped elegantly; her long hands were bare and startlingly white against her pelisse. Sabrina could just make out the woman's voice, low, lilting.

Suddenly the man's head jerked back. He went rigid, stared at the woman. Sabrina's breath suspended. She'd seen a fox look at a vole just like that. Right before it seized it in its jaws.

The man abruptly pivoted and strode away from the woman in long angry strides.

The woman's laughter followed him, a thin silvery sound. Merry as sleigh bells.

Good heavens!

She wondered what on earth the woman had said to cause such a pronounced reaction from such a very large man. Such passions. How uncomfortable it must be to be at the mercy of them.

And with that thought, somehow she knew: this man was the earl.

Sabrina tried to force her interest and trepidation back into the clothes of compassion, but they wriggled back out again. She couldn't help but take a tiny involuntary step back toward the carriage, for the man's anger came with him as he approached the fountain.

And then he seemed to truly notice them, and immediately his posture changed as though he'd thrown off a cloak. All was welcome, ease, grace, smiles.

And when he finally stood over them, and Sabrina looked up into his face, her lungs ceased to draw in air.

This was the only sort of man who could possibly suit this house.

Much more imposing from a mere few feet away, he was lean but broad-shouldered, more than a head taller than Sabrina, and she wasn't a tiny person. There was a hint of Geoffrey in the deep-set eyes, but his jaw was angular, his cheekbones cut decisively higher, the planes and hollows of his face starkly, in fact rather uncompromisingly, defined. And his eyes were startling: blue, pale, crystalline. Brilliant with light. His brows, severe dark slashes over them.

The Libertine.

Absurdly, she thought: *Debauchery suits him.*

Somehow she'd expected a softer man, with Byronic curls and haunted eyes and perhaps an air of dissipation.

"Welcome to my home. I am Lord Rawden."

And his voice: low and elegant, resonant as a cello. Not raw from too many cigars or too much drink.

Mary and Sabrina curtsied as he bowed low.

But beneath the grace, Sabrina could sense the remnants of his anger, and something else, too. Her eyes darted toward where the woman had been standing; she saw, in the distance, the scarlet pelisse retreating deeper into the front garden.

And she knew what she'd sensed. Whatever the woman had said to him had been intended to cut, and Sabrina suspected it had.

And as Sabrina watched him stride over to issue instructions to the housekeeper who had come to stand on the stairs leading up to the house, compassion was the least of a crowd of unfamiliar things, many of them uncomfortable, this man had prodded up in her in an instant.

She sensed it was all second nature, the grace and the manners, no more effort for him than breathing; she also sensed that he had taken her in with a glance of those fiercely intelligent eyes, summed her up, silently dismissed her, and had moved on to other far more interesting things in his mind.

She decided then and there that the Earl of Rawden would most definitely take note of her before this house party was over.

CHAPTER TWO

Granted, as scandals went, it had been a particularly bad one—beginning with champagne, progressing to being prodded from the nude, fragrant embrace of a countess by her livid husband, and culminating in a duel—but for Rhys Gillray, the Earl of Rawden, it really ranked no worse than any of the other scandals gleefully attached to his name over the past few years. And the scandal had done nothing to actually aggravate his reputation. After all, when one poured more whiskey into a glass of whiskey, the whiskey didn't become more potent. The glass only became more full.

Then again, if one *ceaselessly* poured whiskey into the glass, it would inevitably spill over and create a bit of a mess.

With the addition of this latest scandal, angry husbands and infatuated women had seemed everywhere underfoot in London, which had made going about the usual business of amusing himself more awkward than he preferred.

In short, he found himself at last confronted with a bit of a mess.

Serendipitously, shortly after the duel—during which nothing but pride had been wounded, as both men were crack shots but tacitly interested in continuing to live—word had reached him that La Montagne was finally, after so many years, officially his again. Restored to the Rawden title.

La Montagne. The home's name amused the poet in him. He'd planned and executed its acquisition the way a mountaineer planned an expedition. It represented the pinnacle of his dreams. It was as vast as a bloody mountain.

And so forth.

On the whole, Rhys preferred his metaphors more subtle. His own were said to seep into a reader's bloodstream like a fine wine: stealthy, intoxicating, perhaps even a bit dangerous. Seduction on the printed page.

He understands women, women crooned.

What bloody nonsense. He understood *seduction.* The two were not necessarily the same.

Regardless, he would ensure that La Montagne never again left Rawden hands. And if at the cornerstone of his fortune and his struggle to regain the Rawden lands were blood and a secret more than a decade old, Rhys told himself that everything came with a price. He'd made a difficult choice years ago to regain all he had, and some days he could convince himself that life was like war: bitter, desperate choices were often made in the name of survival, and some inevitably survived at the expense of others.

Other days it haunted him, cost him sleep, until he needed to do something, anything, to drown out the voice of it. But this, he decided, was the price. And it was a price he could endure, for there was nothing to be done about it now.

In fact, a trial took place in London as he stood in his grand home. And the trial might have worried him more had he not known that his secret was buried as deeply as La Montagne's ancient cornerstone. He paid as little attention to it as possible, the way one might avoid staring a wild animal in the eye.

Still, he would not be displeased when it was over.

He'd disguised his retreat from London as a house party by inviting Wyndham, an artist so cheerfully debauched that he might just consider a country house party a novelty. Lady Mary and her friend came by virtue of an old school chum, Lord Paul Capstraw. And his cousin Geoffrey had sent a note round begging an audience, and Rhys expected him with a certain impatience and wry resignation.

But in a regrettable fit of madness, he'd also invited Sophia Licari.

Bloody Sophia.

So he hadn't precisely fled the *ton*. But in truth, he thought, rather darkly amused, he could not find fault with the timing of the news. Because there were other reasons he'd decided to leave London.

A few nights earlier, as he'd marked off the paces of the duel, and stood to fire at the other earl he'd cuckolded, it occurred to him even then—even *then,* as he pointed a pistol at a man, and the other man pointed a pistol at him—that he was bored. That his pulse had scarcely increased, that the outcome scarcely interested him.

This succeeded in unnerving him, and it took a very good deal to unnerve Rhys Gillray.

The other reason was that he hadn't been able to write a word in weeks. And this unnerved him, too.

The inside of the house was just as vast and echoey as the outside; the sound of their footsteps bounced from the smooth marble floors and all those other hard, gleaming surfaces up to the endless ceiling as Sabrina and Mary were led into it and ushered up a flight of marble stairs to their rooms. On the way they passed rooms that had no specific purpose Sabrina could discern but that were nevertheless stocked with curving, complicated furniture, paintings, and myriad shining things. The sheer size of the rooms exerted an almost dizzying pull; it was like peering from the shore out onto the sea.

Sabrina exchanged a glance with Lady Mary, who inhabited one of the larger homes in Tinbury. The entirety of which could have fit neatly into La Montagne.

Mary's eyes were wide. "Cor!" she mouthed to Sabrina. Louder, she said, "And look, Sabrina! Here's the library! I imagine we will lose you to books while we're here."

Sabrina peered in as they passed, gained an impression of soft darkness, then moved on lest she indeed become lost. For Mary knew her well, and was very likely correct.

They were taken in two separate directions on the third floor, and Sabrina was left to discover her room on her own.

She circled it almost tentatively, like an animal sniffing out new territory. It was snug by the standards of the rest of La Montagne, she suspected. A healthy fire leaped in the hearth, and it had been burning for some time, she surmised, as the room was filled with warmth. Shades of lavender and gray surrounded her—in the carpet—which proved plusher than spring grass and featured fringed ends, and in the chairs and counterpane and curtains, which hung in heavy twilight-colored folds, gleaming dully. Sabrina fingered them; they looked like ball gowns. She began to wonder just how many dresses she could make from one.

And then she playfully wound herself all the way up in one and stepped out to admire herself before the mirror. She turned this way and that.

She did have a best dress packed in her trunk. It was about five years old, but the color was timeless, or so she'd been assured, and tremendously flattering, as it was a sea shade, and made her eyes shine almost as green as new leaves. It was cut low enough to show just the top of her bosom, the sleeves were puffed, and it was in fine enough condition, as she seldom wore it in Tinbury. There was a spot near the hem from a splashed ratafia last Christmas, but one would only notice it if one were perhaps admiring her slippers. She hoped no one intended to examine her slippers, as they were rather older than her dress.

Sabrina smoothed the curtain down in front of her. She decided that she looked well in mauve, too. She smiled at that decision. And then glanced up only to meet the eyes of the housekeeper in the mirror.

She whirled about. "Oh! Mrs. Bailey!"

She blushed and reflexively curtsied, inadvertently using the curtain instead of her skirts, which made her eyes burn with horror. Mortified, she released the curtain, and watched, helplessly, as it spiraled and whipped from around her as though she were a mummy being unwrapped.

It fell back into place against the window with a soft rustle.

Mrs. Bailey watched the curtain fall back into place with no discernible change of expression: no censure, no twinkle of amusement. Sabrina had the sense that she might have been discovered stark naked, sawing away at a cello, and Mrs. Bailey still would not have flinched. Then again, if Mrs. Bailey was employed by The Libertine, and if any of the rumors about him proved to be true, she'd no doubt seen things a good deal more thrilling than a girl in a curtain dress.

"May I bring up some tea and refreshment, Miss Fairleigh? You'll find a basin of water in the corner. Dinner will be served at eight o'clock. The earl will dine with you then."

Meaning, perhaps, that the guests would entertain themselves until he deigned to join them.

"Thank you, Mrs. Bailey. I should like some tea, if it's not too much trouble." And then she nearly bit her lip, because the job of housekeepers such as Mrs. Bailey was to take trouble for guests, and she suspected she'd revealed how callow she truly was.

"I shall bring tea, then, Miss Fairleigh. Will there be anything else?"

Did she dare ask the question?

"Can you tell me whether a Mr. Geoffrey Gillray has arrived?" Sabrina tried not to sound too eager about it.

"He has not yet arrived, Miss Fairleigh, though he is expected today."

Sabrina wondered if she had been indiscreet in asking, but then realized the housekeeper probably cared little about the affairs of a girl she'd never before seen and would likely never see again after this fortnight had passed.

"Thank you, Mrs. Bailey."

Rhys strode back into the house, back into the sitting room where Wyndham was enjoying a cigar and waiting for Rhys to join him for a promised game of billiards.

Wyndham took one look at his face, plucked his cigar from his mouth, and asked, "As usual, I see she's done wonders for your temper. Why in God's name did you invite Sophia?"

Rhys gave him an incredulous, speaking look.

Wyndham smiled slightly. "Besides that."

"Because she'll . . . prevent me from being bored. Because she might sing. If the moon is in the correct phase, that is. If the color of the room suits her."

"If the dinner is to her liking," Wyndham contributed.

"If the temperature is just so," Rhys added.

There was a pause.

"God, why *did* I invite Sophia?" Rhys groaned.

Wyndham laughed.

He'd invited Sophia because she was his talisman against boredom, he supposed, and he had a horror of boredom. Ever since the publication of *The Secret to Seduction*, trembling, fawning women were everywhere he turned. He hadn't lacked for feminine attention before, of course, as he was an earl, and a war hero, and far from ugly. But with that bloody book of poetry, he'd inadvertently robbed himself of the pleasure of conquest.

Apart, that was, from Sophia.

With Sophia Licari . . . well, he was reminded of the time he'd dangled a watch so a cat could chase the dancing reflection of it. The beast would pounce on the spot of light, only to lift its paw in surprise to discover it had caught nothing at all. But when the reflection darted away again, the cat had continued the chase. Dazzled in spite of itself. Chasing just to chase.

He suspected Sophia had no substance, that she was all reflection, a vessel for a glorious voice, but he never could quite put a finger on her charm. It was the wondering that made him come back, that kept him curious enough to play her games. He supposed she had a right to keep from being bored as well. Perhaps experimenting with prodding his temper was *her* way of entertaining herself.

And Sophia was to singing what The Libertine was to poetry. He could forgive her almost anything when she sang.

"And who are the women who have just arrived?" Wyndham wanted to know. He put his boots up on the little table stretched out before the settee. Rhys scowled at him.

Wyndham swung them down again.

"Oh, they scarcely count as women, at least not of the sort that would interest you, Wyndham. Lady Mary, the twittery blonde, is married to Lord Paul Capstraw. Capstraw has been visiting relatives in the Midlands, and he sent a note round asking whether he could meet his wife here, as La Montagne is between his uncle's house and Tinbury. Old school chum, Capstraw. Doesn't seem to mind that I've a dastardly reputation, or perhaps he assumed I'd like nothing to do with his wife. If so, he assumed correctly. And the friend . . . Miss Serena somebody? She's the daughter of a vicar. Or so I'm told."

Rhys turned and stared out the window, wondering if Sophia was still out there somewhere, strolling the grounds. No: it was too cold, and her voice would suffer from it. She would have considered her point made and reentered the house by now.

Why should he care whether Lord Levenham had bought the scarlet pelisse for Sophia? It wasn't the pelisse so much as the way Sophia had slid it into conversation. Rather like sliding a stiletto between his ribs.

His pride was hurt.

At least something hurt.

"Tinbury? Where the devil is that?" Wyndham wanted to know.

"Does it matter?" Rhys said idly. "Come, Wyndham, I'll show you the solarium. It'll be a brilliant place for you to paint. And then we'll head to the billiard room."

The tea was delicious and accompanied by a slice of un-asked-for but entirely welcome lemon seedcake. Sabrina wondered if it was a particularly fine blend of tea, or whether the fact that it had been served in an exquisite little china pot painted all over with blue milkmaids and brought to her by a servant had anything to do with it.

She'd divested herself of her warm wraps, the bonnet and scarf and pelisse, and swabbed her face and the back of her neck and her armpits with the water in the basin, which turned out to be scented with lavender. Feeling considerably fresher, she thought she might try to find Mary.

But she'd neglected to ask for Mary's room when she'd been so brazen as to ask after Geoffrey.

And the hours between now and dinner stretched before her with the dizzying, nearly wasteful luxury of those rooms she'd passed by on the way to this one. As she'd never before been asked to a great house party, she'd never before been presented with expanses of time to fill with frivolity. Her life hadn't been entirely *free* of frivolity. But she was ever busy at the vicarage, visiting the elderly and sick, managing the household budget and planning meals, sewing and mending and cooking and tending the garden, rallying the villagers of Tinbury to donate cast-off clothing to the housebound and poor and drunken. Of the latter, fortunately, there was only one— poor Mr. Shumley, who was convinced he was King George. The villagers generally cheerfully indulged his delusion, bowing when they saw him and inquiring after His Majesty's health. He slept in barns, typically, during the warmer months; in the winter, her father occasionally allowed him to sleep in the vestry.

And once a year a fair was held in honor of the church, and everyone attended. It was great fun. Sabrina was content; it all kept her very busy. There were assemblies and dances, as well. But it wasn't until Geoffrey Gillray had arrived to serve as her father's curate that the assemblies took on a frisson of something else besides gaiety.

She decided to wander downstairs and listen for voices; perhaps other guests would have arrived, and Mary, the most social of butterflies, would have found them by instinct. But at the foot of the stairs just past two sitting rooms, she passed the library.

She couldn't help herself. It drew her in.

Reading was the one activity she wanted to do a great deal more of in Tinbury, but given the other demands upon her time, most of her reading took place just before she fell asleep. Candles were dear, so she confined herself to a strict twenty pages per evening. And while it took her ages to finish reading a story in this fashion, it made the story last longer, too.

The library was large, of course, but altogether more subtle than the other rooms she'd so far seen. The only gold in the room glowed tastefully from the words etched into book spines and from the bowed legs of a little table near the fire. The shelves and furniture were fashioned of dark woods and fabrics; the curtains pouring to the floor were the color of chocolate and corded in silk ropes of black; the carpets were patterned in twined scrolls of brown and black and were, coincidentally, just as soft beneath her feet as the carpet in her bedroom.

She couldn't hear her own footfalls as she entered the room, and for a moment she felt disoriented, as if she'd suddenly become a ghost, and was haunting La Montagne rather than visiting.

Two dark leather chairs with backs like fans and a long settee striped in black and brown faced each other near the fire. The servants seemed determined to keep the entire house warm, and the very idea of this boggled—Sabrina and her father pored over the vicarage budget as though it were a battle plan and the vicarage expenses an enemy to vanquish, and they relished discovering strategies for conquering them. She had a very good idea of how much warming a house this size would cost.

Arrogant house, arrogant man, arrogant budget.

Compassion, she reminded herself. She recalled his anger this morning, and the hurt she'd sensed beneath it. She wondered who the woman was: his mistress?

Good heavens, was she really under the same roof as a *mistress?*

The bookshelves were generously laden with tomes bound in deep somber colors—blue and dark green and brown and burgundy—and organized by subject. Philosophy stretched over one shelf, history another, novels over another. Lady novelists were well represented along with the men. And—

What was this? Poetry?

A prickle of thrill touched the back of her neck. Would his infamous poetry be here? And would she dare to read it, if it was?

Nervously, swiftly, she read the names on the spines: Yeats. Coleridge. Southey. Keats. Chatterton. Wordsworth. Lamb. Brentano. And Byron, of course. Now *there* was a chap who was easily as scandalous as The Libertine, at least in his everyday life, but was rumored to have fled the country to fight in some misguided foreign war. Poets and their wayward temperaments. She'd always half suspected they had clouds for brains. Sabrina shook her head. What a relief it was to not be a poet.

But she was spared from the decision about reading the earl's poetry: it wasn't on the shelf. It seemed an odd omission, but then again, perhaps it was so scandalous it was kept locked away from curious guests.

At last, Sabrina chose a novel by Miss Maria Edgeworth because the title seemed appropriate to her current setting and she thought she might perhaps learn a thing or two: *Tales from Fashionable Life.* She tested the chairs and the settee with a moment of sitting in each, and decided upon the settee. And as there was a clock nearby, she didn't worry about missing supper.

Besides, Mary had known her long enough to look for her in a library.

"And here's a room you won't be spending very much time in, Wyndham," Rhys said as they passed the library on the way to the billiard room.

Wyndham began to laugh, then muffled it as he peered in.

"You're stocking females in your library now, Rawden? Is this your way of persuading me to spend more time with the philosophers and poets?"

"Am I? Is there?"

This was interesting news. The earl peered in, too.

A shining head could indeed be seen over the top of the settee. The woman's hair was dark, with copper and gold strands threaded through it—the firelight told him this—and it was pulled simply up and pinned in a casual little heap on top of her head. A few loose spirals traced a delicate profile. She seemed to be squinting a bit as she read, or frowning over a sentence; her brow was knit.

She hadn't at all noticed them standing in the doorway, staring at her as though she were part of the furnishings; the book had engulfed her.

Rhys recognized the volume, as it was the only one he owned bound in burgundy leather. It was the Maria Edgeworth novel. An intelligent woman, Miss Edgeworth, and a fine writer, but given a bit to preaching between the lines and a bit overfond of realism. These days, he wanted to take in only words that sang and soothed or aroused; he'd had enough lessons and grit to last a lifetime. But he kept the volume out of consideration to Miss Edgeworth, whom he'd met and whom he'd liked.

Given the choice of novel, Rhys felt certain he knew who this was.

"It's only the vicar's daughter," he whispered to Wyndham. "Let's leave her to her sermons."

Wyndham stifled a laugh, and they went on their way.

CHAPTER THREE

IT'S ONLY THE vicar's daughter.

Sabrina knew she was supposed to feel compassion, but they were now seated around a long dinner table, and what she still felt was rankled. Slightly *less* rankled than she had been earlier this afternoon, but rankled nevertheless. The man had all but looked through her this morning as though she were vapor, and this afternoon he had dismissed her with a whisper. She'd heard it as they left, saw his tall dark frame striding away from the library with his friend.

Why she should care was a bit of a mystery. How on earth such a man could be related to Geoffrey was yet another mystery.

And this was worrying, too: Geoffrey should have arrived hours ago, and he was nowhere to be seen.

Sabrina shifted her elbow a little to allow the attentive footman next to her to add peas to her plate.

Above the table hung chandeliers dripping crystals sharp as fangs; slim silver candelabra topped with tiny flames marched down the length of snowy linen. Everywhere out of the corner of Sabrina's eye things glinted: forks, tureens, the jewels about the throat and wrist of

Signora Sophia Licari, who turned out to be the woman who had so incensed the Earl of Rawden earlier today, and who was apparently the famous opera singer and alleged mistress of the earl.

Miss Licari's gown was copper silk, and somehow magically, precisely matched her eyes. Those eyes were long and almond-shaped, and she regarded the world through languorously lowered lids, as though her thick lashes were too heavy for them.

To Sabrina's right was a Mr. Wyndham, who, she'd been informed as they were introduced earlier, was a painter. On her left was a man who played the cello, a Mr. Mumphrey, and the woman who traveled with him, Mrs. Wessel, who, Sabrina had been fascinated to learn, apparently gave dramatic readings and also played the flute. Sabrina wasn't fooled: this meant Mrs. Wessel was an *actress* who played the flute. This was somewhat alarming. But Mrs. Wessel didn't look particularly immoral; she was handsome, heavy, and cheerful; it was possible her hair was hennaed, but she wasn't otherwise garish. No mention had been made of whether they were married to each other, though Mr. Mumphrey seemed pleasant enough for a man who might very well be living in sin with a woman. He devoted himself to the pork and peas with almost religious fervor, and inquired pleasantly about Tinbury.

Mary and her husband, Paul, who had arrived this afternoon, were at the other end of the table, near the earl. Mary, as usual, seemed to be talking ceaselessly while her husband nodded and beamed at intervals.

The earl was nearly as lazy-lidded as Signora Licari, but then Mary's chatter *could* occasionally have a stupefying effect, particularly upon men.

In fact, Sabrina thought she'd never seen a man look so bored, though his face was arranged in an expression of polite tolerance. Somehow, everything else about him radiated tension, as though he was poised to spring at the appropriate provocation.

The food was splendid, however, and she intended to take full advantage of it while she was here.

"Oh, did you hear, Rawden? Viscount Bedford took a ball in a duel," Mr. Wyndham said suddenly.

Sabrina's fork froze halfway to her mouth.

"Was it over a woman?" the earl asked, as though discussing the price of hay.

"*Ma naturalmente,*" Signora Licari murmured. "What else would it be? It is Bedford we speak of, after all. His name suits him . . . so many beds."

"The Countess Montshire," Wyndham clarified.

"Ah," the earl said, as if this explained everything. "And how is her husband taking it?"

And at this, Sabrina set her fork very, very carefully alongside her plate and stared down at it. It was rather a large dose of sophistication to take in all at once: Countess? Duel? *Husband?* And all delivered in that accent of offhand irony.

Even Mary's chatter had slowed, and her lashes were batting rapidly, as though something had been splashed in her face. Paul looked less distressed, but he'd shot a warning look at Wyndham. Wyndham shrugged and smiled, as though he could not be held responsible for what popped from his mouth.

And then, to Sabrina's chagrin, the earl seemed to notice her stillness.

"Our apologies, Miss Fairleigh. Do we scandalize?"

There was that voice again, as deep and elegant as a cello. She somehow doubted he was sorry if he'd scandalized. But his words had been polite, and delivered directly to her, and he was their host.

She cleared her throat. "It must be terribly uncomfortable to be at the mercy of the sort of uncontrollable passion that leads to duels."

There was a silence as everyone's head swiveled in unison to regard her.

"Do you really think so, Miss Fairleigh?" This came from the earl again. It was unsettling to suddenly be the focus of his blue gaze. A bit like having two comets aimed in her direction. But his question seemed sincere enough. That is, if one discounted the curious glint in his eye.

"Oh, yes." She said it gently, in case he thought she was judging him. Too late realizing he'd allegedly killed a man in a duel.

"So you've never been 'at the mercy of uncontrollable passions' yourself, Miss Fairleigh?" The earl sounded gravely, solicitously curious.

She lifted her fork and turned it in her hand nervously. Round and round. "I count myself fortunate to be possessed of an even temperament," she said modestly. "It is simply how I was born. However, I feel great compassion for those who suffer extremes of feeling. I imagine it is dreadfully inconvenient, at times, and must cause considerable pain on occasion."

The earl was now staring at her with the oddest expression. Something akin to fascination.

Next to her, Mr. Wyndham coughed once into his fist.

"You are very gracious indeed to offer compassion to those buffeted by their own animal natures, Miss Fairleigh," the earl said somberly, at last.

Sabrina wasn't certain how to respond.

"Thank you," she decided to say, tentatively.

Mr. Wyndham coughed again.

"Lady Mary tells me you hail from Tinbury. Your father is the vicar there?"

Well, apparently she'd at last captured the earl's full attention. She was no longer certain that she wanted it.

"Yes, Lord Rawden."

"And what sort of pastimes do you enjoy in Tinbury, Miss Fairleigh?" Another sincere-sounding, easy-*sounding* question. And yet there was little of ease about this man. Something restless, probing, hummed beneath the surface of every word.

"Well, I like to visit the poorer families in town, you see. We collect clothes and food for them at the vicarage—everyone in town brings them round—and then we take them round to people like Mrs. Dewberry, and Mr. Shumley, who"—she cleared her throat again—"who drinks." She lowered her voice a little, and said the last word delicately.

"A sinner is Mr. Shumley, then?" The earl had lowered his voice, too, to almost a hush. One of his dark brows made an inquisitive upward leap.

Given that the earl was allegedly versed in a multitude of sins, Sabrina suspected she would need to answer gingerly. "Drink happens to be Mr. Shumley's particular weakness, Lord Rawden. That, and he believes he is King George."

There was a burst of laughter at this at the table.

"Coincidentally, he *does* have that particular weakness in common with His Majesty," the earl said, and smiled at her.

That smile had washed the carefulness and boredom right from his face, and the stark beauty of it was as startling as a slap. Sabrina's eyes flew wide. And then she quickly looked down at her plate again, an attempt to regain her composure.

"And do you enjoy life in Tinbury, on the whole, Miss Fairleigh?"

So he hadn't quite finished with her yet, then. She wasn't entirely a fool: she doubted a man who lived in London would be terribly interested in life in Tinbury.

She looked up at him again, braving that handsome face. "It's quiet and very pleasant," she said politely. "I should be content there for the rest of my life, if I did not also hope to do some good as a missionary in a faraway land, perhaps in Africa. I should like to help others less fortunate, you see, as a missionary."

"Helping is indeed commendable, Miss Fairleigh." The earl raised his glass to her.

How would you know? She was tempted to ask.

"Missionary is a wonderful position," Wyndham volunteered somberly.

Mary was beaming at Sabrina, apparently proud she was the subject of the earl's praise.

But Sabrina wondered why Signora Licari looked so very amused, her sable eyes bright as lit candles. She might be a country girl, but she didn't particularly enjoy being the subject of mirth she didn't quite understand. Particularly from this beautiful woman.

Compassion, she reminded herself.

"Speaking of helping, I should like another helping of pork," Wyndham said cheerily.

* * *

After dinner, Sophia Licari was importuned to sing. The request came from Mr. Mumphrey, and was humbly delivered.

Signora Licari placed a delicate index finger against her chin and tilted her head, her eyes going abstracted. Pondering the question, perhaps.

"I do not think tonight," she pronounced at last, as though she'd been asked to predict whether or not it might rain.

And so instead Mr. Mumphrey set about playing the cello and Mrs. Wessel played the flute, and a pleasant little Bach composition that Sabrina recognized floated out over the grand drawing room. But no one seemed to be obliged to simply sit and listen. The other members of the party took up quiet pastimes. Mary and her husband had agreed to play cards with Signora Licari and Mr. Wyndham, but Sabrina had never learned the game they were playing, so she decided to read instead, in the room with everyone else, because it seemed the companionable thing to do.

She had found a comfortable chair, and had fetched the Maria Edgeworth book.

She'd read two pages when she'd looked up to find that the earl had settled down at a small, elegant desk very near her, a quill between his fingers, foolscap spread before him.

Instantly, for some reason, it seemed more difficult to breathe. It was as though he took up more air than the usual person, and so there was less of it to breathe now that he was near. Or perhaps it was just that the air seemed sharper, somehow, like the air outside when they'd arrived this morning.

He seemed to take as much notice of her as he did the lamp on the desk as his quill began to dance over the page. So Sabrina ducked her head and began to read again.

She'd only managed to get to the bottom of the second page when some sort of disturbance in the atmosphere caused her to look up.

He was staring at her. Directly, unblinkingly, fixedly at her.

Good heavens, but his eyes were astoundingly blue.

She smiled tentatively.

His expression didn't change. He, in fact, didn't blink.

"Are you . . . are you writing a poem?" she ventured.

The earl blinked then. And the faintest of creases appeared between his eyes, as if he couldn't quite place how he knew her, or was surprised that she would dare to speak to him at all. As though a dog or a cat had just asked him about his poetry.

"Why, yes." He sounded mildly amused. Indulgent. "I *am* writing a poem." He looked at her a moment longer, almost appraisingly. "I was trying to think of a rhyme for skin."

Whoosh. Heat scorched Sabrina's face from her collar to her hairline.

The earl returned his gaze to the page. But not before she saw the flash of a tiny smile.

The *devil.*

"No, you weren't, Lord Rawden," she said firmly.

He looked up, surprised. "Wasn't I?"

"No. If you'd said, perhaps, that you were trying to think of a rhyme for 'lemon,' I might have believed you.

Shin, din, grin, sin," she added pointedly. "I believe you were trying to be . . ."

She trailed off when she realized, to her horror, she was actually scolding the earl.

He was smiling a little. "Incorrigible?" he completed helpfully. "Very well. Lemon, did you say? I shall take that under consideration the next time I decide to be incorrigible."

And then he lowered his head to his work again, and it was clear she was once again forgotten.

A bit belatedly Sabrina recalled that she perhaps ought to ingratiate herself with the earl, in order to help support Geoffrey's petition for funding of the mission she hoped to share with him.

She took a deep breath, and gingerly, as if holding her hand out for a bear to sniff, she ventured a conciliatory question. "Do you find writing poetry pleasurable, Lord Rawden?"

He jerked his head up again, his eyebrows drawn ever so slightly together. As if he wondered that she dared interrupt. "God, no," he said dismissively. "It eases pain."

He dropped his head.

Sabrina stared at that handsome head bent over his page of foolscap and knew an unfamiliar ire. She knew he wasn't *precisely* obligated to be polite, as he was an earl and a notorious one at that. Still, she wasn't accustomed to being completely ignored or dismissed—quite the opposite in fact, at least in Tinbury—and she was a little surprised to discover how much she minded.

" 'It eases pain,' " she mimicked under her breath. "How very dramatic." She lowered her head to her book again.

The earl's head came up very slowly this time.

"What did you say, Miss Fairleigh?"

Oh, no.

She stared at him in what she hoped was an artless way. "I . . ." She stopped.

"It rather sounded like: 'How very dramatic,'" he encouraged on a drawl.

Sabrina was unwilling to corroborate this. She was certain her scarlet cheeks were all the answer he needed, anyway.

"Have you read any of my poetry, Miss Fairleigh?" A mild question.

"No!" she said rather vehemently, before she realized her vehemence might be construed as impolite. Then again, it was best she make it clear precisely what sort of female she happened to be.

"Good. I daresay you wouldn't understand it, and it would only confuse you." The earl dropped his head again to his page. His pen scratched a few more words across the page.

She should leave it at that. She really should.

"I read English well enough," she said coolly.

"Passion is another language altogether." He tossed this out without bothering to lift his head from his foolscap.

She'd been in the presence of this notorious man scarcely a day, and already one of the seven deadly sins had her firmly in its grip. Later, she would blame pride for what she said next.

"I'm tempted to roll my eyes, Lord Rawden, but then I would be unable to read my book."

The earl lifted his head slowly, slowly up then. He studied her at length. And finally, a faint smile began to hover about his mouth, and his face registered a peculiar sort of approval.

"Unable to read your book? You haven't turned more than two pages since you've sat down, Miss Fairleigh. Do you read so very slowly? Or does my presence disconcert you? If it's the latter, I do apologize."

She'd thought poets possessed clouds for brains. This one possessed a rapier.

"You're not sorry, Lord Rawden," she said evenly.

Oh, and at that, he smiled fully. And what a smile it was: genuinely, brilliantly pleased with both her and with himself. The kind of smile that made his eyes all but vanish and lines ray from their corners.

And *smack*: just like that, her wits scattered like billiard balls.

"No, I suppose I'm not sorry." He continued to smile at her.

She really ought to look away, or smile in return, or say something. Anything. But she hadn't any wits left. Staring was all that was left to her.

Before her eyes, his smile drifted away, and his expression became more pensive.

"Since we are chatting, Miss Fairleigh, and since you are, as you say, familiar with the English language, I wonder if I might trouble you for some assistance with my poetry."

It was very nearly a humble entreaty, and helping was more familiar to her than sparring. "I know very little about poetry, Lord Rawden, but I should be happy to try."

"Well . . . ," he began almost diffidently. "I am writing a poem about seduction."

He might have said: "I am writing a poem about forks." It made the word less dangerous, somehow. Which in a way, she knew, made it even more dangerous. Still, this was the sort of language this man used. And as she would with luck become a missionary on another continent one day, perhaps she ought to view it in a "When in Rome" light, and try to speak his language.

"I'd thought you'd already written a book about sed . . . seduction, Lord Rawden."

Too late she realized that this revealed she knew all about his scandalous volume.

He leaned slowly back in his chair then, with the air of one settling into his favorite topic.

"Oh, one can never really finish writing about seduction, Miss Fairleigh. I find I've a good deal more to say on the topic." He made it sound nearly academic.

Sabrina thought of the kiss she hoped she'd get from Geoffrey one day, and of the shadowy things that took place in a marriage bed, which were giggled about and spoken of only in the very, very broadest of euphemisms among the girls she knew.

But then there had been a girl in the village of Tinbury who had disappeared under a wave of whispers and scandal: she'd been ruined, it had been said. All because of seduction.

"But . . . why do you want to . . ." Sabrina cleared her throat. "Seduction implies . . . enticement. Luring someone against her will. Does it not?"

"Are you saying it isn't . . . well, *nice* to write about it, Miss Fairleigh?" He sounded concerned. "I thought . . . well, I truly thought that within every woman is the will to be seduced. That they in truth *want* to be seduced."

"Within the unfortunate women, perhaps," she corrected gravely. "The ones possessed of weaker wills. There are others of us who are blessed with more fortitude."

She knew nothing at all about seduction, but she did know a bit about sermonizing.

"Ah. So what you are saying is that *you* cannot be seduced." The earl nodded sagely, mulling this. "Because of fortitude. And that you think seduction has to do with 'will,' and the possession or lack thereof."

Sabrina suddenly realized how often the word "seduced" and its variations had been used in the last minute or so. She had the uneasy suspicion that she was being lured out into the middle of a sticky, silky web woven of the word, but wasn't certain how to scramble back to safety.

"But we are not animals, Lord Rawden," she said gently. "We possess the ability to control our actions, and I'm fortunate in that I've never experienced difficulty doing so in any circumstance. And as I said, I've been blessed with an even temperament, and I've nothing but—"

"—compassion for those of us afflicted by tempestuous animal natures. Oh, yes, I recall. Pray, will you answer a question for me, Miss Fairleigh?"

"I shall certainly try."

"You hail from the country, yes?"

"Yes, Tinbury is a country town. Nothing at all like London." She only realized she'd made "London" sound like "Babylon" when his mouth tilted up a little.

"Very well, then. And in the country . . . do you see animals adapt to their circumstances? Grow longer coats for winter, grow spots so as not to be seen by predators, or coloring to attract others of their species?" He had a thoughtful little crease between his eyes.

"Well . . . yes. I do. For instance, the cattle have all grown longer coats this year, for winter. And the squirrels have begun gathering more nuts, and Mrs. Dewberry believes this means this winter will be early and hard."

He nodded in a satisfied manner. "Very well, then. But here is the question I've been pondering." He leaned slowly toward her, so close she could see how very thick his eyelashes were, and that his eyes featured more than one shade of blue.

He clasped his hands on his knees thoughtfully. "Why, Miss Fairleigh . . ."

And without warning, his voice slowed, the timbre of it changed—and just like that, it wound around her senses like a silken rope and held her fast.

". . . why do you suppose a woman's skin is so soft . . . so very, *very* soft . . . if it isn't meant to . . . tempt? If it isn't meant to be . . . touched?"

The last word was very nearly a whisper. It landed on Sabrina as surely as a breath blown softly against the back of her neck.

This was when her lungs ceased to take in air.

His blue eyes refused to relinquish hers. She was well and truly caught.

That voice went on. "And if we aren't meant to take pleasure in our own skin, Miss Fairleigh, why then can so *very* much pleasure be had from touching it . . . and from being touched?"

She felt his words somehow everywhere on her body.

He waited. But she couldn't speak. She breathed in deeply, appalled to hear how uneven her breath was, how she struggled to take it. Like a genie freed from a bottle, his words entered her mind and took shape there, filling it with images she'd never before entertained.

The earl nodded, as though he'd confirmed something.

"We are *all* animals, Miss Fairleigh." He said this mildly.

And sat back in his chair, dropped his head again to the page, that little smile playing over his lips, and his pen began scratching away as though this conversation had been naught but a pause to yawn and stretch.

He'd lured her into his web and made his point as surely as if he'd thrust a sword into her. And he'd done it, she suspected, purely for his own diversion. She, as far as The Libertine was concerned, was child's play.

Sabrina remained silent. And then she turned about ten more pages of her book, not reading or seeing any of them. She finally decided that ten pages' worth of pretending to read was enough to salvage her dignity.

And finally she stood and moved across the room to get closer to the fire. The leaping blaze seemed far less dangerous than the Earl of Rawden.

Later, after all the guests had gone up to bed, Rhys bent over a billiard table across from Wyndham. His shot was true; the little triangle formation of balls scattered across the table, finding the pockets he'd meant them to find.

"Good start, Rawden." Wyndham bent to take his own shot. "Your mood seems to have improved. What brought it about? Did Sophia grovel or beg forgiveness or do some other significantly more pleasant thing to cause you to relax?"

Rhys's mouth twitched. "Hardly. Take your shot, Wyndy."

Wyndham took his shot, and it was splendid. "Ha!" he said pleasantly to Rhys, and stood upright, leaning upon his stick.

"No," Rhys continued, "it has naught to do with Sophia. But I think I may have discovered a cure for boredom."

"Has it anything to do with the righteous but pretty Miss Fairleigh?"

"Pretty?" Rhys repeated idly, as if he hadn't noticed at all.

Of course he'd noticed. He'd gazed at her long enough today, and had been vaguely irritated with the conclusion. Upon close assessment of her features, no other conclusion could be drawn, really. Her eyes were spectacular, a disconcertingly direct and clear green, a bit tilted, long dark lashes fanning from them. A mouth full and gently curved, soft-looking, just barely pink. The color of her skin when she blushed, her lips were. It hardly seemed necessary for a vicar's daughter to have eyes like that, or a mouth like that, or skin so luminous it seemed to create its own light.

And he couldn't shake the sense that there was something familiar about her. Perhaps it merely had to do with her timeless sort of beauty.

"Well, yes," Wyndham continued. "I thought it was why you'd paid Miss Fairleigh any attention at all. You don't think she's pretty, Rhys? You can scarcely call her anything else. Despite her unfortunate years-old frocks and her pious plans for her future. Or . . . is that what you like about her?"

"She's clever," Rhys said mildly, not addressing the question of whether or not she was pretty. Or mentioning the fact that he had, for a moment, been genuinely entertained by his exchange with Miss Fairleigh. "But she's also more than a little self-righteous. I think it will be diverting to prove a point."

"What precisely did you have in mind?"

Rhys straightened and cupped his hands over the top of his cue, rested his chin atop his hands. "She claims she cannot be seduced."

"You *cannot* have sat in the corner and discussed seduction with the proper Miss Fairleigh while I played cards with her friends and Sophia." Wyndham said this with awe. He'd acquired a good deal of respect for Rhys's power over the female of the species.

Rhys laughed, but opted to remain cryptic. "Let's just say I think it will be diverting to broaden Miss Fairleigh's horizons."

"How will *I* know when her horizons have been broadened?"

"She'll blush in my presence. She'll stammer. She'll fawn. She'll be speechless." Rhys ticked off the list, sounding bored.

"Oh, I see. The usual way." This was how women behaved near Rhys typically, anyhow.

"And then she'll go back to Tinbury ever-so-slightly enlightened, and she might just pleasantly surprise whoever eventually marries her."

"Good God, Rawden, you don't propose to—"

"Relieve her of her virtue? No. But I do intend to relieve her of a little of her innocence."

Wyndham took his shot. An abysmal one. He shook his head regretfully. "How do you propose to do it?"

"I haven't yet decided."

But he knew that he could. Miss Fairleigh didn't know it, but she was proud. She was clever. She was proud of *being* clever. He also suspected she possessed a temper and an imagination, for he'd watched her listen to him today, her eyes abstracted, taking in his words. *Feeling* his words.

A clever man would know how to take advantage of the clues Miss Fairleigh offered to what other aspects of her nature might lie dormant.

Rhys smiled to himself as he sank the ball of his choice in the pocket of his choice.

He was a very clever man.

CHAPTER FOUR

A ND AT BREAKFAST the following morning at last, there was a familiar lean figure in somber clothing helping himself to kippers from the sideboard. Sabrina's heart gave a little leap.

Geoffrey turned and saw her, and looked startled. "Sabrina! What on earth?"

"Are you surprised to find me here, Geoffrey?" She said it almost breathlessly.

"I confess I am. But may I also say that I'm pleased?" He smiled at her, recovering nicely from his surprise.

Geoffrey had such a pleasant way of speaking. Her father occasionally allowed him to give the sermons, and he chose many pretty words to make his point. "You may." She smiled back at him.

He lowered his voice. "And good heavens, what brings you to the den of my scandalous cousin?"

Sabrina dimpled a little. "I am a guest of Lady Mary Capstraw. I am traveling as her companion."

She saw Geoffrey look puzzled for a moment, and then his face registered the cleverness of her strategy, and became peculiarly speculative. It seemed he had just realized what she might be about. He smiled a little . . . and good heavens, it was a bit . . . well, *sultry*.

"I would have arrived sooner, you see, but our carriage suffered a small accident," he told her. He was certainly helping himself to a good deal of eggs, she noticed. Possibly he didn't get enough to eat at the vicarage. "I've only just arrived an hour or so ago."

"Oh, dear! A carriage accident? Are you sound?"

"I am perfectly sound, thank you for your concern." He paused in his dishing of eggs and turned to study her a moment longer, and a glimmer of sorts seemed to move over his eyes. He lowered his voice a bit more. "Sabrina . . . might I beg a private meeting with you?"

She loved the intimacy of his lowered voice and his intense gaze. House parties were most *definitely* exciting, she decided then.

Sabrina tried not to glance over her shoulder, where Lady Mary and her husband and Mr. Wyndham were happily devouring their breakfasts. Presumably Sophia Licari was having a late morning lie-in.

Perhaps with The Libertine himself, as he wasn't present at breakfast, either.

She mentally brushed aside the very idea of it. One conversation about seduction, and see how quickly her thoughts fell into his way of thinking? He was a dangerous man, indeed.

"Certainly, Geoffrey."

"There is a sitting room all done in yellow in the back of the house. I recall it from when I was a boy. Follow the black-and-white-tiled hallway to the small table with the gilded turned legs, and turn right. If you find yourself in a gallery of sorts featuring portraits, you've gone too far. Once we've finished breakfast, excuse yourself and wait fifteen minutes. You will find me there."

She was a bit startled by how briskly and efficiently he planned what essentially amounted to an assignation. But as intrigue was unfamiliar to her, she found it quietly thrilling, too.

"Have you spoken to the earl about our—" Sabrina corrected herself just in time. "Your mission, then?"

They now stood across from each other in the room Geoffrey had suggested. Yellow indeed. Wallpaper that reminded Sabrina of eggs—white and yolk-yellow—striped the wall, and made her a little dizzy. She looked at Geoffrey instead, because he typically made her a little dizzy, too, in a pleasanter way.

Geoffrey's gaze was wandering the yellow sitting room, over velvet, marble, ormolu, rosewood, up the walls to the endlessly high ceiling. The filigreed hands of a grand clock glided forward to land upon eleven. It pinged out the hour tastefully.

"I've an appointment with him tomorrow to discuss it," Geoffrey finally said. "He's expecting it."

"As formal as that, are you?" she teased. "He's your cousin. Shouldn't you just discuss it on a stroll to review the horses, or whatever it is men enjoy doing together?"

Geoffrey's eyes returned to hers. "We . . . aren't very close now, I'm afraid." The words seemed carefully chosen. His expression was odd. As though he were trying with some difficulty to disguise a stomachache.

"Were you ever close?"

Geoffrey didn't answer; suddenly he was more restless than Sabrina had ever seen him. Gingerly he picked up a small vase splashed with delicate pale pink roses, turned it in his hand. Worth a fortune, and would break if one sneezed, no doubt. A lovely, unthinkably frivolous thing, the result of someone's painstaking labor to create.

All for displaying flowers.

Geoffrey settled the vase carefully back onto the stand that seemed specifically made just for it.

At the vicarage, Sabrina usually stuffed bowls and jars with flowers, when there was time for such frivolity. Being poor required so much time. All the careful economies, the picking of threads out of dresses to resew them with the worn and faded side inside, using one poor chicken as thoroughly as possible, from eggs to dinner to soup stock to feathers for pillows.

He looked up at Sabrina. "Did you know, Sabrina, that once upon a time Rhys was nearly penniless?"

This seemed impossible, given the house they were now standing in. "Truly?"

"Truly. Many years ago the Gillray family fortune was actually in great . . . disrepair." It seemed a carefully chosen word. "But Rhys came into money when he was about eighteen years old. I never did know quite how it happened. And it seems he has managed to create . . ." Geoffrey paused. "Well, you can see what Rhys has done with it since."

"Is poetry as lucrative as that?" It was a bit of a jest.

"One wonders." Geoffrey wasn't really listening, and clearly not in the mood to jest. He strolled over to the carved mantelpiece and absently traced a finger over it: leaves, grapes, acorns. "He bought a commission. Earned money that way. But no doubt investments also played a role." He sounded faintly sardonic. As though he'd little faith in the fiscal rewards of poetry.

"What was he like when he was young?" Sabrina was surprised that she truly wanted to know. "Did he show any signs of becoming . . . well . . ." She blushed. "The Libertine?"

The young curate immediately stopped his restless perusal of the room and swiveled his gaze to Sabrina with an intensity that reminded her rather suddenly of his cousin.

"Sabrina . . . how much do you know about his poetry?"

Good heavens, but Geoffrey sounded awfully interested. His dark eyes were alert.

"Not very much," she said hurriedly. "It's . . ." She cleared her throat. "Prurient, I believe. That's all I know."

"Salacious, in fact," Geoffrey agreed, with what sounded surprisingly like a certain amount of relish. He still looked rather . . . bright-eyed. He was gazing at her with an expression she was having difficulty deciphering.

"Have *you* read it?" she ventured, since he didn't seem inclined to say anything.

"Some," he admitted. He hadn't blinked in nearly a minute.

She quickly decided to change the subject.

"Is he a generous man, the earl, despite his reputation?"

Geoffrey came a few steps closer. "I truly don't know what kind of man he has become, Sabrina. I haven't spoken to my cousin in years. I can only hope he will find it in his heart to support a missionary enterprise as well as . . . opera singers and painters and actresses and . . . that fellow with the cello and his great redheaded paramour who departed this morning." There was a whiff of judgment about his words.

Paramour. Goodness, Geoffrey was a curate, but he'd used that word nearly as easily as the earl had used the word "seduction."

"When we arrived yesterday, I believe he was arguing with Signora Sophia Licari," Sabrina said in a lowered voice, as though confiding a scandal. Since Geoffrey shared her even temperament, he would probably appreciate the story. "They seemed to be having a rather serious conversation outside in the courtyard, anyhow."

"Signora Sophia Licari? The *opera* singer?" Geoffrey sounded amazed. And truthfully, just a little amused as well, which was a bit puzzling. "Is she here?"

"She is. Geoffrey, do you know whether she is truly his mistress? I heard she was his mistress. I heard that he *lived* with his mistress."

Geoffrey froze. "Where on earth would *you* hear such a thing, Sabrina?"

"Mary," she confessed.

Geoffrey's entire attention was focused upon her now, his eyes strangely assessing. He took a few slow steps closer still. She'd in fact never stood quite so close to him before.

"Sabrina, if you would permit me a liberty . . ." His voice had become low and urgent.

She frowned a little, confused. "It's not a liberty, Geoffrey, if you beg permission."

His hand rose, and he placed it on her arm. Her first reaction was puzzlement; she looked at his hand resting on her arm with a faint furrow of her brow, as if wondering how such a thing had gotten there.

And then all at once it occurred to her that Geoffrey intended to kiss her.

It was done—his head bent, his lips touched warmly to hers for a moment, his head returned to where it had originated—almost before she could realize that it was happening, or muster a shortness of breath or a quicker heartbeat.

And suddenly she put her fingers up to her mouth, a delayed response; her lips still remembered the pressure of his lips. That's when her face, at last, began to grow warm, and she felt a little glow in the center of her chest.

She stared at him. It hadn't been unpleasant. Still, kisses were so very controversial, discussed only with giggles or feigned swooning or dire warnings, Sabrina had expected much more than . . . well, warmth, she supposed.

"Sabrina . . . forgive me . . ." Geoffrey's voice was tense, but he seemed pleased. A bit aquiver. As though he'd very much enjoyed what he'd just done.

She was envious: she'd rather hoped her first kiss would make her feel those things, too.

Perhaps in a few more moments it would.

"There's nothing to forgive, Geoffrey," she said quickly. "After all, you did request permission for a liberty."

He smiled a little at this. Perhaps when Geoffrey was more at ease about his future—hopefully *their* future—he would feel freer to laugh. And she prayed the Earl of Rawden would find it in his heart to support his cousin's dream, so that she might share it, too.

For surely a kiss meant that Geoffrey felt there was an understanding between them. She allowed herself this hope, felt it flame just a little in her chest.

She wondered if it had been *his* first kiss. She gazed up at him for a moment, and felt a peculiar disorientation: for a tick of the clock, he seemed entirely a stranger, and she'd known him almost a year.

She could only imagine how dangerous The Libertine's actual poetry was for a woman who lacked her own strength of will, if a mere mention of it—perhaps in conjunction with the word "mistress"—had heated Geoffrey to the point where he'd burst out into a kiss.

"What do you suppose we'll do this evening for entertainment?" Her way of changing the subject.

"Perhaps you should play for everyone," Geoffrey suggested.

"Oh, I couldn't possibly!" This was his cue to flatter her.

He obliged. "You play very well, Sabrina." Indulgently said.

She occasionally played almost *too* well, in fact, losing herself in the sweep of music, finding fresh pathos in a hymn the Tinbury parishioners had heard dozens of times before, in the process causing eyes to moisten or religious fervor to build to an unprecedented pitch. It was one of those things about Sabrina that caused the Vicar Fairleigh's forehead furrow to deepen.

"I will play if requested, but no doubt everyone here will find my playing rather ordinary. Do you suppose Signora Licari will sing?"

Belatedly she recalled that Signora Licari was allegedly the earl's mistress, and she wondered if mentioning her would make Geoffrey restless again, and result in another kiss. "For I've heard Signora Licari has a splendid voice," she added, because, after all, Sabrina wasn't entirely adverse to another kiss, and she did want to be fully aware of her next one. Perhaps if she were to get better at it there would be more to the sensation.

This particular cue Geoffrey missed. "No doubt. I cannot imagine that even a singer of her fame can refuse an earl if he were to ask her to sing."

"But Mr. Mumphrey asked her to sing last night. She said she could not."

"*Could* not?" Geoffrey looked puzzled.

"Those were her words."

"As though her voice was otherwise engaged for the evening?" Geoffrey sounded mystified, and he was smiling a little.

Sabrina smiled, too, and felt pleased with their concord. They would never understand the caprices of artistic people, and this was as it should be. She and Geoffrey had a higher calling.

It was amusing, Rhys thought, as he backed from the doorway of the yellow sitting room, that he could learn so much about Miss Fairleigh by simply strolling through his own home. Yesterday he'd learned she enjoyed reading.

Today he'd learned she enjoyed his cousin.

It seemed Geoffrey, curate or no, hadn't quite changed his spots.

He hadn't been spying, truly, he told himself. He'd simply strolled by the room on his way to the portrait gallery to make certain the portraits—the ones he'd been able to reacquire—were hung in their proper places. And he'd heard voices, and had peered in just as Miss Fairleigh and his cousin touched lips.

It was all he needed to see, really. It made the game a bit more complex, granted, but that only made it more interesting.

And it shed an intriguing light on his meeting with his cousin.

CHAPTER FIVE

Sylvie Lamoreux-Shaughnessy, ballerina, and Susannah Whitelaw, Lady Grantham, had spent their lives feeling as though they belonged both nowhere and everywhere, and as a consequence, now felt at home almost everywhere they went. Which was why Susannah, the wife of a wealthy viscount, thought nothing of perching on a chair in a dressing room sipping tea while her sister Sylvie bustled about preparing five half-dressed, giggling girls for a ballet performance at The Family Emporium. The Emporium, the brainchild of Sylvie's impossibly handsome husband, Tom Shaughnessy, was a veritable layer cake of entertainment, featuring floor upon floor of diversions for men, women, and children, and ballet was one of them, popular primarily because the king seemed to enjoy it.

But the other reason Susannah was in the dressing room was that she and Sylvie had only just found each other. Each had grown up with a single blurred memory of being awakened in the dark, of frantic movement and weeping, of three little girls and of a woman's soft voice. But neither of them had known what it truly meant. It was Susannah's husband, Kit, a viscount in His Majesty's Secret Service, who had risked his life to solve the mystery of Susannah's birth, a journey that had taken him from London to the country town of Barnstable and then to a little, tucked-away town of Gorringe. Their family, they had learned, had been shattered when their father, a beloved politician, had been murdered and their mother, Anna Holt, was wrongly accused of the crime. Anna had been warned in time to flee for her life, but she'd been forced to leave her three very young daughters behind, and her daughters had been raised in separate families, never knowing of one another.

No one had seen Anna since.

Together Kit and Susannah had managed to gather enough clues to lead them to Sylvie, who had at the same time taken it upon herself to bolt from France in search of her past. And in searching for the truth about their lives and for each other, both Susannah and Sylvie had found love with remarkable men.

Susannah had been married to Kit in the summer, and Sylvie to Tom in the fall, and now winter was upon them.

And now, though Mr. Thaddeus Morley was on trial for treason and the murder of their father, Richard Lockwood, two people were still decidedly missing from their lives. Susannah and Sylvie wouldn't be able to rest until they had done everything possible to find Sabrina, their other sister. They had only one very ambiguous clue: it was thought that a curate had raised her.

They would also never give up hope of finding Anna, though finding her had begun to seem impossible. They knew only that she might have gone to Italy.

"Trials can go on simply for years, Kit tells me," Susannah told Sylvie. "Mr. Morley might literally live for years in the Tower before he swings from a rope." She sipped at her tea, faintly pleased with herself for using

such a grisly expression. Then again, Mr. Morley had
made rather a habit of trying to murder members of her
family, not to mention *her*. Her husband bore scars from
saving her life. She thought she might be entitled to be a
bit grisly.

"But they've evidence, you said, to convict Mr. Morley
of treason and murder," Sylvie said. She was installing
Lizzie the ballerina into a clever pair of gossamer wings
in preparation for the next show. She was a very busy
woman, and for details of the trial she relied upon Susannah, who heard them from Kit.

"But Morley also has a very fine lawyer defending
him at Westminster. He was a politician, you know, and
quite well respected, so he'll have the best defense. And
though the evidence is damning, Kit says, they *will* try to
save him, for that's what lawyers do. They're having better luck proving Mr. Morley committed treason than that
he orchestrated the murder of our father and blamed our
mother in the process. And they've found no evidence that
Mr. Morley actually *paid* witnesses to point the finger of
blame at Anna Holt. They've only the word of that horrible
little man to go by. The one who tried to kill me again and
again. Though you'd think that would be quite enough,
wouldn't you?" A frisson of irony from Susannah.

"Perhaps the trial will not go on as long as years,"
Sylvie suggested hopefully. She wasn't eager to hear
about the trial day after day, either. In a few short months
Susannah and Sylvie had acquired each other, and husbands, and new, extraordinary lives, and they each were
looking forward to the day when they could savor their
newfound happiness unadulterated. "Let us try to find Sabrina in the meanwhile."

But they'd talked of this before, and they didn't have the faintest idea where to begin their search for their sister.

Through the walls of the dressing room they could now hear The General, Tom's partner and choreographer, arguing with Daisy Jones, who had retired from bawdy performance and now shrewdly managed the finances of The Family Emporium, helped plan productions, and mercilessly spoiled young Jamie Shaughnessy, Tom's son. Somehow Daisy contrived to be just as much of a diva in her new role as the old one. The voices rose, and rose, and rose, until there was one inevitable final shout, this time from The General, followed by a low conciliatory murmur from Tom.

Susannah suspected Tom had won the argument. He invariably did.

Shortly thereafter, there was a knock at the door. "May I enter?" Tom's voice came through the door.

Squeals rose up from the dancers, a chorus of playful false modesty. There wasn't a soul in the room who would have minded if Mr. Shaughnessy were to view them in the altogether, with the exception, perhaps, of Susannah. And even Susannah had confessed to losing her breath with her first look at Tom Shaughnessy a few months ago.

Tom and Daisy stood side by side, The General having stormed off, no doubt, muttering. He would forgive and forget, as he always did, as he was in love with Daisy, after all.

"To the stage!" Daisy ordered the cluster of pretty ballerinas, who filed swiftly off in a cloud of powder and a rustle of taffeta.

Daisy settled herself on one of the chairs before a dressing table vacated by a ballerina.

"What are you chatting about, m'dears?" Daisy was an honorary aunt to both Sylvie and Susannah, as she was the only person they knew who had known and loved their mother, Anna, who had once been an opera dancer. And it was Daisy who thought Sabrina might have been raised by a curate.

"We were talking again of Sabrina. We should like to find her."

"Well, love, why don't you ask the vicar in Gorringe if he has a curate? It seems the place to start."

Susannah and Sylvie exchanged a look. It was as good an idea as any.

Sylvie and Tom had come for dinner at the Grantham town house, and over roast lamb and peas, Susannah repeated Daisy's suggestion to her husband. Kit regarded his wife thoughtfully. She might have been born in Gorringe, but she'd also nearly died there—twice. Gorringe was also the place he'd acquired the long scar scoring his biceps, traced there by a knife.

In short, charming though it might be, Gorringe was not precisely his favorite place to visit.

Susannah read his expression. "No one can harm me now, Kit. Especially not when I'm with you."

Kit snorted. His wife knew he could see right through any attempt at wiles, but it entertained her now and again to make the attempt. She smiled at his snort.

"Some of the roads to Gorringe might become difficult until spring. What if something becomes of Sabrina before then?" Now this was a very fine argument, and it came from Sylvie.

Kit sighed. "Very well. Shaughnessy, can you spare a day's worth of travel to speak to a vicar who has very little memory left?"

"It might be longer in this weather, Kit."

"Perhaps we should send a message ahead to the vicar to prepare him for our visit?" Susannah suggested this.

"Do you trust Vicar Sumner to remember reading a message, or to remember to respond to it?"

And this was a very good point on Kit's part, as communicating with the vicar had proved as taxing as communicating with a fog.

"All right." Tom had begun planning. "We'll set out for Gorringe tomorrow."

CHAPTER SIX

LATER THAT DAY Mary and Paul and Sabrina and Geoffrey attempted to tramp about the grounds of La Montagne, which were vast and were rumored to include a labyrinth, but the air had acquired more of a bite and the wind had whipped up, penetrating clothing and setting teeth chattering, driving the visitors indoors once more.

They were brought mugs of chocolate, and a card game was undertaken. Mr. Mumphrey and Mrs. Wessel had set out on the road early this morning, as another engagement in another town awaited them. Mr. Wyndham was off somewhere else in the house, painting, it was rumored; no one knew what had become of the earl.

Funny way to conduct a house party, Sabrina thought. Avoiding one's guests. But his presence on the whole seemed so very . . . pronounced . . . when he *was* present that his absence seemed somehow more notable. She was grateful for a bit of distance from him.

A few minutes after they'd arrived indoors, Signora Licari drifted picturesquely down the stairs and was persuaded to join them for a few games of cards.

Two games were all she seemed to have tolerance for.

"It is a bad hand," she said at last listlessly. She put her cards down and turned her back abruptly and wandered away, as if to punish the cards.

Signora Licari paused and looked yearningly out of the window toward, Sabrina suspected, London.

Plainly, Signora Licari was bored.

So, as guilty as she felt to admit it, was Sabrina. She liked cards well enough, and she liked Mary and Paul well enough, and it was pleasant to be with Geoffrey in another context besides the vicarage, and the house was very grand, but she had begun to suspect she wasn't designed to withstand too much leisure.

And Geoffrey was conspicuously distracted. He said very little; he smiled very little; he laughed not at all. She wondered if he felt a bit of guilt at his sudden kiss. Or perhaps he was worried about his meeting with his cousin.

He took up his new hand of cards, and his hair flopped down over his brow as he studied them. And yet he appeared, somehow, not to see them.

And thus a few relatively pleasant hours were passed until dinner, though they seemed, to Sabrina, nearly interminable.

Upstairs in his chambers Rhys spent the afternoon bent over a piece of foolscap. Scrawling out a word. Then scratching it out again vehemently. Staring out the window. Pacing. Scratching another word. Pacing to the window again. Watching the sun sink lower and lower and lower in the sky.

Watching snow melt would have been a more productive way to spend the afternoon.

Finally, in a fit of petulance that embarrassed him seconds later, he flung the quill across the room.

It wasn't the quill's fault the words just wouldn't come.

Sabrina found dinner a merrier affair, as Mary had pressed the earl to send an invitation to dinner to the Colberts, who lived a mere two hours' ride away from La Montagne. Much chattering over a pheasant done in a sauce of onions and herbs took place. Or, rather, much listening took place, as Mary did most of the chattering.

And after dinner, inevitably, Signora Sophia Licari was again importuned to sing, this time by Mr. Wyndham.

Signora Licari tilted her head back; her eyes closed briefly, and her long lashes hovered against her cheekbones.

She opened her eyes again. "Not tonight," was her languid conclusion. As though her singing voice could only be conjured by a séance.

Sabrina watched the earl and Mr. Wyndham exchange cryptic glances.

"Perhaps Miss Fairleigh is musical?" This suggestion came from Sophia Licari, and there was a hint of whimsy in it. Sabrina disliked being considered whimsical, particularly by Signora Licari.

"Sabrina plays very well," Geoffrey maintained.

Sabrina beamed at his gallantry.

Mary chimed in. "Oh, Sabrina, play something! Do let's have dancing!"

From the expression on Sophia Licari's face, Mary might well have cried: "Oh, do let's have cholera!"

"Yes, *do* play, Miss Fairleigh!" the earl echoed suddenly. "One of the pieces on the pianoforte is a minuet.

Perhaps you'd like to try your hand at it? I would be honored to turn the pages for you."

Sabrina eyed him somewhat warily, looking for ulterior motive in those faceted eyes. He gazed levelly back at her. His enthusiasm seemed genuine enough. Perhaps now that he'd expended the urge to be a devil, he wished to redeem himself by being helpful. This seemed unlikely, but she could hardly refuse his offer of help, as he was their host.

"You shall need some audience members to admire your playing, so some of us will regard you while the others dance," Signora Licari pronounced. Her voice always sounded as if she were stretching luxuriously while she was speaking.

Splendid. Now she was to be "regarded" by Sophia Licari.

"I shall be pleased to play for you," Sabrina conceded at last.

Chairs were gathered before the pianoforte, and other chairs and settees and those ubiquitous little tables pushed aside to make room for the dancing. Mary and Paul and Geoffrey and the Colbert girls gathered across the room, and looked over, faces bright and expectant.

Sabrina approached the pianoforte almost gingerly. It was a grand pianoforte, all gleaming curves of mahogany trimmed in spotless brass, and if she was not mistaken, the keys were made of mother-of-pearl. It was the aristocratic cousin to the battered but stalwart square pianoforte from which she coaxed tunes at the vicarage, nearly an entirely different instrument by comparison, and it seemed almost disrespectful to play reels and jigs on it. But then again, a pianoforte was built for music, after all, no matter how grand.

She settled before it, and the earl stepped up and hovered attentively over her shoulder.

"This one seems a pleasant enough tune," he suggested. He plucked up the music in one of his long-fingered hands, fanned it open for Sabrina to read. She was close enough to smell the starch in his white shirt, and something sharper, lime perhaps. For an instant her senses were dazzled and she couldn't read the notes at all.

He leaned back, and, finally, Sabrina took a deep breath, positioned her fingers over the keys, and began.

The tone of the pianoforte was exquisite, and the keys sank beneath her fingers and bounced right back up again as though they could play the tune entirely without her assistance.

Across the room, Mary, her husband, Geoffrey, and the other game guests had gathered in the formation of a minuet, and with every appearance of gaiety launched into it. And for a time she almost forgot the earl stood behind her, and she smiled softly, enjoying herself, and watched them.

"You would enjoy it more if you opened your mouth a little," the earl said idly over the music.

"Open my mouth, Lord Rawden?" No one had suggested she should sing. Which had been very wise of everyone, as far as Sabrina was concerned.

"Yes. And relax into it."

"Into . . . the song, sir?" she ventured, confused.

"Into kissing," he corrected absently and turned the page.

Scronk.

Sabrina's hands stumbled and collapsed on about five wrong keys. Out of the corner of her eye she saw a few eyes disappear into winces, but everyone recovered with rapid aplomb. No one had expected her to play particularly well in the first place, and now that she'd gotten the first mistake out of the way, the suspense was over, and her audience looked considerably more relaxed.

Sabrina's hands kept moving independently of her mind, which was fixed on the large man leaning over her with the pretense of being solicitous and the intent of being a devil.

"I'm certain I don't take your meaning, sir," she managed coolly.

"There I was," he continued into her ear, "merely strolling from one room to another, enjoying my wonderful home . . . and what should I find but my cousin and Miss Fairleigh engaged in an . . . indiscretion."

Of all the deuced rooms in this house, the master of the house happened to stroll past the one they were in.

"It was a private moment, sir." Her frosty tone was beginning to tremble and thaw at the edges. Temper licked at the edge of it.

"There are no *truly* private moments at a house party, Miss Fairleigh."

Ignoring him. Perhaps that was the solution to enduring those of his temperament. She would ignore him; he would grow bored of toying with her if she didn't respond. Figuratively speaking, she would roll up like a hedgehog, and not rise to his goads.

She willed her scorching face to cool. She played on.

"Did you enjoy it?" There was his voice again.

"Dinner? Dinner was lovely, thank you." She said it firmly and a little desperately, to give him an opportunity to locate his manners.

"The kiss."

She should have known.

She realized she'd played the same passage three times over, and the dancers had circled each other three times, and would soon be in danger of toppling over from dizziness.

Sabrina drew a long breath in through her nose then exhaled. "Will you turn the page for me now, Lord Rawden?"

Compassion, she reminded herself. Poets are capricious by nature. Batted helplessly to and fro by their passions.

With all appearance of sobriety, the earl obliged her and leaned forward to turn the page. His mouth was solemn; he even had a convincing little furrow of concentration between his brows. But when her eyes darted sideways she saw that his were crackling with mirth, and something more determined.

The earl, she realized, once again intended to make a point.

Sabrina played on, giving each note its due, though a truly discriminating listener might have noted significantly more . . . *feeling* in her playing now. A discriminating *viewer* might wonder why her face was crimson.

The dancers across the room sped up a little to match the pace of her song.

"They're *meant* to be enjoyed, you know," he murmured conversationally. "Kisses."

Sabrina felt that unfamiliar something snaking up through her like a fountain of sparks: a temper.

"Why are you tormenting me?" she hissed through gritted teeth.

"Best slow the tempo, Miss Fairleigh. You'll give the dancers apoplexy. And you should probably open it only a little. At first."

"Open *what*?" she all but snapped.

He turned the page, that attentive furrow still in place. "Your mouth. When you kiss."

Plink. She stumbled, picking out another sour note. Sophia Licari's eyebrow leaped upward, and she leaned over and whispered something to Wyndham, who smiled.

"Yes, only a little. Best not give it all away at once, you know. Not the first time, anyhow."

Confusion, pride, and outrage wrestled for control of Sabrina's tongue. But it was a late arrival to her soup of emotions—curiosity—that ultimately won the contest.

"How do you *know* it was my first time?" She tried to say it loftily, but her genuine curiosity seeped into the words.

A muffled crack of laughter escaped him. "You've kissed dozens of young men, have you, Miss Fairleigh?"

Really, she hadn't the faintest idea how to be coy or ironic, so she gave it up. "Of course not."

But how could you tell it was my first time?

Sabrina lifted her eyes from the music momentarily. Across the room Mary danced merrily and Geoffrey danced gamely. Sabrina wished herself desperately across the room.

"I just found it interesting to discover you succumbing to uncontrollable passions."

Ah. And thusly the devil delivered his point.

"I *wasn't* succumb—"

"No? Then what do you call it, Miss Fairleigh?"

She was struck by the fact that this was a very good question. There had seemed little of passion in it at all, given that it had, in fact, been a kiss. She went silent, forced to ponder this.

"Oh, rest easy, Miss Fairleigh," he said a moment later. "'Twas only a kiss." The bloody man was still laughing, albeit silently.

Only a kiss. For her, it had been a threshold crossed, a moment strangely elevating and deflating all at once. In short, it had been a profound moment for her, though in truth . . . well, she'd felt very little, at least physically, in that moment. And this alarmingly handsome man was mocking it.

And as she couldn't best him in this game, she gave him honesty instead.

"I suppose I've never thought of a kiss as 'only.'" She wanted to sound firm and censorious; her voice faltered, and she knew that she sounded wistful instead.

When he said nothing at all, she risked a glance up.

His expression was odd. She couldn't interpret it. Puzzled? Uncertain? She did know that it wasn't guarded, or ironic, or indifferent, or amused. And these were the expressions she'd so far seen him wear.

She had the oddest sensation that she'd somehow bested him, anyway.

"Not all kisses *are* 'only,' Miss Fairleigh." His voice was low in her ear as he said this. It sounded like a concession.

And then in silence for a time she played on, the sweet music more jarring now for the thoughts in her head. He turned the page for her without being asked with his elegant hand, a hand that looked as though it would never do anything so gauche as stumble over a pianoforte note no matter what anyone said into his ear.

"I believe you've played this particular passage three times now. Though I'm not certain our audience cares terribly much. Sophia is flirting with Wyndham, Wyndham is worried that I'll notice and care, and the rest, even my cousin Geoffrey, appear to be enjoying the dance."

His voice was level. He was signaling, perhaps, that he'd finished tormenting her for the moment. She managed a small smile, to reward him for not tormenting her and for attempting to be charming instead.

At last, the interminable piece, along with—hopefully— the torture, came to a finish.

A polite little patter of hands came from Sophia and Wyndham. The dancers, rosy and cheerful from a strangely vigorous minuet, dispersed and moved toward them. Sabrina began to rise from the bench, and was prepared to dart as far away from the earl as would be considered polite.

"Would you play something else for us now, Miss Fairleigh? Perhaps . . ." He sorted through the selection of music and placed a piece in front of her. "This piece."

Sabrina glanced at the piece, and within moments knew the suggestion was tantamount to a challenge. It was subtle, the music, but she quickly saw within it moments of power and poignancy, and as she read the notes, she could nearly hear the lilt of it in her head, almost picture the story it conveyed. It was a far cry from a hymn or a minuet, and she'd never played anything quite like it before. She wasn't certain she could. Or if she dared.

"Oh, do play another, Sabrina, one we might listen rather than dance to. I find I am quite winded after the last dance," Mary coaxed. They all plumped happily into chairs and stared up at her expectantly, Geoffrey included, his complexion rosy, too. His cheerful color was utterly at odds with the expression he turned upon the earl, Sabrina noted. He'd held it only an instant, but it looked very much like something more powerful than resentment. Sabrina decided it must have been nothing more than a shifting shadow, or a twinge from being required to dance the minuet so vigorously.

Rhys gave the sheet of music a questioning tap, awaiting her reply.

She couldn't help but accept his challenge.

"Thank you for your confidence in my playing," Sabrina said wryly to everyone, and placed her hands over the keys. "I should be happy to play again for you."

And she began the piece.

Tentatively, at first. But it swiftly pulled her in: wistful yet ardent, sweet in a way that was by no means cloying. She swiftly found the momentum of it; in moments the piece played her as much as she played it, and Sabrina nearly forgot about her audience. She saw the pages turn before her, but gave no thought to the fingers that turned the corners, or the owner of those fingers.

The piece came to a finish on a single note at the far end of the pianoforte. She tapped it delicately, and let it ring. Then sat quietly, savoring the finish of it.

There was silence.

She finally looked up, blinking as though being shaken from sleep, and was startled by the faces of her audience. Mary had a handkerchief up to the corner of her eye. Wyndham's face reflected unadulterated respect and a peculiar sort of speculation.

But Geoffrey looked . . . well, truthfully he looked rather unnerved.

Sophia Licari was wearing a faint smile that didn't precisely light her velvety eyes. It was difficult to know whether this indicated approval or not. Sabrina wasn't certain whether she cared.

It was the earl who finally began the applause, and as the sound was right behind her it made her start. The small audience took it up fervently. Sabrina's cheeks heated in pleasure, and a sweet warmth took up residence in the center of her chest.

She saw Wyndham open his mouth to say something.

"Rhys, will you play?" It was Sophia Licari, in that voice that made her sound like a stretching feline, speaking before Wyndham could speak. Everyone turned to her. She rose from her seat, slim and elegant as an eighth note, and made her way to the pianoforte, utterly confident that everyone wanted her there.

Interesting. The heavens must have at last aligned properly, if Miss Licari intended to sing.

And thus Sabrina's moment was gone before she could even decide how she felt about it.

From the tense expressions on the earl's and Wyndham's faces, it seemed as though a wrong move or word would frighten Miss Licari back to her seat.

Sabrina stood and surrendered her place on the pianoforte bench to the earl, who scarcely looked at her. His attention was now entirely fixed on Miss Licari, who drifted over and nodded at Sabrina in passing, as if she were a servant.

Sabrina should have known the earl would play very well. He had the fingers for it, those long confident fingers meant for things requiring precision and grace. He began the song with ease; it was a lament in a minor key. Sophia stood with her head lowered, eyes on the ground, and then slowly tilted her head back and—

All the little hairs rose up on Sabrina's arms.

It was a sound unlike anything she'd ever heard in her life. The volume was otherworldly; it seemed impossible for a human, let alone a slight one like Sophia Licari, to produce it. Her voice was an instrument, as surely as a bell or a trumpet or a battering ram. It ascended, trilled, toyed with a single note, then raced back down the register to attend to another note, flirting with it before moving on to seduce and linger over the next phrase. And as it swelled, filling the entire room, Sabrina felt it ringing inside her chest, until she felt of a piece with the song.

As much as she would have preferred not to . . . she surrendered to it. Tears began to well in her eyes, called up by that voice. It was so glorious it almost gave Miss Licari license to behave any way she pleased, Sabrina thought.

Almost.

Sabrina liked to think that *she* would be a bit more gracious, had she possessed such a gift. But perhaps the weight of carrying about such a talent kept one's balance off, and hence Sophia Licari could only behave unpredictably.

Miss Licari finished. Applause seemed almost inappropriate. After all, one didn't applaud a miracle as though it were a magician's trick. But having no other means of expression at their disposal, the audience clapped, and Sophia Licari nodded, accepting her due. *Allowing* everyone to applaud her.

Sabrina felt small and invisible again, and when she saw the awe in the earl's face where he sat motionless at the pianoforte but followed Sophia back to her seat with his eyes, she knew she, the vicar's daughter from Tinbury, had been forgotten. She wondered at the prick of disappointment she felt. She doubted she'd ever see awe, true awe, reflected in anyone's face in response to anything she'd played.

She wondered whether she cared. She had never cared very much about being admired.

Or so she'd thought.

Deuced *pride* once more. And now she was irritated, which meant temper, as well.

She laid the blame for all of this discomfort at the earl's door.

She touched a finger to the corner of her eye to stop the dampness and turned her face toward Geoffrey, curious to see whether he, too, was under the spell of Signora Licari.

But Geoffrey was sitting very still, and his expression was carefully, studiedly blank.

She willed him to look her way. He did not.

So her eyes moved to Mary . . . who caught her glance, and lifted up a gloved hand to hide a feigned yawn. She gave a one-shouldered shrug and a tiny smile and rolled her eyes.

Sabrina stifled a smile of her own. Trust Mary to be impervious to a soprano.

Later, after all the guests had gone to bed, Rhys once again bent over a billiard table across from Wyndham, a cigar clamped between his teeth.

"I've a little test for you," Wyndham said as Rhys took his shot. "What was the most fascinating thing about this evening?"

"Apart from whim seizing hold of Sophia?" Rhys said this around his cigar.

"It wasn't whim that seized hold of Sophia, Rhys. It was the beautiful little Miss Fairleigh and her playing."

"Beautiful?" Rhys idly scoffed. Though once Wyndham had said it, the word began to settle in and trouble him. "I'm the poet, Wynd. I should be the one speaking in hyperbole. Take your shot."

Wyndham did, and gloated, and Rhys removed his cigar from his mouth long enough to hiss disappointment.

"She's a green girl, but—"

Some errant gentlemanly impulse that amused him prevented Rhys from telling Wyndham about how he'd discovered Miss Fairleigh and his cousin in a kiss.

"But? For God's sake, Rhys, you can talk and take your shot at the same time, you know. It's done all the time."

Rhys took his shot, a bad one, which made Wyndham wince and cluck in mock sympathy. Rhys straightened and shrugged. "*But* she certainly played the devil out of La Valle's little composition, didn't she? Miss Fairleigh."

Rhys had thrust it in front of her in part to test her. It was an intricate, passionate little piece he'd commissioned from a musician who was much less appreciated than he ought to be and loved his liquor more than he should. And the girl had sunk right into it. She'd played it with the proper feeling, if not the most accomplished technique. Rhys admitted to himself that he'd been lost in it for the duration. That he had genuinely, without reservation, been moved.

And he knew no performer could move unless they truly *felt* what they were playing. She'd understood the piece, the passion and poignancy of it.

"She certainly did," Wyndham concurred. "And really, Rhys, there could be no other explanation for Sophia's performance tonight. I mean, we hadn't even reached the begging or bribing stages. You can be certain that if Miss Fairleigh were plain, Sophia would not have made the effort."

"I'd had the thought as well. No doubt Sophia needs adulation the way La Valle needs his drink, and perhaps Sophia thought there wouldn't be enough for her should we spare some for Miss Fairleigh. But Miss Fairleigh is hardly any sort of competition for Sophia, in singing or any other aspect of life."

Rhys had leaned his stick against the wall to pay proper attention to his cigar.

"Are you going to tell Sophia so?" Wyndham wanted to know.

"Good God, no. I'm not mad."

Wyndham laughed.

Nor did Rhys plan to pay a visit to Sophia tonight. She would be expecting him of course, thinking all she'd needed to do was wind the golden rope of her voice around him to tug him back into her bed. It was a familiar little game. He didn't think he was tired of it yet.

He did, however, think he might enjoy tinkering with the rules.

He could do without her tonight. One of the advantages of being The Libertine, and a grown man, was that he wasn't at the mercy of his sensual needs. He knew they would be met very nearly the moment he needed them met. It pleased him a little to think that few other men could make a similar claim.

And then he felt restless, because this knowledge did rather shave the sweet sharp edge of uncertainty from desire.

God, but he was tired of feeling restless.

"So how's the painting coming, Wyndham?"

"I've made a tree."

"Good, good," Rhys said absently. "Make some more."

Wyndham bent to shoot again. "Speaking of the fair Miss Fairleigh, we'll be deprived of part of our party tomorrow. Lady Mary informed me at dinner they intend to return with the Colberts for a visit to see Lizzie Colbert's new baby!" Wyndham imitated Mary's breathless tones.

Rhys grinned. "I've nothing at all against new babies. Something needs to replace all the ones that grow to be adults. Here's to Lizzie." He raised his glass.

"And it seems Lizzie Colbert has an ailing father who would appreciate a visit from a 'man of God,' or so those were her words, so your cousin Geoffrey will go along, as well as the fair Miss Fairleigh. Who, as she sat at my other elbow at dinner, told me the winter will be early and hard, thanks to the squirrels in Tinbury, or some such."

"Deuced squirrels," Rhys said idly, and took a long satisfying pull from his shortening cigar.

CHAPTER SEVEN

I DON'T LIKE the look of the sky," Tom said grimly. "It's too still, too even a color. Mark my words, there will be a snowstorm soon."

Living on the street for a good portion of his life had given Tom an animal's instinct for the caprices of weather.

The trip from London to Gorringe had been long and uncomfortable, as the first snows had muddied the roads and other passing equipages had made great furrows of them. The horses slowed to pick gingerly over ruts, but the wheels took them hard nevertheless, and conversation inside the coach began to sound like hiccups from the sheer amount of jolts. Up top, the coachmen availed themselves heavily of the contents of flasks, as much a winter accessory as the scarves and wool coats they wore.

Jamie Shaughnessy had been left for the day with his aunt Daisy and The General, who spoiled him unconscionably, and would probably inadvertently add a word or two to his vocabulary that didn't belong. But they loved him nearly as much as his father did.

And at last the stained-glass windows of the church, bright as jewels, signaled the travelers, and they were there once more. Susannah unconsciously reached for Sylvie's hand, a gesture of hope. She wondered if she would always approach this particular church with hope and trepidation.

Kit pushed open the door. "Mr. Sumner?" he called experimentally. He hoped to find the vicar about and lucid, since it was shortly after Matins, and before the time when the vicar might be dipping into the wine.

"Good day, my friends. Can I be of some assistance?"

They spun about to see the ancient vicar, precisely as Susannah remembered him: a tiny, spotted head, bare of hair, propped by a neck that was all soft folds of skin now.

They exchanged bows all around, and the vicar's eyes landed on Susannah and Sylvie and lit with pleasure. The vicar did appreciate a pretty girl.

And then he turned his attention to Tom Shaughnessy and studied him, mildly puzzled. Unlike Kit, who was quite obviously a lord to his toes, he seemed to have difficulty placing what Tom might be.

"My goodness," the vicar finally said.

Considering this a compliment, Tom swept a deep bow.

"I recall your visit, sir," the vicar said to Kit. "You said you've been known to be a generous benefactor on occasion. You inquired after the birth records here. And pretty girls."

Kit bit back a smile. The vicar, as all vicars were, was interested in anything that might add to the coffers of the church and his own income, and he hadn't forgotten.

"We've returned with another request, Mr. Sumner. To ask another question. This time about a curate, rather than a pretty girl. Have you a curate now?"

"Oh, the curates never linger long," the vicar said with a drifting sort of cheeriness.

This didn't surprise Kit in the least.

"Many years ago, nearly twenty years ago . . . did a curate assist you here in Gorringe?" he pressed.

The vicar's eyes drifted toward the windows, and the eyes of the four travelers followed his there. *Faith, Hope, Charity,* the windows read. The sun pushed through and made a colorful, softly blurred reflection of the words on the floor of the church.

Tom Shaughnessy cleared his throat.

The vicar turned back to them in surprise, as if just remembering they were there. "Fairleigh," he said.

No one seemed certain what to make of this.

"Fairly . . . long ago?" was Kit's careful guess.

Mr. Sumner's fuzzy gray brows dipped, puzzled. "It *was* fairly long ago, son, yes." He said it gently, as though humoring Kit.

And waited.

"Fairly long ago that you . . . that you had a curate?" was Tom's contribution.

"Yes. Fairleigh. Long ago." The vicar's brows had now met, and his forehead had collapsed into four deep puzzled lines.

Another uncomfortable silence limped by.

"The curate's name was Mr. Fairleigh!" Susannah burst out delightedly, as though they'd all been in the midst of a game of charades. "And he was your curate long ago!"

The curate turned a mild expression on her and his forehead smoothed out. "That *is* what I said, my dear."

"Do you know what became of Mr. Fairleigh?" Kit said immediately, to take advantage of the vicar's moment of lucidity.

"He was offered a living in the town of . . . of . . ."

He drifted again, smiled dreamily.

Sylvie possessed the least patience of anyone standing in the church. "Of?" she barked.

"Tinbury!" The vicar looked startled, but the barking had clearly jarred the word loose from his brain.

"Tinbury?" Kit repeated. "That's in the Midlands, yes?"

"I suppose so, son."

"Do you remember when this curate left for Tinbury?"

"He merely told me he'd been offered a living, and as I could never begrudge the young man a living of his own, I wished him Godspeed. So I cannot tell you a year, I fear."

"Did your Mr. Fairleigh have any children, Mr. Sumner? Do you recall?"

The vicar's head creaked up toward the ceiling in thought. And then creaked back down again. And slowly, he shook it to and fro with regret.

As the curate, Mr. Fairleigh, had not been *pretty,* as it were, no doubt Vicar Sumner had relinquished any memories associated with him. Kit imagined it was a pleasant and practical way to rank memories, if you could only keep a few. He rather thought he'd only want to remember the pretty things, too.

A *mission*!

The moment the fetching Miss Sabrina Fairleigh had shyly confided her dream to Geoffrey Gillray on their decorous little walk a few months ago, he'd all but shouted "Eureka!" He'd known it was precisely the story to bring to his cousin Rhys: he'd become a new man now that he was a curate. He enjoyed his quiet life, his sermons, the helping of others. He'd developed a taste for doing good works; he understood now, after a wildly misspent youth, that he had a calling to spread his newfound devoutness and brotherhood to other cultures and continents.

He'd like, in other words, to go on a mission.

And he needed eight thousand pounds in order to do it. For medical and building supplies. Those sorts of things.

This last bit, particularly the eight thousand pounds bit, was going to be difficult to say with a solemn face, and without sweating.

But it was, in fact, the most crucial bit of the story. In truth, eight thousand pounds was two thousand more pounds than Geoffrey actually—urgently—needed, but he'd decided it would be practical to request a little extra, as dear *God* he missed his life in London, and none of the things he missed were inexpensive.

It was safer at the moment not to venture into London at all, of course. He'd wrung a good deal of credit from the Gillray name and the fact that he was cousin to the Earl of Rawden—he was in fact a little bemused at just how *very* much—but the pity was . . . merchants inevitably wanted to be paid for their goods. And men tended to want their vowels honored, too, after a certain amount of time had elapsed. Geoffrey wasn't averse to paying anyone. It was just that it had all caught up to him yet again—it had happened several times before, this snowball of debt, and his father and his cousin had several times been importuned for money—and now the straits were dire, indeed. Merchants had cut off his credit; some had even, to his surprise, resorted to threats of violence.

His father, ill though he was, had managed to secure him a tucked-away position in Tinbury with the Vicar Fairleigh, who happily had a pretty daughter who had proved diverting and pleasant to look at. Geoffrey would have outright languished if he hadn't had *someone* pretty about to look at, even if that particular someone was much too innocent and provincial for his tastes. Tinbury was driving him slowly mad, but it ought to protect him from his creditors for the time being. They were proving to be a determined group, but it would probably be some time before they thought of looking for *him,* of all people, in Tinbury.

And Geoffrey had no intention of remaining a curate. He was a Gillray, for God's sake. He was born to be a bloody *gentleman.*

Geoffrey hadn't been to La Montagne since he was a child, since Rhys's father, the former earl, had lost everything, and sold all holdings that could be sold. And it seemed, through some kind of miracle, Rhys had been able to buy La Montagne back for the Rawden title. Geoffrey had been astounded to discover that nearly everything he recalled from his youth—the fixtures, paintings, statuary—had been restored to its place at La Montagne. Seeing all of it had stirred up the resentment that always waited somewhere in him.

His cousin, it was clear, had money, and plenty of it.

They were so alike, he and Rhys. Geoffrey was younger, but at one time he and his cousin, the earl, had genuinely enjoyed each other, sharing as they did the family sense of humor, the appreciation for all things beautiful, and a gift for, a pleasure in, words. But Rhys had somehow turned those things into tools that served him, and had created a grand life from them. Geoffrey had tried, or at least tried *somewhat,* but he was forever swept along by the current of his own predilections. He didn't enjoy working. He'd worked, and he'd *not* worked, and he vastly preferred the latter.

"A curate, Geoffrey?" were Rhys's first words when Geoffrey sat down before him in his office. "How in

God's name did that come about?" He sounded faintly amused.

Geoffrey struggled to keep his expression neutral, as it was crucial to making his story convincing, but even he was a little amused by the fact that he'd become a curate. "Father found the position for me."

"Well, I suppose it's one way to use that Gillray silver tongue. Up at the altar with a captive audience, no less. Less expensive than talking your way beneath the skirts of parlor maids and actresses."

Geoffrey leaped to his own defense. "It was only *one* parlor maid. And she was unusually pretty."

"And *expensive*," Rhys emphasized. "For me, anyhow. No doubt you've a son in Cornwall now, because that's where she went after I paid her to leave. But her disgruntled employers miss her. Apparently she was the best damned parlor maid they'd ever had."

Geoffrey sighed. Geoffrey was clever, but so was Rhys, and Rhys had always been so bloody quick. Rhys knew precisely why Geoffrey was sitting before him today, and he had deftly seized the upper hand in the conversation.

"I've thanked you for that," Geoffrey said.

"Yes, you did," Rhys confirmed. "As you did all of the other times I've come to your aid with money. And you've clearly something to ask, Geoffrey, so you may as well go about it."

Geoffrey cleared his throat. "Well, you see, Rhys . . . I've learned in my new position as a curate in Tinbury . . . how very much I enjoy the quiet life of service and—"

"Tea? Brandy? Whiskey? A cigar?" Rhys interrupted suddenly, gesturing. A glint in his eye.

Oh, God, all of them, all of them, please. "No, thank you. I don't—"

"Ah, but you used to, Geoffrey." It was partly a tease, and partly a jab, and partly a test, Geoffrey knew. "You used to, and then some."

"But no longer, Rhys," Geoffrey said somberly. "And I cannot, of course, afford to buy cigars, should I care to smoke them."

He couldn't help but add this, and realized it was a bit of a mistake. A faint whiff of bitterness lingered in the air, acrid as the smoke from a bad cigar.

Rhys's eyebrows went up in mock sympathy. "But you've found fulfillment in your latest role, you say. What about Miss Sabrina Fairleigh? She has a 'mission,' too, you see. She wishes to help people abroad, or so she confided this dream to us all at dinner. I find it unusual to play host to all manner of folk from Tinbury."

Geoffrey paused. "She's pretty, isn't she?" he said.

"Yes," Rhys agreed fervently.

And because they were Gillrays and couldn't quite help themselves, they shared a brief moment outside of resentment and grinned at each other.

"But I found her a bit righteous," Rhys continued more somberly, a moment later.

Was this a test? "Perhaps it's just that she doesn't share your predilections," Geoffrey said carefully, and just a little primly.

"Don't you mean *our* predilections, Geoffrey?"

"*Your* predilections," Geoffrey said quickly. "They aren't mine any longer, Rhys, I swear to it. I have—"

"Oh, that's right. A calling. And just to be clear: your calling doesn't include whiskey, cigars, parlor maids, actresses, fast horses, or gaming hells?" Rhys asked with a furrow in his brow.

Geoffrey struggled to keep the yearning from his expression. He felt a bit like a starving man listening to a menu of his very favorite dishes.

"I swear to you, Rhys. I should like to go on a mission. I find it is my higher calling."

"How much will this mission cost?"

Geoffrey inhaled and willed his features to hold very still. "Eight thousand pounds," he said piously.

The earl stared at him, mouth open. "Eight *thous*—" Rhys slapped the desk and barked a laugh. "Oh, cousin, I've missed you."

"But I'm not . . . ," Geoffrey trailed off. He knew already it was futile. "I'm not jesting."

"Geoffrey." Incredulous patience. "I told you the last time I paid off your gaming debts that I wouldn't do it again. Your father found you a position as a curate; I suggest you make the most of it. And Tinbury sounds like an *excellent* place to lie low if you're dodging debt. There's a fair every year, I hear."

His bloody cousin was so damn smug. And now Geoffrey truly was sweating. He remained silent, and gripped the knees of his trousers to dry his hands. That eight thousand pounds seemed to close in on him now, threatening as a flock of vultures.

"I swear to you, Rhys . . . it's a mission. For travel expenses, and medical and building supplies, and—"

"All right," Rhys said calmly. "If you remain a curate at Tinbury for a year at the very least, then return and we'll discuss your mission once again."

Geoffrey stared at Rhys, looking for any give, and of course found none.

A leaden silence followed.

"How is your father?" Rhys asked finally, somewhat conciliatorily.

"Not well," Geoffrey said shortly.

"I'm sorry to hear it."

Geoffrey nodded shortly, not wanting to talk about his father, and they were quiet together for a moment, no longer certain how to speak to each other.

"Rhys?" he said after a moment.

"What is it, Geoffrey?"

"Where did it come from, all those years ago? The money?"

"Money?" Rhys repeated, his expression neutral.

"There was no money . . . your father and mine and the bad investments, and then your father was killed and your mother and sister were—"

"I recall the delightful sequence of events," Rhys said curtly. "You were just a boy."

Things had been bad indeed, then, Geoffrey recalled. Fear had permeated his home like a mold; it had been everywhere in the atmosphere. And then it had been gone, the fear, because suddenly there was money.

The money had come too late for Rhys's family, in some respects. But at least there had been money.

"Where did it come from? The money? The house? I thought you were given a house somewhere."

"It was serendipity," Rhys said after a moment. Cryptically.

"Is that a town in Yorkshire?" Geoffrey asked. A faint bit of humor.

And Rhys did smile a little. "Clever. Cleverness will be useful when you give sermons, Geoffrey. And now, if you'll excuse me? I've as usual enjoyed our conversation, but I've La Montagne business to attend to."

Dismissed. It had always been his cousin's right to dismiss him, and Geoffrey obediently stood, habit winning out over the never-far-from-the-surface resentment.

But he'd never before asked Rhys about the money, or the house. Nor had he ever asked these questions of his father.

And Rhys's evasive answer was *very* interesting.

Later that afternoon, after spending part of the day absorbed in a volume of Greek myths, Sabrina found Geoffrey quietly reading a book in the drawing room. That shock of dark hair was falling over his eyes as he read. Sabrina was possessed yet again of the urge to brush it away. If she became his wife—aw, that was no way to think—*when* she became his wife—she could reach across any table and do that as he looked over the sermon he would give, or as he sat down to the dinner she'd cooked.

She came and sat quietly next to him. He looked up, the memory of their kiss in his eyes, and she felt her face growing warm.

"Did you enjoy Miss Licari last night?" Sabrina asked.

"Did I *enjoy* her?" He looked slightly startled. Almost guilty. "Oh, did I enjoy her *singing,* do you mean?"

"Well . . . yes." What else could she possibly mean?

"Well, I found it . . ." He seemed to be searching for a word.

"Glorious?" she suggested resignedly.

"Loud." He smiled a little.

"Truly?" Sabrina was puzzled. "You didn't want to simply . . . soak in it? To let it take you over?"

Geoffrey smiled a little. "How you do talk sometimes, Sabrina."

"She is beautiful, though, isn't she?"

"Is she? I didn't notice." He glanced quickly down at his book.

"Nonsense, Geoffrey," she teased.

He smiled again, but it was a tight, narrow thing, and his fingers were plucking nervously at his book. Truly, Geoffrey seemed liable to jump out of his skin lately.

"Geoffrey, is aught amiss?" And then she felt uneasy. "Was the earl unreceptive to your request?"

And when she saw his expression, she felt her missionary dreams begin to slip away.

Geoffrey sighed and looked across the room, to where the earl and Signora Licari and Wyndham and the cello player were having what appeared to be an animated discussion. Wyndham was waving his hands about.

"Sabrina . . . I don't think he will offer funds."

"*But—!*" She lowered her voice to a strident whisper when she realized she'd squeaked the word. "But he has so very much! Look at this *house*! How can he possibly refuse you?"

"I think the earl has other priorities and other interests, and many of them are gathered about him right now. Artists and opera singers."

Sabrina blinked in the face of his bitterness.

"But you are so very eloquent, Geoffrey. I cannot see how you would have failed to arouse his sympathy for your cause!"

Geoffrey seemed to gather his composure with some effort, took a deep breath, pushed his shock of hair out of his eyes. "Sabrina . . . he likes you," he began.

"He does?" This was a surprise. She didn't know how this could possibly be true. She considered correcting Geoffrey: *He seems to like* torturing *me*.

"He deigned to turn the pages for you as you played last night."

"That was because—that is, well, he did turn the pages, didn't he? It was kind of him."

"Kind." Geoffrey repeated the world flatly, ironically. But didn't expound. "And he did suggest that you play another piece. So perhaps he enjoyed your playing."

"Yes. Perhaps."

Again, the suggestion that she play another piece was more a gesture of torture than of fellowship, Sabrina suspected. Then again . . .

No. It had been a test. She knew it had been a test. But she'd rather enjoyed the piece, and so, in the end, it had felt like a gift. An uncomfortable gift, in a way. She hadn't known it had resided in her, the ability to interpret a piece so lovely and sweeping. It was something new about herself she was forced to consider. But she hadn't room in her plans for new assumptions about herself at the moment. She wanted to be a missionary, and the wife of a missionary.

"Perhaps, then, Sabrina . . . perhaps you can persuade him to review my cause?"

"Do you really think it would help?"

"I cannot think that it would hurt. The earl is known to be susceptible to"—his gaze dropped to her lips—"feminine charms."

"Geoffrey!" Sabrina said, blushing, casting her lashes down for an instant. This house party had certainly unleashed his more ardent qualities. "Do you really think I'm capable of *charming* him into supporting our—your—cause?" She stumbled, a little mortified by her slip yet again. "He's so very . . ."

Geoffrey didn't appear to notice her slip, or perhaps, now, it was the way he thought of it, too: *our.* It was their future, the future she'd dreamed about for nearly a year now, and it was fading quickly.

"If anyone can charm him, Sabrina . . . it's you."

And then he laid his hand over the top of hers, surreptitiously, so that no one in the room could see.

Why is a woman's skin so very, very *soft, if it isn't meant to be touched?*

Sabrina stared down at his hand, considering the feel of Geoffrey's skin against her skin. It was the very first time he had touched her so intimately, apart from the sudden kiss.

Why then can so very much pleasure be had from touching . . . and from being touched?

It was odd, but she would not have described it as pleasure; pleasure was too strong a word for this contact.

Perhaps the sort of touch the earl had described was entirely different.

Sabrina glanced up. There was heat of a sort in Geoffrey's eyes; she glanced away, and gently slid her hand out from beneath his, with a little smile to tell him she didn't mind. She didn't want to entirely discourage him, after all.

But she did want to think about how it felt to be touched by him before he touched her again.

"All right. For you, Geoffrey, I shall try."

CHAPTER EIGHT

S HE KNEW SHE could wander the grand house for a day and not encounter the earl, so she sought out Mrs. Bailey instead. Sabrina knew she was about to ask a bold question. Then again, perhaps the housekeeper was growing accustomed to bold questions about the whereabouts of gentlemen from the seemingly mild-mannered Miss Fairleigh.

She cleared her throat. "Mrs. Bailey, I wonder if I might trouble you for the earl's whereabouts?"

Mrs. Bailey fixed her with a gaze striking in its impartiality. It tempted Sabrina to say all manner of controversial things. It was a very freeing sort of impartiality, Mrs. Bailey's gaze.

"The earl was last in the portrait gallery, Miss Fairleigh. It is just beyond the yellow sitting room."

"Thank you, Mrs. Bailey."

The portrait gallery turned out to be a large room featuring portraits as tall as actual people, or even taller. As if making them very large would make up for the fact that they were all dead. Between the portraits were sconces, and the room glowed softly, lighting all the painted faces, should someone care to come in and view them.

Oddly, the earl was there, but he wasn't gazing at a portrait rather at a space between the portraits where a portrait ought to have been.

"Why, good evening, Miss Fairleigh." He'd scarcely glanced her way.

"Oh! Good evening, Lord Rawden." She tried to sound surprised to find him here.

In profile, she saw his mouth turn up a little. He knew she was pretending. Still, he didn't attempt to engage her in conversation.

He moved on to a portrait; it featured a man with a pointed beard and dark eyes and long face, his neck encircled by a stiff ruff. A pair of spaniels cavorted at his feet. He looked very familiar.

"Goodness. He rather resembles—"

"Geoffrey. Yes, doesn't he? That's the Viscount Merrivell." He turned to Sabrina. "He was hung for marde. No doubt because he succumbed to untoward passions."

He turned back to the portrait, eyes glinting.

She willed herself to stay composed. "Fortunately, I doubt you shall ever need to worry that Geoff—Mr. Gillray will end in such a manner."

"Is that so, Miss Fairleigh?" Absently said.

"He is admired by the people of Tinbury."

"And by one of them in particular, as I've witnessed."

She took a deep breath. "He very much would like to do some good in the world outside of Tinbury, Lord Rawden."

"That would make for a pleasant change."

She frowned a little. "I beg your pardon?"

The earl ignored her question. "I imagine you sought me out for a reason, Miss Fairleigh. Do you wish to plead the cause of your lover to me, then?"

Her jaw dropped; she quickly clapped it closed again. "He is *not* my lover."

"But . . . you did kiss him." The earl's brow creased in feigned confusion.

"No! Yes! Well, *he* kissed *me*. And—"

"Are you married to Geoffrey?"

"What—I—you know full well I am not, Lord Rawden."

"Well then, are you *engaged* to be married to Geoffrey?"

She hesitated. "No, but—"

"Do you have any sort of understanding at *all* with Geoffrey?"

She didn't quite know the answer to this, but she certainly wasn't going to tell the earl so. She remained stubbornly silent.

"Then he's your lover," he concluded firmly. "And *I* of all people should know what a lover is." He returned his eyes to the portrait. But not before she saw the spark of devilry in them.

Did he suppose she was another Sophia Licari, for heaven's sake? Going about recklessly kissing people? Or was he merely being incorrigible again?

"Geoffrey *can't* be my lover as we haven't . . . we haven't . . ."

She stopped and squeezed her eyes closed.

"You haven't what, Miss Fairleigh?" The odious man was laughing silently at her. "Oh, wait, I recall now. You've a will of iron and cannot be seduced. So of course you . . . '*haven't*.' And I am a scoundrel to suggest such a thing to an unmarried girl. And so on."

"Lord Rawden. I am *not* like you."

"No?" he wondered in an idly insinuating way.

Sabrina bit her lip to keep from retorting. She'd come for a purpose, and she wasn't about to be diverted from it. With some effort, she gentled her voice, as she might when speaking to a nervous animal.

"Lord Rawden, as you've devoted your life to pleasure, I imagine it is difficult for you to understand a man such as Geoffrey, who is willing to make sacrifices in favor of a higher calling. But if you'd only—"

The earl barked a genuine laugh. "Devoted my life to pleasure! Why, my dear little hypocrite, you've devoted your life to pleasure, too."

Sabrina blinked, thinking of the work in Tinbury at the vicarage, the work that kept her moving and thinking swiftly from the moment she rose until her head landed on her pillow again at night. Thinking of her dreams of laboring as a missionary.

She was *incensed.*

"What on earth do you mean?" Her voice thrummed with outrage.

"Don't you take pleasure in judging me? Don't you take pleasure in . . . *helping*? Don't you feel just a little bit superior because you *do* help? Come now. Confess all, Miss Fairleigh."

"I—" She disliked the way he said "helping." Though this was, in fact, very difficult to deny. She would consider the part about "feeling superior" in a moment. She had an uncomfortable suspicion that she wouldn't like what she discovered.

"And why do you do it?" he prompted, very much as though she were a schoolgirl and he a schoolmaster, when she said nothing. "You couldn't even resist *helping* with my poem when I asked, even though it was about seduction—not a very *nice* topic—and even though you think I'm a complete reprobate. Come, Miss Fairleigh. Tell me why."

Oddly, she sensed he was a bit angry now, too.

This wasn't at all going as she'd hoped.

She scrambled for her mental footing, but he'd succeeded in poking her temper up again, which made it nearly impossible. "I cannot speak to how *thorough* a reprobate you might be, Lord Rawden, but—"

He laughed, this time sounding for some reason thoroughly pleased. "Why, then, do you help, Miss Fairleigh? Are you afraid for my immortal soul? Because you're the vicar's daughter, and must always do good?"

"I was adopted," she said curtly. "I'm not the vicar's daughter."

"Ah, well then, that explains *every*thing."

"*What* does it explain?" Her voice was perilously close to shrill.

"Never mind, Miss Fairleigh. Do go on. We were talking about your fear for my immortal soul." He was laughing silently at her again.

"Your immortal soul concerns me very little, Lord Rawden." This wasn't entirely truthful. At the moment, she rather wished his immortal soul someplace that would appall her father.

"Why, then?" he persisted. "What compels you, Miss Fairleigh, to devote your life to . . . helping? I would like a truthful answer before we pursue the topic of Geoffrey and his mission."

"Because—"

She stopped, realizing what she was about to say. He was again right: she helped because it made her uncomfortable *not* to help.

In short: she helped because she enjoyed it.

"Do you do it because you want to, or because you think you should?" he coaxed. She could not recall encountering another man so utterly determined to prove a point.

"Aren't they the same?" She said it rather helplessly, delaying her moment of confession.

"One is about pleasure, Miss Fairleigh, and the other is about duty. Then again, perhaps you take pleasure in duty. I can only imagine you do, if you've dreams of living in penury serving the poor as a missionary. Tell me, once and for all, why do you help?"

She tried for a partial answer. "Because I . . . must. Because it's right."

"Right for whom?" Relentless, he was. Ferocious as any debater who ever stood in the House of Lords. She wondered if he did take his place in debates in the House of Lords. She didn't know where he'd find the time to do it, given his schedule of debauchery.

And in a way it was invigorating to encounter a mind that would never let her dodge a truth. Then again, she could have happily lived without being shown certain truths.

But as she was innately honest, she could hardly avoid answering.

And at last she did. "Right for . . . me." Her voice was a trifle creaky when it emerged.

Like a tiger with its kill between its paws, he all but purred the next words. "Ah. Very well, then. Feel free to make an entreaty on Geoffrey's behalf, Miss Fairleigh, and feel free to judge me if you will, Miss Fairleigh, but judge me honestly. We are not so very different, you and I, in our commitment to pleasure."

Humbled, Sabrina looked up into his satisfied face.

But she suddenly understood something: that satisfaction he felt was only momentary. The rest of the time he was restless and bored and—

"Oh, I fear there you are wrong, Lord Rawden. For helping makes me *happy*."

And it was a pleasure, and not a pleasure, to watch him blink as though she'd slapped him. All the fierce light and satisfaction fled his face for an instant, and unguarded, he looked purely . . . astonished.

His mask was back in an instant, as if the moment had never been.

"You came here to plead with me about Geoffrey, I imagine, Miss Fairleigh," he said calmly. "What is it you wish to say?"

Sabrina could not recover quite so swiftly as the earl from their exchange. She took a deep breath to steady herself. Sparring with him—and his mere presence—was as invigorating and disturbing as a stiff wind. And all the things he made her aware of, things she wasn't certain she wanted to know, crowded into her thoughts now, tangling with her plans and the words she wanted to say.

"He wants to do some good in the world, Geoffrey does," she said quietly, simply. "That's all, Lord Rawden. You have it within your means to permit that to happen."

"And you want to accompany him on his mission." A statement.

She was silent for a moment. "I would very much like to do some good as well. And we are of two minds, philosophically, Geoffrey and I."

"Of even temperament?" he asked ironically.

She didn't respond. Breathed in, breathed out. Her temperament at the moment felt more like waves battering at cliff walls.

It was entirely his fault.

The earl nodded to himself once, as if her silence was answer enough. He eyed the portrait that so resembled his cousin. Spent another moment in quiet.

"Has he offered for you, Miss Fairleigh? Do you yet have an understanding? You didn't answer my question." His voice was level. The question seemed reflective.

She flushed. "Well . . . no, he has not yet offered. But I believe it's because he is uncertain about his future, and he is concerned about what he may be able to offer a wife. I have every expectation that once he knows . . ."

"You've a good deal of faith in Geoffrey's intentions, Miss Fairleigh, have you?" And he was ironic again.

How difficult it must be, she thought, to think so cynically of everyone. What a burden.

"I—," she began, but he held up a hand to stop her, shook his head once, as though he didn't require an answer.

She waited again, as he said nothing for a time. Reflective. He turned to her, looked down at her with those light eyes of his.

"You should know that I have already outright refused Geoffrey's request for assistance. Did he tell you that? Did he send you to plead with me, or did you do it of your own volition?"

Sabrina's heart became a stone, and sank. Geoffrey hadn't said as much, in so many words; he hadn't said he'd been rejected. She did wonder why. Perhaps he refused to believe his cousin's refusal had been irrevocable. She said nothing; she cast her eyes down briefly.

When she looked up again, the earl's eyes were on her, his expression inscrutable. She suspected that he could read her as clearly as any book in his library.

"You've very pretty eyes, Miss Fairleigh, but it takes much more than that to persuade me to part with my money."

It had been flung like stardust, the compliment. Her breath hitched strangely. There hadn't been a shred of flirtation in his statement. It rather sounded like something he'd been thinking for some time.

He sought out her eyes and held them, and in the silence that followed, Sabrina could feel it: the very nearly tidal pull he exerted. It seemed right to succumb to it, to see what might happen.

And she wanted to free herself from it, too.

She didn't know how to go about either of those things.

With some effort, she finally turned her head and began studying another portrait.

A moment later she heard him move away from her, three leisurely steps echoing across the gallery.

She wondered why it was he was here, lingering over each portrait. It was as though he was reviewing his lineage, ascertaining that all his relatives were hanging where they belonged.

He paused at that empty space between portraits once again.

"My mother and my sisters belong here," he said shortly. Almost to himself.

The words "my mother and my sisters" touched on the longing she felt for her own, stirring the memory of a long-ago night.

"I've always wanted a mother and sisters."

He turned to look at her then, interest apparently piqued. "And what did you have instead, Miss Fairleigh?"

"A father and two brothers much older than I. I never knew my mother. My mother died, it seems. Or so I was told."

"So did mine," he said shortly, his voice nearly inflectionless. "So did my sister."

The revelation surprised her. It made that empty space seem somehow more eloquent. She wanted to ask why the portrait was missing, but his silence had an impenetrable quality to it, and her nerve, which seemed uncommonly pronounced when he was about, was lost.

Finally, the earl spoke. To the wall, not directly to her.

"I will consider offering Geoffrey the living at Buckstead Heath, Miss Fairleigh. He may live at the vicarage there, if he chooses. The rest of your future is in Geoffrey's hands. But I shall not finance his . . . mission . . . regardless of your entreaty. And I fear my answer is final."

She'd expected to feel acute disappointment. And she *was* disappointed. But disappointment seemed to be wrestling for her attention with a dozen other thoughts and sensations at the moment, and so its edge was blunted.

She had been a vicar's daughter; she certainly knew how to be a vicar's wife, and in truth, of all the futures she could imagine, it seemed as suitable for her as any. She knew good livings were rare; she knew Geoffrey would be fortunate indeed to be given one. And perhaps when the earl offered Geoffrey a living, Geoffrey would offer for her.

"Thank you, Lord Rawden," she said quietly.

He merely nodded curtly. "And I should like to personally inform Geoffrey of my decision to do so, Miss Fairleigh, when and if I reach it. So if you would be so kind as to not speak of it to him until then?"

"As you wish. You've my word."

The earl said nothing more. A moment later he seemed to have forgotten her. He wandered farther down the gallery, and appeared to lapse into a reverie before a portrait of a woman in a dress featuring an enormous bustle, a narrow-faced dog cavorting at her side.

Sabrina turned to leave.

"Yemen," he said suddenly.

She paused, and turned slowly back to him.

"Yem—? Oh! It's the . . . it's the rhyme for lemon, isn't it?" She smiled a little.

He turned to face her again. "One of the world's oldest countries," he said gravely.

"Part of the Ottoman Empire."

"Ah, so you *do* read English well enough, Miss Fairleigh." And then he smiled at her, an open smile. Genuinely, simply pleased.

Sabrina laughed, feeling a peculiar, breathless rush of delight.

The earl turned abruptly away from her then. Almost as if the sight of her bright face troubled him.

A little stung, she hovered a moment more in the gallery, uncertain.

And when his silence made it clear that he'd finished with her, she quickly left him, listening to her own footsteps echoing across the gallery. She wasn't precisely fleeing. But she knew relief to be away from his restless

games and daunting mind and the charm he seemed to
ration—perhaps because it was so very, very potent.

Late that evening, after billiards and before he retired,
Rhys made his way into the library and examined the
shelves carefully. Mrs. Bailey and her staff were exem-
plary, but they were no match for a very observant earl. He
could see by the slim line of dust remaining on the shelf
between the books—it was a place that no amount of staff
could ever hope to keep completely spotless at all times—
that the volume of Greek myths had been disturbed ever so
slightly. Pulled from its place and read and replaced again,
no doubt, by a girl from Tinbury with misguided notions
about her even temperament and practical ambitions.

   She all but left a trail of clues for him. She had no idea
that poetry and passion lived in her soul, or how open she
left herself to sensual gambits because of it.

   She would know in a day or so.

   She was cleverer than he preferred her to be. She had
an unnervingly direct gaze, when it was more fashionable
for a woman to look sideways through lowered lashes, or
cast eyes modestly down. Her view of the world was uncluttered by cynicism but clouded by naïveté. She didn't
know any better, he supposed, than to look a man in the
eye and deliver stripping truths.

   She'd managed against all odds . . . to surprise him.
Again.

   And it had been as exhilarating—and about as pleasant—
as being pushed off a cliff.

   He supposed it was surprise that caused him to offer to
speak to Geoffrey about the living at Buckstead Heath. He

in truth didn't at all want his cousin to be consistently underfoot, or anywhere near La Montagne. He didn't want his cousin formally beholden to him in the least; he'd in fact hoped to see Geoffrey very seldom for the rest of his days.

Surely he couldn't have considered the idea simply to please Sabrina Fairleigh.

He'd turned to watch her walk away, admiring the elegant line of her body, the curves of her. Achingly pretty was Sabrina Fairleigh. But then, so were so many other women.

Having Geoffrey underfoot might very well mean having Sabrina Fairleigh underfoot as well, if Geoffrey did the honorable thing and married the girl he'd kissed. Rhys's mouth quirked grimly. Then again, the Gillrays made rather a habit of avoiding the honorable thing. He reminded himself that he'd made no promises to anyone. He didn't particularly need to speak to Geoffrey about anything at all when this house party ended.

He glanced down at the book in his hand. Below the shelf where Miss Fairleigh had plucked the volume of Greek myths was the shelf where the poetry resided.

He slid out the volume of Byron, and replaced it with a book bound in somber green leather: *The Secret to Seduction.*

Usually Sabrina slid into slumber's arms effortlessly, as the work of the day thoroughly spent her. When sleep eluded her—as it occasionally did, if the weather was restless—she would lie awake and dream about the future, or wonder about her mother; soon after Geoffrey had appeared in Tinbury, she'd sometimes dared to imagine a future including Geoffrey.

But tonight, rich food, too much leisure, and a controversial earl contrived to prevent her from sleeping, and she found herself wrestling with her blankets as she tossed and turned. At last Sabrina stilled, surrendering to one particular thought, and lay on her back, staring up at the ceiling.

She drew her hand out from beneath the blankets and lifted it up before her in the dark, studying it, turning it slowly this way and that.

And then hesitantly, lightly, slowly, she dragged the fingers of her other hand from the center of her palm, down the silky skin beneath her forearm, then turned them round to brush them up against the short hairs of her arm. She listened to her body as she did it, and felt her own touch echoing in her—a whisper of sensation at her spine, at the nape of her neck, at the crook of her legs—as though something in her had been gently awakened.

And like most things when just awakened . . . it had an appetite. Wanted more.

Why do you suppose a woman's skin is so soft . . . so very, very soft . . . if it isn't meant to . . . tempt?

And then she imagined other fingers on her skin, long, confident fingers, lightly, slowly tracing the very same path.

The thought of him, just the thought of him, was a bolt of lightning at the base of her spine. A conflagration of sensation swept through and stole her breath on its way.

Stunning. It was as though every part of her had leaped to heed a call it had been waiting for.

And if we aren't meant to take pleasure in our own skin, Miss Fairleigh, why then can so very much pleasure be had from touching it . . . and from being touched?

She thrust her hand beneath her blankets again. Curled it into a fist.

There were other ways of being, she knew, just as there were other lands besides England, and one couldn't experience all of them. Not every threshold was meant to be crossed, or every curiosity indulged.

And she did have a strong will. And so she willed her thoughts in other, more familiar directions, and they became more soothing. She drifted to sleep on thoughts of her future at Geoffrey's side, the vicar's wife at Buckstead Heath.

But in dreams will has no jurisdiction. And so she dreamed of another man entirely.

CHAPTER NINE

THE NEXT MORNING Sabrina awoke with a grinding headache, a result of too much food and more wine than she was accustomed to, and perhaps too much opera singing; perhaps those grand notes were still ricocheting about in her head. It was the sort of headache that made her stomach roil, and when the maid came in to build the fire, shuffling and clanking things, Sabrina turned her face into her pillow to stifle a groan of pain. She wondered if this was how debauchers felt every morning, and wondered why they bothered with debauchery, if this was the case.

She staggered out of bed and peered out the curtains, but even the flat winter light stabbed through her eye into her skull. She didn't like the looks of the sky. It looked full and resentful. Portentous.

The sky looked full and resentful? It was just the sort of impression that would have worried her father.

"Sabrina, why aren't you—"

It was Mary, who had burst in to find Sabrina in her night rail, clutching the window frame.

"Speak softly, Mary," Sabrina croaked. "I've a bad head."

"Oh, dear!" Mary whispered worriedly. She approached Sabrina tentatively, as though the bad head might be contagious, and placed the back of her hand against Sabrina's forehead.

"Well, you aren't feverish," she said briskly. "But do you think you can travel?"

"I am sorry, Mary, but I really don't believe a carriage ride over rutted roads . . ." She closed her eyes, picturing it. And picturing it brought a fresh thump of pain and started a swirl of nausea in the pit of her stomach.

"Geoffrey and the Colberts will be so disappointed," Mary said wistfully.

And then Sabrina recalled that a greater disappointment awaited Geoffrey when he returned, which was when she would tell him she'd failed to persuade the earl of his cause.

"You'll return very soon?" she said to Mary.

"In a day or so. It's only a few hours by carriage, and the earl has graciously allowed us the use of his. He's soooo handsome, don't you think, Sabrina? The earl? It's difficult to believe he's so very wicked, because his manners are so fine. Do you suppose Miss Licari and he . . . last night . . ." Mary whispered it.

"*Unnnnh . . .*" Sabrina moaned and put the flat of her own mercifully cool hands on her temples. She didn't want to think of it.

"All right, all right," Mary said gently, but she was clearly a bit disappointed they weren't to have a bit of a gossip. "I'll ask Mrs. Bailey to send up tea and a headache powder. I shall miss you, but I shall refrain from giving you a hug at the moment, as you look as though you might cast your accounts upon me."

"My thanks," Sabrina said wryly. "But, Mary, do be careful. I don't like the look of the sky."

Mary sighed. "Oh, Sabrina." She said it almost pityingly. "Everything will be all right, and it's *not an omen*. The earl will eventually need to do *something* to ensure a place in Heaven, and why shouldn't the funding of Geoffrey's venture be it?"

Ah, Mary. The optimist. Sabrina didn't enlighten Mary about last night's conversation, because it would only prolong the one she was having now.

"Let's get you back into bed, now. I shall see you in a few days."

And so Sabrina was settled back into her bed, and Mary turned the pillow so that the cool side would cradle Sabrina's tender head.

Sometime later the solemn housekeeper brought in chocolate and a headache powder. Sabrina drifted into dreams that were astonishingly vivid, if not restful, as the powder took her headache away.

Later, Sabrina remembered the moment the blizzard struck. A clock somewhere in the vast house had chimed three times—could it really be three o'clock?—and shortly after that, a violent wind flung open the windows and roared through the room, dashing up the curtains and knocking over the fireplace poker.

Sabrina leaped out of bed and threw her weight against the window, struggling with the latch. It must have been open just a bit; perhaps the conscientious Mrs. Bailey had decided fresh air would revive Miss Fairleigh.

Once the burst of activity was over, Sabrina realized she was light-headed, no doubt from hunger, but no longer in pain. The headache powder had done its work.

It was cool near the windows, but the fit of them into their frames was gratifyingly snug, and when she held her hand up against the frame, she felt no breeze.

But a howling wind had filled the sky with a violent swirl of snow, and she could see nothing of the grounds. She pulled the heavy brocade curtains snugly closed, anyway, and wandered to the fire, snatching up her shawl on the way, to heat herself before it.

Part of her was a bit pleased she'd been correct: a blizzard! Early! The squirrels had it right all along.

Then she realized that she was alone in the house with the earl, and Mr. Wyndham, and Signora Licari.

Nausea of a sort returned again at the thought.

She prayed Mary and the others had arrived at the Colberts' safely. They had left so very early this morning, and the Colberts were but a few miles away. In all likelihood they were now ensconced before a fire, chocolate in hands, chatting pleasantly.

Chocolate. She was definitely feeling more herself if chocolate made her stomach growl.

It sounded like a splendid idea. Sabrina eyed the bell that would call for a servant, and wondered if she dared give it a pull. It seemed she hardly had the right. And yet the earl employed a battery of servants for this very reason, and Sabrina hated to think that one of them might be bored.

She gave the bell a pull.

But now another realization settled in: because of the blizzard, it was a certainty that it would be days before Mary and Geoffrey returned.

In moments, it seemed, Mrs. Bailey appeared.

She was carrying with her a tray topped with a pot that steamed a cocoa smell, and laid about it were lovely golden slices—bread and cheese, no doubt.

"Thank you, Mrs. Bailey. You are truly . . ."

She didn't finish the compliment, as Mrs. Bailey fixed her with a mildly reproving look, as if to say she was already fully aware that she was a marvel, and found compliments condescending. She was only doing her job.

"Thank you," Sabrina finished shyly.

"You are feeling more like yourself, Miss Fairleigh?"

No was the answer to that question.

But an infantry battle was no longer taking place inside her skull, and she supposed this was more like herself. "Yes, thank you, Mrs. Bailey. The powder was very efficient."

Mrs. Bailey nodded once, shortly. Sabrina had never seen the woman smile, though she wasn't precisely dour. Just tremendously serious, and difficult to charm. Perhaps the weight of her responsibilities in this grand house dragged her mouth down and made smiling impossible.

"Miss Fairleigh, the earl has informed me that he will be conducting a tour of some of the more interesting rooms in the house, and has settled on half past the hour. He is aware that you've been indisposed and will be happy to hear you are now feeling better. If you should care to join the other guests in the solarium at that time, he should be pleased."

Sabrina doubted the earl had strong opinions regarding her health or her presence, unless he wished to alleviate his own boredom by prodding her a bit more, but she nodded. "That's very kind of him. I shall be happy to attend."

* * *

She dressed in a gown that was only four years old, woolen and high-necked, a deep maroon that flattered her vivid coloring, and at last she ventured down the stairs. She paused on the first landing to listen for voices, but heard none, just the muffled, nearly ambient sounds of servants going about their work and the irritable whine and moan of the blizzard wind as it whipped at the house, frustrated it could find no crevice or crack or open window to enter.

Sabrina decided to make a left turn at the foot of the stairs instead of a right, and ventured toward the back of the house, down the long marble hallway. The marble was the color of eggshell, inlaid with the shapes of stars in a russet shade. She rather liked following a road of stars, and wondered where it would lead.

It concluded in a single vast room, the floor marbled apart from a few scattered carpets, the domed ceiling held up by two grand pillars in the center of it. She followed the pillars up with her eyes and found the ceiling was painted all over in stars. Gold leaf, from the looks of things, and arranged in the shapes of constellations—she recognized them. Arched windows that reached nearly to the ceiling flanked the room, and each window was inlaid at the top with twin exquisite stained-glass images: a midnight-blue field scattered with vivid stars, a solemn-faced moon presiding over each. They were lovely and fantastic, these windows, images from a dream.

A fire burned at one end of the room, and crowded around it was a collection of furniture upholstered in deep blue and ivory and propped up on gilded bowed legs.

That's when she saw Mr. Wyndham. An easel was balanced before him, and he held a paintbrush between his teeth as he stabbed away at a canvas from a palette of colors near him with another brush: *Dot dot dot dot dot dot dot.* And then he transferred the brush in his hand to his teeth deftly and the brush between his teeth to his hand, and went at the canvas with broader sweeping motions, a bit like waving a wand. His shirt was remarkably colorful, splashed everywhere with evidence of previous efforts. No doubt it had once been white. She couldn't get a look at his trousers from where she stood, but she suspected they were in the same condition as his shirt.

Wyndham looked up and noticed her, and plucked the brush away from his teeth to smile at her. "Well, good afternoon, Miss Fairleigh. I hope you're feeling better."

"Yes, thank you, Mr. Wyndham. I don't wish to intrude. I'll just—"

"You shan't be interrupting. Come, tell me what you think of my picture."

She moved closer and ventured a peek at the canvas. She saw trees, two of them, the needled variety, against a twilight sky. There wasn't much else on the canvas yet. She supposed the dotting motion had created the blades of grass at the foot of the trees, and the sweeping had created the sky.

"It's not very good, is it?" He said this matter-of-factly, with no evidence of disappointment, and no sign that he was fishing about for a compliment.

"Well . . . I . . ." She didn't know whether she thought it good or not. She'd certainly seen pictures that pleased her more. She was a fair hand at watercolors, but only a fair hand, as she hadn't much training and truthfully not a good deal of interest in it. And besides, her work at the vicarage left her no time for that sort of thing.

They looked very much like trees, his trees; his sky looked very much like a sky. No doubt it would be an adequate picture when he was finished with it.

"I fear I'm not qualified to judge a painting, Mr. Wyndham."

"Nonsense. Do you like it, or don't you, or don't you know?"

"I suppose I don't know," she confessed.

"Ah," he said cheerfully, folding his arms across his chest. "There you have it. A painting of any merit would have inspired *some* opinion, Miss Fairleigh, and I suspect you have the sensibilities to judge at your disposal, should you choose to use them. I fear I'm average at best, though I would have preferred to own a bit of talent. But Rawden *will* insist on commissioning paintings from me, and his commissions keep me in blunt. He professes to enjoy them, the trees and hills and whatnot. I wouldn't presume to question his taste in that regard. His taste is usually flawless."

"Perhaps you should trust his taste then, Mr. Wyndham. Perhaps you are being too modest."

This seemed to strike him as funny. "*No one* has ever accused me of being too modest, Miss Fairleigh. What I am not is delusional. And I think this may be a pity, because I sometimes believe delusion is the better part of talent. Look at Coleridge, for instance."

"The poet?" she asked, a little uneasy.

"Never a sober day in his life," Wyndham confirmed carelessly. "Opium, alcohol, women." He squinted at his painting for a moment, then lunged forward, rubbed at it with his thumb, then rubbed his thumb on his shirt.

Opium, alcohol, and women. Good heavens. An alarming reminder that The Libertine came by his nom de plume rather honestly, given the company he kept.

"And that little piece you played last night on the pianoforte? You play quite well, by the way, Miss Fairleigh."

"Oh? Do I? I—"

"Rawden commissioned it from a small French fellow named La Valle, who composes quite beautifully when he's not in his cups, and he's usually in his cups. I'm afraid Rhys rather *keeps* him in his cups, given the number of pieces he's commissioned. Otherwise, no one would ever know of him."

"But it was a beautiful piece," she said, half appalled.

Wyndham laughed up at her. "One does not preclude the other. Art does not require sobriety, Miss Fairleigh."

"But what of the earl?"

"Oh, Rhys is quite a different case altogether. He's dabbled in everything that can prevent a man from being sober, of course, but his great tragedy is that he cared for none of it. Came back from the war full of poetry, for some reason. And poetry seems to be his curse and his blessing."

Such drama, all of these artistic people, with their talk of pain and curses. Sabrina was relieved again to think that she wasn't subject to being whipped about by undue passion. It was interesting to hear that the earl had come back from the war full of poetry, however.

"But is he a good poet?"

"He's an extraordinary poet," Wyndham said matter-of-factly. "And I believe his poetry would shock you to your bones, Miss Fairleigh. Do I shock you now?"

"Yes," she said fervently.

Wyndham laughed. "I apologize. I honestly don't know how to speak to proper young ladies, having never spent time with one. But I don't frighten you." This last was a statement.

"Strangely, no." It was a jest.

"What a pity." He smiled at her then, and seemed to look at her fully. She half suspected he'd been *out* to shock her, that his little speech had been a monologue of sorts in part for his own entertainment, for all of these artistic people seemed rather enamored of themselves.

But now he was noticing her in earnest. Mr. Wyndham was handsome, too, she couldn't help but note, with a silent apology to Geoffrey. Lean, as though he never ate very much, not terribly muscular, with russet hair. His nose was a bit strong and blunt—she suspected it had been broken once—but the rest of his face was elegant, and his eyes were narrow and dark, which suited him: they were rather like the crossbow slits cut into castle walls. The intelligence beaming from them was more concentrated for all of it.

Sabrina turned when she heard boots strike marble behind her. And there was the earl himself. She felt her body bracing in his presence, as though all of her faculties needed to be marshaled to take him in.

"Good afternoon, Miss Fairleigh." Such a lovely, low voice. It must be a family characteristic, as Geoffrey was capable of such a voice when he gave a sermon, though his was softer, more of an entreaty than a command. "Are you feeling better, then?"

"Yes, thank you. Mrs. Bailey brought up a headache powder and chocolate."

The earl laughed at this. "Oh, most of the world's ills can be solved with headache powder and chocolate. Did she smile at you? I can never get her to smile, no matter how I try, and she has been with La Montagne for as long as I can remember."

The blizzard wind had triumphantly found the chimney for the room, and sent the fire wildly dancing for an instant. *Everything* seemed to become more extreme in the earl's presence.

"No," she finally remembered to answer. "I fear she didn't smile." Thinking that if the earl couldn't get her to smile, then Mrs. Bailey was an impenetrable fortress.

"Are you troubling Miss Fairleigh, Wyndham?"

"She was offering an opinion on my painting."

"And did she like it?"

"She 'doesn't know.'" Wyndham made it sound like he was quoting her.

"Oh, Miss Fairleigh." The earl mimicked clutching a knife to his heart. "Don't you know that's the worst possible thing you can say to an artist?"

He was teasing.

"As I've said very little to artists before this week, perhaps Mr. Wyndham will find it in his heart to forgive me," she said lightly.

Good heavens. Was she *flirting*? She *was* flirting. Sabrina blinked, disconcerted by this thought. It had just popped out, the flirting.

The earl turned to her. "Your friends have gone on a journey to visit the Colberts, Miss Fairleigh."

"Yes," she confirmed, a bit cautiously.

"And you are alone here."

"Yeees," she repeated.

"Are you concerned about what your father, Vicar Fairleigh, might think, of you left alone without your chaperone?"

How bright his eyes were when he was teasing.

"My father would assume an earl would perhaps be possessed of more manners and scruples than other men, and shouldn't worry on my behalf."

This probably wasn't at *all* what Vicar Fairleigh would think, but it made the earl laugh again. She realized she very much enjoyed watching him laugh.

"I hope you will join us on the tour of the house, Miss Fairleigh. Wyndy, please change your shirt. I won't have you walking about covered in paint."

Wyndham cheerfully stood and began packing away his painting supplies.

"I hesitate to leave you alone with the earl, Miss Fairleigh, but I shall return very shortly. And he only bites when requested."

He winked as he departed.

"And even then, it's rather pleasant," came the purring voice of Miss Licari, who had just prowled into the room.

All this talk of biting no doubt had a prurient meaning. Sabrina decided it was intended to make her uncomfortable, and for that reason she refused to feel uncomfortable.

"The stained-glass windows are very beautiful," she said, pretending she hadn't heard. "The moon looks so pensive."

The whimsical observation was out of her before she could stop it.

"Pensive?" The earl looked a moment, his expression unreadable. And then he looked up at the windows Sabrina had been admiring earlier, at the solemn stained-glass moon presiding over the vivid splash of stars, and appeared to give this serious thought. "I suppose it does, doesn't it? The windows were made in a tiny mountain town in Italy—Tre Sorelle—by a craftsman who does extraordinary work. Signor Giovanni Santoro. I commissioned them because they reminded me of something my friend Damien Russell said at Waterloo. And because, of course, I thought they suited the stars on the ceiling. Signore Santoro and I discussed colors for them, and how the light would shine through them and make a reflection on the floor at very specific times of day."

"He is a cur," Sophia said in her voice that made it sound as though she were just waking up and stretching deliciously. "Santoro. But he makes lovely things," she allowed.

Sabrina never knew quite what to say to Sophia Licari.

The singer was radiant today, an aria in a dress. Fair hair pinned up, a gown the color of mulberries in heavy silk, the neckline of which possessed only a glancing acquaintance with propriety. The mounds of her breasts peeked up out of it like a pair of pearls.

Sabrina cast a surreptitious glance down at her own neckline, which was appropriate to the weather outside. A practical dress. And then she glanced up and noticed that the earl was doing the very same thing at the very same time. His glinting eyes flicked up to meet hers.

Sabrina's eyes flew wide; she turned away immediately, flustered, a little hitch in her breathing.

Wyndham appeared then, a handsome coat buttoned over him, cravat fluffed and white. He flung his arms out for inspection, and the earl shrugged, and began his recitation.

"All right, Wynd. Ladies, Wyndham already knows this, but the room we're standing in is called the Star

Room. The fourth Earl of Rawden was an astronomer by avocation, and the ceiling is in fact an accurate representation of the galaxy, or so I'm told. He built those vast windows on either side of the room to allow in as much starlight and moonlight as possible. To facilitate his view of heavenly bodies, of course." He flicked an infinitesimal smile at Sabrina, who blinked, astonished, as though he'd flicked a spark at her.

Had that been an *innuendo*?

But the earl merely continued speaking. "And as the previous occupants of La Montagne managed to shoot out the upper windows while they were having a drunken go at grouse in the park—and they most definitely weren't members of the Gillray family, I should mention—I commissioned the stained-glass insets you see here. As I told Miss Fairleigh a moment ago, when the light shines through at certain times of day, you can see the reflection of the moon and the stars very vividly on the marble floor."

Sabrina glanced where the earl gestured. The swirl of snow outside was allowing very little light through, but she imagined for a moment she could see the moon and the stars on the floor. She rather hoped she'd have a chance to see them.

"Other occupants? Did you rent out La Montagne to other occupants then?"

"No." A single word.

"But . . . then who shot out the windows?"

"They *owned* La Montagne, Miss Fairleigh," the earl said shortly. He continued speaking as if her question had not been asked.

"The table you see here before the settee, and the chairs, were designed by Mr. George Bullock, who, coincidentally, was also commissioned to design the furniture for a certain emperor who was just exiled to St. Helena. I bought them from Mr. Bullock shortly before he passed a few years ago."

Sabrina's thoughts were elsewhere. So somehow the Gillrays had lost La Montagne, and somehow the Earl of Rawden had acquired it again. Sabrina remembered what Geoffrey had said: that Rhys had been nearly penniless, and that somehow, magically, he'd had money again. And somehow he'd managed to turn the money into a fortune.

Extraordinary to think it: he was probably just past thirty years in age, the earl, and somehow he'd managed to reacquire a magnificent house and all the magnificent things in it.

Sabrina eyed the pieces he was speaking of, inlaid ebony and gilt, simple but striking, gathered about the settee, which was much more ornate by contrast. She tried to imagine Napoleon Bonaparte on St. Helena sitting among his own furniture.

"Chippendale," the earl said, noticing Sabrina's glance at the settee, as if this explained everything. "Not a Bullock."

Sabrina wondered if Sophia Licari considered Chippendale or Bullock curs, but the soprano refrained from comment.

And then the earl turned and strode from the Star Room.

Thus proceeded a tour of a seemingly endless warren of rooms, most of them featuring at least one portrait of someone wearing a wig or a ruff or mounted on a rearing horse. The earl pointed at things, chairs and settees and tables and candelabra, and names flew by Sabrina like exotic birds. Someone with the unlikely name of Grinling Gibbons had carved the gorgeously complicated panels in a predominantly green sitting room; a Mr. George Hepplewhite had made the chairs in another room; a carpet by the name of Aubusson stretched out over the floor of yet another room.

Sabrina was struck by the fact the earl seemed almost grimly proud as he announced the provenance of the various pieces, all of which were spotless, the wood gleaming, the colors in the carpets fresh. She considered that this might be the reason Mrs. Bailey never smiled. Perhaps she went to bed at night thinking of all the dust requiring vanquishing anew each day.

Most of the furniture at the Tinbury vicarage had been made by someone Sabrina personally knew, and was sturdy and functional and *never,* no matter how she tried, truly gleamed. Too much use had been gotten out of every stick of it. The pianoforte had been made by Broadwood, a very respectable maker of pianofortes, but it had been so thoroughly played by numerous previous owners by the time the Fairleighs acquired it that the D key next to middle C needed to be thumped hard to get it to move, and a few of the black keys didn't move at all.

They passed by a small room the earl didn't bother entering, though he did gesture to it.

"Used by my father's man of affairs as an office," he told them. "And no one uses it now."

Sabrina peered in as they passed: yes, everything in there gleamed as well.

"Ah. And this is what I wanted to share with you today."

The earl had paused in the doorway of a gallery of statues. Before them were rows of elegant marble figures

captured in motion or repose, glowing softly in the
daylight.

"The fourth Earl of Rawden began commissioning
sculptures of the gods and goddesses and depictions of
Greek myths. You'll note here we have Leda tussling
with the swan—poor Leda—and here's Jason"—the earl
strolled by and gave a gentle pat to Jason's marble biceps
and moved on—"and here's Diana flanked by a pair of
deer, and this is—"

"Persephone," Sabrina breathed, drifting over to
her.

She was beautiful, Persephone was, her face gently
resigned, more thoughtful than unhappy; a pomegranate cupped in one palm, her cheek cradled in the other.
The toga she wore flowed to her ankles, as fluid as silk.
Her elbow rested on what appeared to be the arm of a
throne.

Persephone, the daughter of the goddess of spring,
compelled to live in Hades six months out of the year for
partaking of pomegranate seeds. Thus denied the warmth
of her presence, the earth experiences fall and winter, or
so the myth has it.

Wyndham was lingering at one end of the gallery and
appeared to be surreptitiously comparing Artemis the
Huntress's bosom with Sophia Licari's. Signora Licari
either didn't notice or didn't care; she was examining the
row statues critically, her gaze taking all of them in, like a
merchant mulling a purchase.

"They are very fine," she pronounced generously. As
though Rhys had been awaiting her opinion with bated
breath.

Rhys said nothing; merely flicked an amused, slightly inscrutable glance her way.

The lovely singer moved on, roving past several more statues, and paused to study an anatomically . . . *thorough* . . . statue of Hercules. Not a modest people, the ancient Greeks. And Sabrina remained near Persephone and the earl, and the latter spoke to her.

"You are familiar with the Greek myths, then, Miss Fairleigh? But they're all rather filled with uncontrolled passion and people behaving badly, wouldn't you say?"

"They're myths, Lord Rawden," she said mildly. "They're *called* myths precisely because they are not about actual people, and didn't actually happen."

Rhys gave a laugh. "Ah, but there's something you should know, Miss Fairleigh . . ." He lowered his voice a little, as though to speak only to her. "This great window here is designed especially to illuminate the statues when the moonlight slants in. And legend has it that Persephone comes to life when the light of the full moon at midnight touches her face."

Sabrina stared at the exquisitely detailed statue, the rounded arms and throat. She could almost believe it.

"What does she do then?" she asked. She was embarrassed when she realized she'd whispered it. She cleared her throat and repeated it in her usual voice. "What does she do then?"

The earl tilted his head in question, smiling a little. "Does your question mean you believe she might very well come to life, Miss Fairleigh?"

"I'm inquiring after the legend, Lord Rawden," she said evenly. "I imagine the legend addresses what she does after she comes to life."

"Well, I don't know that part of the legend, truthfully. I imagine she looks for a way out, like the Persephone of myth."

This suddenly struck Sabrina as terribly sad. She went quiet for a moment. "But the moon will be full tonight," she said softly.

Sabrina peered more closely at the detail of Persephone's face, struck at how yielding the marble could seem until one actually touched it. Her lips and nostrils were delicate; her hair was dressed high in the Grecian fashion, but remarkably fine marble tendrils of it clung to her cheeks.

"She does look soft, doesn't she, Miss Fairleigh?" His voice was soft, too.

She looked up, startled that he should know her thoughts. And lost herself a moment in those eyes.

"Shall I tell you precisely where a woman is softest?" The question was husky, beguiling. More an invitation than a question.

When she didn't answer, for she couldn't answer, he began it as if he were telling a tale around a fire. His voice lowered, and the effect was as if he'd reached over and slowly turned down the lamp.

"There's a place . . . here . . ." So soft, his words, and she watched his hand slowly, slowly rise up; her eyes tracked it. When it landed on the underside of his jaw, she exhaled a short breath; she could feel the echo of his touch on her own skin. And then he drew a finger beneath the strong elegant line of his jaw, lightly, from his chin to just below his ear. "Just here. The skin is delicate as petals, like a baby's skin, as though nothing of the earth has touched it since the day she was born. And if a man touches a woman here, Miss Fairleigh, just so . . . he can feel the beat of her heart quicken in response to him."

Sabrina could not have spoken if someone had fired a musket next to her ear.

The earl's eyes were dark; the blue held galaxies.

"And when a woman's heart quickens, I imagine what she is feeling at that moment . . . everywhere in her body. And imagining this does . . . extraordinary things to my own body."

Sabrina's mouth parted slightly; she could feel her heart leaping, jabbing against her. She wondered if he could see the pulse in her throat.

"Oh, yes," he continued musingly, "there are oh-so-many places to savor. But the softest, most tender places are the sheltered ones. For instance, there's a place just"— his hand moved again, down his torso, leisurely trailing the line of his buttons; she followed it as if it were a compass, as if her eyes were chained to it—"here."

His voice was smoke when he said the word.

And he traced a slow semicircle, once, twice, oh-so-slowly, oh-so-lightly . . . just below his breastbone.

Sabrina's lungs locked.

"Fine gallery, Rhys. And you've recovered all of the statues?" Wyndham had appeared, Sophia Licari at his side, and Sabrina hadn't even heard his footsteps moving closer.

"All of them," Rhys said, transferring his storytelling fingers casually into his pocket. "Did you know it's a full moon tonight, Wyndham?"

"How on earth do you know that?"

"Miss Fairleigh told me so. And we know she would never fib."

Wyndham turned to give Sabrina a gently quizzical look.

"We . . . we harvest herbs at a full moon in the vicarage garden. I always know the cycles of the moon. Mrs. Dewberry . . . well, a woman in Tinbury recommended it. It brings out their most potent qualities."

There was a small silence.

"It is what country people know," Sophia Licari indulged.

"I suppose," Sabrina said curtly. It seemed vastly more useful information to possess than the things *these* people knew.

"Full moons bring out the potent qualities of poets, too," the earl said idly.

"Oh, Rhys! *Siete così divertenti!*" Sophia's fingers brushed the earl's sleeve lightly and she gave a silvery little laugh. Sabrina recalled hearing that laugh float over to her on the winter air when they'd first arrived.

The soprano transferred her gaze to Sabrina. "Miss Fairleigh, good heavens. I do believe you look feverish. Perhaps we've wearied you?" Her tone, at least, sounded concerned.

Wearied her? Sabrina was almost amused. She wondered if Miss Licari had any idea how much effort it took to simply be *poor.*

"Thank you for your concern, Madame Licari, but I am truly . . . unaffected . . . by all the activity here."

She addressed these words to Sophia, but she was gratified when she saw, out of the corner of her eye, a swift little smile touch the earl's lips. Because her words had been meant entirely for him, after all, and they had been meant to be ironic, and irony was not second nature to her.

And they were also a lie, of course. The words.

He knew that, too.

* * * *

Rather than join the earl and Signora Licari and Wyndham for dinner, Sabrina invented a return of her headache. She took soup in her room, relieved to be alone with the soft colors and her own thoughts.

And later, restlessly, she sought out the library, as it was the closest thing to a den that La Montagne featured, with its dark colors and subtle patterns. She felt like a small animal seeking shelter.

She did want to think. She needed something to replace the image of the earl's knowledgeable, illustrative hands, which lingered in her mind, and made her feel nearly as though she'd had too much wine.

Determinedly, she chose a row of books to examine, and ran her finger over the spines: philosophy, religion, history. All written by great and orderly thinkers, all of them men. Any one of them seemed certain to get her mind moving along a more seemly track, if only because of the effort required to plow through them.

But on the shelf just below, the other gold-embossed titles winked at her like coquettes from across a ballroom: Yeats. Byron. Wordsworth. The Libertine.

The Libertine?

Her breath caught. She knew it hadn't been there the previous night, or the night before that. And yet there it was now, looking as though it had always been there, bound in green leather, etched in gold, and as somber-looking as its philosopher brethren on the shelf above.

It was a coquette *masquerading* as a philosopher.

Sabrina ignored the winks for as long as she could. And then her hand dropped slowly, stealthily to the row below. She snatched The Libertine volume from the shelf like a dog stealing a scrap from the dinner table and all but darted over to the settee. And there she curled up, her heart thumping, and opened it to the first page.

> *You are the silk that breathes beneath my hand*
> *I am the pleasure your sighs command*
> *And with breath and lips let our journey begin—*

And so her journey began.

The words might well have been his hands. She whipped her head about suddenly, as though she could feel his palms landing on her shoulders.

She knew then she couldn't read his book here, in the library.

She closed the book over her thumb to keep her place, then made her way up the stairs almost furtively. The sound of low feminine laughter came to her distantly, as impersonal as birdsong heard in a garden.

It was dark in her room apart from the fire, and she curled up on her bed with the book, her face close to the softly glowing lamp. And though with every page her mind told her she should stop reading, her hands, as if of their own accord, turned the next page and the next. Until at last her head swam with the explicit, lush heat of the words.

She knew she ought to stop, and she finally did, because, after all, her will was a strong one. But stopping was like pulling herself up from a deep velvet well. It carried with it the same sort of vertigo.

Gently, she laid the book aside.

Sabrina rubbed her hands over her face as if to reacquaint herself with it, but somehow, even that very act seemed new: she felt as though she were feeling her own skin for the first time. Her hands had become a stranger's hands, her skin a new skin. A canvas to be painted.

She'd awakened to discover she was wearing . . . "breathing silk."

She took a deep breath to steady herself, but the very act of drawing air into her lungs had become a sensual act, and only heightened her awareness.

Oh, Geoffrey was wrong. The poetry wasn't salacious. The word was far too simple. There was a very focused beauty to it, and a subtlety difficult to describe; one didn't read so much as *breathe* his words. In they went, like smoke from a hookah, stealing sense and replacing it with sensuality. And in some ways they were reverent, his poems, but they were also shameless and abandoned. They told the story of a man who indeed understood more than was fair about seduction, a man who lived through his senses, reveled in them.

And there hadn't been a word in the book about love.

At last Sabrina stood and began to undress. She unlaced her gown, slipping out of it. She'd never had a maid to help her with such things, and she didn't give it a thought. She hung it in the wardrobe next to its country cousins, the small collection of thoroughly worn dresses she'd brought with her to La Montagne.

Once nude, she dimmed the lamps, and reached for her night rail.

But then she paused. And for the first time ever, she stood before the mirror and looked at herself, and tried to imagine how someone else would see her. She saw the gentle, curving whiteness of her body as new terrain—the slopes of her shoulders, the mounds of her breasts, the triangle of hair between her legs—and imagined a man's hands exploring it, savoring it, taking unique pleasure in it, in something she'd always taken for granted.

And slowly, hardly daring, she did it: her hand rose and cupped her breast gently. And after a moment's hesitation she traced the same path the earl's fingers had traced earlier today, on his own breastbone.

She closed her eyes.

She learned that the skin beneath was indeed exquisitely soft. A shock. She'd never known. And, oh, the touch raked awake that fierce, unidentifiable want again.

And now it was everywhere in her.

You are the silk that breathes beneath my hand . . .

She stood for a moment longer, nude, before the mirror, until she became aware that her skin was pricking up in gooseflesh from the cold. She slipped her night rail over her head and reached for a shawl, and stood for a moment indecisively.

The curtains had been pulled closed, but a bit of moonlight was forcing its way through. Sabrina followed the shaft of light with her eyes, and thought of Persephone in the statue gallery, waiting for moonlight to awaken her.

And suddenly Sabrina wanted to see her.

CHAPTER TEN

THE WIND HAD ceased for the moment to heap more snow up against the house, and the quiet was so sudden and thorough it very nearly had a texture. Moonlight poured in through the soaring arched windows and washed over the rows of statues.

Sabrina hesitated on the threshold of the room, and this hesitation, as well as the sharp little curl of anticipation in the pit of her stomach, amused her. She approached the statues almost stealthily, until she was a mere few feet away from Persephone.

But it was another few seconds before she mustered the nerve to lift her candle high enough to illuminate Persephone's face.

Persephone's smooth marble eyes gazed back at her.

For seconds of silence Sabrina watched the statue. Seconds ticked into a minute, then two minutes.

How long minutes are when you're waiting, Sabrina thought idly.

Finally, she grew a bit bored and whimsically decided to rest her candle in Perseus's outstretched hand. She stepped back toward the wall to admire it. It looked as though he were bearing a torch.

"For a moment I thought you were Persephone come to life, Miss Fairleigh."

Sabrina's heart didn't precisely stop, though it most definitely did stutter. And when it leaped forward again it was much more swiftly than before.

Perhaps she hadn't jumped out of her skin because she'd almost expected him.

Still, she didn't dare turn around.

"Forgive me for dashing your hopes." She was proud of her voice, even, cool as marble. The voice a statue would have used, she liked to think. Though her heart was now beating so rapidly she wondered it didn't echo in the gallery.

"Given that I came here hoping to be surprised, and perhaps even . . . awed . . . I cannot in all honesty say my hopes have been dashed." Drawled irony in his soft, soft voice.

It washed over her the way the moonlight did. It changed the very room. And her mind knew he was an expert at choosing clever words and imbuing them with innuendo, at all the little things that added up to seduction. In this, he'd proven himself an artist.

Oh, yes, her mind knew it. Still, it was not her mind that surged in response to his voice, or set the hair on the back of her neck standing.

And in that moment, she didn't dare speak.

She remained quiet; and now she began to feel the warmth of him behind her, as surely as though he were a fire burning low; she wondered, absurdly, if he was clothed for day or night. Perhaps he wore a dressing gown and a cap, had come creeping down from his chambers dressed for sleep. It would certainly de-fang him, somewhat. She'd seen her father, Vicar Fairleigh, in his dressing gown and cap. She had difficulty imagining that any man so dressed would pose any sort of sensual danger.

And then it occurred to her to wonder what the wan moonlight was doing to her dressing gown, and heat rushed into her cheeks.

She fought a maidenly impulse to pull the shawl more tightly around her shoulders, but she sensed the gesture would amuse him and confirm for him everything he believed about her. For some reason, at the moment, the thought of this was intolerable. She restrained herself.

"What . . . what would you have done if you'd seen her?" she found herself asking instead. She was genuinely curious. "Persephone?"

"Take her to Hades with me at once, of course." He sounded surprised that she needed to ask.

This startled a short laugh from her. "Or to London, at the very least."

"Is there a difference?" He made it sound like a serious question.

"I wouldn't know. Is the entrance to London guarded by a dog with three heads?"

She thought he might laugh.

Instead, it was quiet again. The candle flame snapped upward, tugged by a draft.

"You've never been to London?" He said it softly, but he sounded so thoroughly, genuinely astonished—as if she'd admitted she'd never learned to read, or to eat with a fork, something *just* that fundamental—that she couldn't resist smiling.

And she finally turned, slowly, to face him.

Which of course required looking up a significant distance.

No dressing gown and whimsical cap. White shirt, open at the throat—it took a moment to get beyond those few open buttons—and those blue eyes fixed upon her.

His expression disconcerted her. He didn't seem inclined to blink, for one thing; his gaze on her face was nearly as steady as the statue's . . . if considerably more warm. The warmth she could see even by the combined light of moon and candle. But she would also have called it . . . bemused. It was as if two very different notions were warring inside him, and he was puzzled by at least one of them.

"I've never longed to see London." She heard the prim note in her own voice. Perhaps it was for the best.

He simply continued gazing. She refused to be the first to look away, and so an absurd moment passed during which they merely gazed.

When he spoke, she almost started.

"Miss Fairleigh, do you have a mirror in your chambers?"

"A mirror?" She was puzzled.

He didn't clarify the question for her; he smiled faintly as if at some private joke, and gave his head a slow shake, to and fro. And then absently, almost affectionately, he reached out and gently tugged the ends of her shawl more snugly around her. As though tucking a child into bed.

Just as her own hand had gone up to do the same.

A shock: the backs of his fingers touching hers. His skin against her skin. He was startlingly warm, flame-warm. And this simple touch sent a buzz through her blood and flashed like lightning in her mind, obliterating thought. She went motionless, astonished, and looked up at him, absorbing the sensation. Confusion shredded her thoughts, and a tide of heat rose toward the surface of her skin.

* * *

Rhys knew an opportunity when he saw one, and he'd brilliantly orchestrated this one. Those lovely full lips were parted just a little; her muslin wrapper fell softly over the slim lines of her body, hinting at lithe bareness beneath. Her dark hair should have been twined in a missish braid to keep it from tangling as she slept, and instead it spilled in dark silken handfuls over her shoulders. Her eyes were wide and soft, stunned at the contact of his hand, lulled by the moonlight.

He'd kissed myriad other women for much less provocation.

And so he swiftly calculated his angle of approach, and did it.

He'd meant it to be a swift touch of the lips, just enough to scandalize her and to satisfy his own half-whimsical impulse, to prove to himself that he had won: he had lured her here, and his reward was to be a kiss.

But when his lips met hers, something went terribly wrong.

Or perhaps it was just that something went too terribly right.

Because . . . oh, God. Her mouth was a dream beneath his. So softly, surprisingly welcoming, it was as though she'd been anticipating this kiss her entire life.

Pragmatically, he thought it more likely it was because she *hadn't* expected to be kissed, and therefore hadn't had time to do the sensible thing . . . which would be to stiffen and slap him in indignation. He knew he had an instant's worth of advantage, and regardless of whether it was sensible, he wasn't about to relinquish it. His arms went around her loosely but decisively and he pulled her into his chest before she could do something silly, like stop him.

Her forearms folded up, her hands bunched softly near his collarbone, her head tipped back. And now that she was gently trapped, he lowered his head. And he kissed her, not as though she was a virgin, or the vicar's daughter, or the almost fiancée of his resentful cousin. He kissed her the way a woman ought to be kissed: with absolutely no quarter.

His mouth played insistently over the vulnerable softness of hers, helping her to discover the exquisite sensitivity of her own lips, to sense the universe of possibilities in a simple kiss. And when her lips parted—and they did, because his own determined lips had given her no choice in the matter—he breached them with his tongue, tasted without preamble the velvety heat of her mouth, and plundered.

It was a kiss calculated to shock, to melt bones. He meant her to feel it everywhere in her body, to arouse her so swiftly she would be able to respond only with whatever instinct she possessed.

Odd that he should feel this supposedly calculated kiss everywhere in his own body.

Her mouth softened with his, her surrender nearly complete.

"Here." He whispered the rough order against her mouth, taking her wrists in his hands and lifting her arms up to fit around his neck. Quiet triumph surged when her hands clasped there, and her shawl drifted to the floor. In the moonlight he saw the dark of her nipples peaked against her night rail, which was so worn it was nearly as soft as skin itself. He spanned her slim waist with his hands, savoring the supple warmth and curves of her.

"Kiss me, Sabrina," he ordered in a hoarse whisper, nuzzling her silky cloud of hair aside to touch his tongue to her ear. The heat of her swift breathing against his throat, the brush of her fingers against the crisp hair at the back of his neck, made him frantic. "Kiss me back."

He returned his lips to hers. And glory of glories, she kissed him back. She found the rhythm of it, and they eased together into the hot languor of the kiss, the kind of kiss that dissolved time and seemed to become its own world, that demanded more, more, more.

He lifted his lips, feeling oddly drugged.

It's only a kiss.

"My lord, I . . ." Her voice was frayed and dazed.

No quarter.

He touched his lips to her throat and tasted her delicately, felt the fine wash of gooseflesh rise. A tiny sound caught in her throat, a whimper of pleasure. Her fingers moved instinctively through the fine hair at the nape of his neck, and her body pressed against his, and desire nearly cleaved him in two.

"Are you wondering what you're feeling, Sabrina?" he murmured against her throat and kissed her pulse. "Are you wondering what you want? What your body wants?"

"I—" A choked whisper.

"It's this," he said hoarsely. He cupped her buttocks and lifted her abruptly, just a little. And then he let her body slide down slowly and hard against his erection.

And she moaned, a choked sound of raw pleasure, and clung to him.

No quarter.

"And it's this, Sabrina." She leaned against the wall now, and he scooped a hand beneath her thigh and swiftly lifted her leg and thrust against her, moved his hips in a slow grind against her night rail, against where he knew she was hot and slick, against where he knew her body craved him.

Her head fell back and she sucked in a sharp breath, and her nails dug into his shoulder.

"Move with me, Sabrina. I swear to you, there's no danger of anything but pleasure." His voice was a shamelessly wheedling rasp. He was dangerously close to begging, like a damned boy rutting with a chambermaid. "I swear to you, it will be exquisite." He whispered it, made it a promise. He nuzzled her ear again, breathed his next words there, made sure his cock still fit snugly at the crook of her legs. "Take it, Sabrina, what your body wants. Take it now. Or I'll walk away, and you'll never know." And this last was a threat.

He felt the trembling tension in her, and with a strength of will he didn't know he possessed, he loosened his arms. He wanted her to choose. He wanted to know which was stronger in her: passion or propriety. And he wanted her, God help the scoundrel in him, to choose passion, because he wanted somehow to conquer her, to prove his point to this too-clever girl. To somehow make her understand the way he lived his life.

Mostly, he conceded, he just wanted with an unreasonable, unconscionable ax-edged want.

She tipped her head back, looked up at him, her swift ragged breath echoing his, her lashes lowered, eyes heavy-lidded, inscrutable in the dark. He wondered if she hated him in that moment, or hated herself. He wondered whether he ought to mind.

And then her head dropped and rose, twice, the shallowest of nods. She wanted.

And he knew only triumph.

And this time it was he who groaned when she rocked her body against his, taking, as he'd urged her, what her body wanted. A low primal sound dragged up out of him as he buried his face against her throat, and pulled her closer still, tightly against him, pushed his fingers up through her hair, opened his lips again against the delicate skin beneath her chin. He knew no man before him had ever before pressed his lips to that soft, soft place.

"Yes," he rasped. Found her mouth again. She'd learned already how to demand from him. Lips meeting and blending again, tongues tangling, her fingers in his hair, his hands roaming her back, holding her tightly against him. Silvered in moonlight and striped in shadow, with an audience of marble statues, they rocked against each other, and somehow, for Rhys, this slow, clothed, adolescent dance was more erotic than if he'd mounted her nude.

Very quickly he could feel her begin to unravel in his arms, feel the tension tightening her limbs, hear her breathing coming rough, staccato. Her movements against him swifter, more precise, as she found the source of her pleasure; he knew her release was coming upon her.

So lightly, lightly, he touched her nipples, skimmed them with both palms. She arched, gasping.

He wanted her to know there was more. And perhaps it was cruel, but when this was done, he wanted to leave her wanting, wanting. Wondering.

And even so, he felt the enormous tension gathering within him, and he was astounded. He knew he was about to spill in his trousers in a way he hadn't since he was thirteen years old, and it could not be helped, and he didn't want it to be helped.

"*Rhys—*"

He cupped a hand behind her head and pressed her face against his chest so his name wouldn't echo through the gallery. Her body shook with its first ever release, and he held her, reveling in it, even as moments later his own shocked him, racked him with a bliss unexpected, with a sweet lightness.

"*Sabrina.*" The name emerged from him involuntarily. A whisper.

He held her, rested his cheek against her hair, as the two of them fought for even breath again.

It was he who released her finally, opened his arms, stepped back. And from his distance he watched carefully, to see if she would flee, or scream.

He could hardly believe he'd done what he'd just done. And yet he couldn't find it in himself to be sorry.

She backed away a little farther from him, and stood quietly, as though stunned, her eyes lowered. And then she covered her face with her hands.

For a quiet moment, she stood there, her breathing settling. And he simply watched, as emotions he could guess at warred within her, and she struggled with them, quietly, with dignity. He knew admiration then.

He also, again, knew triumph.

"And that's what it feels like, Miss Fairleigh, to lose control," he said softly.

She dropped her hands and her head jerked up, and she stared at him. He wondered if he should prepare to be slapped.

Instead, he saw her jaw set.

"It wasn't I who lost control, Lord Rawden. I believe it was *I,* in fact, who had it the entire time."

She watched him as the truth of this sank in. Rhys froze, realizing it.

And then she turned swiftly on her heel, dipping to gather her dropped shawl, and walked swiftly from the room, wrapping it around her.

He would have thought her downright composed had she not left her candle burning in the hand of Perseus.

Sabrina didn't know how she'd found her room again in the absence of a candle; some internal homing instinct must have led her there while her mind and heart ricocheted between horror and exhilaration. She slid the bolt on the door and walked to her bed, sat down on it almost gingerly.

She thrust her knuckles against her mouth to stop a hysterical laugh. Or was it a sob?

Well, now she understood. She'd been thoroughly humbled, in fact.

She'd been twined with him, her mouth joined in heat, her body straining to be closer, closer, wanting to climb inside him. Some primal wisdom in her had taken over and had known, somehow, that it was in his power to give her shattering release. Her body had understood everything his poetry described, seemed to possess its own wisdom and will and wants, even as her mind couldn't fully give shape to them.

And that devil had given her a *choice.* He'd known she would take it, because he was, after all, The Libertine, and he possessed the secret to seduction. He'd read her like that piece of music by La Valle and had all but orchestrated, leading her little by little—oh, she could see it now, all those little moments—to that moment in the statue gallery.

He was a dangerous, dangerous, bad, bad man. Bad man.

Oh, dear God, he tasted heavenly.

She lowered her face into her hands and breathed deeply into them. And yet that was a mistake, because she could still smell him on her hands, the masculine musk of sweat and salt and desire.

She wanted him all over again.

We are all animals, Miss Fairleigh.

And because her hands smelled of the Earl of Rawden, she once again did what he'd done. She skimmed a hand lightly over her own breast, to see if the shock was the same. And it was similar, but it was not the same, of course. Because it was a man she wanted.

Not once the entire time had she thought of Geoffrey.

And instinctively she knew she would never experience that sort of pleasure with the curate. And not once had she thought of Sophia Licari, and whether the earl might have gone from her to the soprano.

It hadn't mattered. She hadn't cared. Thought had played no role whatsoever, let alone will.

So much for will.

She breathed in deeply to steady herself. Breathed out again. She didn't know how she could possibly face him again.

And then she looked up and caught a glimpse of her face in the mirror, flushed, agitated, distressed, delighted. And it was entirely his fault. And suddenly this made her angry.

She was made of sterner stuff than that.

Things would go on. And if the Earl of Rawden had a shred of decency in him, he would leave it be. He'd made his point. Thoroughly.

As he'd done, no doubt, with dozens of women before her.

CHAPTER ELEVEN

SYLVIE, WE'VE HAD a message in return from the vicarage in Tinbury. The vicar is away at present—something about performing last rites for some poor soul?—but the housekeeper has sent a message back to us. She says he does have a daughter named Sabrina, whom he adopted when she was a very little girl. But she isn't at home, either! She has gone to visit a Lady Mary Capstraw. How does the vicarage manage without anyone in it, I ask you?" Susannah groused.

"Do you know Lady Mary Capstraw?" Sylvie asked Susannah. They were seated across from each other on matching velvet settees in the drawing room of the Grantham town house, imbibing strong tea.

Susannah turned to her husband, who had just strolled into the room, dressed for an evening at White's. "Kit, do you know a Lady Mary Capstraw?"

"Capstraw . . . Capstraw . . . oh! Lord Paul Capstraw. Pleasant chap. Military type. Has said scarcely a word since he's been married, but I'm not certain he misses the need to talk. Besotted with his wife." He smiled at Susannah, as this described him, too. "She travels rather a lot, from what I've heard. Dragging Paul along with her. Haven't seen Capstraw in ages."

"Shall we next send a message to Lady Mary Capstraw?" Susannah asked eagerly.

"I'll try to learn where to send it. Capstraw hails from the Midlands, as I recall. Still, finding Mary may seem a bit like chasing the wind, Susannah."

"We have to try," she said firmly.

"Of course." Kit's answer was blithe. "And we shall find her."

As cool, as penetrable, as opaque as a glacier.

Rhys chewed his lamb, regarded Miss Fairleigh over the tiny flames of the dinner candle, and let the metaphors slide through his mind the way a pious man might slide rosary beads through his fingers. An attempt to soothe himself. She was laughing at something Wyndham had said—it hadn't been too terribly funny, but she was polite, Miss Fairleigh was—and she'd spared a glance or two for the earl during the soup. A cool, impenetrable, opaque *glance*. She'd said something about the flavor of the soup, and he'd said something inane in agreement.

"We'll have mud to contend with when the snow melts. I wonder when again the roads will be passable?" Sabrina said to Wynhdam.

"Determined travelers will find a way," Wyndham said cheerily.

Four *days* of this. No blushing, no stuttering, no hiding in her room feigning illness, no weeping, no fawning. Four days since that evening, and somehow she had contrived to always be in the presence of a servant, or of Wyndham or Sophia. He saw her at meals. He saw her for cards. She retired early. He was never alone with her.

Not that he wanted to be.

It was very nearly insulting, he thought in amusement. He'd conducted an experiment with a girl who allegedly could not be seduced, which had concluded with the two of them grinding against each other in the statue gallery. She seemed entirely unaffected. Perhaps the green hills of Tinbury bred girls with stiffer backbones after all.

Or perhaps she considered the earth-shattering experience of climax akin to tasting a new soup.

He remembered her fingers at the nape of his neck, her warm body softening against his, and how she kissed, quickly learning the heated give-and-take of it. How rapidly things had escalated beyond the grasp of his own control, and how she had arced as though shocked when his hands slid down to cover her breasts, her nipples peaked against—

He dropped his fork to his plate, and the resounding clatter made the other three members of his party jump.

He smiled, a slightly strained smile. "My apologies. Do continue being witty, Wyndham."

Wyndham pretended to be aggrieved. "Ah, but you've ruined it, Rhys. I cannot perform on command. Artists, and comedy, are at the mercy of the muse, are they not, Sophia?"

Sophia. Rhys had scarcely looked at Sophia throughout dinner. He looked now. She was fondling the stem of her glass of wine. Idly stroking and circling the length of it between two fingers, as though she'd never before felt such a thing. Her spine had all but collapsed from boredom. She wore a ruby-and-diamond necklace, the teardrop-shaped stone pointing like a prurient little arrow to the deep shadow of her cleavage. Rhys wondered who had given it to her, and was surprised that no little surge of jealousy accompanied the thought, as it normally would have. Her stays had contrived to raise her breasts nearly entirely up out of her dress, and the diners were presented with a view of a luscious, candlelit shelf of bosom.

"*Sì*," she said finally. It sounded more like a yawn than a word. She met Rhys's eyes, widened her own eyes in entreaty. *Please, dear God, make the boredom stop,* her expression said.

Sophia was not a creature made for country house parties.

Only then did Rhys notice that Sophia's idly moving fingers were performing a reasonably accurate imitation of one of her *other* skills. She saw him notice; a smile, tiny, sultry, just for him, lifted the corners of her full mouth.

He smiled a little in return. He considered the possibility of easing his own boredom with a vigorous midnight visit to Sophia.

He turned then, and saw Miss Fairleigh's green eyes on him—Lord knows he'd seen her best dress often enough during her visit, but it did rather collude with the candlelight to set off her delicate shoulders and neck and those very astute, very clear green eyes.

She dropped her gaze to her plate and frowned a little, studying her lamb avidly, as though the world's fate depended upon which slice she decided to put next in her mouth.

"Did I mention, Wyndham, that I located a beautiful volume of the history of the world's countries? Wonderful illustrations. It was tucked away in one of the suites on the third floor."

"Umm . . . no. You haven't yet mentioned it." Wyndham seemed uncertain what to do with this information.

"Yes. I've transferred it to the library."

"Have you? Capital." Wyndham was clearly hoping this particular topic was to be a short one.

"A beautiful book belongs with other beautiful books, don't you think?"

"Yes, I imagine so." And Wyndham gave Rhys a puzzled frown. He'd probably begun to suspect that boredom was a contagion, and that Rhys had caught it, and intended to bore him from now on.

Before he retired for the evening, Rhys carried the book in question to the library, leaving it on the polished dark table that sat between the two settees.

And then loosened his cravat, and stopped, staring at himself in the mirror, giving some thought as to whether he wanted to sleep in his own bed, or in a bed sweatily entwined with the fragrant and inventive Sophia Licari.

No: he rather thought he could wait for an apology from Signora Licari. He rather thought he'd wait for her to come to him out of sheer frustration, or boredom.

As this had never before happened in the history of their association, he suspected the wait might be a long one. But the idea was novel, and it amused him, and strangely he found his usual need for Signora Licari was tonight outweighed by a need for sleep.

And by wanting, first, to lie awake and picture Miss Fairleigh in her room having difficulty sleeping from thinking of him.

The next day dawned almost aggressively, defiantly clear, and brilliant blue skies glared through every window as Rhys passed through La Montagne's hall. The snow would be slush in no time beneath these rays.

He'd had a light, almost impatient breakfast alone; he'd risen late. He was irritable; he'd had enough of country confinement. He wanted to read the London papers, watch London performances, speak to artists and poets and musicians, drink liquor in London clubs, explore the latest amusements in the darkest bowels of the city, be cosseted by the accommodating beauties that populated The Velvet Glove. Surely the furor would have ebbed a bit by now, the irate husbands pacified, the ardor of all those infatuated wives cooled by his absence? Perhaps it was time to return.

But this morning, first, he had an objective.

He made sure his footfalls were quiet as he approached the library, but he suspected it almost wouldn't have mattered if he'd galloped up behind her. She was leaning against the arm of the settee, feet tucked beneath her, the big book open in her lap. She supported its spine with one hand; she had the little finger of the other against her bottom lip, and she seemed to be nibbling absently on her nail.

It had almost been too easy.

"Imagine finding you in the library, Miss Fairleigh."

She jerked a little in surprise, the book slipping from her grasp. She recovered rather neatly.

"You knew you'd find me here, Lord Rawden." Dryly said.

She'd startled a laugh from him. Four days of her coolness and he'd somehow managed to forget how very direct Miss Fairleigh could be.

"It's a beautiful day for a walk," she said meaningfully. "Clear at last. Perhaps you'd like to take the air."

"Are you trying to banish me to the outdoors, Miss Fairleigh?"

"I just thought I would point it out." She sounded a little disappointed he hadn't leaped upon her suggestion.

"I find I'm in the mood to read. History, perhaps. Don't let me disturb you. A wonderful book, isn't it?"

She seemed reluctant to answer. "Yes," she said at last, sincerely. Almost resignedly.

"Very good."

He said this noncommittally and strode over to the nearest bookcase, where he spent some time perusing the row of blue spines. Behind him, he heard the rustle of a page turning.

"Pretending something didn't happen doesn't quite mean it didn't happen, you know," he said idly. "It's not quite the same thing, is it?"

He didn't turn. Not yet.

But the silence was interesting. He wondered if her face had gone that lovely pink, or whether she'd stopped breathing.

"But pretending it didn't happen helps hasten the process of *forgetting* that it ever happened," she told him, in an admirably steady voice. "In fact, I've very nearly forgotten it already."

"Have you?" he said absently, then knelt to study the books on the row below.

"Of course," she said idly.

He let a silence go by. Long enough to allow her to perhaps relax a little.

"You've forgotten how my lips felt against your throat, and how your body felt pressed against mine?"

This he said conversationally, his voice almost drifting, as he pulled a book from the shelf, leafing through it slowly. Romans, this one was about.

Ah. He thought he could hear her breathing now. Still, he didn't turn around.

"And"—he mused, turning a page, in the voice he would use to inquire politely after one of her relatives—"you've forgotten how you begged me with my own name? And how very, very hard I was against you, and how good that felt?"

He cast a glance over his shoulder then. Brilliant color rode high on her cheeks; the rest of her face was pale. Her eyes glittered. She was staring at him.

"As far as I'm concerned, nothing of any import happened, Lord Rawden." The words were thin, but steady enough.

"Very good, very good," he murmured. "I just thought I'd verify that, as I felt very little, too. I should dislike for one of us to pine for the other in vain."

He stood and turned his full examining gaze on her, giving her no choice but to meet it.

Ah, the transparent Miss Fairleigh couldn't disguise outraged pride, and she had just bitten her lip to stifle some sort of retort. Her eyes fair snapped lightning.

He turned his back to the shelf, leaned against it casually. "Let me be blunt, Miss Fairleigh," he said, with all evidence of good humor. "I don't believe for a moment you were unaffected."

"No?" It was an attempt to sound bored. It failed, as her voice was scarcely audible, as though he'd just truly caught her out.

"No. I think you returned to your room that evening and relived each moment again and again. I am virtually certain, in fact, that you *touched* yourself as you relived these moments, and I don't believe your body will ever feel the same again now that you've lost control of your . . . animal nature."

What a pageant of emotions crossed her face then: outrage, guilt, horror, astonishment, and—oh, yes—longing. Because now she knew how it felt to be touched the way a woman should be touched.

"Moreover," he mused relentlessly, "I think that you'll be dreaming of me perhaps until the day you die."

She clapped the book shut then and stood abruptly. "It was only," she ground out, "a kiss."

"Was it?" He was laughing now.

"And *moreover*," she all but growled, "you, Lord Rawden, murmured my name rather feverishly into my throat, as I recall."

His smile disappeared. Good God, but a man didn't like to be reminded of the things he did or said in the heat of passion. She was a very good player. He eyed her somewhat cautiously.

"And you were breathing rather like a bellows," she continued. "Like a mating bull."

"A mating *bull*?"

Trust a country girl to arrive at this particular analogy. How deftly she'd seized his weapon from him.

He closed the distance between them, as if he intended to seize it back. "Interesting recollections, Miss Fairleigh, considering you couldn't *remember* any of it."

"And I do believe you groaned a bit toward the end there, Lord Rawden."

Sweet merciful—

"And . . . if you were entirely unaffected, Lord Rawden, why are you here in the library now?"

"'Tis my library," he said mildly. He held up the Roman book. "And here is my book."

He took yet another step toward her, and now he stood so close he could see flecks of gold in those eyes. Her scent rose sweetly up to him. Odd how familiar it seemed now; he suspected he would know it anywhere.

"If you were entirely unaffected, then my proximity shouldn't trouble you in the least. And yet . . . you're quite a distinctive shade of pink. Do I trouble you, Miss Fairleigh?" His voice had become that low rumble, persuasive, coaxing as a stroking hand.

Her bodice was definitely moving a little more quickly.

"Not . . . not in the least." Barely words. Then she squeezed her eyes closed. Angry at herself for stuttering.

She opened them again quickly.

"Ah. I think I know a way we can prove that we've both been entirely unaffected by the events of that evening," Rhys murmured.

"What is it?"

"Kiss me again, Sabrina."

Silence as she stared up at him, seemingly unable to look away. "Are you *mad*?" Her outrage was very unconvincing, as she'd whispered the words.

"Of course, I can go to my grave thinking that you cherish the evening in the gallery more than anything else in your crusading life."

"You're insufferable." Another whisper.

"I regret to inform you that you're not the first to make that discovery."

"You're so certain there isn't a woman who can resist you. You're here because your pride is wounded, that is all."

She rather had a point. Still, he had a point to make as well.

"Very well, Miss Fairleigh," he said softly. "Feel free to resist me."

It was difficult to say how it happened; but his head was lowering, her hands were pressed lightly against his chest, then sliding up to clasp behind his head, their lips were touching, his arms pulled her closer, closer. And now that their bodies were familiar to each other, knew how to fit and mold against each other, the kiss took fire rather rapidly, and became much, much deeper, much more quickly than Rhys had intended.

And oh . . . it was divine.

Which was why they were in too deep to hear the footsteps on marble or the low murmur of voices.

"Sabrina! We've returned, and by *sleigh,* if you can imagine! We brought your father from the Colb—"

A veritable windstorm of gasps.

Followed by a silence as resounding as a thunderclap.

Rhys and Sabrina leaped apart.

In the doorway stood Lady Mary Capstraw, the Colberts, Geoffrey, and someone who could only be, God help them . . .

Sabrina's father.

CHAPTER TWELVE

APART FROM WYNDHAM, all of the other witnesses had scattered like grouse when a shot is fired, including Miss Fairleigh, who had somehow burst out of the library door and vanished in the hubbub. Leaving Rhys and his friend alone to contemplate the aftermath of the disaster, and the consequences, and what he intended to do about it.

Wyndham settled himself on a fawn-colored velvet settee and gingerly lifted his heels up onto the eighteenth-century table with the bowed gilt legs. "I'm not quite certain what to say, Rhys. Congratulations? The vicar's daughter is human, after all?"

Wyndham sounded amused, but the amusement had an edge. Apparently not even Wyndham took the public ruination of a vicar's daughter lightly.

"What were you thinking? In the middle of the library? In the middle of the *day*?"

Rhys fixed him with a brief baleful glare before returning his attention to the landscape.

"Ah. I gather from that glower that you *weren't* thinking. With your head, that is."

"Careful, Wyndham," Rhys said absently.

Wyndham quieted. He knew that tone. Rhys was teetering on the edge of fury.

"Does Sophia know yet, do you think?" Rhys wondered. Hers was the one face he hadn't seen in the doorway.

"Oh, someone is bound to inform her. She'll probably be amused."

"No doubt." Sophia was invariably amused, when he would have liked her to be jealous, or kind, or to cling, all of which would have been at least a change of pace. Ironically, it was her very changeability that had drawn him to her in the first place.

Rhys stared out the great arched window. The blue sky was gone; when had that happened? White now met white in sky and ground. Bare trees speared the snow, branches sharp and glittering against the sky. As stark as the decision that faced him.

Bloody hell. It had been just one little kiss.

Admittedly, one very badly *timed* little kiss.

Ironically, as he'd said to Miss Fairleigh: not every kiss was only a kiss. This one had the power to change futures.

How on earth had he managed to best himself at his own game?

He relived that moment now in his thoughts, the way he might relive a fencing match or a chess game to find the moment it had gone wrong. Soft lips against his, soft body against his, the beginning of that delicious slow heat—

Then the door swinging open, the cheerful announcement of Lady Mary cut sharply off by the shock of seeing the earl and Sabrina entwined. And then the row of expressions, each branded distinctly in his memory. Several horrified, one delightedly awed and scandalized— that would be Lady Mary Capstraw—and one saddened and strangely resigned. He supposed this was the Vicar Fairleigh. Mary had said they'd brought Sabrina's father along.

His cousin Geoffrey's expression had been altogether more difficult to discern. It had almost been . . . triumph.

Rhys's mind circled and circled the problem, and the more he circled it the more he felt entangled in it. Sabrina Fairleigh was the adopted daughter of a poor vicar—nearly redundant, those two words side by side—and he'd all but robbed her of her prospects and future and the only thing a woman of her status had, really—her reputation—by indulging in that one little kiss. He supposed he should be amused that his game had turned on him like a domesticated wild beast might turn on its master.

For so long he'd done precisely as he pleased, as if to test the temper of the title he'd worked so hard to restore to glory. Duels and affairs and gaming hells and reprobate friends from all walks of life . . . he'd indulged in every imaginable pleasure and emerged relatively unscathed, even more glamorous if scandalous, as he was an earl, after all. But never before had he been foolish enough to compromise an *unmarried* girl.

His restlessness had driven him to the ultimate recklessness.

And quite simply—and this surprised him—he disliked himself for it. Profoundly.

"Well, Wynd?" he said quietly. He turned to his friend, then dropped his eyes and leveled a speaking glance at Wyndham's feet.

His friend swung them from the antique and very valuable table. "I hate to say it . . . but I fear you may have to make this right, Rhys."

This was what Rhys was beginning to fear as well. And he didn't think he could pay Vicar Fairleigh to forget what he'd seen. There wasn't enough money in the world to pay every witness to today's events to forget what they'd seen. Sabrina was most definitely ruined.

His mouth tipped up in a humorless smile. Odd to think that he of all people would meet such a mundane fate. Trapped. He supposed there was a modicum of drama in doing the honorable thing, even if the remainder of his life he was tied to a woman who thought London the equivalent of Gomorrah.

He'd known he would wed in time, of course.

Of all the women in England, he'd somehow managed to compromise perhaps the only one who would *not* be pleased to marry an earl—let alone the infamously seductive Libertine. Some distant part of him was aware that this was also funny.

Though, when encouraged, this particular woman could kiss like sin. And it was his fault that she knew how to do that now.

Rhys shifted restlessly, inhaled a long breath, as if the room had suddenly become stifling.

"Well, you had to marry someday." Wyndham was trying to find a silver lining.

"Yes."

"You can't have thought to marry *Sophia*?" Wyndham said suddenly.

"No. But I suppose I rather had an aristocratic wife in mind. Not a penniless . . ." He trailed off.

Though he doubted a marriage would deprive him of Sophia's favors, should he choose to avail himself of them. Sophia. Now there was another awkward conversation he was going to need to have very soon.

He inhaled deeply, exhaled.

"Well, I suppose I have two choices. I can wed Miss Fairleigh to salvage her reputation. She can have the country life here at La Montagne, and I suppose I'll live in London much the way I always have. We can live our lives separately, in the fine tradition of aristocracy, and famous poets. I believe Will Shakespeare kept his wife rather tucked away. Or . . ."

"Or?" Wyndham encouraged.

"Or I can pay her to go far away. On her mission. She might prefer it."

And so, Rhys thought for a moment, might he.

Wyndham was silent. "And what of your cousin? Was he attached to Miss Fairleigh? Will you now be called out by a curate?"

Oh, God. He doubted Geoffrey would have the nerve or even the inclination. Geoffrey valued his own hide a little too highly. Nor did Geoffrey possess the passion for it.

"I'll offer Geoffrey a living at Buckstead Heath, as the vicar. He's not all bad, I suppose. And God knows I seldom intend to be in this part of the country."

He didn't turn to look at Wyndham, half suspecting, for some reason, he'd find a censorious look.

"Do you know what I find rather funny, Rhys?"

"Very nearly everything?"

Wyndham's eyebrows pitched upward. "*Today,* what I find rather funny, is that when we all came upon you in the midst of your . . ." He paused to search for just the right descriptive word. The word, in other words, that would annoy Rhys the most.

Rhys spared him the trouble. "Yes?" he snapped.

"Well . . . I could swear she was standing on her toes."

Rhys went still. "Her toes?"

"Oh, yes. Quite as though she were . . . well, let us say, saving you the trouble of bending all the way down to her face to get a kiss. As though she was getting a kiss of her own."

Another way of saying she was a willing participant in the fiasco.

He supposed he had himself to blame for that, too. Miss Fairleigh now knew what it was like to be properly kissed, and she also knew she had enough pride to rise up to whatever challenges he threw down.

Bloody hell.

"*And* . . ." Wyndham wasn't through.

"And what?"

"Your hands were on her arse."

Rhys shot him a filthy look. "That's where hands inevitably go in the midst of a kiss."

"The funny thing is . . . ," Wyndham continued as though Rhys hadn't said a thing. "They looked right at home there, your hands. Rather as though they'd been there before."

Rhys gave Wyndham his best enigmatic expression, while Wyndham gave him his best wickedly knowing expression. And then Rhys turned his face back toward the window. He realized, suddenly, that they might be talking about his future countess, and regardless of how reluctant he was to marry her, he also wasn't eager to hear another man discuss her arse, and he wasn't about to discuss the evening in the sculpture gallery, because he wouldn't quite know how to put it into words. Somehow he suspected Wyndham wouldn't approve, and it would sound ingenuous to say, "In the moment, it seemed I had no other choice but to kiss her."

Rhys finally turned from the window. "Well, Wyndham. Wish me luck."

Sabrina had managed to bolt from the library, and Lady Mary Capstraw detached herself from the crowd of shocked watchers to follow her, her slippers echoing on the marble behind Sabrina.

Sabrina turned blindly into one of the seemingly dozens of drawing rooms at La Montagne. This one was predominantly green. An enormous portrait of a woman wearing a tall complicated white wig and a tiny satisfied smile took up nearly the entire wall over a fireplace. Sabrina flung herself onto a settee before the fireplace. A fire was leaping, full and bright, even though the room was unoccupied. Such untold extravagance. It reminded her once again of whom she'd actually been kissing. Someone who could afford to burn wood profligately to keep a portrait of some unknown ancestor warm and maids employed to keep the pointless fire burning.

Sabrina sat, silent and motionless apart from her fingers, which anxiously wove in and out of one another. And for nearly five minutes, Mary, who could outchatter a chickadee, did nothing but stare at Sabrina, eyes enormous. Her face was brilliant with awe.

"I do wish you would say something, Mary," Sabrina said finally, irritably.

"Cor!" Mary blurted finally.

"Oh, thank you, Mary. Very helpful."

But the dam had apparently broken.

"There you were, Sabrina . . . you were"—Mary paused, and issued the next word in a dumbstruck whisper—"*kissing* . . . The Libertine!"

"Yes." Through gritted teeth. Though it hadn't been much of a kiss, in truth. They'd been interrupted before it could become one. And Sabrina had the earl to thank for the fact that she knew there was more to kissing than that.

"Kissing him!" Mary reiterated.

"I believe we've established that, Mary."

And then silence again. Dozens of questions were clearly clamoring for Mary's attention, and she was having difficulty choosing one out of the crowd.

"Are you in love?" she ventured dreamily, finally.

"Oh, for *heaven's* sake, Mary."

"Were you . . . were you"—Mary lowered her voice—"overcome with passion?"

Sabrina whipped her head around and glared at her friend ferociously.

Mary was undaunted. "Did he"—a delicious little pause—"*ravish* you?"

"*Mary.* Please! Don't you see? It's too terrible for words."

Silence. For a moment Mary looked sympathetic and troubled, but it wasn't an expression she could hold for long. Sabrina could practically *see* the next question as it bubbled up out of her.

"What precisely happens when you're ravished? You see, I'm married, but I don't believe I've ever been properly *ravished*, as it were."

Sabrina moaned and dropped her face into her hands.

Mercifully Mary ceased asking questions for the moment.

Suddenly Sabrina looked up again and parted her hands like shutters.

"Mary, what about Geoffrey?"

Mary's jaw dropped. "Oh, poor Geoffrey!" she said, aghast, as though it had just occurred to her.

It was a very good thing Lady Mary Capstraw had no intention of ministering to the poor, Sabrina thought. She had no instinct for comforting.

"And why on earth was my *father* with you, Mary?" she groaned.

"Oh! Lizzie's mother sent for him. He was summoned by the Colberts some days ago to speak to her father, who is very ill, and possibly dying, you see, but they could not be sure. And there isn't a vicar nearby, and Mr. Colbert is acquainted with your father. They didn't know Geoffrey would be visiting La Montagne."

Another silence.

And then Mary said, quietly, as though it had all at last solidified into a single realization: "Good heavens, you are right. Sabrina, you are quite ruined."

"Are you only now realizing this, Mary?"

Mary was silent then, questions spent, the magnitude of Sabrina's predicament thumping down over her like a great net.

She and Sabrina stared at each other helplessly.

And then Mary moved to Sabrina's side and took her hand and squeezed it.

And then released it and then moved a few inches away from her.

Then scooted back over again and took her hand again and squeezed it.

Clearly Mary Capstraw wasn't quite certain what to do with Sabrina now that she'd been ruined, as none of her friends had ever before done anything quite so interesting.

At last, they fell into a silence that began to feel permanent. And the fact Mary could find nothing else to say confirmed for Sabrina how very grave her circumstances truly were.

Leaving Wyndham, Rhys had immediately asked the inscrutable Mrs. Bailey to find and send Vicar Fairleigh to the yellow sitting room.

Now Rhys stood in the doorway of it, bracing himself for a conversation he'd never dreamed he'd need to have, and studied Sabrina's father. The vicar looked the way vicars over England seemed to, face as furrowed as a winter road, skin reddened and wind-roughened. A peaceful face for all of that, despite the air of bewilderment. His shoulders were squared, as though he was braced for something. Looking at the vicar's weathered, resigned face, Rhys had never felt more like a bounder in his entire life, and Lord knew he'd made something of an art of being a bounder.

Rhys's catalog of experiences was extraordinarily diverse, but since he'd never before kissed a vicar's daughter in a library before an audience of fascinated onlookers, he was at a loss as to how to begin this particular interview.

"Mr. Fairleigh," he decided upon, first of all. He said it quietly.

The vicar stood quickly and turned to look up at Rhys, and dignity, worry, and indignation warred with guarded respect for Rhys's station in his expression. He waited a distinct moment before he made his bow. A point made.

Rhys knew he deserved the small, dignified slight. He bowed, too, and gestured for the vicar to resume sitting.

There was a quiet, as the two men sat across from each other. Rhys knew he ought to speak, but the vicar began.

"I . . . didn't know she was here, you see," the vicar began, his voice strained, sounding faintly bewildered. "Not until Lady Mary told me, and then I . . ." He looked down, and clasped his hands tightly in his lap, overcome with some emotion. Anger? Shame? "She's a good girl," he said quietly, sounding puzzled.

And Rhys suddenly desperately wanted to spare this man shame. He didn't know how he could possibly, with any sort of grace, raise the possibility of paying his daughter to go thousands of miles away. The vicar had raised a good quiet girl—a good quiet girl at least *outwardly*—who might even have remained that way if The Libertine hadn't taken it upon himself to show Sabrina Fairleigh the truth of her nature, out of sheer boredom.

Bloody hell. Rhys felt the bottom officially dropping from beneath his feet. But he didn't lack courage, and he was a man of words, was he not? He would find the right ones.

"Sir, I would like to apologize for what you witnessed a moment ago. I never meant to—"

The vicar looked up swiftly, eyes flaring with disbelief, and a hint of outrage. And Rhys knew an excellent and truthful way to end that sentence would be, "—be caught kissing your daughter," but this was out of the question in the circumstances. He hurriedly continued. "That is, please let me assure you that I never intended to"—he cleared his throat delicately—"dishonor Sabrina. And I would like to assure you that your daughter and I have formed . . . an attachment."

Well, that was one way to describe it.

The vicar's taut expression began to gradually, warily give way to relief. And then he waited, and when Rhys said nothing more, the Vicar Fairleigh's expression softened further and became almost . . . gently sympathetic. As though Rhys were a callow young man confessing to a first love.

Good God. They were in the realm of the comical now. But he'd gone forward, and once he said the words officially, Rhys knew he wouldn't be able to retract them.

He leaped.

"I do intend to do my duty by your daughter, sir. And I should be honored indeed if you would consent to"—Rhys paused, to savor one final moment of freedom—"consent to give me Sabrina's hand in marriage."

He said the words stiffly. He could scarcely believe they'd left his mouth. He was distantly aware that the sensation seemed to have left his limbs.

The vicar paused, tipping his head in thought, and fixed Rhys with a gently bemused gaze. "Though I'm sure we are agreed that the circumstances under which we have met are not ideal, sir, I should be pleased to give my consent to your marriage. I was young once, Lord Rawden. I am inclined to forgive young love—"

Good God.

"—since the outcome is now all we could have hoped for."

There were a million things Rhys could have said in response. He was wise enough—and numb enough—to refrain from saying any of them.

* * *

Not knowing what else to do, Sabrina sat with Mary and watched the pendulum on the clock swing hypnotically to and fro, her stomach a cauldron of misery. She thought of Geoffrey, who could not possibly marry her now, and the odd expression on his face when he'd seen her leap away from Rhys: bitter triumph. Of her father, who looked both heartbroken and strangely not at all surprised. Perhaps this was the thing he'd been expecting Sabrina to do all along: kiss a notorious earl. Sabrina wished now that the vicar had warned her specifically about his suspicion, if this was indeed the case, so she might have avoided it. She wondered where her father was at this moment.

And she thought of all the other witnesses, who would be only too delighted to spread the word.

That clock pendulum had swung dozens and dozens of times before a butler appeared at the door and bowed low to the two of them.

"Miss Fairleigh, the earl would be pleased if you would join him at half past the hour in the window room."

Sabrina's heart immediately balled up like a hedgehog facing a predator. That was an hour from now. What was the earl doing *now*?

"Thank you," she said faintly to the butler's impassive face. He nodded and backed from the room. She didn't wonder how she'd been found. She imagined the servants saw and knew everything, even in this maze of drawing and sitting rooms that was La Montagne. They were everywhere, and as indispensable as the wall sconces, as the walls themselves.

Lady Mary, on the other hand, looked quite cheerfully alert again.

"Talk to me of other things, Mary, for the next few minutes. Please. Of Lizzie's new baby."

And so Mary talked and talked, and Sabrina listened but didn't hear, until the hands moved over to the hour designated for her to meet her fate.

Rhys paused in the doorway. Sabrina Fairleigh was sitting in the center of the settee looking very small in that enormous room, her head turned toward the window much as his had a moment before, as though she were getting her last glimpse of freedom.

He wondered if she saw the expanse of colorless snow as metaphorically as he did.

He closed the door quietly behind him and she gave a start. She was on her feet instantly, smoothing her palms against her skirt.

She curtsied, swiftly, and he offered her a bow.

Awkward as strangers, the two of them, suddenly. When their lips and arms and bodies had been touching a mere hour or so before. And then it had seemed a game.

Only a kiss.

The cool light illuminated her fair soft skin, those lovely clear eyes that were too observant, too direct, which no doubt meant she could also be too easily hurt. How very young she seemed, standing there in her best day dress, faded and poignantly outdated. And as Rhys stared at Miss Sabrina Fairleigh, soon to be Sabrina Gillray, the Countess Rawden, the woman who would bear his name and his sons, he realized, ironically, that she had been right. His own passions and inclinations toward indulgence had led the two of them to this moment.

He wasn't about to confess this to *her,* however.

He wondered how on earth they could possibly go beyond this awkward moment, from this mistake, and proceed with the rest of their lives.

His cravat suddenly felt too tight, his lungs too shallow to take in a proper breath.

"Miss Fairleigh, I have spoken to your father," he began without preamble. "I have made abject apologies to him"—he ground these words out with some difficulty, as it was not every day a proud earl was forced to make abject apologies to an impoverished vicar, nor to admit to it—"and have professed an attachment to you. I have assured him that I intend to do my duty by you. You may find some comfort in the fact that he is inclined to forgive"—he paused, and framed the next two words in fourteen-karat irony—"young love."

She made a soft snorting sound. At least she appreciated irony.

During their excruciating interview, the vicar had in fact assured the earl that Sabrina could easily run a great house, as she ran the vicarage and half the town, and really, the vicar didn't know how he would do without her.

Though of course the settlements would go a long way toward hiring help.

Why on earth *did I decide to touch this unmarried girl?* Rhys wanted to throw something, or run.

Instead, he located his sense of honor. It was bred into his blood after all, even if he hadn't exercised it a very good deal lately. He took a deep breath and said the words with the proper gravity, as he thought every young woman deserved a proper proposal.

"Therefore, Sabrina, I would be pleased if you would do me the honor of becoming my wife."

She regarded him unblinkingly, those disconcertingly direct eyes studying his face. He thought he saw a glimmer of dark humor there.

If she made noises about doing her duty by *him,* he would quite simply go mad, he decided. He would go off to fight a foreign war.

"I thank you for your offer, sir, and in light of the circumstances, I am . . . just as pleased and honored . . . to accept your offer of marriage as you are to offer it."

Perhaps the most ironic marriage proposal ever made and accepted. Not at all what the world at large would have expected from The Libertine, who could make words sing on a page and women swoon.

This one didn't look inclined to swoon at the moment.

Their gazes held a moment longer. Well, they had that in common, at least: mutual disenchantment.

Sabrina's cheeks burned pink as she gazed at him, but her spine was straight and her shoulders square. He'd recognized the pride in her from the very beginning, and he wondered if it was an inconvenient thing for her, the vicar's daughter, with her plans of ministering to the poor alongside insufferable Geoffrey. He considered someone harboring the pride so evident in her stiffened spine might have very likely made an unsuitable wife for his cousin Geoffrey, too.

Or perhaps it was he who brought out the stiff spine, and perhaps Geoffrey would have had a perfectly amiable partner in her, if Geoffrey had ever really intended to wed her.

He wondered if she actually loved Geoffrey.

He wondered if her heart was breaking.

He wondered what that felt like, if so.

It was difficult to say. She just seemed . . . pale and proud and resolute. Trying, the same as he, to come to terms with how irrevocably and quickly her future had changed.

In other circumstances, this would have been a moment for a tender kiss. He didn't feel inclined to touch her at all at the moment, when, funnily enough, he could scarcely take his hands from her a moment ago, let alone the other night. Moonlight, myths, and nearly transparent night rails could do that to a man.

"And so I believe you now know the price of succumbing to your animal nature." She said it somewhat sardonically, as though concluding an argument.

Ah, Miss Fairleigh. She never could resist.

But nor could he. He rose to it. "Oddly enough, Miss Fairleigh, I have kissed dozens of women and managed not to enter into any engagements."

"Dozens? Oh, my. I fall more in love with you by the minute."

It was time to reveal his hand. "*I* believe *you* stood on tiptoe, Sabrina."

Hot color crept into those pale cheeks. "I *beg* your pardon?" She sounded outraged.

Hmmm. A bit *too* outraged. Hadn't the bard written something about protesting too much?

"What I mean to say, Sabrina," he clarified relentlessly, on a drawl, "is that you met me halfway today in the library. You *wanted* a kiss."

Her hands knotted against her skirt, but those green eyes flared hot, briefly, in anger, and something else: guilt. Ha! He thought it intemperate at the moment to point out that tempers were an untoward expression of passion, too.

And granted, it had been ungentlemanly of him to point out that she had met his kiss, that she, in fact, shared the blame for their predicament. But then, being gentlemanly wasn't how he'd managed to get himself engaged, and being gentlemanly now wasn't going to undo it.

She protested no further, which in itself seemed a concession. If nothing else, he could count on Miss Fairleigh to be honest. It was a rare enough quality in any human.

"I will send for a Special License at once, of course," he said, somewhat awkwardly, when she remained silent.

"Of course," she repeated, her voice faint. She turned her head away toward the window again. He thought he saw despair shadowing her face briefly; it was gone again as swiftly. It echoed his own, played upon his guilt. And guilt made him angry, both with himself and with her.

Bloody hell.

But he had done the right thing. He wouldn't be the first man to have a marriage foisted upon him, and she wouldn't be the first dissatisfied woman.

How on earth would they get beyond this awkward moment and go on with the rest of their lives?

"I think it shall be clear for the next few days. No snow. The Special License should arrive in a timely way," she said finally, surprising him.

"How can you know?"

"I've learned a thing or two in Tinbury." She said it with a wry smile, almost to herself.

CHAPTER THIRTEEN

And so when Sabrina finally saw her father an hour or so later, she was engaged to be a countess.

Mrs. Bailey, who seemed to know all, directed her to the room where her father sat. She paused in the doorway and watched him a moment turning as he slowly scanned the glories of the wallpaper, the vases, the fireplace carvings. Sabrina smiled as she watched the vicar shake his head slowly to and fro in bemusement.

And then he turned and saw her. He hesitated a moment before stepping forward to kiss her on both cheeks, then held her hands in his. They settled side by side on the settee.

"Papa . . . are you ashamed?" She burst out with it, needing his forgiveness, his comfort.

The Vicar Fairleigh looked at the young woman he'd raised from a very little girl so many years ago.

"Oh, my dear Sabrina. How could I ever be ashamed of you? I confess I *was* surprised to find you here at La Montagne, and . . ." He couldn't quite finish his sentence, so Sabrina finished it for him in her own mind: *standing on your toes and kissing an earl.* "But I only wish for you to be happy. I never dreamed you'd one day be a countess."

"Nor did I, Papa. It isn't what I thought I wanted."

"But is *he* who you want? This earl?"

It would only make her father unhappy to tell him the truth. Surely she would be forgiven this one little lie.

"He is what I want."

The relief on the vicar's face was her reward. Sabrina suspected the relief was rather like that on the faces of the audience when she'd made her first pianoforte mistake: now that the mistake was over and done with, the strain of *anticipating* the grand mistake was over, too.

The thought of the pianoforte made her ask her next question. "Papa?"

"Yes, my dear?"

"I have a memory . . . of standing near a pianoforte near a woman I think is my mother. And I've a memory of other little girls. It's all very blurry, now, you see. That's all I know."

"You've never told me this before, child." The vicar smiled gently.

"Do you truly know nothing at all about my mother?" It was a formality, really. She knew he'd told her all there was to tell.

She could tell he was searching his mind for something, anything to tell her. She was on the brink of the rest of her life, and wanted to know something of her mother.

"Well, her name was Anna, as your miniature says," he began.

"Yes," she confirmed. This she knew.

"And we can surmise other things about her, too, Sabrina, by just looking at her daughter. That she was beautiful, and kind. Perhaps she played the pianoforte well."

Perhaps she was proud and passionate. Perhaps she had a temper.

Sabrina smiled at her father. He'd never complimented her so specifically before; he had always been careful to guard against vanity. Apparently now that she was about to be a married woman and a countess she could feel free to become as vain as a peacock.

But all her life Sabrina had sensed her sheer conspicuousness had made the vicar nervous. All Vicar Fairleigh had ever wanted was a quiet life. Perhaps all along he'd suspected she wasn't destined for anything ordinary.

"And the night I was brought to you?" she urged.

"Shall I tell you that story again?"

"Please, if you would, Papa."

It was a very short story as there was little to tell, and Sabrina knew it well, like a much-loved bedtime story. A man, a well-dressed, grieving, gray-faced man, had brought Sabrina to him. He was not a handsome man, the vicar said. But he'd seemed quietly determined.

"Was the man my father, do you suppose?"

"I wish, my dear, I could tell you. But he looked not at all like you. And you never once called him 'Papa.' You were crying for your mama."

And suddenly, though Sabrina had no memory of that moment, she felt like that little girl. On the day of her wedding, she would have liked her mother to be with her.

Her father honored her silence a moment longer.

"I don't know how I will do without you, my dear, but your husband has been a generous man." The vicar was wry. Poverty was the besetting trial of nearly every vicar in all of England. "I hope you will be happy, my dear."

"I shall be, Papa." She had no way of knowing if this would ever be true, but these words were her gift to Vicar Fairleigh for taking her in so long ago.

* * *

Later, Sabrina's future husband would remember the days
that followed the kiss in the library in terms of a series of
excruciating conversations, each one life-changing.

From Sabrina, he'd immediately asked Mrs. Bailey
to locate Signora Licari. He wasn't quite certain what he
would say to *her*, either, but he was certain he needed to
do it quickly.

Ironically, Rhys realized that he and Sophia had conducted their affair, such as it was, more or less like an
opera. It had always been dependent upon emotional
crescendos for its momentum, which were linked by
passages of relative, if somewhat wary (on his part, anyhow) calm, during which they shared tastes in the arts
and ironic conversation about members of the *ton*. But
now Rhys felt a bit like an actor who had toppled from
the stage into the audience, and he almost felt like apologizing. Not for being a cad and compromising another
woman entirely under his own roof during a house party
to which he'd invited her, but for interrupting their ongo-
ing performance—which had suited both of them—with
an unscheduled bit of clumsy reality.

And because their relationship was comprised primarily of strategy, Rhys strolled into the yellow sitting room
a good hour after he'd asked Mrs. Bailey to send Sophia
there.

He found the singer arranged on the settee, slim fingers
drumming a leisurely tattoo against her velvet-draped
thigh. This drumming might have been an indication of
pique, which would be slightly gratifying, as keeping
people waiting was typically Sophia's specialty. Or it

might simply be her way of keeping time to whatever music she was listening to in her head. One never knew with Sophia.

She rose gracefully when she saw him and extended her hand, one eyebrow winging upward in sardonic appreciation. She knew why he was late.

Rhys bent over that immaculately kept hand, struck by a memory of how soft and skilled her hands were in general. They'd roamed his body on numerous occasions; he'd bent to kiss them formally countless more times. Odd how he hadn't truly given them a thought for days, though those skilled hands had, in part, been the reason he'd invited her to the country at all.

The jewel that hung around her neck now—a jewel he hadn't given to her—was evidence that her hands roamed *other* bodies, too.

"I'm going to be married," he said when he was upright again.

He hadn't meant to say it quite so directly, not really. But once the words were out, he was glad he'd done so. He watched her, genuinely curious to see how she would respond.

She didn't even blink. "Most men of your station do marry." She sounded amused.

And this irritated him irrationally.

"I am going to be married to Miss Sabrina Fairleigh as soon as a Special License arrives. I shall be wed within days." He said it curtly.

Ah. A swift widening of the eyes. Her lips parted a little.

And then silence, as Sophia fully absorbed that he wasn't jesting. Briefly she turned her head away, then turned it back again.

For a moment he regretted his curtness, because he wouldn't take pleasure in hurting her feelings. Still, he wasn't certain whether he *could,* in fact, hurt her.

He waited. He watched the thoughts moving over her face, and then saw her draw conclusions about his announcement. Sophia was worldly, and knew his temperament. And as she knew he was not one to become overcome with *love,* she would also know he must have been overcome with something else altogether. And he must have been caught at it.

In short, she could probably guess exactly what had happened.

That's when he actually felt himself flush.

"My congratulations," Sophia said finally, softly. She regarded him evenly. He could have sworn she was even a little amused.

"Sophia—," he said swiftly.

He stopped. He didn't know how he intended to finish his sentence. He hadn't intended to hurt her or even wound her pride, as she was a proud woman, and rightfully so. And she didn't appear to be hurt. Then again, it was often impossible to know what Sophia was thinking. All the delicious, dramatic spikes of their relationship had spared them the necessity of honest communication. Which, in part, was why the relationship had suited them both.

"I shall depart straightaway," she said briskly.

He didn't argue with her. "It might be best. You may use my carriage."

She nodded. She had taken this for granted, of course.

"And I will see you in London?" She smiled. This she took for granted, too.

Relieved that at least some things would continue as always, Rhys's smile was warmer. "Of course. Very soon."

He raised her hands to his lips as a promise.

And so there passed several days that taxed the manners of all present, but everyone seemed to tacitly decide that the most comfortable solution was to forget that Sabrina had been caught kissing the earl and had perhaps dashed the hopes of another man, and to rejoice in the approach of a wedding. After all, an earl, even a notorious one, was a much better catch than a curate, and even the curate—soon to be vicar—in question was expected to accept this.

Geoffrey had removed himself to the vicarage at Buckstead Heath. The pleasant collective delusion did not extend to expecting him to perform the wedding ceremony, or attend it, for that matter. Apparently he had quite graciously accepted the living extended to him by his cousin. Another clergyman from a town some distance away from Buckstead Heath had been pressed into service, as her father would be a guest.

Her husband's alleged mistress had also discreetly disappeared, returned to London for an important singing engagement, or so the rest of the company was told.

Sabrina saw her future husband only at dinners with the other guests, where he was politely solicitous but not attentive, and where much discussion of the weather (cold) and the house (pretty) took place, and very little was eaten by the bride-to-be.

Sabrina both wished she knew what the Earl of Rawden, Rhys Gillray, her future husband, was thinking, and was glad she didn't know.

*   *   *

Being an earl had its distinct advantages, and despite the
bad weather, the Special License arrived quickly. The
wedding, small and quiet, was held early in the morning
at the ancient church at Buckstead Heath. Sabrina wore a
walking dress, and in her bodice she'd tucked the miniature of her mother, for she would have liked her mother to
attend her wedding. The groom wore fawn-colored trousers, tall boots, and a dark coat that somehow made his
eyes more vivid, his face more pale.

And of her wedding day, Sabrina knew she would remember this: his blue eyes fierce but otherwise enigmatic,
his warm hands gripping her cold ones, keeping them
from trembling. A ghost of a rueful smile on his mouth
as he looked down at her. He never did look away from
her, in fact. It was such a little thing, but it somehow gave
her strength, for he alone perhaps understood what moved
through her mind at the moment, as similar things doubt-
less moved through his.

And then the words were said, and it was over, and she
was a countess.

She'd always thought her wedding, when it was held,
would be held in spring, with the air soft and warm, and
blossoms just beginning to break out on the trees. Not
this still, cold day, with a sky so blue it made one blink to
look at it, and snow becoming muddy and gray lining the
roads, and the branches of the bare trees surrounding the
church looking as complicated as snowflakes. The winter
had indeed come early and hard.

Another thought crossed her mind: It *had* been an omen.
Silly as it was, she felt somehow vindicated.

* * *

"Don't go, Mary." Sabrina knew this was a futile request, and didn't precisely mean it. Still, out the sentiment came. Mary's trunks were being packed for her by a competent maid, so Mary stole some time alone with Sabrina after the wedding breakfast.

"Oh, Sabrina. You know I cannot stay. You're a wife now. *And* a countess," she added with relish. "I must say I'm awfully pleased to be on such intimate terms with a countess." Mary squeezed her hand. "Where is your handsome husband?"

Sabrina sounded desperate. "Mary, I never *wanted* to be a countess. And I never know where my 'handsome husband' is." *Husband. Husband husband husband.* She wondered if the word would ever feel natural emerging from her lips. It didn't now, particularly since she'd for some time pictured an entirely different man in the role.

"I never wanted to have blond hair that would never curl, but it's what I have, isn't it?" was Mary's fractured philosophy. "We must make do. Although, I must say, I think you're doing considerably better than just making do. Will you go on a honeymoon journey?"

Sabrina stared at her incredulously. "*Mary.* For heaven's sake. Everyone seems to forget that this marriage wasn't precisely planned by either of us. The earl and I are *hardly* lovebirds, no matter what you saw, and no matter what he told my father. The earl merely did his duty by me in order to salvage my reputation."

"As he should, as he ruined it by kissing you, did he not?"

Sabrina was not inclined to take the blame for anything at the moment, so she remained silent.

"And that's no excuse not to make the best of everything, now, is it?" Mary persisted.

Sabrina sighed. She thought again of that miniature of her mother and wondered, not for the first time, whether there might be anyone else like her on the planet, or if she had been her mother's only child. She loved Mary for her essential cheerful goodness, but everything always required a good deal of explanation with Mary.

"Well, I suppose someone ought to talk to you about your wedding night. I ought to tell you what happens, since your mother isn't here to tell you. And he *will* want to come to you tonight, no doubt, as his duty as an earl is to get an heir, of course."

Sabrina suspected she had more than an inkling of what would happen. But now she was as alert as a spaniel.

She waited.

"Well . . . they lie on top of you and"—Mary cleared her throat—"you know." Mary said this somewhat hopefully, with an air of finality, as though she hoped she needn't explain it in more detail.

Sabrina did rather know. She'd seen chickens, dogs, and cattle at it; she knew that the way in which she and Rhys had melded together just the other night wasn't the entire story.

But after a moment of silence, she couldn't resist.

"Mary . . . I think there's more," she whispered.

Mary gaped for an instant.

"I *knew* it! He *did* ravish you!" Mary said triumphantly.

"He didn't." Ravishing implied that something had been *done* to her, when in truth it had all been rather mutual.

There was a pause.

Mary narrowed her eyes shrewdly. "All right, then. Very well. You're right. There *is* more," she revealed, slowly.

Sabrina waited, half in hope, half in dread.

"But not a very good deal more," Mary expounded with some resignation. "And it's over quickly enough, so you needn't worry. I typically use the time to plan the next day's dinner." She sounded cheerfully matter-of-fact about it. "And I am so fond of Paul that I don't mind it overall, as he seems to enjoy it so thoroughly. We've become quite great friends. And it's my duty as a wife, you see, as it shall be yours."

Sabrina stared at her friend, boggled yet again. She couldn't help remembering the Earl of Rawden's words: *Perhaps you take pleasure in duty.*

Then again, whereas before she could have slapped the Earl of Rawden for kissing her, now it was her duty to accept whatever attentions he intended to bestow. And yet . . .

What about the need that comes up on you so suddenly that you feel as though you'll explode from it, and then you do explode from it in the most extraordinary pleasure you've ever known? Sabrina wanted to ask. Just to watch Mary's expression change.

It occurred to her that it was probably different for every man and woman. Not every man can be The Libertine, with his intimate knowledge of how to please a woman, or the women of London wouldn't trail him about and cast their virtue to the wind, as rumor had it. Nor would he be accompanied by famous, beautiful opera singers.

And not every husband and wife will be fond of each other, or become great friends. Or know each other's whereabouts at any given moment.

Sabrina felt a quiet sense of desolation then. She wondered which she preferred. The pleasure, or the friendship.

She did know she would very much like to not be lonely anymore.

"Do you love Paul, Mary?"

"Of course," Mary said, blinking in surprise.

And then Sabrina was sorry she'd asked, because it just made her feel lonely again.

And then Mary and Paul were gone, and her father left soon after. He gave her a hug, and kissed both cheeks, and with them went the last of what Sabrina knew of Tinbury and her old life.

CHAPTER FOURTEEN

M ARRIED.

Rhys regarded his reflection in the mirror. He didn't feel particularly different. Well, apart, that was, from the feelings of guilt, resentment, and nerves. All of *those* were fairly new for a man who had grown accustomed to doing precisely as he pleased, when he pleased, with whom he pleased.

And he'd never before felt any of those things before bedding a woman.

But, oh, yes. He couldn't deny there was also anticipation. And lust. That was more pleasant.

They were all gone, Lady Mary and Lord Paul and Vicar Fairleigh and even Wyndham, who, surprisingly, drew the line at staying under the same roof with a newly married couple. He'd returned to London along with Sophia.

"See you in a day or so, old man," he'd said, with a tip of the hat and a tilted smile. "I'll keep the secret of your wedding for as long as you'd like me to."

How amused the whole of London would be to discover The Libertine in his chambers, downing brandy, mulling his reflection, postponing the inevitable, when a beautiful young woman waited for him in the adjoining room. He could hardly avoid doing his husbandly duty by his bride, nor did he precisely want to avoid it.

But despite his reputation, he'd never before taken a virgin.

He worried that Sabrina would be afraid; and in a way, he resented the very fact of his worry. He rubbed the back of his neck distractedly, and then drew in a long breath.

At last he seized the brandy decanter and two glasses, and prepared to step forward irrevocably into the rest of his life.

Sabrina dressed for bed in her night rail, the only night rail she currently possessed, and unpinned her hair with unsteady hands, shaking it out. There would be a maid to do this for her if she'd like, and to help her dress, she'd been told by Mrs. Bailey, and yet she couldn't imagine employing a person whose sole purpose was to treat her like a child, to dress her and undress her, to groom her. But then again, she was a countess now, and perhaps it was her duty to employ as many people as possible to do as little as possible. There would be more dresses, and lovely fine things to sleep in, too. She'd been told that a modiste would be in to see to it. She was to choose new fittings for her use if she disliked the fittings currently in her room; she could choose from any of the furniture in this grand house.

She hadn't the faintest idea whether she liked or disliked her fittings. She wasn't entirely certain she knew what the word "fittings" meant. She did know the room was immense, comfortable, warm, and lonely.

This entire room was just for her, and the earl supposedly would sleep in his own chambers adjoining hers, to visit perhaps when the mood took him. Perhaps, as far as earls were concerned, wives were fittings, too.

The shades in the carpet, the curtains, the counterpane, the plump soft chairs, were soft green and gold, forest shades. She liked the colors, she decided. Feminine and soft in the leaping firelight. And so different from the life she'd dreamed of.

Oh, she was nervous. Her conversation with Mary lingered in her mind, and the evening in the statue gallery lingered in her mind, and she didn't know what to believe or think about what would transpire this evening. In truth, she was a little afraid. And in this moment, she was willing to undergo just about anything for the company of another person. At the vicarage in Tinbury, Vicar Fairleigh had slept alongside his wife until the day she died. And Mary and her husband, Paul, had formed a friendship. Sabrina wondered if she dared hope such a thing would come to pass for her and the earl.

An ivory-handled brush and comb, lovely things, lay side by side on the vanity table before a mirror. She took up the brush. The fire beckoned; the pelt of some soft dark animal was spread before it. Sabrina sank down upon it and dragged the brush through her hair in the first of what would be one hundred strokes, hoping the homely familiarity of the act would make her feel a bit more like herself. And as she brushed, she began humming a tune, one of the tunes she'd played on the pianoforte in Tinbury. She tried to remember the words, inserting hums as she sang where she couldn't remember the proper lyric. *One stroke. Two strokes. Three—*

She froze midbrush, abashed, when she noticed Rhys standing in the doorway that connected their two chambers, half in shadow.

She wondered how long he'd been standing there, listening to her fractured song, watching her brush her hair.

He was wearing light trousers and a white shirt open at the throat, his sleeves rolled to his elbows. Coatless, bootless. Not nearly as undressed as she was, but nevertheless, about as undressed as she'd ever seen a man she wasn't related to.

He gripped two glasses in one hand and a decanter in the other, a brown-gold liquid filling it part of the way up.

"Good evening," Sabrina managed at last. Appalled to hear her voice emerge thready.

He smiled a little at her formal tone. "And good evening to *you,* Countess. May I join you?"

"In the song?" It was a jest, an attempt to rally her nerves.

He lifted up the decanter, a gesture. "I'll have to drink a good deal more than this before you can persuade me to join you in a song."

It was her turn to smile a little. "You've had a bit to drink, then?"

"I've had a good *deal* to drink," he corrected somewhat ruefully.

An awkward silence ensued.

And uncertain as to what she should do—fling herself upon the bed?—Sabrina began to rise.

"No, do stay where you are," he said hurriedly. "I find I'm rather in the mood to sit upon a fur in front of the fire."

She sank to her knees again, and refrained from folding her hands into fists in her lap. She wasn't certain what to do with them to make it appear as though she wasn't outrageously nervous.

"Would *you* like something to drink?" he asked.

"Oh, I don't think—"

"It's brandy, Sabrina. Not poison. And you may want it." Lightly said.

He tipped some into a glass, held it out to her. After a moment's hesitation, gingerly, she took it.

She sniffed at it; the fumes made her blink. He was watching her, so she tipped it into her mouth; it was smooth, and burned just a little, pleasantly as it touched her tongue. And as it traveled down her throat, tendrils of fire fanned slowly out in her veins, nicely blunting the edge of her nerves.

Ah. So *that's* why he was drinking.

Here was a man who was said to have made love to dozens of women, all of whom had wanted him, no doubt. All probably as sophisticated as Sophia Licari. And for a wife he was now tied to someone as green as the hills in Tinbury, who only had an inkling of what to do with a man, and that only because he'd shown her one or two things the other night in front of a statue of Persephone. Oh, and she'd read about some of the others in his own book.

No wonder he was nervous.

Or perhaps he drank because he suspected she would bore him.

Rhys was still terribly quiet. His eyes had gone dark, watching her, his pupils large in that sea of blue. What she saw in his eyes was unmistakable: they wandered over her, his eyelids somewhat lowered, over where she knew her thin night rail hid very little, and where he now had a right to peruse. It made the intent of his visit to her unmistakable. Which made his next words almost startling.

"Shall I brush your hair for you? I seem to have interrupted you at it."

"Oh!" She blushed. Good heavens, would she ever cease blushing before this man? "Well. I suppose so. If you'd like."

He smiled a little and held out his hand by way of answer, and she placed the handle of her brush in it.

He slipped down from the chair and knelt behind her. Odd how potent his presence was even when she couldn't see him at all. She pretended, for an instant, that she was blind. What words would she use to describe him? Large, definitely. A tart, rich smell: brandy, a hint of smoke—wood and cigar. Something else, a scent clean and sharp, soap perhaps. But the overall impression was one of warmth, and strength. She somehow knew she'd always sense him if he were near, even if she were blind, even if a room were dark as pitch.

"Hmmm . . . ," he mused, teasing her a little. "How does one go about this?"

"Perhaps you should think of grooming your horse."

He made a soft sound, a laugh. "Ah, but thinking of Gallegos won't put me in an amorous mood."

The matter-of-factly stated "amorous" reminded her of why he was in her room, and she lost her ability to jest. Her nerves fought their way up through the brandy. She took another sip as Rhys at last dragged the brush slowly from the top of her scalp to the ends of her hair.

And . . . *oh*. The stroke seemed to send tiny sparks dancing everywhere over her skin.

She'd never dreamed how delicious such an everyday thing could be when someone else did it for you. Let alone a scandalous poet and newly minted husband. Suddenly hair-brushing took on an entirely new dimension.

He paused. "Like that?"

"Yes. I believe you've the knack." The words were a bit distracted.

"Very good, then." She could hear the smile in his voice.

He set himself earnestly to the task, dragging the brush slowly from the top of her head to the ends of her hair, which fell just above her waist. Each stroke of the brush was somehow more soothing and less soothing than the next. Each one seemed to slow time, lulling her into soft- ness, quieting her thoughts and rousing her body until she seemed aware of every inch and corner and curve of it.

"You've a good deal of hair, haven't you?" Wryly, softly said.

"Mmm."

She'd lost her ability to form complete words several strokes ago. And besides, speech would have distracted from the pleasure. Her eyes were closed. She wondered when she'd closed them. She couldn't recall.

"Beautiful hair," he added, his voice gone lazy and dark, as though he was lulling himself as well.

At last, she heard him, slowly, set the brush aside. Her eyes remained closed.

And then he slowly gathered the silken mass of her hair in his hand, gently, gently lifted it in his fist, let it spill from his hand over one of her shoulders. Her entire body was alert to sensation now; her own hair poured down over her like a caress.

And then lightly, lingeringly . . . he placed his lips against the place on her neck left bare by her hair.

The kiss spiked through her veins, hot and drugging as the brandy. She remembered this about kissing: languor and lightning in equal parts, the sense of the boundaries that defined her slowly dissolving.

Rhys brushed his lips over the nape of her neck, opening them so she could feel the heat of his breath, then the brief heat of his tongue, then his breath again. Gooseflesh washed over her arms and back, and she sighed. And then his large hands slid gently down her back and looped around her waist. Covered in his heat, it seemed she had no choice but to melt against him. She leaned into this warm wall of a man, and when she did, she felt the hard prod of his erection against her buttocks. But his breathing was still remarkably steady compared to her own, which she could hear rushing in her own ears, uneven, rising and falling like the tide of sensation in her.

When his lips traveled to a tender place where her pulse beat, she found herself arching her neck, artless as a cat, so he could reach it. And as she did, his palms slid up over her breasts.

Her breath hitched raggedly. The shock of pleasure all but made her sway.

She tipped her head back against his shoulder, her eyes closed, and his hands leisurely traced the contours of her breasts through her night rail, dragging the silky fabric over her almost painfully sensitized skin, his thumbs circling over the bead-hard peaks of her nipples. And then he slowly slipped his hands beneath the loose neckline, and they were hot on her bare skin.

"*Oh.*" She sighed the word. Pleasure was everywhere in her, skeins of hot light furling and unfurling as he stroked the silky curves of her breasts. She found herself arching under his touch, encouraging it, moving with it, and a sound very like a whimper slipped from her.

She could hear, feel, that his breathing was now as uneven as hers, rapid; surrounding her now was the musk of what she knew was his desire. She pressed her back into him, moved against his arousal instinctively, and his touch became more fierce. His tongue found the whorls of her ears, and then his voice was there.

"Sabrina," the word was husky and strained. "My God."

He became a man of purpose then.

Rhys withdrew his arms from her long enough to gently lower her to the fur, and before she knew it he had gently but swiftly dragged the night rail from her shoulders, slipped it over her slim hips, and stripped her of it, until it was nothing but a limp bit of fabric in his hand. He tossed it aside.

Not his first time at this sort of thing, she suspected.

She was entirely nude before him, but before she could marvel at this he was stripping out of his trousers, and she saw, curving up toward his belly, his enormous swollen shaft. But before she could take in his nudity, or form a thought, or even widen her eyes, his strong hot hands were on her, running purposely up the length of her calves, stroking the tender skin inside her thighs, places no person had ever before touched her. He was so certain of himself, of her. He coaxed her thighs wider with long, delicate, determined sweeps of his fingers, and she quivered and tensed a bit. But her tension eased away beneath his hands, because her body wanted him, and he knew it.

When her knees parted for him he knelt between them. And then she felt the head of his cock against her, and then he pushed inside her, beyond the reflexive clenched resistance of her shocked body, and filled her, slowly. She gasped, arched to accommodate him.

Her husband drew in an audible breath, closed his eyes briefly. The pleasure seemingly so intense it very nearly hurt him.

They opened again, stared down at her, eyes gone dark. A conqueror. Allowing her to become accustomed to the feel of him, watching her eyes, perhaps, for what she thought of it.

For the life of her, she didn't yet know.

And then his fingers reached out and massaged very deliberately just where she joined with him, where she needed to be touched, and she did know: bliss ripped through her, total and breath-stealing. She moaned, and his mouth curved, satisfied. He drew back then, and thrust slowly, his fingers playing skillfully over her, then drew back again. Her own body found the rhythm, joined him in it, rising up to meet him.

"*Oh* . . ."

"Is it good, Sabrina?" A murmur.

"Rhys—," she choked. *So good.*

"Is it good?" he demanded, his voice dusky, the cadence of his hips even, relentless, each stroke banking that unidentifiable need in her until it was immense and demanding, and she began to beg him, and he obliged her, his thrusts becoming more swift and purposeful. The rush of his breath told her his own excitement was building, and then she saw his eyes begin to go opaque, his face taut. He was racing toward his own pleasure now, intent on it as well as her own.

But she needed him to ease hers.

"*Rhys . . . please . . .*" Pleasure roiled, built, gathered. The friction of him inside her, the pressure of his fingers outside, was exquisite, and then necessary—and then everything.

When release finally broke over her, it was shocking, extraordinary. She heard her own hoarse, near-silent scream as the force of her release bowed her body upward, and shook her. And still Rhys plunged into her, swiftly, his breathing a roar, sweat now shining over him.

At last he went still; the pleasure of his own release tearing a groan from him. His eyes closed; his head tilted back. And she felt it: the warmth as he came inside her.

And surely she'd left her body, because she felt lighter than air, and limp with peace.

Rhys at last withdrew from her, and stretched out alongside her on the fur. Then gently, he took her into his arms. He closed his eyes again; his chest still moved hard with his breathing.

Well. Sabrina supposed she was now officially a wife.

She tried to think about what this meant to her, about what had just taken place, but her thoughts only drifted across her mind like clouds across the sky, separate somehow from her. She couldn't seem to grasp hold of one. She could only feel. It was strange to lie here with this man, blissfully spent, nude, slick with perspiration, his arms wrapped around her. The soft fur against her back yet another caress.

She did have one faintly pleased thought: *Mary was wrong*.

Distantly she wondered if Rhys had made love just this way many times before, if he'd known precisely what to do to lull her, to seduce her, had anticipated her response.

She wondered whether she cared.

Just a kiss, he'd said just a few days ago. Would he say to her, "It was just lovemaking, Sabrina"?

"You were very competent," she said inadvertently, aloud.

Rhys gave a short laugh, startled. "Damned with faint praise!"

She flushed. "Oh! I'm terribly sorry. I meant to say that you seemed . . ."

"As though I knew what I was about?" His voice quivered with restrained hilarity.

She remained silent, squeezing her eyes closed. God help her, she should not have said anything.

"As though . . . I might have even done it . . . before?" he pressed, giving the words a slightly scandalized intonation.

"I just . . ."

"Sabrina?" he said solemnly.

"Yes?" She turned to him, worried.

He whispered, "I confess I've done it before."

She threw an embarrassed arm over her eyes. "Forgive me. I've never before made conversation under these circumstances. I'm not certain of the etiquette."

She thought he might laugh, but he said nothing. She could hear his breathing, slow and even now. The damp heat of his skin against her own warmed her.

Suddenly Sabrina had a concern. "Did I do it correctly?" she wondered.

When he said nothing, she'd begun to suspect he'd fallen asleep. She peeked out from beneath her arm to find him propped up on his elbow, gazing down at her wearing that expression she'd seen before: as though she were some new creature he'd discovered, or he were experiencing some sort of alien sensation in his body and trying to interpret it. Disconcerted. A soft expression, for all of that.

He didn't answer her. He lowered his head and kissed her gently between the eyes.

It wasn't an answer, but it would do for now.

He cleared his throat. "Did you enjoy it?"

The expression that accompanied his question was carefully neutral.

"I . . ." What did he expect to hear, this man who supposedly caused women to cast off their dignity, who wrote odes to sensual moments—whole odes to parts of *bodies,* for heaven's sake? Who'd "done it before"?

This man who was her husband now.

"Mostly," she confessed. "And then . . . well"—she blushed, rubbed her forehead self-consciously with her hand—"rather."

Such an inadequate word. But all the other words she could think of at the moment made her feel both shy and wanton.

But he was smiling faintly down at her again. " 'Rather'? As good as that, was it?"

She supposed she should be grateful she could consistently amuse her husband.

Something else occurred to her then.

"Did *you* enjoy it?" she asked worriedly. Wondering if he'd asked for her opinion because he hadn't.

He gazed down at her. He did have beautiful eyes. Blue like the sky. She wished they were as expressive of his internal weather as the sky was of the external.

"Rather," he finally said gently.

He reached out and plucked a strand of hair away from her face where perspiration had glued it; he smoothed it behind her ear.

She smiled up at him a little. Which oddly made his smile fade to seriousness again. And then he surprised her: he lifted one of her hands, kissed her palm, and placed it gently against his chest.

His skin was so surprisingly soft, the hair fine and crisp over his chest; beneath it ran hard muscles; steel beneath silk. Such beauty. She'd thought other men handsome before; she thought Geoffrey was handsome. She hadn't known that male beauty could be so very thorough, so heady and strange.

Her hand began to wander as if he'd just set it free. She traced the distinct lines of it, each hewn muscle, the ridge of his collarbone, tangled her fingers through the fine hair that curled over his chest and ribs, and in the process she discovered his heartbeat. Her hand hovered there, lingered over it; the speed, the hard thump of it, surprised her.

And then she realized his breath was all but held.

She stopped, feeling suddenly shy, looked up into his face. Saw tension, his eyes darker now. He gently placed his hand over hers, stopping her exploration.

"Perhaps we should sleep." His voice was husky.

"All right," she faltered, after a moment.

But he gave her a faint smile, and cupped the back of her head with his hand, shifted her to rest her head against his chest, folded his arms around her. She pressed her body against his, and when she did, she could feel that he was very hard again. Ready again for her. And the tension in his body, in his face, told her that for some reason he was holding himself back from her.

He remained quiet, and with her body pressed against the heat of his skin, her cheek pressed against the sway of his breathing, the beat of his heart, it was nearly impossible not to drift to sleep. And she did.

He hadn't meant to take her so quickly, so very nearly roughly, with all the finesse of a boy.

He hadn't expected to *need* to take her so urgently. For need to rise up and crest over him like a rogue wave, sweeping him along with it. It had been so long since that sort of thing had happened.

Well, at least since the night in the statue gallery.

He *had* intended to make her nearly scream with pleasure, however, and he had.

His wife, the Countess Rawden. He watched her sleep, one arm flung up over her head, mouth parted a little. What a beautiful little body she had, this country girl from Tinbury. Long slim legs, a scar from some childhood mishap, no doubt, shining white on her knee. Tiny waist. Lovely full breasts that tilted up, tipped in palest pink. A small mole in the shape of a crescent moon above one, a sweet punctuation mark, of sorts. He knelt to place the lightest kiss on it now, and she scarcely stirred.

A blend of vulnerable naïveté and stubborn, irritatingly astute observation, all covered in skin like cream silk.

He hadn't expected to want to take her again the moment she touched him. To be so hard and ready to take her at once.

Or to linger here in this room, when he would rise early tomorrow to leave for London.

Was he now so very jaded that he found innocence erotic?

He fought back a strange sense of impatience. There had never been anything he couldn't parse with his formidable mind. And whatever he felt now eluded him.

She would be tender in the morning, and it would have been selfish to take her again. Or so he'd told himself. But a part of him worried that he wanted her so very badly. Just as there was a part of him that still resented her for being in his life at all.

The fire was burning low, and he'd begun to feel the coolness of the room.

He rose, knelt, and slid his hands beneath his bride, scooping her gently up, amused to find she wasn't precisely a feather in his arms. But she was strong and lithe and warm. She didn't wake; she merely sighed and muttered an incoherent complaint and frowned a little. He half smiled. Ah, so he'd worn her out.

He tucked her into her great bed, pulled the blankets over her around her nude shoulders to avoid titillating the maid when she entered in the morning to build up the fire. He poked up the fire to make sure it would last until then.

And as he'd done his duty by his wife, he went back to his chambers so he could return to London tomorrow.

Sabrina woke with a start to the sound of coal shuffling and a determined shaft of sunlight penetrating the divide between the curtains. Then realizing with another start that she was entirely nude, she pulled her blankets up tightly around her shoulders and peered down at the maid busying herself with reviving the fire, her white cap bobbing efficiently atop her head as she moved about.

The maid must have noticed the change in her breathing, and realized she was awake, because she cast a worried look over her shoulder. " 'Tis sorry I am t' disturb ye, Lady Rawden."

Who was—

Oh: *she* was Lady Rawden, wasn't she?

"Oh, you didn't disturb me. The sun woke me, truly." It was a lie, but the sort that wouldn't send her to Hell, Sabrina was certain.

She sank back against the bed, as soft as a pillow itself, and knew before she looked that Rhys wasn't there. She slid a hand over to where he might have slept; the bedding was cool. The pillows were still round and plump, not flattened by a sleeping head.

He'd taken her on a fur in front of the fire. And then he'd tucked her into bed.

And then he'd left, duty done.

She sank her head back down against her pillow, and the maid darted from the room to perform the rest of her morning chores.

Sabrina decided to give the fire an opportunity to warm the room before she stirred. She shifted her limbs a little, and they slid over the softest linen imaginable, and she felt stiffness in them, a pleasant heaviness and soreness in her muscles. She recalled last night with extraordinary vividness. Heat rushed over her body at the thought of it.

And then she felt a weight in her chest. So odd to join with a man so intimately and then for him to simply leave.

Perhaps not so odd for him.

There was a warning tap at the door, and Mrs. Bailey entered, accompanied by the scent of steaming chocolate and something warm and yeasty.

Despite everything, there were definitely going to be advantages to being a countess.

"Good morning, Lady Rawden."

She was ready for the greeting this time. "Good morning, Mrs. Bailey."

Perhaps he was in his own chambers, or taking breakfast, or moving about his vast property. She wondered at the hope she felt, as they'd had an agreement, after all. And she knew all along he'd intended to go back to London, for his life was there.

Life at the vicarage had always been full. She knew precisely what to do and when; her schedule had been governed by the needs of others, and she'd been happy enough to oblige. For the first time in her life she hadn't the faintest idea what to do with her day.

And suddenly it yawned ahead of her like a year.

Thus her life as a countess began.

CHAPTER FIFTEEN

O N HER FIRST day alone at La Montagne, the army of servants commanded by Mrs. Bailey lined up to be introduced to Sabrina. Among them were girls her own age in soft white caps and snowy aprons; they blushed and curtsied deeply when Sabrina repeated their names in order to remember them. But Sabrina sensed that Mrs. Bailey had it all in hand, that La Montagne would continue on as it always had regardless of whether she or even the earl were on hand to see to it. She would love nothing more than to make improvements, but the machinery of La Montagne's staff made this nearly impossible. Everything was flawless.

She contemplated writing to Mary and begging her to return, but she knew Mary had fluttered off to collect nectar from another social flower, dragging along her willing husband, and would be very nearly impossible to locate.

So she imagined, again, she had sisters. In her mind an image of two little girls remained. Sometimes she lingered over the pianoforte, and played the beautiful instrument, because there the memories were the strongest.

There they seemed to want to bob to the surface through the accumulated memories of her other years.

Maybe, in this quiet house, she would finally remember them.

She poked about in the library. She poked about the halls and in the rooms of La Montagne, until she'd memorized every curve of every statue in the gallery and every face on every painting. She could almost picture the paintings that belonged in those eloquently empty spaces on the walls.

She visited the windows in the gallery where Wyndham painted, but she never seemed to be there in time to see the moon and the stars reflected on the floor.

And at night, alone in the large, soft bed, she thought of one thing only: her husband. With ambivalence and a new, uncomfortable physical yearning that she partly resented, because the yearning would never have been there at all if not for him.

If she'd married another man she might never have known this remarkable pleasure. But she might have known peace, and she might not have been alone.

On the fourth day, magically, a modiste appeared.

Madame Marceau was a tall, briskly cheerful woman with a regal, homely face, and she came armed with bolts of fabrics and books of fashion plates and complaints about the roads on the way to La Montagne from London.

She had been charged by Rhys to dress her as she would any countess, and she set to her task with zeal. Sabrina was examined and measured and clucked over, and a dizzying array of fabrics and choices were laid out before her to rub between her fingers and hold up under her chin as she faced the mirror. Sabrina remembered being caught in a curtain dress on her very first day at La Montagne, and asked Madame Marceau, with all seriousness, her opinion of the curtain color, bringing her into the small room.

Madame Marceau thought perhaps a deeper purple would be even better. She had just the satin. And she was right: the deeper purple made Sabrina's green eyes brilliant when she held it beneath her chin.

Sabrina was promised dresses of wool and of silk, pelisses lined in fur, chemises and night rails of softest lawn, silk stockings and gloves and boots and bonnets—all inside a fortnight. She had made her own clothes almost since she could wield a needle, and the very idea of this bounty arriving so quickly seemed as likely as Madame Marceau's gathering up all the stars and bringing them down from the sky.

Then again, it had begun to be clear that there was very little the Earl of Rawden's money couldn't make so.

Sabrina couldn't help but wonder whom the beauty would benefit. Then again, she would be like the other things in the grand house: beautiful, polished, decorative. And perhaps this was the point.

And when the modiste left to return to London, she took with her color and chatter, and Sabrina felt more alone than ever before.

This was when, out of desperation, Sabrina asked Mrs. Bailey to find a ball of wool and a pair of knitting needles. She hadn't done anything productive in days, and she had come to realize that her very nature centered about organizing and producing and . . . helping.

Mrs. Bailey didn't seem surprised by the request. No doubt years of serving the aristocracy had drummed the capacity for surprise out of Mrs. Bailey.

"What color would you like, Lady Rawden?"

Of course there would be a *choice* of colors here at La Montagne.

Dyed wools in brilliant shades danced in Sabrina's imagination. She considered asking about red . . . she did like red, and it was cheerful on winter days. White was simple, and elegant. Gray was practical, and would be—

No: blue. It needed to be blue.

She might knit a scarf to the length of a hundred ells before she saw her husband again. And even when she did, she wondered if she would have the nerve to present him with a scarf she'd knitted to match his eyes. She also wondered at the impulse, except that they were undeniably beautiful, his eyes, and she had almost nothing else to do.

Finally, at the end of the first week at La Montagne, the snow had melted enough to make the roads to Buckstead Heath passable, and Sabrina decided she could ride out to the town. A groom insisted upon accompanying her, saying it was more than his life was worth to allow her to go alone, which would have been what she preferred.

She glared at the man in what she hoped was a countess-y way.

"Mr.—"

"Croy," the groom supplied patiently.

"Mr. Croy, I've ridden entirely on my own since I was a very little girl, and I lived in a town very much like Buckstead Heath before I came to live at La Montagne."

The groom, however, had more than twice her years, a few daughters of his own, satisfaction in his pay, and a healthy respect and fear of the very large Earl of Rawden.

"Aye, but ye're nay a little girl anymore, are ye?" he said mildly. "Ye're a countess. I'll saddle a mare fer ye, Lady Rawden, and I'll ride wi' ye into town."

In Tinbury, riding was a necessity, a way to get from one place to another. They kept a mule at the vicarage, and the versatile beast pulled plow and carts and carried Sabrina on errands on the occasions the weather was too brisk for a walk. Sabrina's legs only just fit over its broad back, and he lifted his feet high and put them down hard, the mule did. She'd always felt every inch of the road when she was riding him, every shift of his great haunches.

But the mare she rode now flowed beneath her with a gait as smooth as water. Sabrina wondered if one day she would become accustomed to such luxuries, a brown mare with a delicate, tossing head and slim legs, a mare that might very well be pleased to fly, it seemed, if only Sabrina would allow her to.

Mr. Croy was taciturn; clearly he believed his duty was confined to steering her in the proper direction and seeing that she kept her seat. After a few vain attempts to engage him in conversation, Sabrina abandoned the attempt and instead took in deep gulps of country air.

Buckstead Heath came into view over a rise, little cottages scattered about, smoke wisping up from chimneys, and a central street where Sabrina suspected the shops in the town could be found.

But it was the church that caught her eye. Modest, a few hundred years old. Built of sturdy tawny stone with thick walls, inset with simple stained-glass windows, a shining cross finishing the tall, narrow spire.

And she knew, before she did anything else, before she rode farther into town, she should speak to Geoffrey, whom she hadn't seen since the disaster that preceded her wedding. She wasn't quite certain what she would say to him, but if they were to be neighbors, they ought to at least be friends.

"We're going to church, Mr. Croy."

The groom nodded and touched his fingers to his cap.

It was just shortly after the time Matins would have been spoken. The people of Buckstead Heath, if they had attended church this morning, had already left, and it was empty and quiet with the sort of hush that only churches seemed to contain, as though the walls had been soaked with centuries of worship.

Sabrina stood in the doorway and saw a man standing near the chancel. For one disorienting moment—his height, the way he held himself, the color of his hair—he recalled Rhys powerfully, and a strange clutch of hope tightened her chest.

Geoffrey turned and saw her then.

"Sabrina." He sounded startled; he stared for a moment. "Oh, my apologies. Lady *Rawden.*" He bowed deeply.

Sabrina blushed. "Oh, Geoffrey, please don't. It makes me feel silly. I am always just Sabrina to you."

He smiled a little at her, and an awkward silence tripped by.

"Geoffrey, I came because . . . Geoffrey, I'm so sorry for . . ." She paused. What did she intend to say? *For kissing your cousin in the library in front of numerous neighbors and then marrying him?*

They approached each other, then; met in the nave, stood a few feet apart.

"No, Sabrina. It's my fault. I was the one who encouraged you to ingratiate yourself with the earl. I had no idea his lack of scruples ran so very deep, though I should have suspected."

Sabrina wasn't inclined to take any of the blame for the change in her circumstances at the moment, though she knew she wasn't entirely above reproach. She decided not to illuminate matters for Geoffrey any further.

She merely said, "Have you settled in here at the vicarage, then? Is the house comfortable?"

"Yes. It's comfortable enough. And the surroundings of a vicarage are familiar now, of course. Perhaps I shall never go on my mission, but at least I shan't be penniless, thanks to Rhys's largesse."

There was something else in Geoffrey's face: a hard sort of resolve and irony, which Sabrina didn't quite understand and couldn't quite place, as it seemed somehow unrelated to the disaster at hand. He also didn't seem heartbroken, and her newly discovered pride chafed a bit at this. She would have liked him to be angry with her, at the very least.

She admitted to herself that she wasn't precisely heartbroken, either.

Still, it was undeniably good to see Geoffrey. He was familiar; he was of Tinbury; she liked him. He had been her first kiss.

Her life would be considerably different at this moment if only she'd had the sense to allow him to be her *only* kiss.

"I am glad you will be near, Geoffrey. Perhaps we can be friends again one day, if you can forgive me."

"There is nothing to forgive, Sabrina." He smiled faintly, echoing her words when he'd kissed her in the sitting room. "And I hope we will always be friends. I should have known that someone of your nature would be no match for someone with his, should he determine to behave as . . . well, as he always has."

And at this, Sabrina felt a startling but increasingly familiar sizzle in her rearing up: *How could you possibly know my nature, Geoffrey?* I didn't even know it until I arrived here.

She'd never dreamed she had a temper until she'd arrived at La Montagne. She'd never dreamed she was so proud. She'd never dreamed she could be tempted into a passion she'd never known existed, that would open a door onto a life she'd never wanted. A door that could never be closed again.

There was something else, too: no matter what, Rhys was her husband now. And the instincts for loyalty in her stirred. She didn't precisely wish to defend him, but at the same time it was strangely uncomfortable to hear him criticized.

She offered Geoffrey a conciliatory smile and, hesitating a moment, held out her hand.

He took it in his, looked down at it. He looked up intently into her eyes then, his dark eyes searching for something in hers, or perhaps attempting to silently communicate something of importance.

Sabrina grew puzzled, and considered that Geoffrey might perhaps be more disappointed about her marriage than he thought right to show her. Perhaps his feelings for her were stronger than he'd ever expressed.

She allowed him to hold her fingers a moment longer. He released her hand just as she'd begun to consider giving it a subtle tug.

"Perhaps one day soon you can persuade Rhys of the worthiness of my cause, Sabrina, and he might relent and provide the funds."

"I shall try, for your sake, Geoffrey," she promised. "But he will likely be in London much of the time."

"And will you live at La Montagne?"

"Yes, it's my home now."

"Then you shall come often to visit me, so you will not feel lonely," Geoffrey urged. "I shall always welcome you, and who knows better than the two of us how demanding the life at a vicarage can be? Perhaps you can offer advice."

Sabrina was uncertain about the propriety of visiting Geoffrey often, though he was a relative now, and she did very much enjoy giving advice.

"I should like that, Geoffrey."

And she supposed she should feel grateful to have a friend living nearby, since she hadn't the faintest idea when she'd next see her husband.

She did feel a bit more at peace now that her relationship with Geoffrey was settled. She glanced about the church, and felt the tug of familiarity. Life at a vicarage was a life she knew, a life she would have known how to live. So unlike the one she had now in the grand house over the hill.

"It's quite chill in here, isn't it, Geoffrey? The carpets are so tattered, and it smells of mildew. The church seems to have been neglected."

Geoffrey nodded as he walked alongside her, up the nave to the chancel, and she gestured, pointing at things.

"The parishioners have been making do with a visiting clergyman on occasion or by attending services in other villages, so the church has been a bit neglected, it seems. They were delighted to hear there was a vicar in residence now. They seem to think Rhys is a hero for appointing me."

Sabrina thought of La Montagne, and all those rooms scarcely used or occupied, filled with beautiful objects.

And then she recalled one particular room. *No one uses it,* Rhys had said about the office of his father's man of affairs.

Inspiration struck.

"Geoffrey, speaking of advice . . . I have a splendid idea!"

Rhys had been married for precisely eleven days when the message arrived at his London town house. He'd been invited to a performance Sophia Licari was giving at the home of the Duchess of Caraday, and he was dressing with care for it—black coat, a silver-and-cream-striped waistcoat—as the *ton* hadn't seen him in a while, and he'd caught wind of murmurs about his retiring from London for a life in the country, and wished to dispel them instantly. He also thought it might be time to ascertain for himself whether the quotient of irate husbands and fawning women had somehow decreased in his absence. It would be pleasant to know he could move about London safely.

He'd returned to London with a certain amount of relief, knowing he need only step outside the door of his town house to lose himself in the universe of amusements on offer. Yet, for some reason, he'd not done much since his return apart from putter about his town house, feeling restless, testing the idea of various amusements in his mind, shying away from them irritably. He read. He drank. He ventured out to his club; everyone and everything there irritated him, too.

It made him uneasy.

There. The cravat was perfectly tied now.

He'd wondered if perhaps the invitation to Sophia's performance was tantamount to an apology, which amused him. He hadn't partaken of her since he'd returned to London.

Nor had he partaken of anyone else, truthfully. Not since he'd partaken of his inconvenient wife.

He hadn't abstained long enough to actually worry about the reason for it. He had, however, begun to wonder why his thoughts returned again and again to one image: a tiny mole in the shape of a crescent moon above one particularly silky breast.

His thoughts went there now and lingered, almost hesitantly, testing. And yes, again he felt it: the swift tightening of his lungs, the tightening in his loins.

He shrugged roughly, to free himself of the image. *Poetry,* he thought. The image appealed to the poet in him. The man in him would enjoy vigorously reconciling with Sophia tonight, and—yes, he could have sworn loin tightening accompanied that thought as well.

Rhys returned his attention to the message in his hand. He didn't recognize the handwriting, so he swiftly broke the seal and read it.

* * *

Dear Lord Rawden,

I thought it best to inform you that the countess is giving away the carpets.

Yours sincerely,
Mrs. Margaret Bailey

What in God's name—?

What on earth could this possibly *mean*? Rhys had a sudden chilling vision of Sabrina, his wife who enjoyed helping, holding a biblical sort of bazaar in the courtyard of La Montagne for the villagers of Buckstead Heath.

He swiftly unbuttoned his waistcoat, flung it aside for his valet to attend to, and rang for his butler at the same time to give him a command.

"Send a message to Signora Licari telling her I shan't see her this evening. I must away to La Montagne."

CHAPTER SIXTEEN

THE JOURNEY FROM London to La Montagne required a day and a half over snowy, difficult roads, a stop at an inn, poor food, and a lumpy bed. Not even an earl could entirely control conditions during a sudden road trip.

Fortunately, no one was holding a bazaar in the courtyard when he arrived. Still, Rhys stood before Mrs. Bailey in a foul humor.

"She's giving away the carpets." He said this flatly. A statement, not a question.

"To the vicarage," Mrs. Bailey confirmed evenly.

"To the *vicara*—" He stopped, and wondered what other sort of largesse Geoffrey might be experiencing. "Which carpets?"

"The office once used by your father's man of—"

But Rhys was already on his way before Mrs. Bailey could finish her sentence. "Find the countess and send her to me," he snapped over his shoulder.

Sure enough: the carpet was gone. The bare marble floor was a pristine white, and Rhys's impatient footsteps echoed across it, and no doubt made marks for a member of the army of servants to clean.

It was a small room, featuring a desk and some modestly stocked bookshelves, a small settee, globe, and of course a clock, because one must always know the time even in a room never used.

Even his thoughts were becoming sarcastic.

Sabrina found her husband standing in the middle of his father's office, and halted in the doorway.

He bowed low. "Sabrina." He'd drawled the word by way of greeting, making it nearly an entire sentence long.

Drawling seldom boded well.

"Rawden!" She faltered. "I wasn't expect . . ."

Of course she wasn't expecting him. He hadn't even told her at all that he'd intended to be gone when he'd left her the day after their wedding, and he hadn't said good-bye to her when he left; why would he tell her when he would return? Her sentence seemed foolish in light of that, so she said nothing more.

They regarded each other in silence. It had been nearly two weeks since she'd been parted from her husband. And now it was difficult to know how to greet him, or what to say to him.

There was an advantage to being parted, to some extent, because despite what seemed to be contained fury emanating from him, his presence, the sheer force and beauty of the man, tugged at her like a fresh wind, as it had from the moment she'd met him.

"Word reached me that you were giving away the carpets." He said it sardonically.

I missed you, too, she thought, just as sardonically.

Aloud, she said, "Car*pet*. Not carpets. I gave away only one." Something devilish in her made her add: "So far."

He stared at her. His mouth opened a little, then closed. He gave his head a shake, as if to clear it. "Sabrina . . . that carpet was a *Savonnerie.*" He enunciated every syllable of that last word with pure incredulity.

She studied him warily. No matter how slowly or sarcastically he said it, *Savonnerie* still meant nothing to her.

"It was *one hundred fifty years* old," he added, his voice going tauter. Like a bowstring being pulled back.

More silence. He seemed to be waiting for her to say something.

"And?" she coaxed, finally, gently.

"*And?*" The arrow flew. "*And? There is no 'and,'* Sabrina. You gave away a valuable carpet. To the *vicarage.*"

She wondered if he was going to begin waving his arms about. Such passions.

"Nobody was using it," she said mildly. In the hopes that a calm voice might settle him a bit. It was difficult to maintain a steady voice in the face of this large blazing man, however.

"It was covering the floor in this *room,* Sabrina. One might say the *room* was using it."

"A room which you said no one," Sabrina ground out, the temper she'd discovered thanks to him beginning to rise up, "*uses,* and I doubt anyone has used until you decided to use it to bellow at me."

"But the carpet belonged in this *house,* Sabrina."

"Have you seen the church, Rhys? It's neglected, and tattered, and smells of mildew in the vestry and . . . Well, people need a proper church. The people of Buckstead Heath should have a proper church. And it's your town to look after."

She'd thought it a wonderful idea. Sabrina had demanded Mr. Croy tell her the names of the people in town who might be persuaded to carry a carpet from La Montagne to the vicarage, and Sabrina had subsequently recruited three brothers, Mr. Ferris, Mr. Ferris, and Mr. Ferris, to help remove the carpet from the office of Rhys's father's man of affairs, the room he'd said was seldom used.

"I'm no expert, Sabrina, but I'm fairly certain a church can still be considered a proper church without an antique carpet in the vestry."

Gilded in sarcasm, that sentence was.

"Yes—but—tell me, is there a carpet in this house worth less than the one I gave away?"

There was a silence.

"No," Rhys conceded at last. The word clipped and all but edged in flame.

"And are there carpets in this house worth more?"

"Yes."

Interesting that he should know the worth of the carpet precisely, Sabrina thought. She stopped and flung her arms out, as though the logic of this should end the argument.

Unfortunately, he was still staring at her with the same bald incredulity. "Sabrina." Exaggerated patience, as though her very name was too heavy for his mouth. "That carpet was *very* valuable."

"That carpet is a *carpet*," she explained just as patiently. "It's meant to be used. It's meant to cover a floor.

Whoever made it *meant* for it to *cover a floor.* And now it's covering the floor at the vicarage."

Rhys made a wild little frustrated noise and swept a hand through his hair.

"Well, several floors at the vicarage," she modified. "The carpet was rather large, so I imagine they cut it to fit properly in the various rooms."

He froze as if she'd just produced a weapon from beneath her skirts.

And then gave a low moan and sank down on the settee, leaned back and closed his eyes.

A silence ensued, weighty and resigned.

"Sabrina, it wasn't yours to give away." He sounded weary.

She was a little unnerved by his reaction. Then again, she was no less stubborn than she was when he'd left for London. "I was told I could choose from any of the fixtures in the house for my own use. And this is my own use for the carpet. I wish for the vicarage to use it."

His eyes snapped open then, and he turned his head slowly, slowly toward her. He gazed at her for a good long time.

She met his eyes unflinchingly, those crystalline, see-everything eyes. Which was much harder to do than one might think.

And at last, surprising her, a slow reluctant smile crept over his lips, and he shook his head slowly.

Good heavens, he looked like a boy when he smiled like that. It felt like the sweetest sort of pincers around her heart, his smile.

"Are you certain you were raised by a vicar, Sabrina? I'm beginning to suspect Mr. Fairleigh was a lawyer, instead."

Sabrina smiled a sweet little smile in return. "You can request that Geoffrey return it, of course. The parishioners will, of course, miss it, as they are delighted with it. But they will probably understand if the earl wants to take his carpet back."

His smile vanished, to be replaced by an expression of patent respect.

And then he turned his head away from her and leaned it back against the settee again.

They sat in a sort of silent stalemate for a moment; détente, if not complete peace.

"Rhys . . . may I ask why it is so very important?" she ventured. "It's one carpet. And you have . . . you have so many." She tried not to betray how this felt to her: the great regiment of things that surrounded her in this house. All of which were pretty, and few of which were necessary—to her, anyhow. She felt them like weights.

But as Rhys was a clever man; he heard it anyway.

"Sabrina . . . people *want* their earls to be wealthy. People want their earls to have . . . things. It's expected of us. You should want them, too. They're now an emblem of your station in life."

"But shouldn't we take pride in being able to give things away?" Odd to say we, but they were a "we" now, despite the nature of their marriage.

He leaned back against the settee again. And then he sighed. "But I'd only just . . . gotten all of it back." He sounded rueful.

She risked the question: "Gotten all of it back?"

He seemed to consider whether to speak. And then he turned to her. Something in her face, perhaps, helped him decide.

"My father lost La Montagne years ago, Sabrina. He lost everything that wasn't entailed to the title, in fact, and the properties that stayed in the family soaked up every last shilling we had. There were bad investments, and . . . well, I've spent so many years attempting to restore to the title everything he lost. Tracking it down, purchasing things when and as I could. Everything here at La Montagne is part of the Rawden legacy, and has been for three hundred years, and as long as I'm alive, will never again leave this house. And as far the carpets in the house are concerned . . . the carpet you gave away was a relatively new carpet. But it was ours. It was Rawden."

She remembered now. Geoffrey had said they were poor, and had marveled at how Rhys had managed to rebuild a fortune.

And then she remembered that achingly blank spot on the wall in the portrait gallery, and understood something in an instant.

"It was a lovely carpet, Rhys," she said gently. "But it won't bring them back."

He snapped a startled expression toward her. He stared for a moment, and she saw again on his face astonishment. Which was shuttered quickly. He turned his face away from her again.

Perhaps it was best she didn't make any pointed observations for a moment or two. She allowed a beat of silence before she spoke again.

"Rhys?" She liked his Christian name.

"Yes?" At least he hadn't snarled the word.

"You've made dozens of people inordinately happy with one carpet."

He made a sound then, and it was almost a laugh. Shook his head resignedly to and fro slowly.

"It looks very well at the vicarage," she offered, encouraged by the laugh.

A soft snort. "Oh, I'm certain it does." But he didn't sound angry anymore.

The quiet that followed was more peaceful, if not entirely comfortable. The clock bonged out the hour, and Sabrina couldn't help but notice the sound had a bit more resonance, now that the room was no longer carpeted and there was nothing but marble and hardwood for sound to bounce from.

"I didn't mean to make you angry, Rhys. I would never have if I . . . I just wanted to—"

"I know. Help."

She went quiet again. She couldn't interpret his tone. Not censorious, at least.

"I'm sorry I neglected to arrange for an allowance for you," he added. "I shall have my solicitor arrange for a substantial one. You may spend all of it on carpets if you wish."

Humor in the words now, at least.

They were quiet together. It struck Sabrina that, from the very first, they seemed to have little to say to each other when they weren't sparring.

He turned to look at her, his eyes lingering on her face, then taking in her new cerise gown in heavy silk. "The modiste has been to see you."

"Yes." She smoothed down the skirts.

"You look like a countess." A crooked smile.

"That was the object, was it not?" She was teasing, but then she saw his expression. How quickly it changed to inscrutability again.

Confused, she added quickly, "They're all very beautiful. More beautiful than anything I've ever before owned. Thank you for your generosity. I would not have known how to dress, you see, and Madame Marceau knew precisely what I should have."

"Have you hired a maid? You can ask Mrs. Bailey to send in a selection of girls to interview."

"I will"—she was going to complete the sentence with "dress myself, for heaven's sake," but she saw his face again. It all seemed so important to him, the title, the trappings of it—"speak with her about it soon."

He nodded once, shortly. And then instead of saying anything, he continued to gaze at her, and gradually his expression went faintly, gently mystified. Seeing her finally as a woman, and his wife, perhaps, and not as a carpet thief.

Sabrina took advantage of the quiet, too, to reacquaint herself with the contours of his face. The emphatic punctuation of his dark brows over his light eyes. The sharp line of his jaw merging with the hollows of his cheeks. That wide firm mouth, so stern sometimes in repose. Which made his smiles more brilliant and startling when he gave them.

And then solemnly, slowly, as though he couldn't help it, Rhys reached out and drew a finger along the stylish neckline of her new dress, lightly, lightly over her skin, across the swell of her breasts.

"So soft," he murmured, almost ruefully.

His finger had all but left a trail of flame. She had no choice but to close her eyes.

So simple, so unfair: with just that touch, she was his.

Odd how passion seemed to create its own sort of time inside of time; instantly, it seemed, a dense, sensual net surrounded them. She went easily when Rhys almost languidly gathered her into him. And then slowly but decisively, as though he'd planned it all along, his dark head ducked and he closed his mouth over her nipple, already peaked and hard against the fabric of her dress. She sucked in a breath at the sudden, sharp pleasure of it; it rayed instantly through every part of her body.

And then with his fingers he gently tugged the neckline of her dress just a little lower to free her nipple entirely, and he closed his hot mouth over it, tracing it with his tongue, then sucking gently.

Dear heaven.

Sabrina's fingers combed into his hair, clinging, stroking, encouraging his tongue. And his hands were busy gathering up her skirts, sliding them up until the fabric bunched at her hips, and then his fingers were feathering up the vulnerable skin of her thighs.

"Why, look at this . . . lovely new stockings, too," he teased, in a voice like night.

"The servants . . . ," she breathed.

"No one uses this room, remember?" More teasing.

She laughed a little, breathless, in awe of his expertise, of her own curiosity, of how willing she was now to surrender to it. Still a little afraid of how potent all of these sensations were.

He eased her back against the settee, her skirts gathered around her waist, the silk rustling as it bunched and moved together like a sigh.

"I want to show you something, Sabrina."

When he spoke to her in that voice, she thought she might do anything. It could charm snakes, that voice; it was the voice his poetry would have used if it could speak.

And it was his right to take her, she thought; he was her husband.

But even as something in her reared up against this, rebelling at the thought, her thighs were parting for him. She wanted to know everything he could teach her.

His warm hands, skillful hands, were on her thighs again, his touch coaxing and soothing, and then . . .

Oh, God . . . His tongue slid hard against the moist heat of her.

She gasped; the pleasure shocking.

Tentatively, he did it again. And this time she moaned her approval.

"More?" he queried softly, sounding half amused. And waited.

The devil. "Yes, *please* . . ."

And so she became a feast for him, the sinewy heat of his tongue so unlike anything she ever could have imagined, dipping and stroking, over her, into her, as talented and deft as his hands, and soon she was arching with the strokes of it, aiding him.

He paused again. "Sabrina . . . is it . . . ?"

"Don't stop." A curt command.

He laughed, and the low hum of his laugh against her flesh was erotic, too. "You taste wonderful," he murmured. "Like spring."

Like spring? But now she didn't care if servants intruded. They could have pulled up chairs and watched and applauded the outcome. All Sabrina cared about now was the outcome.

Her arms flung back, her neck arched against the arm of the settee, she moved with him, and stray fevered thoughts popped like bubbles in her mind. *How does he* know . . . *dear God this is wicked . . . dear God this is heavenly . . . how many times has he done th*—oh, more, please more there, there . . .

He knew the right places to taste and touch just as he'd known there was passion in the core of her supposedly temperate nature, because he did, after all, possess the secret to seduction.

And then there was no thought, just the great tide of her release crashing over her, shaking her, and the sound of her own voice keening softly with it coming from somewhere, it seemed, outside her own body.

Rhys rose up over her almost leisurely, his trousers already unfastened, and he was lifting up her hips, and guiding himself expertly home.

Lucidity returned to her somewhat as she watched her husband braced over her, and his eyes never left hers. She wondered what he saw in hers. She knew what she saw in his: fierce pleasure in the taking of her, and something else that fought through—a sort of wonder, a sort of surprise. For a moment she suspected he was nearly as helpless in the matter of passion here as she was, but then the moment was gone, and his eyes closed tightly as every bit of him went taut, and he drove himself swiftly to his release.

What if my children are conceived in a room without a carpet? Sabrina wondered.

Silently he withdrew from her, carefully, gently brushed her skirts down. Refastened his trousers. She fussed with her neckline, straightening it.

Rearranged, they sat side by side on the settee.

"Welcome home," she said wryly, trying a jest.

He gave a short laugh. It sounded almost pained. And then he went closed and quiet, a quiet she didn't quite understand, and for some reason didn't dare breach.

He finally turned to her again. "I've things to see to here at La Montagne. If you'll excuse me?"

He said it gently, but the words were so formal in the wake of feverish intimacy that Sabrina blinked.

"Of course, my lord." She couldn't disguise the irony in the words.

He simply rose and nodded shortly to her, and left her in that carpetless room.

He'd vanished into his office to do whatever it was he did at La Montagne, and she didn't see her husband at all for the rest of the afternoon. But later, an invitation came in the person of Mrs. Bailey.

"The earl would be pleased if you would join him for dinner this evening."

Such a peculiar way to live, Sabrina thought, even as the invitation undeniably pleased her. How peculiar to be invited to dine with someone in her own home. To be formally invited to dine with her own *husband,* for that matter.

"I am pleased to accept his invitation," she'd replied with mock solemnity.

And she dressed for him, knowing, thanks to Madame Marceau, what colors suited her: the purple, to make her eyes bewitching and her skin glow like a pearl. Cut to gently skim her curves and reveal a soft expanse of skin and the shadow between her full breasts. In the wicked hope that her husband, while he was here, might want to pay attention to them again.

"Wyndham said you came back from the war full of poetry."

It seemed a place to begin a dinner conversation, anyhow. But for some reason the question made Rhys go quiet, and Sabrina worried she'd ended the dinner conversation before it could truly begin.

Finally, he smiled a little. "Wyndham talks far too much."

There was a *chink* in the silence that followed, the sound of his fork stabbing into a bean and missing and striking his plate.

"I've read your poetry," she confessed tentatively.

Rhys stopped and his eyes blazed humor at her. "For heaven's sake, *I* know that."

Her mouth dropped open. And then, indignantly, she said, "So you *did* lay a trap."

He seemed to consider this for a moment.

"A trap is only a trap," he finally said, "if one's quarry, by nature, *wants* the bait." And then he grinned at her.

She couldn't smile back, because his smile took her breath away. And then she was sorry, because his smile was soon gone again.

"Did you . . . like it? The poetry?" he wondered. He wasn't looking at her. He was slicing his beef into little rectangles.

He was trying, she realized, to appear as though he didn't mind what she thought.

"Yes," she said fervently. "I didn't want to, mind you, but . . . it's extraordinary. Not . . ." She skipped the word she might have used, which might have been "shocking," and he looked at her then, his brow leaping upward sardonically. "It's magical." The word embarrassed her, but he seemed to take it as a matter of course, being a poet, she supposed. "I found it so, anyhow. Though I know very little about poetry."

He ducked his head briefly. Sabrina thought she saw him hiding a tiny pleased smile, a flash, there and gone. And he said nothing else.

"I suppose you cannot experience it the way a reader does," she continued.

"No," he agreed, his eyes upon her again. "Particularly since most readers seem to be women." Another smile.

She was ready for it this time: she smiled, too, enjoying his teasing. "Will you write another book?"

He snorted a soft laugh, not an amused one. "I don't know. I haven't written a word of poetry in months."

Her fork paused in midair. "But . . . but . . . at your house party you were looking for a rhyme for skin!"

"No, I wasn't. I was writing a letter to my solicitor."

She stared at him. "I believe the word you used that night was 'incorrigible'?"

"Yes."

"Still fits," she muttered, and ate a pea.

He laughed.

And then there was a quiet. Not an awkward quiet. Sabrina felt the change in its texture. It was like the rest in a piece of music. They were learning to talk to each other. And tentatively, skittishly . . . they were enjoying it.

"Have you found your mother's portrait?" she asked.

"The search continues," he said shortly.

"I've a portrait of *my* mother," she volunteered shyly.

"Should we hang it in the gallery?" He asked it lightly.

She smiled. "It's only a miniature. It's all I have of her. Her name is Anna, or so it says on the back of the image, in script. She looks very like me, or so I'm told."

And Rhys went strangely still. Something flickered over his face, something Sabrina couldn't interpret. It was almost as though something had hurt him.

Perhaps he'd swallowed a pea too hard.

"I always wanted to know her," she added softly.

He finally stirred again. "Do you know how you came to live with Vicar Fairleigh, Sabrina?" She watched his hands fuss with his napkin.

"I only know I was brought to him one evening, shortly before he left for the living in Tinbury. He was told my mother had died, and that I was an orphan."

"Do you know what year this was, by any chance?"

"Of course. It was 1803. Are you trying to learn my age?" She smiled at him.

Rhys smiled a little, too, but now he seemed distracted. He tipped more wine into his glass, sipped at it while appearing to admire the room, then returned his gaze to her, seeming to decide she was more interesting.

"I remember only . . . ," she began. "I remember being awakened in the middle of the night, and there were other little girls there, too. And we were crying. And I remember the voice of a woman, soft. But I don't know whether it was my mother or not."

Rhys stared at her as if she'd just confessed to making love to King George. Or something *just* that shocking. Perhaps the memory stirred his own memories of his mother and sister, both of whom had died. Perhaps he was feeling keenly again his own losses.

She changed the subject. "I've noticed you've no paintings by Mr. Wyndham hanging here at La Montagne."

"Have you?" he asked idly, looking down at his plate.

"And yet you've commissioned quite a few. Mr. Wyndham doesn't think he's a good painter, but he thinks that you believe he is."

Rhys helped himself to another slice of beef. He chewed for a bit. Swallowed.

"Wyndham is a good *friend*," he finally allowed, the words careful.

Sabrina's mouth dropped open. She clapped it shut, realizing something. "You—you—"

"I?" Rhys coaxed, amused and a little puzzled.

"You like to *help*, too! You commission Wyndham, and La Valle, and—because you want to help them! You *help*!"

This seemed to give Rhys pause.

"For God's sake, don't tell anyone," he finally said, sounding abashed.

She laughed, delighted.

Rhys had bid her good evening after dinner, perhaps vanishing into his office; Sabrina had retired to the library to read, but found herself taking up her knitting needles, adding more rows to the blue scarf she would someday, if she'd the nerve, give to her husband.

If he'd wished to find her, he could have looked in the library. He did not.

So Sabrina retired to her bedchamber. But now it was late, and the lure of bed was strong. She began preparations for sleep, plucking up her hairbrush. She began to brush out her hair, and remembering the night of her wedding, her strokes slowed. She half hoped Rhys would appear to do it for her again. She'd been so afraid that night, and lonely, and he'd managed both to soothe and seduce her with the homely little act, though he'd left her the following day. He was an observant man. She was beginning to believe he might also be a kind man.

She was beginning to—dare she say it—like him.

But a hundred strokes later, her hair was gleaming in a sheet to her waist, and she was still alone.

Sabrina pulled a night rail over her head, this one warm and very fine, a new one. And like the night of her wedding, she waited. Tensed in anticipation, and in a peculiar hope.

But the door between their rooms never opened.

Ah. So perhaps he thought he'd done his duty by her for this visit.

A knot of desolation in her stomach pulled tight, and her hands went there protectively, covering it. She remembered what Mary had said about thinking about what to serve for dinner the following day when she was lying beneath her husband, and for another instant Sabrina rather wished someone like Paul would come through the door.

Finally Sabrina slipped beneath her blankets and tossed and turned, restless as if she'd gone to bed without supper. It was a new and different sort of appetite, however, that remained unsatisfied, and her new unhappiness was born of having a brief taste of happiness.

At last she drifted, as the fire grew lower, to a fitful sleep.

He didn't know why he resisted.

He'd prepared himself for sleep, stripped himself of clothing and built the fire up higher than necessary, and fully intended to *only* sleep, so he might rise early and be on the road again to London in the morning very early, because there was a soiree he should attend. A new young poet would be reading, and Rhys could add his own cachet to the event.

Actually, it wasn't entirely true: he did know why he resisted.

Everything he'd tried in the name of curbing restlessness—alcohol, opium, music, poetry, gambling, sport, woman after shockingly skilled woman—he'd been able to leave behind. He'd known pleasure. Sometimes *acute* pleasure. He'd known oblivion. He'd accumulated a store of extraordinary memories, memories few other men could afford or would ever have.

But not one of those things had ever felt like a *need*.

And this . . . this had begun to feel perilously like need.

He didn't want to ever need again.

So he doused his lamp, and lay in the dark and waited for the oblivion of sleep.

He didn't know how much time had passed before he realized that sleep would be denied him. That he would have to, for perhaps the first time in his life, surrender.

Sabrina had been sleeping for some time when she awoke and stirred groggily, realizing that a warm body had slid beneath the blankets next to her. She stirred into a dreamlike wakefulness when his arms went around her, and turned up to face his shadowy face in the dark; instinctively, as if of their own accord, her arms reached up to wrap around his neck. He was bare; his skin was fire-warm. His mouth found hers, and her lips fell open beneath his, and he tasted a little of brandy, felt like warm velvet. She kissed him hungrily back, reveling in the taste and texture of him. Her body moved to fit beneath his, wanting him. He gathered up her night rail until it bunched around her waist, and his hands were hot and urgent against her skin, skimming across her belly, over the curve of her hips and waist, filling impatiently with her breasts, stroking, until her body was exquisitely awake, even as she half felt she was dreaming.

"*Yes*," she whispered, and arched into him, abetting him, asking for more.

And like this, in the near-total darkness, Rhys made love to her, swiftly and without words. In the dark he was hardly more than a shadow; it was like making love to night itself. He braced himself above her and then he was inside her, and her hips rose up to meet his driving hips, knowing now how to take her pleasure from him, and the low roar of breath and the meeting of their flesh were the only sounds.

And then it was done, his breath against her throat lulling as he lowered himself again to lie next to her.

"Rhys," she murmured.

Spent, she drifted to sleep again, his body stretched out next to hers, his arms around her.

The next morning she awoke in an empty bed, to the sound of a maid poking up the fires. Sabrina slid a hand over, and found the sheets cold.

He might as well have been a phantom.

And for a disorienting moment, she felt a bit like a phantom, too.

CHAPTER SEVENTEEN

IRONIC THAT THE sunlight forcing its way into his cell should land a beam on the floor in the shape of a cross, Morley thought, given that the slits had been cut in the Tower wall for some soldier's arrow centuries ago, and were meant to abet the shedding of blood.

Two hatches, vertical and horizontal, bisecting. A symbol of God, a symbol of war.

He grimaced at the direction of his thoughts. There wasn't very much to do in the Tower, so his mind had begun to fix upon minute things, dissecting them hungrily for every particle of meaning and distraction, rather like a man tearing into a small loaf of bread. He almost sympathized with Bonaparte exiled in St. Helena. A man of action and intelligence and leadership, Bonaparte was reduced to a quiet retirement, which seemed rather a pity for such a resourceful and energetic man. He'd wanted to be exiled to London, once, Bonaparte had. The very idea had always struck Morley as very funny: London never could have contained him. He would have escaped, or started a revolution.

Morley imagined a peaceful exile would make short work of the emperor.

Of course, the emperor would not be facing the gallows.

He'd been in the Tower for nearly a month now. Sir Walter Raleigh had lived for thirteen years in the Tower, and he'd managed to write his memoirs and conduct scientific experiments before they took off his head. Morley wondered if he would live in the Tower long enough to write his own memoirs. In the long moments of silence and solitude, he'd run through his memories, thinking to find distraction or ease, but they'd begun to all feel the same: all of them, the pleasant and less pleasant, made him restless, only reminded him that the balance of his life would be lived out inside a cell of whitewashed walls.

He would not apply the word "regret" to any of his memories; he had always done what he'd needed to do to achieve his ends. He'd accomplished more, acquired more, than many men would ever dream. He'd done some good in the world; he'd done some bad in the world.

He'd had many political allies at one time; some members of the Commons considered him a friend. He'd dined with earls and viscounts. He'd made love to some of the *ton*'s most beautiful women, and he suspected he'd loved only one of them.

None of them had come to visit him in the Tower, of course. Not when the son of the powerful Earl of Westphall, Kit Whitelaw, had been the one instrumental in arresting him.

He leaned heavily on his cane and turned to his lawyer, Mr. Duckworth, who had been ushered in by guards. Mr. Duckworth was a juiceless man, with a permanent-looking pallor born of spending nearly the entirety of his life indoors. Thin lips, thin arms, thinning hair, as befit a creature who willingly deprived himself of sunlight. Morley briefly thought of the roses on his country estate, which would be dormant now, but which unfolded to greedily drink in the sun in late spring.

England's profligate king, always desperate for money, had no doubt seized his estate.

Duckworth's spectacles glinted in the light from the narrow slit, so that Morley couldn't see his eyes. But they were brown, Morley knew, and shrewd.

It was Mr. Duckworth who'd been presented with the thankless task of defending Morley against the extraordinary charges against him: conspiracy to sell information to the French, and conspiracy to murder Richard Lockwood, a beloved politician, seventeen years ago.

Treason and murder, in other words.

"The evidence is exceptionally damning, Mr. Morley. The documents found by Viscount Grantham are thorough and convincing and the witnesses could not be more credible. And your assistant, the little man, Mr. Horace Minkin—"

"Horace Minkin?" Morley frowned.

"You call him Bob, Mr. Morley."

"Ah, yes. Mr. Minkin," Mr. Morley said soberly. He'd never known Bob's actual name. He'd never wanted to know it.

"What Mr. Minkin lacks in character and credibility, he more than makes up for in the sheer volume and detail of his stories. Coaches and adders, Mr. Morley?" Mr. Duckworth shook his head.

And Bob, Morley knew, had rather a lot of stories to tell. Until he'd encountered Kit Whitelaw, Bob had been remarkably useful.

"In short, in all likelihood, you will rapidly be convicted of murder and treason."

"Rapidly?" Morley repeated ironically. "In an English court? And I've only just begun enjoying my trial."

The lawyer offered him a thin smile. Appreciating the dry wit. "I believe you know the punishment for treason and murder, Mr. Morley."

I wonder where they will hang me? Morley thought. In public, as an example for anyone tempted to treason, or on the Tower Green, as befitting someone who had also managed to do some good for his country, despite the way he'd set out to do it?

"Did you come here to tell me what I already know, Mr. Duckworth, or because you enjoy my company?"

Mr. Duckworth turned toward the shuttered windows and gestured. "May I?"

Morley nodded. Apparently Mr. Duckworth was having difficulty with the confines of the cell. It had taken some time, admittedly, to become accustomed to them. Morley kept the shutters closed; the cold air in the cell made the ever-present ache in his leg nearly unbearable.

He opened one, and the gust of cold air, painful in its reminder of the world outside, rushed in. Morley blinked in the sun, an assault of light.

"Far be it from me to say that I do not enjoy your company, Mr. Morley. But I fear today's visit is not a social one. I've come with an option."

And Duckworth turned a faint smile toward Morley. Mr. Duckworth might harbor as much belief in Mr. Morley's guilt as he did in the existence of a Creator, but he was still, at heart, a lawyer. And Morley, for the first time in weeks, began to feel a prickle of anticipation of a more pleasant variety.

"Do share, Mr. Duckworth."

"I have done some discreet questioning on your behalf. His Majesty would, of course, be fascinated to learn of any other members of the Commons or Lords who may have—shall we say—an ambivalent relationship to the law, or who might have assisted you in any way in your allegedly criminal activities. Particularly those of, shall we say, higher station. His gratitude for relevant information would of course be reflected in your sentence. Perhaps even the charges brought against you. Depending, of course, upon the nature and magnitude of the revelation."

And suddenly the fresh air gusting through the cell was a promise, and not a taunt.

In other words: hand us a lord on a platter, Mr. Morley, and we might consider not hanging you. Perhaps you'll even see your roses again.

Morley smiled faintly. "Were you born a lawyer, Mr. Duckworth?"

Mr. Duckworth merely smiled his thin-lipped smile. "Since you've a good deal of time to review your memories and associations, I suggest that you use it wisely. I stand ready to hear anything you wish to share, when and if you wish to share it."

Sabrina almost wished he hadn't come at all. That he *wouldn't* come at all. But wishing wouldn't undo her marriage or the circumstances of it, and if there was anything she'd learned in her life, it was how to make do. She would learn how to make do.

She didn't know what Rhys did in London, but she truly wanted no part of it: the very idea of hordes of people living stacked virtually atop one another, skies dimmed with smut from thousands of coal fires, crime and squalor. She knew Mary considered it glamorous. And perhaps there were things she would like to see and do there. Museums. Galleries of art. But for adventure, Sabrina still would very much have preferred to visit another land populated by people who *weren't* English. She preferred room to run and stretch.

But her days eventually, haltingly, acquired a rhythm of sorts. She stopped in to speak with the cook and the housekeeper about meals; she read, glutting herself on the library until she thought her head might pop from the diet of words; she rode out to Buckstead Heath to the vicarage to visit with Geoffrey, to listen to him rehearse his sermons and offer up her opinions on them. She liked to think they had settled into a friendship, she and Geoffrey. And as they were related now, it could hardly be considered improper, could it?

And each time she left, Geoffrey asked whether she'd spoken yet to Rhys about his mission.

Geoffrey was growing thinner, she noticed. He jumped at loud sounds. Perhaps he needed more beef in his diet. She would speak to the cook and have some sent to him.

Or perhaps he was pining the loss of his dream. His hope tore at her.

"The next time I see Rhys, I shall speak to him on your behalf," she promised Geoffrey.

And God only knew when that would be.

At the end of the week she stopped into the kitchen to discuss the evening meal with the cook and Mrs. Bailey— she would be dining alone, of course, but it was a pity to not take advantage of the wonderful cook, and she'd tried all manner of delicious new things since she'd married the earl. Again, she could not discount the myriad advantages of being married to an earl.

"Poor old Margo Bunfield has lost part of her roof," Mrs. Bailey was saying to the cook just as Sabrina arrived.

"I beg your pardon, Mrs. Bailey, but who is Margo Bunfield?" Sabrina asked.

"Oh, Lady Rawden!" The two servants spun about and curtsied. "Mrs. Bunfield is an elderly widow who lives at the edge of Buckstead Heath," Mrs. Bailey told her. "And her roof was damaged in the blizzard. Nearly gone, in fact."

"Oh, dear! Did much of the village sustain damage, then? It truly was a rare storm."

"A number of roofs, Lady Rawden. And I've heard the mill suffered, too."

Sabrina heard the siren song of people needing help. "My goodness, perhaps I should see to them."

Mrs. Bailey apparently had no opinion on this subject, for she remained silent.

And then Sabrina dared to ask the housekeeper the question that had taken up lodging in her mind.

"Mrs. Bailey, did you send a note to my husband about the carpet?"

"Yes, Lady Rawden," she answered without a moment's hesitation.

Sabrina needed to ask her next question, though she suspected the answer had something to do with the fealty the housekeeper felt. It was the earl, after all, who paid her wages. Still, the faintest sense of betrayal was in her tone as she asked.

"*Why* did you send a note?"

And here there was a pause.

The housekeeper answered surprisingly gently. "He came, didn't he?"

Sabrina went still, staring in wonder at Mrs. Bailey.

And when it became clear the countess didn't intend to say anything more, Mrs. Bailey curtsied and strode purposefully away to see to the business of La Montagne.

Rhys jammed his hat onto his head as he departed White's. He had an hour or so to prepare for a soiree at which Sophia Licari was performing. She'd extended yet another invitation, a direct, explicit one; once again, he saw no reason not to accept.

He swiveled suddenly in the street. A woman had walked by on the arm of another man, and something about her—perhaps her slim shoulders—called Sabrina to mind.

He stared after her a moment, felt a peculiar pierce of something that felt like—

"Heard you just returned from the Midlands, Rawden. What takes you to the country these wintry days?" It was Lord Cavill, emerging from White's at the same time. "Surely the amusements in London can keep a man warmer?"

"Business at La Montagne," Rhys answered curtly.

"Would that business be a . . . wife?" The man raised furry brows. And then actually wagged them.

Rhys glared at him. Though he wasn't precisely trying to keep his marriage a secret—in fact, some women vastly preferred dalliances with married men—he hadn't made any effort to announce it, either. How on earth had word got out? Wyndham? No. More likely word of the issuance of a Special License to the Earl of Rawden had spread. No doubt everyone in the *ton* was amused.

"Carpets," he said shortly.

There was a message waiting for him at his town house, along with the perspiring messenger, who had been sent with it posthaste, apparently.

Rhys now recognized Mrs. Bailey's script. It was the writing of someone who only trots out her ability to write for dire or special occasions. He sincerely doubted Mrs. Bailey was inviting him to a birthday party.

He broke the seal.

Inside was more of her script:

Dear Lord Rawden,

I apologize for troubling you, but I thought it best to inform you that Countess Rawden has been seen on the roofs of the Buckstead Heath.

Your servant,
Mrs. Margaret Bailey

Sweet *merciful* God. Rhys flung the note down.

What on earth could that possibly *mean*? Had Sabrina gone mad, imagined she was a pigeon and was perching on roofs? Was she threatening to dash herself off one in sheer protest of not being able to give away the carpets?

Granted, both of these scenarios were remarkably difficult to imagine, given how sane and frank Sabrina tended to be. But the message was precisely cryptic enough to give him no choice in the matter, and he wondered if the bloody housekeeper had intended it that way. He wondered if housekeepers were capable of that degree of subtlety.

Bloody hell. And here he'd thought he'd acquired a *quiet* wife. She was proving more capricious, in her way, than Sophia Licari could ever dream of being.

He'd been in London a mere fortnight, and now he was forced to return again. He turned to the messenger, fishing in his pockets for coins with which to pay him.

"Would you kindly bring a message to Signora Sophia Licari to tell her I will not be attending her performance this evening? I must away to La Montagne."

He arrived at La Montagne by midday, a little later than he would have liked, but melting snow had played merry hell with the accessibility of the roads, turning some to pools of mud and forcing them to seek out different routes, or to occasionally get out of the carriage and walk.

He arrived disheveled, perspiring, muddy to the knee, and seething.

He rang for Mrs. Bailey immediately, and the stout, solemn woman greeted him with a curtsy.

"On the roofs, Mrs. Bailey?" he demanded without preamble.

The woman didn't even blink. "The blizzard, sir. The countess discovered that the storm damaged some of the roofs in Buckstead Heath."

"And so she climbed up *on* the . . ." It was too absurd a sentence to complete.

Rhys read no approval or disapproval in the housekeeper's face. She was merely relaying information. "So I am told, Lord Rawden."

He didn't ask: *told by whom?* He knew how gossip spread in a town like Buckstead Heath.

"Is the countess in?"

"I'm afraid not, Lord Rawden."

He drew in a breath. "Do you know," he drawled, "where she *is*?"

Please, God, don't say "on the roof."

"I believe she went to see to the mill, Lord Rawden. The mill seems to have suffered some damage, too. The roofs in town have already been seen to."

CHAPTER EIGHTEEN

FIFTEEN MINUTES LATER, Rhys had sponged his face, handed his boots over to be cleaned and pulled on fresh ones, changed his coat, retied his cravat, and mounted Gallegos bound for Buckstead Heath, in search of the mill.

Far be it from him to look like anything less than an earl, ever.

In a sense, Rhys knew the mill on Buckstead Heath was in part responsible for his existence: it was centuries old, and had ground the grain that both fed and filled the coffers of the Gillray family. Still, Rhys needed to keep his eyes on the horizon in order to find it, because pride had kept him from visiting the town until he was lord of the manor once again. He expected the mill would have been built on a mound to best take advantage of the wind, so despite the thick growth of trees, he was optimistic he'd be able to spot it.

At last in the distance he saw, turning like a great Saint Andrew's cross high in the sky, the sails of the mill, a post mill, a brilliantly whitewashed little dome against the blue sky. He spurred Gallegos into an easy gallop, but slowed as he drew nearer: one of the mill sails had been snapped, the bottom half dangling sickeningly. One of the blizzard's victims.

And that's when he saw the now-unmistakable-to-him figure of his wife, hands on her hips, head craned back, standing alongside a man as squat as the mill. This person, Rhys assumed, was the miller. His head was pointing upward, too, and his hands waved about illustratively. Recounting the story of the disaster, no doubt. He saw the miller make a snapping motion with his hands in the air. Sabrina's bonnet had tipped from her head, and it bobbed behind her as she nodded along with the miller's tale as though she found it fascinating.

They both swiveled abruptly as Gallegos galloped up, and in one smooth motion Rhys pulled him to a halt, swung down, and strode toward them, leaving the horse's reins to dangle. The miller took a reflexive step back, and Rhys was distantly amused. His expression must be speaking indeed.

The miller recovered himself swiftly and bowed low, because though he'd never seen Rhys in his life, there was absolutely no question about who he was: potent rays of aristocracy all but radiated from him, along with, Rhys was certain, his temper.

"Rawden," his wife said faintly.

She curtsied, a little belatedly. She looked a little guilty. Ah, he thought ironically. At least she knew countesses do not typically tread out to discuss mills with millers.

"Countess." He made the word a warning.

She cleared her throat. "Rawden . . . this is Mr. Pike, the miller for Buckstead Heath and the surrounding villages. Mr. Pike . . . the Earl of Rawden."

Mr. Pike bowed again. He seemed rather pleased to have an earl to bow to.

"Mr. Pike and I were just discussing the—"

"Yes," Rhys interrupted abruptly. The word cleared her sentence in two like an ax.

Sabrina fell silent.

Mr. Pike was unaware of any tension; his mind was focused on a more immediate grief. "Snapped right badly, din't she, Lord Rawden?" Mr. Pike said mournfully. He reached up a hand the size of a lamb shank and gave the dangling blade a stroke. "The windshaft is splintered, too, and willna 'old the sails should the wind get stiffer. Built in the year of our Lord 1540 by Pikes, and we Pikes 'ave been millers 'ere e'er since yer family first built 'ere. Nivver seen a blizzard the likes of the one what came through. Polly was no match for it."

"Polly?" Rhys frowned. "Who the devil is—"

"The mill's name is Polly," Sabrina told him quickly.

A tall ladder leaned against the side of the mill. Or rather, Polly. And the ladder made Rhys immediately think of roofs. His wife, rosy-cheeked from the chill or perhaps guilt, eyes bright from no doubt treading all the way to the village from the Montagne, stood looking up at him, the wind whipping the hem of her green wool pelisse about her ankles. He suddenly had a vivid image of her up on that ladder, the wind making a sail of her pelisse at that height, catching it, yanking Sabrina's feet from the rung, the pelisse fanning out behind her as she plummeted to the—

"Were you about to go up the ladder to look at the sail?" He directed this, with deceptive mildness, to his wife.

"No," she answered quickly.

"She just come *down* from lookin' at the *windshaft,* din't she?" the miller told him cheerfully. "Knows a bit about mills, she does."

Sabrina shot a belated quelling glance at the oblivious miller.

It seemed there was no end to the things there were to learn about Sabrina.

"You've been on roofs as well, I hear." Rhys's voice was growing milder and milder. The only way he knew to keep his temper in control. Sabrina's eyes were beginning to kindle a bit with temper of her own.

"Just the one!" Mr. Pike interjected quickly, in the spirit of clarity, no doubt. "Margo Bunfield's roof is gone by half. Rufus Curliss lost the roof of his cottage, and the blizzard took the roof right off the barn at the Jenkins' farm." The miller ticked these off his fingers. "That's all I know fer now. The countess, she were looking into it, ye see."

So while Rhys was compromising a vicar's daughter and getting himself married, disaster had struck in the little town of Buckstead Heath, and his countess had recently climbed up on roofs to see it.

Rhys gazed up at the handsome, sturdy mill, and almost unconsciously took a step toward it, laid his hand on the fractured sail as though in comfort. Some instinctive sympathy for the machine. "The mill is a few hundred years old, but I'll wager the sails are newer?"

"Aye, Lord Rawden, we've the sort what closes and opens, now, like shutters. Built 'em meself, when the cloths looked ready to give way. Learned it from a chap in Sussex."

Rhys was intrigued. "Ah, I see. So you can open and close them as necessary, to best utilize the wind. Rather like the blinds in Venice, isn't it?"

He studied the cunning construction of the sails, absently tried his hand at opening and closing them.

"I canna speak fer the blinds in Venice, Lord Rawden, but the sails do a bonnie job of turning to grind the grain. I can take best advantage of the wind as she comes, can't I, this way? But we Pikes might 'ave built a tower mill a century ago, like, rather than this little post mill, if we knew we'd 'ave blizzards like the one a fortnight or so ago."

"Clever of you, Mr. Pike, to move with the times with regard to the sails."

The miller glowed.

Sabrina, for her part, was wisely silent. Her hands were clasped behind her back.

"And I do believe that blizzard was a once-a-century anomaly, Mr. Pike." He glanced at the miller. "A rare occurrence," he revised for him as he set foot on the bottom rung of the ladder, testing it for his weight and height. It was sturdy, too, and Rhys scaled it quickly.

At the top he had a view of miles, and everything, he knew, as far as his vision could reach, now belonged to him, to his family, once again. Dizzying, exhilarating. He could see La Montagne, a stretch of tawny stone, aged, glowing against the white landscape; uneven fences surrounding snow-covered pastures, older cottages built a few decades after William the Conqueror had reached English shores scattered among newer cottages. And beyond those cottages, land that had not yet been built or planted, and could be used for grazing, for another field of corn, grist for Polly. He drew in a breath; the air seemed sharper, cleaner at that height, than on the ground, so clean it nearly hurt. He imagined that it all but scoured his lungs.

He glanced down: the windshaft, to which the sails were attached and which turned them when they were set free in the wind, was indeed badly split; perhaps the force of the wind that took off the sail had borne down on the axle, too, and the weight had proved too much for it.

His coat did whip about his legs, and he gripped the ladder to keep his balance. Silently he swore again, picturing Sabrina up there doing the very same thing.

"Is Polly in good repair otherwise, Mr. Pike?" he called down to the miller.

"All's fair with her, as far as I can see," the miller called up.

"I think we'll need to replace the windshaft." He was scarcely aware that he'd used the word "we." "I don't think it can be patched or repaired." He was accustomed to giving orders. Out it had come.

"My thoughts, too, Lord Rawden." The miller sounded pleased to be in accord with an earl.

Just then three men, well fed, warmly clothed in patched coats, and looking remarkably alike with their round heads and blunt wind-reddened noses, trudged into view up the mill mound. One of them carried a long wooden box by a handle.

"'Eard ye'd a wee problem on yer 'ands, Pike!" one of them called. "Ye've a man to see to it, then? We've come to 'elp, as we can use yer 'elp wi' the roof. We've covered it fer now, but me wife dinna fancy snow in the parlor, ye see."

Rhys began to back down the ladder.

"Snow doesna match wi' 'er new settee!" one of the other big men explained, and they all laughed.

"Oh, 'tis the countess!" one of them said, noticing Sabrina. "Good day, my lady."

"Good day, Mr. Ferris, Mr. Ferris, and Mr. Ferris," she replied solemnly, as they each bowed in turn.

"Could 'ave bought a good mule for the price of that set-tee!" one of the Mr. Ferrises continued. It was a sore point, clearly. "I tell ye, the cost of making a woman 'appy is—"

He stopped abruptly as Rhys landed softly on the ground, and they all got a good look at him.

And then all was stares and silence.

"Gentlemen," Sabrina said gently. "Lord Rawden, the Earl of Rawden."

Simultaneously, the three Ferris brothers bent swiftly in bows.

Upright again, their faces were somber but pleased, and a little shy. It occurred to Rhys that they'd all been rather missing the presence of a Gillray family member.

"Albert, Georgie, and Harry Ferris, at your service, your lordship," one of them ventured.

"A pleasure to meet you, gentlemen."

A bit of an awkward silence.

"Has Polly gone to her reward, then, Lord Rawden?" The one called Harry asked this with no apparent sense of whimsy.

"Oh, she's some life in her yet, I think," Rhys reassured him thoughtfully. "I imagine a number of men working together can get her repaired. What do you think, Mr. Pike?"

"Well, it willna be a simple thing, but I do think ye've the right of it, Lord Rawden. 'Twas men what built the sails in the first place."

"Shall we, then? Have you tools, Mr. Ferris?"

"Aye, Lord Rawden."

"Good, then. And I'd rather like to see how you build those shutters, Mr. Pike."

In minutes, Rhys, former military man, current erotic poet, had organized the men with precision and was issuing orders. With the help of Mr. Pike, he gave out tasks and instructions, and soon the sound of sawing, hammering, swearing, jests, and syllables of triumph filled the air as the new sail and windshaft took shape.

A half hour or so into the labor Rhys shed his coat and strode over to Sabrina, handing it to her without a word. She took it with a raised brow, but wisely held her tongue. She folded the coat neatly over her arms, and silently stepped aside, taking up a seat on a nearby log to watch the work.

She was all but forgotten soon enough, but this suited her. She didn't particularly want to actually *build* a sail for the mill, after all. And it gave her an opportunity to watch her husband work in his shirtsleeves. He'd appeared looking nearly as groomed as he did for dinner, but now the fine linen of his shirt was damp and clinging to his broad-shouldered frame. His forearms were strong and corded; his hands wielding tools deftly, as though he'd done it dozens of times before.

He had taken charge so effortlessly, and his command had been quickly accepted by these men, who seemed to have no difficulty finding a sort of language that involved both bonhomie and deference for Rhys's rank. Men always bemused her, the sort of effortlessness they found around a manly pastime. She watched her husband confer with Mr. Pike about the construction particulars, but he seemed to grasp the process quickly. He understood form and composition, after all, and his hands were efficient in so many other ways, so graceful and confident.

She dallied a minute over thoughts of those *other* ways in which Rhys's hands were efficient and skilled and confident. Instantly she forgot about the cold.

He was so certain of himself. Sabrina knew he would feel certain of himself no matter the circumstances. Such were the privileges of his birth.

She wished she could make him understand that she would never be able to share that same certainty. She would only be able to throw the role of countess over her and button it up, like a pelisse. She didn't know how to be a countess. She knew only how to be herself.

He must be terribly angry with her; since she'd taken his coat from him, he hadn't glanced at her more than once. And then his blue eyes had flared enigmatically, and returned to the job at hand as if she'd been naught but a tree or a fence post.

Several hours later, a gratified cheer went up when the new sail was lifted up to the new windshaft and tested. It caught the wind beautifully, and the sails spun round and round.

They stopped it, as they wouldn't be grinding today, and Mr. Pike made certain it was in the position that put the least strain on the sails, the Saint Andrew's cross.

Rhys grinned and swiped the back of his hand against his brow. His hair, soaked through with sweat despite the chill, clung where he'd pushed it. They'd all worked hard.

"Can I offer ye some cider, the countess and yerself?" Mr. Pike seemed loath to relinquish the company of the earl.

"My thanks, Mr. Pike, but I best take the countess home." Rhys spared Sabrina a glance then. There was nothing of reassurance in it.

"I thank you for your help, then, Lord Rawden. Will we see you atop Margo Bunfield's roof?"

Rhys merely laughed. A noncommittal laugh.

And then he stood back with all of them and admired their collective handiwork one more time.

Rhys had watched in silence as Sabrina exchanged farewells with the men, and then he'd lifted her up into the saddle in silence, and nudged Gallegos forward. And he'd been silent the entire journey.

This was when Sabrina decided it was safe to assume that he was very angry. Either that or he was rehearsing the speech to end all speeches, and now that they'd returned to La Montagne, she was about to be the fortunate recipient of it.

"In here," he said to her curtly when they returned to La Montagne. He motioned her with his chin into the library.

He didn't invite her to sit once they were in the library.

"You like this room, don't you?" he asked without preamble.

She studied him, found no clues in his face. "Yes," she answered carefully.

"Why?"

"Why?" she repeated innocently, to give herself time to decide what he meant.

"Yes. That's what I asked. *Why* do you like this room, Sabrina?"

"It's unpre—" She stopped herself just in time from saying the word "unpretentious" as she saw his face darken. "It's cozy. There are books here. I love books."

He inhaled deeply, exhaled just as deeply. "You were about to say it was unpretentious."

She refused to confirm or deny this, which of course was tantamount to confirming it.

"Sabrina . . . ," he began, his voice heavy with patience. "You're a countess now. You will be a countess until the day you die. This house belongs to you, whether you like it or not, and you'll be happier if you learn to like it. And I must insist that you *behave like a countess.* Surely you understand that countesses do not climb about on roofs."

Of course she understood his point. Still, all of his "insisting" was rousing her stubborn streak. "You said we should live our lives as we wish."

He shook his head roughly. "So sayeth the lawyer in you. Nevertheless, I'm afraid you cannot climb on roofs and confer with a miller like a *hired worker,* Sabrina." His voice had risen a little; he paused to take a deep breath and lowered it. "In fact, this may come as a shock to you, but some women actually consider it an advantage to marry a wealthy earl, precisely *because* they'll never have to labor again." He said it ironically.

The absurdity of having to explain this struck both him and her at the same time, along with a slight sense of futility.

And there was a quiet.

And in the quiet Sabrina's senses rallied, and she could smell him: his linen, the tang of something clean, with that tart edge like lime, a little sweat: he was still warm from his labor at the windmill. And perhaps from exasperation.

"And you could have been *hurt,* Sabrina. On the roof, on that ladder . . ." He trailed off.

She was inordinately pleased that her husband didn't rejoice in the idea of her plummeting to her death.

"I have marvelous balance," she reassured him. An attempt at a jest.

He made an impatient sound. "There must be other ways to help, Sabrina, that don't compromise my family dignity or your life or give the village men an opportunity to peek up your skirts."

Her mouth dropped open. "They wouldn't!"

"They're *men*." He was thoroughly exasperated now. "And I wouldn't blame them in the least. But then I'd have to shoot the lot of them, and *then* who on earth would grind the grain at Buckstead Heath?" He had given full rein to his sarcasm now; he was half enjoying himself, but he was fully angry. And just a little despairing.

And then Sabrina realized: his pride was again wounded. Everything here at La Montagne was something he had earned, won hard, unlike so many others of his station who had been born to it and never lost it. His own recklessness may have saddled him with a wife he hadn't asked for, but now that he had her, he wanted to give her these things, too. Wanted her to appreciate them, to take pride in who she now was: a Gillray, and Rawden.

"It's just . . ." She stopped. "I've so little to do, Rhys."

"*Do?*"

"Do! I was ever busy at the vicarage. I felt needed. I . . . my days were full. And now . . ."

Rhys took this in silently.

Well, his days were full, too. With beauty and smoke and music and liquor and clever, bored people and expensive things and outrageous pastimes. He had plenty to "do."

Being sarcastic in his thoughts was becoming quite a habit.

"You enjoyed yourself today," she said suddenly, when he said nothing.

She was doing it again. Those sudden observations of hers stung like shrapnel. Surprised, he carefully answered: "Yes."

"They enjoyed seeing you, Rhys. They're your people. They're good people."

"Perhaps. But I can tell you that I don't intend to make a habit of laboring, because, quite simply, I no longer need to. And I am telling you now, Sabrina, that *you shall not,* either."

He'd issued an order.

Silence. He saw rebellion flicker over her face.

And yet . . . it did make her genuinely happy, he understood. Helping. It was her nature, at the very core of her.

She sighed her acceptance. "I'm sorry," she said faintly, at last. "I just—"

"I know. Wanted to help. Can you find another way to help that doesn't involve climbing on roofs, or giving away parts of the house?"

She smiled a little. "Yes, very likely, I can."

She was ever apologizing, Rhys thought. And they were ever frustrated with each other. Two people never meant to be together, now linked for life.

His lovely, hopeless, stubborn, inconvenient wife. Lashes thick and dusky over those green eyes lit with her smile. The soft, soft mouth, pink as—

Well, he *was* a poet. Or had been. He should be able to think of some metaphor for her mouth. Except, at the moment, he could not.

Instead, on impulse, he took her hand in his, gently turned it palm side up, rubbed his thumb over it. A pretty hand, the fingers long and straight and slim, the nails short. But the palms weren't satiny smooth. They weren't tended hands. They'd been used a bit.

"Not the hand of a fragile woman," he murmured.

"No," she agreed softly, after a moment. The word a distracted-sounding little syllable.

And there was a silence. And as the silence stretched, it seemed to gather a charge.

He'd only meant to hold her hand, touch her, let it go. But he gazed down at her, and his thumb continued to move slowly over the mounds of her palm, tracing a feathery pattern. As if this were the map to Sabrina.

And what had begun almost absently became, as it did every time he touched her . . . intent.

As he watched the warm color rise in her cheeks, that nearly irrational want surged in him. Dear God. And he'd only *touched her hand.*

He lifted her palm up to his lips and pressed a lingering, hot kiss in the center of it. Sabrina's breath was shorter now, softly audible, her dusky-lashed lids growing heavier.

And then Rhys drew one of those slim fingers into his mouth, and gently sucked.

Her eyes fluttered closed, and stayed closed. "Oh." It was a surprised, cracked whisper. All pleasure.

And he was hard, just like that, and he needed to take her *now.*

Rhys moved his mouth farther down her wrist, his hand gliding below it. His thumb found her speeding pulse, and he pressed his lips there, the silky skin a tantalizing reminder of how silky the rest of her was, and he lingered there long enough to watch the gooseflesh stand the little golden hairs of her arm on end.

And then his mouth moved to land hard on hers, and she met him hungrily, stretching her arms up to wrap around his head, her mouth open and hot and sweet, taking his plunging tongue and twining it with her own. He pulled her tightly against his body, and lifted his mouth from hers briefly.

"Sabrina—too many clothes—" God, he could barely speak. He was choked with desire.

His hands fumbled desperately at her pelisse, her skirts, found practical woolen drawers; he swore colorfully and dragged them down, mercifully finding, at last, cool smooth skin, and his hands were on her thighs, stroking up them. She gasped her approval, and her fingers scrabbled at his trouser buttons. Together, half laughing, they worked to quickly free him, and when at last he sprang, painfully hard, into her hand, he swore softly with pleasure.

"Like this," he said roughly, his voice a rasp. He turned her abruptly so that the wall braced her back, and he pushed his knee between her legs, lifting her smooth thigh in one hand, his other hand searching, testing the damp curls between her legs, and he found her as ready for him as he was for her. And this time she helped him guide himself in, gasping when he was seated.

Oh, God.

His hips took over instantly, plunging into her snug heat again and then again and again and . . . *so good.* He heard her frayed breathing in his ear as her arms went around him tightly, clasping behind his neck, her hips arching upward to meet his, and his mouth landed on hers again, his tongue imitating his swift deep thrusts.

His hand dragged down over to close hard over one breast, and she gasped, jerked her lips from his, hoarsely said his name. *"Rhys . . . yes . . ."*

Again and again he drove into her, until the bliss was a white light exploding in his head, and he saw Sabrina throw her head back, the cords of her neck tense. Just in time he covered her mouth with his hand, gently, and she hoarsely sang out her release into his palm as his own tore through him. He buried his face against her throat, gasping, as his body convulsed from it.

Unthinkably good. Terrifyingly good.

He'd written a book on the art of seduction, a book composed of one feverishly, precisely chosen word after another, the process, in a way, a metaphor for the way he'd conducted all of his seductions.

And yet he'd just taken his countess against the wall in the library as though he'd had no choice at all in the matter, while one of his ancestors beamed down enigmatically from a mahogany frame. Looking smugly pleased. They were everywhere, those smugly pleased ancestors. Rhys glanced over at the clock.

Seven whole minutes had passed.

His lean, young, virile body felt as limp as a cotton rag.

"You *do* have marvelous balance," he murmured at last, with some surprise.

Her laugh was muffled against his shirt. A wonderful sound, her laugh.

He didn't understand this. It unnerved him. And so he didn't speak, just held her quietly, spent, but still gently sheathed in her. They were both too worn to move just yet. He took the moment to breathe her in. The spice and lavender and female musk at the nape of her neck. The scent that said "Sabrina" to him now.

The clock chimed, a sound like fairies tapping a bell with tiny mallets. What a lot of bloody clocks there were at La Montagne.

"Rhys?"

"Mmm?"

There was a pause so long he began to wonder if he'd imagined her speaking.

"Is it . . . is it like this for every married man and woman?"

She'd tilted her face back to look at him, and her usually direct gaze was shaded a bit. The question embarrassed her, but he understood why she'd asked. He knew she meant: Did every man and woman all but burst into flames the moment they touched each other?

He hesitated. "No." He said the word carefully. As if giving her a gift he wasn't certain she could handle, like a musket or a wild stallion.

She said nothing in response to this; he saw her eyes go abstracted as she took a moment to consider what this meant. And then, to his surprise, she drew her finger across one of his eyebrows twice, gently smoothing it.

"It was mussed," she explained. And smiled.

He felt some strange sensation inside his breastbone, something as sharp and clean and exhilarating as that air he'd breathed today atop Polly, the post mill. As though he'd just been jerked up by the collar to some dizzying height, and from there could see eternity.

His expression must have gone odd, because her smile faded.

"Rhys?"

This time he merely looked at her, because he feared the next question.

She took in a deep breath. "Is it always like this for . . . you?"

And suddenly breathing was difficult.

This clever, tender woman easily saw as much as he did, he knew now, only through a different lens. He preferred the shelter of being cleverer than everyone else. Of keeping the world at bay with words, words, words. Words and things.

And the word was reluctant, and the word surprised him, and he preferred not to say it until he knew what it meant for him, or how he felt about it. But it was true, and she had asked.

"No."

He said it shortly, gave it no intonation. A way of discouraging any more such questions. For the more accurate answer would have been: "It has never been like this for me."

She looked down, and frowned a little, faintly. Such delicate brows. Two little auburn wings drawn together.

A few moments later he pulled gently away from her, smoothed down her dress, and she laughed a little self-consciously, as though they were both finding sobriety again after a debauch. He reassembled himself in his trousers, freshly amused that he was reassembling himself in the library. It was probably the least sensual room in all of La Montagne.

He noticed something then on the settee: a soft coil of blue. "What's this?"

She flushed as he picked it up and ran it curiously through his hands.

"It's . . . it's a scarf. I knitted it for you." Casual words, yet strangely weighty in import.

"Oh." A blue scarf. Knitted for him. He hefted it almost as though he'd never seen such a thing before. For some reason, he didn't feel he could meet her eyes in that moment.

"I'll see you at dinner, Sabrina," he said gently, at last looking up from his gift.

He gestured for her to precede him out the library door.

She looked at him once, searchingly. And clearly she didn't find what she sought, because her face went closed and polite.

And they went their separate ways again in the grand house.

Sabrina wondered if she would ever cease marveling at the appearance of food she hadn't cooked. Domed tureens had been left for them in the dining room; no footmen were in evidence. They were to serve themselves this evening, apparently, which she could certainly manage. A pair of candles lit the table and their faces, and the great chandelier was dark. It made the grand hall much more intimate.

"Do you dine out in London, frequently?" she asked him as they took their places across from each other.

"Not lately. Lately I run to and fro La Montagne and London to pluck my wife down off windmills and rescue my carpets."

She smiled, which for some reason made him go very still, and just . . . watch her. With a pleased sort of mystification. His eyes darkened a bit, too, which made her wonder whether her smiles perhaps did to him what his did to her.

The thought made her momentarily breathless.

"Have you heard Signora Licari sing lately?" It was a bold question, and she asked it while dragging her fork through some sauce. She thought the timing right, however, if he was mystified by her. She looked up for it.

It took him a while to answer.

"I haven't seen Signora Licari at all," he finally admitted. And the words were delivered carefully again.

She glanced down at her plate and bit her lip to keep from smiling. It was a gift, his answer. But somehow it was funny, too.

"Why did you begin writing poetry?" she asked when it seemed he wouldn't speak again, and was only intent upon gazing at her.

He looked startled for a moment. He tipped his head to the side, as if giving serious consideration to his answer.

"Do you remember the man I mentioned? Damien Russell? Scottish lad, but it was my misfortune that he ended up in my regiment—"

She smiled at the affection she heard in his voice. "Your regiment? What did you do during the war?"

"I was an officer under Wellington. Bought a commission after my mother died," he said shortly. "Damien was a foul-mouthed, cheeky bugger, very funny, the best soldier you could hope for. Never complained. Always knew precisely the right filthy thing to say to cheer the men up." Rhys smiled a little. "He was a gambler, but he never won. He was bad at every game of chance he tried. Never could manage a face for bluffing. But I caught him one night, scratching away with a pencil. And wouldn't you know it . . . he was writing a poem. And I told him I'd tell everyone in camp about it unless he let me read it. So he did, of course. Besides, I was his commanding officer, and he hadn't a choice."

"You were a tyrant," she said gravely.

He shrugged modestly.

"Was it good, his poem?"

"Oh, no. It was dreadful. Quite lurid. But lively enough. And it planted the idea, you see, when I'd exhausted other options. War is boredom interspersed with terror, typically. Poetry was something to do."

She thought of his extraordinary poetry. "Something to do," indeed.

"Did Damien come home from the war?"

"Yes."

"Do you still see him?"

"Oh, we've a reunion once a year in Little Orrick, a tiny town with marvelous fishing. Northumberland."

It seemed such a very tame thing for The Libertine, of all people, to do—the fishing—that she smiled again.

And Rhys frowned a little, as if embarrassed by his own disclosure.

"Do you have regiment reunions from time to time, then?" she asked him, thinking he'd be more comfortable talking of war. "The men in Tinbury do."

"Damien and I were the only ones from our regiment who came home." So matter-of-factly said.

The words knocked the breath from her.

And she didn't know what to say, but the realization struck her just as hard: he'd come back from the war full of poetry, sensual poetry all about the pleasures of the flesh. Nothing of ugliness, nothing of emotion. They were odes to the senses, so potent they'd acted on her own senses like opium. When no doubt he had seen bodies shattered and limbs torn, watched all of his men die but one.

And somehow he'd managed to create from that ugliness something that made the women of London cast off their dignity and trail him about. Poetry was his own form of anesthesia. He'd created something beautiful, remarkable, from blood and terror. And he'd taught her something miraculous in the process. He'd brought her fully alive.

And now he couldn't write.

But perhaps it was gone, then. Perhaps, with words, he'd exorcised whatever had haunted him.

He poured more wine into her glass, just as though he hadn't handed her the key to himself.

And later, once again she dressed in her night rail, and began to brush her hair, and though as usual she half hoped he would appear and finish the job for her, she found herself hoping just as strongly that he wouldn't.

She'd made love with her husband a mere four times now. But each time he'd left her it had taken her longer to find her way back to a semblance of nonchalance, to the pragmatic acceptance of the nature of their marriage, regardless of the pleasure they took in each other's bodies. And even as she found herself yearning for him, she resented what she knew would follow: the struggle to regain her equilibrium in his absence. The struggle to swallow her pride.

And so when Rhys did appear in the doorway, she didn't turn to see him, and the words emerged from her before she could consider the wisdom of or motivation for them.

"Will you be returning to London in the morning?"

"Yes."

The man actually sounded *puzzled* by her question.

Rhys came to stand behind her, so closely that she could feel the warmth of his body. His hands landed lightly on her shoulders, and he ran them down her arms, lowering his head to kiss the nape of her neck.

She stiffened.

Astute as ever, Rhys lifted his hands up. Was silent for a moment.

"What's troubling you, Sabrina?" His voice was quiet, even.

She inhaled deeply. She hadn't the courage to put it into words. She perhaps hadn't even the right to put it into words. And yet—

"It's just . . ." She stopped.

"It's just?" he urged. Tension in his voice now.

"You appear every few weeks and you . . ."

"And *what* do I do?" He'd begun to sound impatient.

"I'm sorry. Please forget what I said."

She moved restlessly away from him, pretending to fuss with the brushes on her table.

In silence he watched her.

"Complete your sentence, Sabrina." Coldly now. An order. "Let me remind you how it began: You said: 'You appear every few weeks and you . . .'"

"I know what I said." Apparently anger was contagious, for she was angry now. "All right. It's just that . . . you never ask. You just . . . take."

She turned then to look him bravely, evenly in the eye. Odd how his beautiful eyes could be so very nearly terrifying when he was angry.

"I take." He drawled it, and she heard the contained fury building in his voice. And oddly, accompanying it was something she could have sworn was fear.

"Me," she clarified, her own temper quite obviously fanned by his. "You take *me*. And I do know it's my duty—"

He flinched as though she'd slapped him. "Is that how you see this, Sabrina? As a *duty*?" The words were incredulously choked.

"I . . ." She was struggling, and his obvious fury wasn't making it any easier for her. "Well, isn't it? Isn't it my duty to be here to take as you wish and when you wish, and for you to leave when you wish?"

She lifted her hair, pushing it up away from her face awkwardly.

He stared, his breathing hard and fast now.

"What the bloody hell else do you want?" This said low and cold.

Silence now. Rhys watched her shoulders rising and falling, saw the soft unhappiness on her lovely face.

"Please forgive me, Rhys. I'm sorry I said anything."

And as he watched her, that panic welled, along with the irrational fury. And he didn't understand why he felt either of those things.

"I didn't ask for this marriage, either, Sabrina."

She jerked her head up then. "Oh, I know that very well, Rawden."

She could do sarcasm now as well as he could, it seemed.

Silence.

Inwardly Rhys flailed. He was at a loss with a woman for perhaps the first time in his life.

"You . . . enjoy it," he said. "This." And he meant every-thing that took place in this bedroom—and the library, and other rooms—between them. He'd said it almost accusatorily. And there was a hint of plea in it, which he despised.

There was a long pause.

"Yes." The word was a desolate little syllable. Delivered with a rueful smile.

She met his gaze evenly for a moment. And then she dropped her eyes.

"Bloody hell," he finally said quietly.

He spun on his heel and left the room, shutting the door hard behind him.

CHAPTER NINETEEN

And so the days resumed a sort of rhythm. Sabrina woke to chocolate and warm bread brought in by Mrs. Bailey; she rode out or walked out to visit Buckstead Heath to sit and chat with Margo Bunfield, and to visit with Geoffrey.

And she cursed her pride.

She supposed she was luckier than many, many a woman. She was comfortable and wealthy. Her every need was met, and good heavens, she had more carpets and tables and portraits of ancestors than anyone could ever want. She wasn't entirely neglected by her husband. He appeared every few weeks to service her and to scold her.

Ah, and there was her temper again.

She would never have known about her temper, or her pride, or her passion, without that bloody man. She wouldn't now be hurting, and seething, and longing, and confused . . .

And at last, learning to be resigned.

Oh, yes. If she'd never met the man, she wouldn't now feel more alive than she'd ever felt, and she wouldn't now feel as though something very lovely, something promising, had been yanked away.

She hadn't seen Rhys in weeks. She'd begun to wonder whether she would see him again.

Find something to do to help, he'd said, that didn't involve climbing on roofs or giving away the things in the house. All those bloody *things* that made him feel so complete.

And so she had.

They knew her in town now; she visited with Margo Bunfield, and with Mrs. Perriman and her four children, and with three other elderly women who never left their homes because of age or infirmity.

Three weeks with nary a word or sign of the earl. Though, of course, she wasn't behaving in any sort of scandalous or embarrassing manner, which seemed to be what mattered to him, and so there was no need for the earl to rush away from his life in London.

And because she was lonely, she found herself drawn more and more often to the familiar surrounds of a vicarage and of a church, and to Geoffrey.

She'd just listened to Geoffrey rehearse a sermon, a fine, eloquent one about the dangers of the pleasures of the flesh, delivered with such feeling Sabrina wondered just how much Geoffrey knew about the pleasures of the flesh. The thought gave her pause for a moment.

"Nicely done," she complimented finally.

"It was rather, wasn't it?" He smiled, but for some reason she didn't want to see his smile, as there was an echo of Rhys about it. "Thank you for sending the beef," he added.

"Oh, you're welcome." He still looked twitchy, however. Perhaps someone in the village could make him up a simple for his nerves. Though what could possibly trouble his nerves in Buckstead Heath eluded her.

"Sabrina . . . we're friends, are we not?" Geoffrey was watching her with something like speculation.

"Yes, of course, Geoffrey."

"Forgive my presumption in saying so . . . but you seem unhappy." He said it evenly.

She was struck by the observation. Then again, she wasn't precisely an enigma, never having perfected the skill of irony, so perhaps she shouldn't feel quite so struck. It was kind of him to care, however. She thought it kind of anyone to take an interest in how she might be feeling at the moment.

"I'm sorry, Geoffrey. I shall endeavor to smile more in your presence," she teased.

But he merely looked thoughtful. "I beg your pardon for asking, Sabrina, but I feel I must. Is . . . is Rhys unkind?"

Is Rhys unkind? Rhys wasn't anything in particular, it seemed, besides absent.

"My life is here, and his life is in London. He has provided a generous allowance so that I may buy all the carpets and the like I desire. It's a fair arrangement. I've naught to complain about." It was an honest enough answer.

Geoffrey fixed her with his dark gaze. His face so like Rhys's, and yet unlike his. Geoffrey seemed even more nervous lately; he was growing thinner still, and she'd noticed that sudden movements and noises made him start. She was certain the living Rhys provided him with was generous; she couldn't imagine the earl deliberately starving his cousin. She wondered if she ought to arrange for a nerve tonic to be sent to Geoffrey as well.

And then, startling, Geoffrey turned swiftly and reached for her hand. "Sabrina . . ."

His eyes were so intent on hers; his skin warm, his hands smooth. She stared at it again, knew a moment of sadness, and a strange sense of disconnection. How odd that one man could simply turn her inside out with the barest touch, and the other inspire nothing, unless it was warmth.

"Do you ever still long to be a missionary?" he asked.

And when Geoffrey said it, Sabrina felt the loss of her dream freshly. And wondered how her life would have been if she'd been able to travel across the world with the man who now held her hand. She felt a bit like Persephone, who had partaken of the pomegranate seeds and paid the price of her weakness.

"I have thought of it from time to time," she admitted.

"If you are ever so unhappy, Sabrina . . . I want you to know . . . I would assist you in your mission."

She frowned a little. "But, Geoffrey . . . I'm married now."

"But you've an allowance now, an income of your own, is that not right?"

"Yes, but—"

Almost eagerly he said, "If you chose it, Sabrina . . . you *could* leave him. It would be a very bold step, but I would . . . I could accompany you. We could always go to Africa as we planned and do some good. I would help you to leave, and Rhys would never find you."

It was an *astounding* suggestion. Sabrina stared at him and was tempted, briefly, to laugh.

But Geoffrey looked so earnest. His silky dark eyes were so understanding, so very nearly persuasive, and she could almost picture it: the leaving, the satisfying work on another continent.

And then it occurred to her that Geoffrey still held her hand in his, and he was standing a little closer than he usually did. She took a hint of a step backward.

He was merely trying, she realized, to help ease her unhappiness, rash and extraordinary though his suggestion seemed. And she did feel an ache: for an instant, she saw herself again, several continents away, useful, busy, working side by side with someone who shared the same dreams. A hard life, but a thoroughly lived life. The one she'd thought she'd wanted.

A scandalous thing it would be, to leave her husband. Then again, her husband had made a habit of leaving her.

"Thank you, Geoffrey. You're so kind." She faltered a little. And it was all she said.

How much more peaceful life would have been had she married Geoffrey instead. He never had offered for her; then again, he hadn't been given a living until after she'd nearly made love to his cousin by moonlight in the sculpture gallery, and so it was impossible to know whether he would have or not. And unfair, she thought, to ask him whether he might have.

"When will Rhys next return?" Geoffrey wanted to know.

"I don't know."

And in the wake of these three lonely little words was a moment there where Geoffrey could almost have persuaded her to abandon everything. For she was young, and her life stretched ahead of her, lonelier for what might have been.

She was Egyptian and Irish, Louisette was, and born in France. Sloe-eyed, silky-haired, lips as inviting as a velvet pillow, and all but entirely spilling from her gossamer gown were a pair of breasts the color of milk and honey stirred together. She was redolent of strong perfume, too, and as she had chosen to drape herself over Rhys, her hands sliding down his chest, her soft breasts pressing against his shoulders, he knew *he* would be redolent of her perfume by morning.

He could feel her breasts shift against the back of his neck every time he reached for a card. She breathed softly in his ear as he reviewed his hand. It was physically impossible to be unmoved. He did smile a little for her benefit, which prompted her to touch her tongue to his ear.

You just take.

Oh, and how she'd looked when she'd said it. That diffident hand playing in her hair, her face flushed and unhappy. So arrestingly lovely, she was. So generous with her passion, a passion *he'd* shown her she possessed. So generous with her trust, a trust he'd never really earned.

A similarly exotic girl was draped all over Wyndham, who sat across from him holding a hand of cards, and Wyndham looked more aware of the girl than the cards. His hand had risen to settle companionably on the girl's breast. He gave it a pat. All the girls were accommodating here at The Velvet Glove. They'd all been particularly sympathetic when they'd learned the earl had been recently married. And since his wife was not in evidence, it was assumed it was a marriage of convenience, the sort foisted upon men of his station at his time of life.

Louisette, Bettina, and all the other ladies at The Velvet Glove stood ready to help him satisfy any appetites a wife was disinclined to satisfy.

What the bloody hell did she want?

He *had* taken. He'd taken advantage of her innate passion, her innate generosity, her capacity for pleasure . . . Because he'd never thought it anything but his right to do so. Because he thought she'd wanted it, too.

Because it was all he knew how to do and give.

"Rawden, are you ever going to play?"

He paused, his gaze moving from his cards, to the sultry room at The Velvet Glove, to the girls sprawled in shadowy embraces with the men who had the money to pay for their attentions.

"I fold."

He lowered his cards. Louisette's hands trailed back up his chest to tangle in his hair. He turned his head to look at her, and found hope in her dark eyes.

And it wasn't that he wasn't tempted. He studied her, picturing vividly the hour or so he could spend upstairs with her. She tilted her head invitingly.

He'd spent so many hours like that, in so many arms like that, and—

He swiftly lifted her hand and kissed it gracefully. "Good night, darling."

His last view was of Wyndham's astonished expression as he pushed himself away from the table, away from Louisette, and called for his coat, leaving all of them behind.

What was the use of being an earl if one couldn't depart abruptly and rudely on occasion?

A breath of joy arrived at La Montagne along with a message from Lady Mary Capstraw: she had completed her social migration and was now winging her way back to Tinbury via Buckstead Heath.

And now she was breezing into La Montagne, a silent, beaming Paul in tow, while footmen took care of her trunks, and Paul excused himself to freshen up.

She seized Sabrina in a great hug.

"Countess! Shall I curtsy? I aver, *look* at you! Show me all your new clothes, if you please! We can stay just the evening, I fear, as I've promised to move on to visit the Gordons by next week, and if the weather turns dreadful again, we shall be stuck in the coaching inn outside of Buckstead Heath, and the food there wreaks havoc upon Paul's delicate digestion. And oh, let us call for some tea in your cunning green sitting room. Where is your handsome husband?"

"London," Sabrina answered shortly.

"Ah, London! How very exciting. Sabrina, that reminds me! I just visited with Katherine Morton—"

Sabrina could scarcely keep up with all of Mary's acquaintances. "Blond hair and freckles and two boys?"

"*Red* hair and freckles and a new little girl," Mary corrected. "She'd been to London and she'd brought a copy of the *Times*. I didn't mean to read it—"

Sabrina couldn't imagine Mary voluntarily reading a newspaper. "No? How on earth did it happen?"

"But there was a very exciting story in the paper. And Sabrina, I thought of you. For it came out that the mother of the Viscount Grantham's wife, Lady Susannah, was the mistress of a politician named Richard Lockwood, many years ago, and she was accused of murdering her protector, but they never did find her, and they say she's innocent."

Sabrina didn't particularly want to hear about mistresses at the moment, given that it was all too easy to picture her husband once again in the arms of Sophia Licari.

"Mary, really. I think many men have mistresses." She tried to sound blasé. It wasn't a sentence she could have uttered with any ease or authority just a few weeks earlier.

"Oh, so I've heard. I'm certain yours has given up his, however." She gave Sabrina a pat. "But, Sabrina, it's truly the oddest thing. It came out in the trial that Anna Holt, the mistress, had three daughters. One of them is now Lady Grantham, the other is married to the most divine man—it's Katherine who told me that he's divine—who owns The Family Emporium in London, and the other is still missing. And you'll never guess what her name is supposed to be."

Mary paused, a taste for drama taking over, and leaned forward, her entire face an exclamation point.

Sabrina decided to indulge her. "What is her name supposed to be?"

"Sabrina."

Sabrina's cup of tea paused halfway to her mouth. She frowned a little.

"Like . . . my name? Sabrina?"

"*Just* like your name. Sabrina." Mary was aquiver.

"And the mother's name was . . ." Sabrina knew, it was just that it seemed so . . .

For the first time in days a ray of light penetrated her heart.

"Anna Holt!" Mary nearly shouted in delight. "Anna, Sabrina! Her name was Anna! And that's what it says on the back of your miniature. You might be the daughter of a *mistress*."

She said this with particular relish.

Sabrina remembered Rhys's words when she'd snapped that she was adopted: *Well, that explains everything.* He'd said it to be incorrigible, of course. But she wondered if it did explain why she'd all but mounted the man in the statue gallery the first time he'd touched her. Or her temper. Or . . .

She was dizzy with the wonder of it.

"Well, you're certainly too pretty to be the daughter of a vicar," Mary added as she sipped her tea.

"Mary!"

"Really, Sabrina, you should see the daughters of Mr. Wilson, the vicar in St. Wilberforce where Katherine Morton lives. A pair of horses, the poor things."

Sabrina wasn't proud of it, but she laughed. "Mary, you must be kind," she insisted. "It has naught to do with the fact that their father is a vicar, I'm certain. But you read about this in . . ."

"The *Times.* Which is the most reputable newspaper in London. Perhaps the only reputable newspaper. Paul knows these things, you see," she said proudly.

"And *why* was it in the paper?"

"A trial. It seems Anna Holt supposedly murdered her protector many years ago, but now they know she did not. A Mr. Morley did. Or had it done. I cannot recall. But no one has seen Anna Holt since." Mary delivered this last sentence with a good deal of dramatic flair. "Paul might be able to tell you more, but he doesn't think it proper for me to know such things."

Paul didn't quite think it proper for Mary to fill her head with too many things from books, and was a bit confused by Sabrina's penchant for doing just that. But

Sabrina seemed to make Mary happy, and so he didn't complain overmuch.

Sabrina was quiet, looking about the room. She wondered if one day she would look at this room and think: *This is where I finally learned who I am.*

"A good many people are named Sabrina, Mary."

"True enough," Mary agreed.

"And a good many people are named Anna."

"And that is also true." She'd begun to sound a little disappointed.

"But it's an interesting coincidence," Sabrina allowed.

Mary brightened. "Isn't it? Imagine. You might very well be the daughter of a *mistress*." Her enthusiasm was gaining momentum again. "My goodness. The sister of a viscount! The wife of an earl! You are proving so much more interesting than Paul would prefer you to be."

The last words trailed off a little, as if the momentum had carried them out of her mouth against her volition, and she looked a bit guilty.

Sabrina merely patted Mary's knee, as this hadn't been a surprise at all.

"Tell me about Katherine's girls."

Sabrina could listen to Mary chatter without saying much of anything in response. Mary's chatter was like pleasant familiar music played in the background while she retreated to the privacy of her thoughts.

She'd never told anyone apart from her father of her memory of two other little girls, and a dark night. Of a kind woman with a soft voice and a pianoforte. Fragments of memories, worn away by time.

And she wondered if, perhaps, she ought to write a letter to Lady Grantham, or if the very idea of it was too absurd. The hope was so sweet, so unexpected, she almost hated to risk it by seeking the truth.

"What are you regarding so closely, Rhys?"

Wyndham, invited to White's by Rhys, was bored, as *he* would rather not be reading, and Rhys was clearly absorbed in a book. Wyndham peered over Rhys's shoulder. "It looks like . . ." He sounded alarmed. "It looks like a number of drawings of windmills."

Rhys glanced up at him balefully.

Wyndham fixed Rhys with an intent gaze, brow furrowed in concern. Rhys returned his gaze to the book.

Wyndham continued to stare at him.

"Ask your next question, Wyndham," Rhys said absently.

"*Why?*"

"Because I think that if I build a tower mill opposite the post mill on Buckstead Heath, I can grind the grain, plant the land that hasn't been used, and sell the excess for profit."

Wyndham was silent.

"Madame Galeau at The Velvet Glove has a new girl," he finally said. "And she does things you would *not* believe."

Rhys looked up from his book, interest mildly piqued. "Does she?"

"Ah, there you are, Rawden. I was just trying to ascertain if you were still in there somewhere. You've not been yourself of late."

What on earth is "myself"?

"I don't know whether she has a new girl, truly. But she generally does," Wyndham said cheerfully. "Will you be joining me?"

"I'll join you," Rhys said absently.

Wyndham lifted up Rhys's glass, sniffed it, shrugged, and finished it for him.

Rhys returned his gaze to his book of windmills, and seemed lost for another moment.

"You know, Rhys, perhaps a little country air will do you good." Wyndham said this gently.

The gentleness made Rhys irritable. "I prefer the city." He clapped the book closed.

And that evening—or rather, that dawn—Rhys staggered out of his carriage and up the steps of his town house as the sun was rising. Madame Galeau had indeed taken on a new girl, and there had been quite an extraordinary performance of sorts featuring several girls, and then all the men had been invited to—

Which was when Rhys had called for a carriage and left. The *ton* was talking, he knew. About him, and why he hadn't touched a woman in weeks.

The Libertine is besotted with his wife.

It made him furious.

He made it up the steps to the door, which was opened by his very accommodating butler.

"Tea," he croaked. "And draw a bath."

He wanted to clean the scent of The Velvet Glove from him, and soak in a bath, and not think.

And when he was clean again, and sober again, he discovered a letter was waiting for him. The handwriting on it was unfamiliar.

And for a moment he knew disappointment that it wasn't Mrs. Bailey's dutiful hand.

Rhys took it with him to his study, and over the pot of tea he broke the seal and read it.

He went still. Surprise and sadness swamped him with startling suddenness.

There were only a few words, but he read them twice, just to make certain he'd read them correctly. Just in case it wasn't true.

But they read the same the second time, and he was forced to believe them. He sat with them, and thought, and remembered.

At another time he might have reached for the brandy decanter. He might have gone back to his club. He might have gone to Manton's to shoot until his arm ached from holding up a pistol. Instead, he gazed out the window for some time at the streets of London coming awake.

And then he called for his carriage.

CHAPTER TWENTY

WHEN THE CARRIAGE rolled into the cobblestoned courtyard of La Montagne, Rhys leaped out and all but dashed up the steps. He rang for Mrs. Bailey immediately, and moments later she bustled toward him as he stood in La Montagne's vast foyer.

"My lord! We—"

"Weren't expecting me. I know. I apologize, Mrs. Bailey. I regret I didn't leave you enough time to sound the trumpets and strew flowers in my path."

Mrs. Bailey offered up a strained but dutiful smile. Poor woman, to be saddled with an employer such as he who *would* insist on jesting.

"Where is the countess, Mrs. Bailey? I'd like to speak with her."

The housekeeper hesitated. Her face had gone just a little wary. "The countess isn't in at the moment, sir."

He disliked her hesitation and the wariness. "Where is she?" He tried and failed to keep it from sounding like a demand.

Mrs. Bailey folded her hands against her apron, and pursed her lips a bit before answering, as if deciding upon what to tell him. "You can find her at the vicarage, sir."

Was he imagining the faintly accusatory tone?

Rhys studied the housekeeper with narrowed eyes. She gazed levelly back at him. She was in her fifties at the very least, Mrs. Bailey was, and her hair was almost completely hidden beneath her cap, but a few spiraling ash-colored strands peeked out at the temples. Her complexion was ruddy, her flesh and drooping, dragging the corners of her mouth down, forming pouches beneath her eyes. Those eyes were surprisingly lovely. A shade of turquoise, ringed in gold. It made him wonder if she'd stories to tell. One could hardly go through life unscathed with a pair of eyes so lovely.

And was the accusation for him, or for Sabrina?

He wanted to ask, "Is Sabrina often at the vicarage?" when he realized how this would sound: a confession that he, the Earl of Rawden, knew little of the habits of his wife; had thought, until now, so little of the habits of his wife. Did Mrs. Bailey suspect he would disapprove of Sabrina's being at the vicarage? Or did Mrs. Bailey know for certain that Sabrina was up to something of which he would never approve?

But it was his own fault, if that were the case. He'd given Geoffrey the living in part as a gift to Sabrina, so she would have a friend near. He hadn't particularly cared what sort of relationship his cousin and his wife shared.

But now . . . now he intended to learn a good deal about the habits of his wife.

"Thank you," he said stiffly.

Mrs. Bailey nodded once. Waited for him to dismiss her.

He turned to leave, then paused. "Mrs. Bailey?"

"Yes, my lord?"

"Has anyone ever told you that you have very pretty eyes?"

Mrs. Bailey's face went utterly immobile, and she drew in a sharp breath, as though the compliment had been a fist to her ribs.

And then before his eyes, a soft pink slowly stained her skin, and everything about her softened and glowed. And she was beautiful.

"No, sir."

He smiled a little. "We've all been remiss, then."

And *that,* Rhys reminded himself, was the power of words, whether or not he ever wrote another one.

Sabrina had been sitting and dutifully listening to Geoffrey's sermon when Geoffrey abruptly stopped talking, and stared toward the entrance of the church. Sabrina was surprised to see a quick flush darken his cheeks.

She whirled around. Her hand went up over her heart, as if to restrain it from leaping right out of her. She was on her feet instantly.

"Rhys!"

He stood in the doorway, hovering as though deciding whether to enter. He was turning his hat this way and that abstractedly in his gloved hands. His face was unreadable from where she stood, but she saw the light of his pale eyes from where she stood, and his gaze was fixed rather decisively on her.

"Mrs. Bailey told me I could find you here." His voice was low and even, giving away nothing of his mood. And then, as a seeming afterthought, he added, "Geoffrey." He directed this to his cousin and gave a curt shallow nod.

Sabrina saw Geoffrey's eyes flicker an instant, a bright and startling flash of resentment. And then he bowed, conscious of his position, aware that a mere nod would never do.

Sabrina realized she was halfway up the aisle to Rhys. And then she slowed when she was closer to perhaps read his features, to better gauge his mood.

It wasn't one she'd seen before on his face.

"Is aught amiss?" Her voice was fainter than she'd like it to be.

"No," he said shortly, and extended his arm. She hesitated a moment—the hesitation won her an uplifted brow—and she looped hers through it, cautiously.

And then Rhys turned and strolled arm in arm with her out the door of the church, through the yard of tilting headstones, to where Gallegos was tethered at the gate and puffing air from his nostrils.

Sabrina realized belatedly that neither of them had bid Geoffrey good day.

"Have you come for a visit, then?" she began cautiously.

"Yes."

More silence from her husband. But it wasn't the seething sort. He seemed . . . reflective.

"How did you get here, Sabrina?" he asked after a moment.

"I walked."

"Walked!"

She smiled at his astonishment. "'Tisn't far, my Lord Barouche. I enjoy the exercise. And 'tis safe enough to walk alone here in town. Everyone knows me."

He smiled a little, but the weight of whatever occupied his thoughts seemed to prevent smiles from lingering overlong. He fell quiet again, and he replaced his hat atop his head. He looked altogether rumpled, his coat and trousers wrinkled, which was surprising, when normally he was flawlessly groomed. Sabrina suspected he'd come nearly straight from London to the vicarage, and hadn't even paused to freshen himself before he took Gallegos out.

"It's cold today," he said.

"Yes." She said nothing more. She'd decided to leave the conversation uncluttered, to allow him room to say whatever it was he'd come here to say.

And then a terrible little suspicion struck: Did he suspect that she and Geoffrey . . . ?

The thought horrified her. She felt her cold cheeks heating; a tiny, nauseating concern twisted in the pit of her stomach. Still, she would have expected fury, or cold rejection from him, if that were the case. This man of passions. Not this abstracted, stilted conversation.

And then Rhys turned, absently reaching out to twine the ends of her muffler more tightly about her throat, tuck them into her pelisse. A proprietary little gesture, and it made her heart give a sweet little kick. She looked up at him questioningly, but he'd turned his head again. He was looking toward the village, his light eyes squinting against the hard winter light, deepening the fan of lines around them.

She waited. The wind plucked at her muffler and yanked an end from her pelisse, batting it about. She retrieved it, settled it back into place.

Rhys didn't seem to feel the cold, oddly enough, though he was bundled against it, a thick, woolen scarf beneath his chin.

And then she noticed: it was the one she'd made for him.

She felt as though he were wearing her favor into battle.

"Damien died. A letter reached me yesterday about it." He said it almost conversationally.

Sabrina's breath caught. She felt his loss in the pit of her stomach. And she was silent.

But through the silence, and the weight of the loss, came a quiet, dawning elation:

He'd come to her. Rhys had come to her.

"Very recently?" she said gently.

He still didn't turn around, but she could see his half smile in profile. He tipped his head back a bit. "Oh, the letter reached me only yesterday, but it seems he's been in the ground for some time. He was ill. Left me his poetry manuscripts and ten pounds in his will, with instructions to wager it on a black horse."

"Ah, then you must of course do so at the first available opportunity." She said it lightly, as she suspected the lightness would be easier for him to bear right now.

He grunted a short laugh. "I'll lose. He had terrible instincts."

"But he took joy in employing them. And he always remembered you. Perhaps you can pay your respects in Little Orrick."

Rhys turned slowly then, looked down at her, his brows close together, his perusal very nearly scholarly in its seriousness. As though if he studied her long enough he could find the answer to some question he was having difficulty forming.

She wanted to touch him; but she tentatively reached up and fussed with the coils of the muffler around his neck instead, though it didn't need arranging.

He caught her wrists in his hands, gently, and she thought for an instant he might kiss her. She saw the flare of intent, then indecision flicker in his eyes. He held her gaze a moment, then gave her hands a quick squeeze and released them, turning from her.

"Will you ride back to the house with me on Gallegos? Or would you prefer to walk?"

"He can carry the two of us?"

"You're not precisely a sylph, but he'll manage."

Sabrina laughed. "Ah, my silver-tongued husband."

He smiled, too. And what a beautiful smile the man had, a smile precisely designed to break hearts.

He lifted her up so that she sat astride, and then his warm body was in the saddle behind her, his arms tucked around her, and he took the reins up in his fist. His now-familiar scent had become somehow less sensually disturbing but more comforting, more deeply arousing. The two of them fit a bit snugly together on the saddle. She tilted her head back against his shoulder, against the pillow of his scarf and cold smooth cheek, because she sensed he needed the contact.

And as they rode back to La Montagne, they passed the mill.

"Looks to be in good working order now," Rhys commented. "I'll call on Mr. Pike this week."

It was his way of saying he intended to stay.

When they returned to La Montagne, Rhys asked Mrs. Bailey to send chocolate into the library for himself and the countess. Sabrina gave him a questioning look. She seemed a bit wary, and he could hardly blame her.

He turned to her. "Will you join me?"

"But of course," she told him politely.

Out of duty, or because you want to? He didn't say it aloud. But he'd seen her face when he'd appeared in the doorway of the vicarage, and he'd seen her face when she'd come to him down the aisle. This was a woman who could hide nothing. And when he had seen her face the question that had clouded his mind when he'd headed to the vicarage had vanished as surely as a clean wind had swept it away.

The chocolate arrived with Mrs. Bailey, who left them again.

"Sabrina . . . may I ask you a question?"

His wife regarded him somewhat warily, as though he'd replaced her husband with a polite stranger. It was distantly amusing to him.

"Yes, of course."

"Were you in love with Geoffrey?"

"Oh." The sound escaped her, a puff of shocked breath.

Clearly not the question she was expecting. She watched his face for a long time, and he watched the passage of thought over hers. Saw the color leaving her cheeks.

"Rhys . . . you don't think I . . . that Geoffrey and I . . . at the vicarage . . . I swear I . . ."

"No," he said quickly, adamantly. Because her face had told him. He'd known at once. "No," he repeated softly.

She closed her eyes briefly in relief, opened them again.

"I wanted to know, Sabrina . . ." This was a difficult question for a very proud man to ask. "I wanted to know . . . if you're . . ." Good God. What was the proper word here? "Disappointed."

That she now had a different life, a different man, a different way of being, than what she'd always wanted.

Either she was thinking about it, or she was deliberately making him wait for it. Watching him with those clear eyes.

"No, Rhys," she said, finally. "I'm not disappointed."

Oh, and that smile of hers. A dangerous, soft smile that wrapped all around him, warm as her skin after lovemaking, warmer than spring sun.

He gave a short nod, exhaled.

When he seemed disinclined to speak again, Sabrina turned toward the bookcase, pretended to be perusing the books.

"Sabrina?"

She turned away from the bookcase, a query in her face.

"I should like to make love to you."

Her eyes flew open wide. And he watched, with interest, as that lovely shade of rose made slow progress from her collar to her hairline. He heard belatedly how formal he'd sounded. How like a pronouncement it had been.

Sabrina gave a little laugh. "You sound as though you are ordering up lamb for dinner."

"Do I? My apologies. Nevertheless, I should like— *very* much—to make love to you."

A certain firm vehemence in his delivery. He was very much enjoying making her blush.

She looked at him a moment, utterly, beautifully disconcerted. And then her eyes dropped swiftly as if her composure could be found somewhere on the floor. She looked up again.

"I should like that, too." She said it gravely. Then added: "Very much." In a tone that rivaled his own for sultriness. Mischief sparking in her green eyes.

And he was suddenly weightless. And for some reason, for nearly a minute, he could only smile at her foolishly. And she smiled back at him.

He realized, at last, he ought to say something. "Good," he finally managed. And continued to smile foolishly.

But then her face grew serious once again, and he felt a twinge of trepidation.

"I should like some clarification, my lord."

"Clar—"

"Yes. When would you like to make love to me?"

"Oh. Now." Quite adamantly said. He was doing a remarkable job, if he said so himself, of restraining his rampant passions. "In your chambers. If you're amenable to that."

He smiled crookedly as he watched her hands fidget in her skirt for a moment. He could see she was already breathless, her shoulders moving more quickly.

"Well," she said thoughtfully, "we cannot very well bolt the room together straight up the stairs for your chamber, or the servants will know what we're about."

Ah, his practical wife. He was teetering on the brink of hilarity now. Imagine, The Libertine negotiating the logistics of lovemaking as though planning a dinner party. "Do you truly think there's ever a time when they don't know what we're about, Sabrina?"

She tilted her head in thought, and didn't answer the question, as it was obviously rhetorical. "I shall go up to our rooms first; you shall wait ten minutes, and then you shall follow me." As decisive as a general.

He blinked. "Very well," he agreed equably.

And then she was across the room and at the door with a speed that gratified everything male in him.

She paused there and turned. "Rhys?"

He looked up, heartbeat arrested.

"It will be a long ten minutes."

She threw a tiny crooked smile over her shoulder and slipped out of the room.

And his blood turned to lava.

He arrived to find the room brilliant with sunlight, the heavy curtains pushed aside all around; a fire leaping high in the grate.

Sabrina was standing in the center of the room, and smiled shyly when she saw him. She glanced toward the curtains.

"Leave them open," he said suddenly. He could not recall making love to anyone in brilliant daylight. And suddenly it seemed the best way of all to make love to Sabrina.

He came and stood before her, looking down into those clear green eyes for a long moment, as though seeing her for the first time, and she met his gaze, shy but bold at the same time.

It was she who raised her arms toward him, hesitantly at first, and then her hands landed on the knot of his cravat. He stood still while she loosened it slowly, pulled it gently from his throat, folded it in her hands, set it aside. She turned so he could loosen the laces on her gown.

With tender solicitousness, in silence, they undressed each other, buttons and laces and boots. Slowly, as though they had all the time in the world. And this unhurried prelude to lovemaking contained a passion as pure and brilliant as the light pouring in the window.

And when they were undressed, he stood back to admire his wife. All this lovely, vulnerable softness just for him. Her skin glowed lustrous, pale and blue-veined, all sweet curves: those full upthrust breasts tipped in palest pink, those round hips. His hands finally decided to rest on her narrow waist, because the place seemed simply made for his hands. When he did, Sabrina's eyes closed and she drew in a swift uneven breath. And then she gave a short laugh, as though she was half amazed, half embarrassed, that his simple touch could so easily undo her.

And this undid him.

He pulled her closer, until no space remained between their bodies, until they were skin to skin. She melted so easily into his arms he almost wanted to tell her such total trust of *any* human being, let alone him, was unwise. But even as it made him feel ferociously protective, it aroused him so fiercely it was a physical pain, and his breath snagged in his throat.

And then he kissed her, finding her soft mouth with his own, sinking into a kiss so sweet it was barbed, and echoed everywhere in him.

He tipped her gently to the bed, and the sunlight was almost a third partner in the room, enveloping the two of them as they set out to make love with quiet, joyful ferocity. Rhys's hands moved over every texture of her, the silky density of her hair, the taut smoothness of her skin, the crisper, curling hair between her legs, and there his fingers delved lightly. To his profound satisfaction, he found her satiny and wet.

And when he did, she gasped and took his earlobe lightly between her teeth. The sensation sent such a shock of pleasure through him that he laughed, startled, and turned his head to find her smiling, pleased with herself.

He covered her smile with a kiss, then caught her wrists in one hand and levered them slowly back, pinned them above her head. "Minx," he murmured against her mouth. His fingers dipped again, lightly, and her legs dropped apart to allow him better access. He caressed, expertly, precisely, long enough to drag a moan of pleasure from her. And then stopped long enough to elicit a protest:

"Rhys—*please*—"

Far be it from him to make the vicar's daughter beg.

He was a poet: he understood rhythm and pattern, he understood beauty and crescendo. He watched her, and listened to her breathing, and his fingers played her like a conductor until she was writhing, arching into his touch.

And then coming apart with a soundless scream, bowing up toward him.

Beautiful.

He propped himself up on his elbow to admire her for a moment, glowing and flushed, lips rosy and swollen from kisses, eyes still dazed and warm. The fire popped and spit sparks behind them. Sabrina touched his face lightly with the backs of her fingers. A gesture so tender his heart kicked.

"Come here," she whispered. She captured his waist with her thighs, pulling him closely against her. Her hands smoothed down the long muscles of his back, cupped his buttocks, pressed his erection hard against her. "Now, Rhys. Please, now."

He braced himself above her, took her with swift even thrusts, no finesse, just primal intent. And as he moved over her he gazed down at his wife, her hair tangled over the counterpane, head thrown back, her eyes fixed with his. He watched her reveling in his pleasure until he could see her no longer, and his own release rushed upon him, all but seized him from his own body, and he cried out the wonder of it.

"Again?" he whispered hopefully.

They were lying twined, spent, and Sabrina hardly knew her limbs from his. Sabrina trailed a hand down his damp chest, down the dark line of hair that bisected his ribs, to investigate. Sure enough: he was enormously, flatteringly hard.

She gave him a mildly incredulous look.

He smiled a wicked little smile, pleased with himself. And shrugged a little shrug with one of those beautiful, muscled shoulders.

She surprised him with a kiss, a soft one, openmouthed, because she loved the way he tasted. Warm and tart and dark, reassuring and arousing all at once. And when she did, she saw something in his eyes then that made her want to protect him, somehow. He didn't disguise as much as he thought.

He took her face in his hands, swept back her sweat-dampened hair, and kissed her his way. And for a long while it was only this, the tender play of tongues and lips over each other, a leisurely feast that nevertheless fueled the need that seemed to hover always just below the surface for them, the ravenous beast in the cellar, demanding satisfaction. Their bodies inevitably began to strain together again, and their hands reached for each other in deliberate caresses.

And boldly, she found the warm hard length of him and dragged her hands over him until he buried his face against her throat, and his breath became ragged against her.

"*Sabrina,*" he whispered.

It was wondrous, this power she had.

Oh, so slow now. As though they merely wanted to be joined.

Sabrina floated, and thought.

"Happiness" was such a vibrant word when you said it and thought about it, Sabrina reflected; it had always seemed like such an *active* word. She'd never suspected happiness was in truth a simple thing comprising quiet and warmth: the warmth of the sun upon her bare skin, the warmth of a man's long body pressed against hers as he slept, the sound of his breathing, deep and steady and sated, his ribs rising and falling against her back. Comprising all of that . . . and hope.

She was in love with her husband.

She suspected that her husband—The Libertine—was falling in love with her.

She supposed it was possible she was just a novelty for him. This was a man who sought out and had experienced an extraordinary array of diversions, after all, and no doubt was running out of new things to distract him. The man who wrote so beautifully about passion, and never about love.

But love wasn't an experience that could be sought. Love finds you, Sabrina thought. Love really gives you no choice in the matter.

She suspected that when Rhys came to her today, he was responding to some impulse within himself he didn't fully understand. But she thought he'd found whatever it was he sought, and it wasn't just solace in a woman's body. And it was why he slept so peacefully now. Was, in fact, snoring just a little against the back of her neck.

She was fairly certain he didn't know how he felt. It didn't matter, for she knew how she felt. They had forever, now, for him to decide how he felt.

And for her to discover precisely how *often* he snored.

CHAPTER TWENTY-ONE

R HYS STAYED. She slept in his arms at night, she woke entangled with him in the morning. Sabrina learned every bit of his body by touching and tasting it, marveling at it, the muscles and scars, his eyelashes, his moles (two on his arm, one on his thigh, one at the nape of his neck), that one strange little hair springing from his biceps. She learned all the male smells of him, the musk and sweetness and all the less-pleasant ones, too. Memorized the faint lines beneath his eyes. Learned all his moods, the mischievous, the impatient, the irritable, the quiet, and perhaps, most particularly, the passionate.

They argued. He was occasionally pompous and proud and dictatorial.

So was she.

She forced him to tell her the stories of all his scars (war, and hunting, a riding accident, a dog bite), and he wanted to know about the one on her knee (a little reckless sledding with her brother and a collision with a beech tree). Had he killed a man in a duel? (No.) Had he ever lived with his mistress? (God, no.) Did he spend profligately on his reprobate friends? (Of course.)

They rode out to Buckstead Heath to see to the roofs, and the drainage ditches, and simply for the pleasure of riding in the open air together.

And at last Sabrina saw Santoro's stained-glass windows, the pensive moon and vivid stars, reflected on the floor of the Star Room. For of course Rhys knew precisely what time of day it would shine there. They shared a moment of quiet and awe.

They made love in nearly every room at La Montagne. It was appalling, really. Shameless.

Glorious.

For now. And little by little, Sabrina allowed herself to believe it would be glorious, or at least very close to it, for always.

The week stretched into two weeks, and into three, and still Rhys felt disinclined to return to London. He also felt disinclined to think about the reasons why. He didn't want to *think* at all about why he wanted to be here. He only wanted to be. He wanted to enjoy his wife, this astonishing gift of a woman, and his land, and this newness that seemed infinite in its variety. Part of him was braced for the return of the restlessness that drove him to always seek something to feed it. Part of him suspected it was only a matter of time. And yet, at least for now, there was something about the fullness of their days that was poetry and wine and music all in one.

He couldn't write. He'd ceased to miss it, somehow.

He slid into bed next to Sabrina. The fire had been built up high, because neither of them troubled with night rails or dressing gowns anymore, as they rapidly came off anyway. He pressed himself against her soft warmth.

"Isn't it about time for Lady Mary Capstraw to come for a visit again, Sabrina? She migrates rather like birds, doesn't she?"

Sabrina laughed. "She *was* here, Rhys, and you missed her, more's the pity. Because if you'd been here, you would have learned about Paul's delicate digestion, and other such fascinating things."

"My own digestion is of tempered steel," he said solemnly.

"That's not the only thing of yours made of tempered steel," Sabrina purred, her hands wandering south of his torso.

"*Sa*brina!" Rhys's mouth dropped open in mock scandal. She was a revelation every moment. He shifted his legs to aid her exploration just a bit.

She giggled again, rolled over onto her back so that her breasts rose tantalizingly just above the bedclothes.

"And Mary told me the most remarkable thing, Rhys. Of a trial in London. A politician named Morley is accused of murder and treason, and it has something to do with Viscount and Lady Grantham. But it came out that Lady Grantham had two sisters—one is named Sylvie, and the other is Sabrina! And they cannot find Sabrina anywhere. The funniest part is that their mother's name was Anna Holt! Anna, like my mother. Isn't that funny?"

It was remarkable how smoothly he was able to react to the moment. Even as his stomach turned to ice.

"Funny," he managed to say convincingly. "Perhaps it's a coincidence."

"That's what I thought," Sabrina said. "But still, it seemed funny." Her voice was so wistful. "I've longed for sisters all my life."

Rhys didn't believe in coincidences.

"Have you heard of the trial?" she asked him when he said nothing else.

"I have," he said. And didn't expound. He waited a moment, and said the words idly. "Sabrina, would you show me the image of your mother?"

She slithered out of bed and dashed, a vision in curving white nudeness, to her wardrobe, and retrieved it, then wriggled back into bed next to him.

"Here," she said softly.

He took it in his hands. He stared.

He turned it over, saw the script: *"To Sabrina Charity, her mother Anna."*

"How did you get this?" He heard his own voice almost distantly. He was pushing it out through the weight of memories, of disbelief. Of the struggle to disguise astonishment, and guilt. For something in him had suspected for some time now.

"It was left with me when I was a very little girl. I don't really remember her. Isn't she pretty?"

"Beautiful," Rhys agreed faintly, after a moment. "She looks just like you."

She smiled up at him. He couldn't quite smile back.

He'd once said to Sabrina: *Pretending something didn't happen doesn't quite mean it didn't happen.*

But at the moment, he didn't know what else to do. And here at La Montagne, in the country, in this shocking moment, he pretended that it was possible for the past not to ever touch them.

When a certain trial concluded in London, this might even prove true.

"What's the matter, Rhys? Is it your digestion?" she teased. "Your face has gone awfully funny."

He was quiet for a moment longer.

"It's just that I want you so very much, Sabrina," he finally said.

He pulled her over him, and slowly, thoroughly, proceeded to show her the truth of this, as if this were the last opportunity he'd ever have to touch her.

"We've a message from the Capstraw home!" Susannah told Kit as he crawled into bed for the evening next to her. She was propped up with the message on her knees, savoring it.

"What does it say?" Kit dragged a finger up her arm, and let it wander in the soft curls spilling from her nightcap.

Susannah was focused on the message. "Lady Mary has gone to a house party at La Montagne, it says. And she has taken along a Miss Sabrina Fairleigh."

"*La Montagne?*" Kit was incredulous. "The Earl of Rawden's home?"

"Is that the Earl of Rawden's home? Isn't he . . ." Susannah paused, and said the words delicately. "The Libertine?"

"Oh, yes," Kit confirmed, sounding impressed. "He certainly is. Perhaps Lady Mary has hidden depths. Perhaps we should invite her to visit. Then again, I've heard he's acquired a wife he can't get enough of, and the *ton* hasn't seen him in ages, or so the rumor goes. Really very embarrassing for the man, if it is indeed true. Still, let's have Lady Mary in for dinner."

Susannah gave her husband a playful swat. "I want to go there, Kit. Sylvie and I should go straight to La Montagne. No one mentioned how long Sabrina Fairleigh and Lady Mary intended to stay at La Montagne, and she may not remain for long. And we may never catch up to her again!"

"Can you wait for her to return to Tinbury and Vicar Fairleigh? She's bound to, you know, as she'll eventually run out of places to visit."

"What if she doesn't? What if she's beset by . . . *high-waymen*, or Lady Mary Capstraw drags her about on an endless round of social calls, and we follow her in circles forever, but we never, *never* catch up—"

"Susannah," Kit said softly, stemming the tide of her anxiety. He pressed a kiss against her shoulder. "We'll find her."

Susannah sighed. "But Sylvie and I should go," she insisted. "As soon as possible."

"It's nearly a two-day journey from London to there, Susannah, and the weather—"

He saw the bald entreaty on her face. He knew he would have to let her go.

"I need to remain in London for Morley's trial. And I know Tom can't afford to leave The Family Emporium yet again. But you and Sylvie will take a full complement of armed footmen."

"Thank you," she said softly. "You're the very best husband."

"I know," Kit sighed. "It's such a burden."

He moved his kiss up from her shoulder to her throat.

"Kit?" she said softly.

"Mmm?"

"Have you read The Libertine's poetry?"

He hesitated. "Yes."

"Will you read it to me someday?"

"I have a better idea," he murmured. "Why don't I show you what it says?"

As days went by, and the business of La Montagne continued to be consuming, Rhys allowed himself to ease into believing everything would continue on as it was.

A week had passed when Mrs. Bailey came to Rhys in the morning. She found him in his study poring over ideas for the land three miles south of Buckstead Heath. It was decent grazing land; then again, they might plant it, and take advantage of the two windmills that would soon spin in the village. He'd spoken to Mr. Pike about it.

"I've been informed by the footman that two young ladies are in the drawing room, Lord Rawden."

His first reflexive response, the response of the Rhys of old, was faint, pleased surprise: *Funny, but I don't recall sending for young ladies this morning.* Sending for "young ladies" hadn't been out of the realm of the possible for him only a few months ago.

Given how he felt today, it might as well have been a lifetime ago. He'd been another person entirely.

"They are inquiring after a Miss Sabrina Fairleigh," she expounded.

He frowned a little. "Are they from the . . ." He was about to say, "village." But suspicion faded his words.

"Did they present cards, Mrs. Bailey?" he finally managed to ask calmly enough.

"Yes. They are Lady Grantham and a Mrs. Shaughnessy, Lord Rawden."

He hadn't expected to need to address it so soon; perhaps, somewhere deep inside, he hadn't expected to need to address it at all. A desperate, futile hope, he recognized now.

He needed time to think, regardless.

He wanted to ask the housekeeper more questions. *Do they resemble her?* These women Sabrina has looked for, longed for, all her life? To his knowledge, he'd never met either of them. Though he was acquainted with their husbands. Tom Shaughnessy from the deliciously infamous White Lily Theater. Kit Whitelaw . . . a former soldier, a former officer, like himself.

And it was possible, feasible, in this world, that Sabrina, his country girl, would never cross paths with any of them. He'd kept one secret this long; he could accommodate yet another, he told himself.

Instead he said, "Extend your apologies, but do inform them that the earl isn't in at present, and that the woman they are seeking isn't at La Montagne."

And he congratulated himself, darkly, that it wasn't entirely a lie.

CHAPTER TWENTY-TWO

DISAPPOINTMENT MEANT THAT it was quiet inside the Grantham carriage as it pulled away from La Montagne.

"'The woman you seek isn't at La Montagne,'" Susannah repeated slowly to Sylvie in the carriage. "Where do you suppose she *is*? Do you suppose she's moved on? Had she *ever* been at La Montagne? Not terribly helpful, was she, the housekeeper? I suppose we could have insisted upon staying and waiting for the earl to return. What a long way to come in order to be disappointed." Susannah was sounding nearly peevish.

"Perhaps she has simply moved on to another visit?" Sylvie wasn't terribly enthusiastic about country living. She'd lived in cities the entirety of her life, and vast open spaces made her a bit uncomfortable.

"Kit said Lady Mary Capstraw is known for ever visiting. And if she has Sabrina Fairleigh in tow, we might chase them in circles for ages."

"Then let us return to London straightaway," Sylvie suggested gently. "We shall send an urgent message to Lady Mary's home stating that Viscount and Lady Grantham wish to see her. And we've already left a message at the home of Vicar Fairleigh as well. We're very close, Susannah. We shall see her yet. And we'll know soon if she's *our* Sabrina."

Sylvie squeezed her sister's gloved hand, grateful for the reassurance, and hers was squeezed in return.

"Do you suppose we'll like her?" Susannah wondered tentatively. They had both experienced the serendipity of liking each other from the very first. The very idea that they might have never met horrified them.

"She has been raised by a vicar, Sabrina. Perhaps she's very quiet and sedate."

This was such an appalling thought that they both fell silent again.

Susannah leaned forward suddenly and pointed. "Look, Sylvie, a little church! It looks so like the one in Gorringe. I wonder if they have a funny little vicar, too. Shall we have a look inside before we continue home?"

Matins had just been read, and Geoffrey thought he might have a bite to eat and maybe a nip of wine when he looked up and saw two women in the doorway of the church.

He blinked hard. For a moment he thought he was seeing two of Sabrina, but he hadn't been so pleasantly, thoroughly foxed enough to see two of one person in much too long. But something about the way these two women stood, their height, their very presence, called Sabrina strongly to mind. One of them, in fact, could have been her twin.

He assessed them quickly. Fine clothes, from head to toe, both of them. Expensively dressed in fur-lined pelisses, hands tucked into fine muffs, a brawny pair of footmen hovering protectively behind them. Not only were they lovely, they were wealthy, and very likely titled.

"Good afternoon," he said in his best mellifluous Gillray voice.

They curtsied, a pair of flowers bending, and despite his myriad other concerns, he was charmed. Bloody hell, he missed wealthy, titled women. When he'd last been in London, before his father had rescued him and consigned him to a peaceful purgatory as a curate, he'd found the Gillray name and his association with Rhys very useful when it came to charming and courting and bedding the willing married ones.

But now . . . there wasn't a single parishioner in Buckstead Heath who approached Sabrina for beauty, and as Sabrina for some reason hadn't paid a visit in weeks, he was rather starved for it. Because he was a Gillray in that respect, too: beauty was their nectar.

Beauty was their nectar. Now *there* was an image that rivaled any Rhys could conceive, Geoffrey thought, pleased with himself.

"Good day," the one who could have been Sabrina's twin said. "I am Lady Grantham, and this is my sister, Mrs. Sylvie Shaughnessy. May we have a look at your pretty church?"

He frowned a little, and then realized he was frowning, and stopped. The names were familiar, somehow.

"But of course." He bowed to them. "You honor our little church with your presence."

And it had been too long since there had been someone worthy to charm. They smiled at him, and strolled up through the nave, footmen following—burly footmen, Geoffrey noted—studying the carved rood screen.

He refrained from introducing himself; he wondered if they noticed. He'd realized just in time that he was rather nicely hidden away here at Buckstead Heath, and he didn't want any of his creditors to gain an inkling of his whereabouts. One of these young ladies, who no doubt hailed from London, might very well mention it idly on her next visit to the glovemaker's.

"What brings you to Buckstead Heath?" he asked pleasantly instead.

"We are returning to London, and our carriage is passing through your town," Lady Grantham told him.

And then it struck him: *Grantham!* As in *Viscount* Grantham. The other . . . well, he suspected this was the woman Tom Shaughnessy had married. Geoffrey had been to Shaughnessy's theater, The White Lily, on many a happy occasion, until his tastes had acquired an edge that even The White Lily couldn't quite satisfy.

Good God, but up close these women were beautiful.

"Which fortunate resident of our fair village is paying host to you?" It felt wonderful to employ his charms upon someone worthy of them.

"Oh, we've just come from a brief visit to La Montagne. But we were informed the earl is not in residence at present."

This was intriguing, as the earl most certainly *was* in residence at present, as far as Geoffrey knew.

"Isn't he?" he merely repeated idly.

"We are looking for a young lady named Sabrina," Mrs. Shaughnessy told him. "We were told she might be visiting La Montagne. Have you perhaps met her, or heard anything of her? Her father is a vicar." Eagerness in her tone.

This was very, very interesting. Something was amiss.

He'd been away from London for a few months now, but suddenly Geoffrey remembered precisely why the names of these women were so freshly familiar: in his last peek at a London paper, he'd read about Mr. Thaddeus Morley, the politician arrested for murder and treason, his alleged crimes committed many years ago. He was now standing trial. The scandal was undeniably succulent.

But Lady Grantham's name had been mentioned in connection with the trial. And hadn't he read . . .

He *had*! Lady Grantham had been the daughter of Richard Lockwood's mistress. And she'd two other sisters who had never been found. Geoffrey didn't know for certain, but he would warrant that Mrs. Shaughnessy was one of Lady Grantham's sisters.

He could guess who the other sister might be, and these two women were in search of her.

A thrill of intrigue traced Geoffrey's spine. They had come to La Montagne looking for Sabrina, and they'd been told that no such woman lived there. Geoffrey wondered whether Mrs. Bailey had been instructed by the earl to lie to these women about Sabrina.

Some instinct in Geoffrey made him decide to hoard the information and do a little investigating of his own. Because he instinctively suspected whatever he discovered might be worth something in terms of blackmailing his cousin, and God knew he needed some sort of capital desperately.

"No, I fear I don't know anyone named Sabrina."

He saw their lovely faces go briefly downcast.

And a few minutes later, Mrs. Shaughnessy touched Lady Grantham on the arm, and they thanked him and bid him farewell.

* * *

Geoffrey hated coming here; he hated the perpetual darkness, the empty bottles of futile potions everywhere, the incense lit to disguise the smell of encroaching death. The curtains were always pulled closed, as though dying were something to be ashamed of, or as if light would somehow hasten it. When he visited, which was rarely now, Geoffrey was always tempted to yank them back again, to prove there was a world outside this stifling room.

They weren't close; they hadn't been for years. His father and he were too much alike in many ways, and Geoffrey resented that he'd inherited many of his father's weaknesses. His father was dying of drink. He'd conquered his other weakness, and was managing to die with a certain amount of dignity, with enough money to pay a nurse to attend him, but Geoffrey had inherited his other weakness: the taste for gambling.

And it was this weakness that made him desperate enough to enter this home of the dying.

His father had been handsome, once. All the bloody Gillrays were handsome, unless battle or a duel took off a limb or blinded an eye, as it had upon occasion over the centuries. But his father's skin was yellow, his body shriveled in some places and bloated in others, his dark eyes sunken into pools of red.

"Geoffrey." His father's voice was ironic, even in its weakness. "To what do I owe this pleasure?"

"I just wanted to see you, Fath—"

The voice was surprisingly strong. "Don't lie to a dying man, son. I know you too well. Tell me why you are really here. You want something. What is it?"

Geoffrey sat next to his father's bed. "I'm afraid, Father."

It was a blurt, and perhaps the most honest thing he'd said to anyone in some time.

"Are you in debt, son?"

Geoffrey didn't answer; "debt" seemed like such a small word for the danger he now faced. His hands had gone cold.

"I asked Rhys for money, Father. He won't give it to me."

And it wasn't the full truth, but it aroused his father's sympathy just a little, which was what he needed now.

"He always had a streak of righteousness, Rhys. But he isn't pure as the driven snow, is he, son? Has quite a reputation, doesn't he still? Duels and whatnot?"

Geoffrey disregarded this for now. "I need you to tell me something, Father. Something I've always wanted to know."

"What is it, Geoffrey?"

"Years ago . . . Well, first there was no money; and then we were all comfortable again, all the Gillrays. Where did the money come from?"

His father was silent for a long time.

"You were only fifteen years old then, Geoffrey."

"But I remember being afraid, because there was never any money. And then there *was* money. But no one spoke of it. And Rhys . . . well, you should see what he has now, Father. La Montagne and everything in it. And I have nothing."

His father was silent, and stared at him with those sunken, bleeding eyes. His breath was fetid, and Geoffrey struggled to keep from wincing.

"You've had your share of it, Geoffrey. And you've traded on our name to support your way of life for a good long time. I've given you money. You've squandered it."

He sounded more sad than accusing. "That's why you have nothing."

And Geoffrey's palms began to go cold. "Papa . . ." The word had slipped out of him.

His father stared at him.

"Mr. Thaddeus Morley is on trial for murder and treason, Father."

There was a silence.

"Is he?" his father murmured. "Is he now?" And that was all.

Geoffrey waited.

"Rhys might be a scoundrel, but still you haven't his character, Geoffrey. You want to blackmail him, don't you?" He sounded half amused, half sad.

Sick and dying, and his bloody father still read him like a book.

"I simply want to know."

A snort. "Oh, I'll tell you, son. But what I'm giving to you isn't a gift, it's a burden: the burden of a secret. Because if you share the information with anyone else in the world, it will destroy the family name, and thus whatever benefit, whatever capital you might have gained from the secret, will be gone, too. And Rhys knows that. So you can blackmail him, but if you ever tell the secret, it will be the end of you, anyway. Do you still want to hear it?"

At the moment, Geoffrey simply didn't care. He would find a way to sell it, and he would begin life again somewhere else.

"Many years ago, son . . . Rhys and I did a very bad thing."

* * *

She'd been so absorbed in her husband that she'd nearly forgotten about Geoffrey, and Sabrina immediately felt a twinge of guilt. As she rode into town to visit Margo Bunfield, she slowed her mare near the church.

He'd been so kind to her when she was so lonely. And deep down she knew she'd been avoiding him in part because he'd witnessed her vulnerability. And now that Rhys was here, and seemed inclined to stay, she didn't want a reminder of her former unhappiness. A new dream was beginning to take shape, so different from the old one, yet somehow similar: she once wanted to visit new lands. And this dream . . . this was an entirely new *universe*. She was protective of it; it needed the sunshine and shelter of hope—and not the shadows of an old disappointment—in which to thrive.

Still, there the church was, and as she rode home from Margo Bunfield's house with Mr. Croy behind her, she saw Geoffrey in the doorway of it. He began to lift a hand, then seemed to think better of it and dropped it to his side, and the aborted gesture tugged at Sabrina's guilt.

But she had, she decided, enough room in her bubble of happiness to extend a little of it to Geoffrey. She would visit him.

"We shall stop in at the vicarage, Mr. Croy."

Mr. Croy touched his cap and nodded.

The first thing she noticed was how terribly thin he'd become. Those striking Gillray bones were more prominent in his face now, his dark eyes more hollowed.

"Sabrina." He kissed her hand, a courtly gesture no doubt bred into him by the Gillray blood, and one not typically associated with a vicar. "I've missed you."

She could not truthfully say the same, so she merely said, "It's a pleasure to see you. But, Geoffrey, are you eating well enough? Perhaps you need a wife to fatten you up." She was teasing, all but giddy with happiness.

And it was all Geoffrey could do to keep from snapping: *Eight thousand pounds would fatten me up, you fool.*

He regarded her silently. The unhappiness that had dimmed her light weeks before, that had weakened her resolve so that he could sense imminent triumph, that had very nearly enabled him to convince her to donate her no doubt formidable allowance to his cause and leave the country with him . . . had become radiance.

She was beautifully, obliviously, fully happy. Geoffrey suddenly knew panic.

"You look very well, Sabrina." He heard the accusatory tone in his voice.

She blushed. "Things are wonderful, Geoffrey. Rhys is . . ." She paused, as if she was embarrassed to confess the source of her glow.

As if Geoffrey didn't already know.

"Rhys *is* at La Montagne, then," Geoffrey said musingly. Though of course he knew his cousin was in.

"Yes, he's been here for a few weeks now."

And of course, three weeks ago had been the last time he'd seen her at the vicarage. And if Rhys had stayed in the country—if Rhys had decided to give up *London*, the source of all his pleasures previously—then it was because of Sabrina.

And the blushing, radiant happiness of this girl he'd barely given any thought to was suddenly an affront, and a symbol of everything wretched about Geoffrey's life. Even this girl, this marriage that Rhys had clearly never wanted and had stumbled into, had turned out brilliantly for him. *Everything* always turned out brilliantly for Rhys.

And the pressures of the secret Geoffrey held and of his fear of ruin and of struggling with his own nature finally imploded.

He turned away from her for a moment, abruptly.

"Geoffrey, is aught amiss?"

Her voice grated. So soft with genuine concern. *Is aught amiss? Every bloody thing is amiss.*

He turned slowly back to her, and with cold resolve, began.

"I cherish our friendship, Sabrina. As such, you should know that your happiness is my own."

"Thank you, Geoffrey." She sounded tentative. He'd made it sound like the beginning of a story, so she waited.

He continued. "Two young ladies visited the church a few days ago asking to see it, as it reminded them of another church with which they are familiar. They were very fine, these young women, of quality; I've seldom seen a finer carriage in these parts. They said they had been to visit La Montagne."

Sabrina frowned a little, puzzled. "How odd that they would say so! We didn't have any visitors."

Geoffrey went on. "Sabrina . . . I was struck by how much these young ladies . . . well, they looked very much like you. One of them could have been your twin."

Sabrina sucked in her breath. "Oh, Geoffrey, you mustn't tease me in such a way. Could it be true? But why would they say they had visited La Montagne?"

"Perhaps you weren't in when they visited. Or . . . perhaps Rhys *chose* not to tell you of the visit."

Sabrina frowned a little. "Why on earth would he do something like that?"

Geoffrey reached for her hand and gripped it in his, and she gasped, a little startled, jerked away reflexively. He held her tightly.

"Why don't you ask Rhys, Sabrina. Ask him why he sent these two young ladies away when they came to your home, for that is indeed what he did. Ask him why he never told you they'd been to see him. Ask him how he came by his money so many years ago, and how he managed to restore this fortune, and who gave him the home and money so many years ago, and why."

The blood left Sabrina's skin. "Geoffrey . . . you're frightening me." She attempted to tug her hand away from him. Geoffrey continued to hold it fast.

"Ask him . . ." Geoffrey paused. Inhaled deeply, and decided he might as well finish it. "Ask him if he knows who Anna Holt is."

Sabrina backed a few steps away. Her voice was faint. "But I did ask and . . ."

She trailed off. She gave her head a shake. She was breathing quickly now.

"Ask him, Sabrina, or risk living a lie. I tell you only because your happiness is as my own. I tell you so that *you* may decide what you need to do with your future. Ask him."

CHAPTER TWENTY-THREE

SABRINA GALLOPED THE brown mare home, causing Mr. Croy to struggle to keep up with her. She dismounted and threw the reins to him, and all but ran for the house. She found Mrs. Bailey in the kitchen speaking with the cook. They both turned with a start, and made swift curtsies.

"Good afternoon, Lady Rawden. We were discussing whether you might wish to serve fowl or pork for dinner."

Dinner was the last thing on Sabrina's mind at the moment. Indeed, at the moment, she suspected she might never eat again.

"Mrs. Bailey, can you tell me: Did two young ladies visit La Montagne recently?"

"Why, yes, Lady Rawden."

Sabrina's eyes closed briefly; she prayed, but somehow she knew her prayers would not be answered. "Did they by any chance inquire after me specifically?" She kept her voice light, gave it a lilt. She didn't want to arouse suspicion in her astute housekeeper.

"Yes, Lady Rawden. That is, Lady Grantham and Mrs. Shaughnessy sought a Miss Sabrina Fairleigh. Lord Rawden told me to tell them that the woman they sought was not at La Montagne."

Sabrina was numb now. Her fingertips had gone cold.

Such a clever way for Rhys to put it. But then, he was always clever.

"Ah. Very good." Her own voice came to her as though through a distance.

She remembered his face when she'd shown him the miniature of her mother. How still he'd gone.

She could hardly feel her limbs as she went to find him, and she went slowly. Because she sensed somehow that when she did find him that this precarious happiness she'd known for so short a time would be over.

"Rhys."

The tone of her voice started a cold prickle of warning against the back of his neck. He looked up from his work and saw Sabrina standing before him.

And the expression she wore was one he'd never before seen on her face. She was very still, her face white and guarded. Her eyes too bright and staring. She was regarding him as if he were a stranger. She was still wearing her pelisse, her mittens, her scarf, and tendrils of hair clung to her temples with perspiration, as if she'd had a hard gallop or a hard run.

So she'd come directly in from Buckstead Heath to him without changing her clothing. Which was his second warning that something was amiss.

And then she moved forward and very gently placed the miniature of her mother in the middle of his desk.

He stared down at it, and suddenly felt as though he were plummeting into a chasm.

"What aren't you telling me, Rhys? You'd best tell me everything now, because I assure you I will find out on my own, if you do not."

He stood suddenly, reached out his fingers to touch her arm. "Sabrina . . ."

She backed away a few steps, just out of his reach. "Please, just tell me the truth."

He could feel that the color had left his own face. His fingertips were cold; his limbs had gone numb.

"Very well, then." She sounded unnervingly emotionless. "I will ask the questions. Did two women come to visit a few days ago?"

He hesitated. "Yes." A soft word.

"You knew those women must be my sisters. Lady Grantham and Mrs. Shaughnessy."

And once he made the admission, he would never be able to unmake it, but he didn't ever want her to hear him lie outright. "Yes."

"And you knew when I first showed this to you that the woman in this miniature is Anna Holt. My . . . my mother." Her voice faltered over that last word. And he saw the spasm of anger in her face.

He hesitated. "Yes." His voice still soft. As though to cushion her from the blow of his own betrayal.

"*How* did you know?" She was breathing more quickly now.

He inhaled deeply, seeking strength, breathed out again. "Because I've seen her before."

"But why didn't you tell me so when I first showed her picture to you? You knew even then. Your face went so . . . odd. But you didn't say anything. You *never* said anything."

Ah, his astute girl. Rhys stared at her, trying to decide what to say. But there was nothing he could say that would make it better.

"Rhys . . . *why didn't you tell me?*"

Oh, God. She sounded so frightened.

He took in another long, fortifying breath, exhaled every bit of it. "Sabrina . . . please sit down and—"

"No."

She stood before him, spine rigid, her eyes pinning him motionless.

Rhys didn't know where to begin. He only knew that he must. He was about to tell her a story he had never in his life told a soul. And telling her was his only prayer of making Sabrina understand why he'd done what he'd done . . .

He glanced about the room. Remembering it as it had been just a few minutes ago, when he'd been happier than he'd ever been in his life.

He returned his gaze to his wife's implacable face.

"I've told you before how . . . well, how, Sabrina, my father lost everything. There was a series of bad investments, and he lost everything. We were so poor. And poor in a way difficult for those born of modest means to understand, because it came with a . . . a wrenching shame. My father sold off everything that wasn't entailed, and then he gambled away the earnings from those sales. The only Rawden home not entailed was small, decaying . . ." He looked up at Sabrina.

"We burned furniture for heat," he said flatly.

She gave her head a rough shake. "Rhys—just tell me what you've done." Her voice was a tight, thin thing.

He took a breath and continued. "When my father broke his neck jumping a horse—while drunk, mind you—it was left to me to care for my mother and sisters. And my mother became . . . seriously ill. And then my sister. There was no money at all, Sabrina. I was so afraid . . . things had never been more desperate. And a man came to me and told me . . . he told me . . ."

Rhys remembered that moment vividly now. He'd prayed as only a boy could pray, promising all manner of rash things to God if only his life didn't collapse about his ears.

It seemed only the devil had heard his prayers. But by then, he'd no longer cared who answered them, as long as they were answered.

"This man told me simply that he would pay me a sum of money and deed a home in Yorkshire to me, and that I could do whatever I wished with the home—sell it for profit, live in it, rent it to someone else. It would all be very discreet. In exchange, all I had to do . . ." He took a deep breath. "All I had to do was to tell the authorities that I had seen Anna Holt fleeing Richard Lockwood's town house."

He'd never said those words aloud to anyone in his entire life, though they had formed the foundation of everything he now had.

"So you knew he'd been . . . was going to be . . ."

Murdered, the unspoken word.

"No," he said quickly. "I didn't know. But of course . . . when Richard Lockwood was killed . . . I knew what had happened. And when it became clear what the consequences would be if I did *not* carry through with my end of the bargain . . . I carried through with my end of the bargain. My name was never in the papers; because of my title I was never publicized as a witness. But I was such a credible witness, with my title, and my manners, and my family history—as was my uncle, Geoffrey's father, who was offered the same devil's bargain—that the authorities became convinced Anna was their culprit. And so they hunted for her."

Ceaselessly, he might have added.

Silence. Then:

"Oh." It was a sound of pure heartbreak from Sabrina.

Rhys carried on, saying the horrible words aloud. "And I was indeed paid. I was indeed given a house, an estate in Yorkshire. And my mother and older sister died, for it was too late to save them, but my other sister lived. And with the money I bought a commission, and I rebuilt the family fortune, and she made a good marriage. And she's safe and alive today."

Silence. Odd how he could hear servants moving about in other parts of the house. It seemed impossible for anything ordinary to be taking place anywhere near him.

"So you sacrificed my family . . . for yours."

Her voice was faint. She gave her head another little shake, as if the knowledge had lodged somewhere in her mind, a jagged thing, hurting her. Rhys regarded his beautiful wife, her face so taut with confusion. She simply could not understand that this man she had made love to, and had laughed with, and was building a life with . . . had committed this astounding betrayal. Had done this unforgivable thing to her.

For he knew that it was precisely that: unforgivable.

"Sabrina . . . what would you have done in my place?" He managed to say it quietly.

"I don't know what I would have done, Rhys, because, thanks to you, I never had a mother or sister to worry about."

Cold and even in tone, but the words lashed like a whip. They were ironic. He supposed she'd learned how to be ironic from him.

"Sabrina . . . I swear to you, I wanted to tell you all of this. I was glad Anna had disappeared. I was glad she was never caught. I prayed for her, I swear to you. But I never knew whether she'd been killed, or whether she had managed to escape. And I never knew what became of her daughters."

Sabrina's mouth parted for an instant; no words emerged. Just an airless sound. And then, finally:

"All of my life, Rhys. My mother . . . it's the one thing I have wanted all my life, to know who my true family was. I was so lonely all my childhood. And you knew it. I told you. And oh, God, Rhys . . ." She stopped, her voice breaking. "And you made love to me that night I showed you her miniature."

How could he defend the indefensible? He could only try to explain.

"Sabrina, as a child you were cared for and loved, and I thank God for that. But until you find yourself in the position I was in . . . I ask that you try to not judge me too harshly."

"Not judge you?" She made a sound, an incredulous laugh. "You helped destroy a family. If I hadn't found out—if he hadn't—you might never have told me."

And then as the full realization sank in, she repeated it, her voice stunned.

"You might never have told me, Rhys. I might . . . I might never have known. I might have lived happily here in the country with you. I might have lived my whole life without knowing what manner of man you are."

And though he hadn't a right to it, he was suddenly furious. It swept up from somewhere inside, someplace it had been lurking for years. Furious at the choice life had required him to make, perhaps, and what that choice might now take from him.

"What manner of man I am?" he ground out ironically. "I know full well what manner of man I am, my righteous little wife. And so did you the first time you kissed me, and so do you every time you take your pleasure in my arms. You've always known. From the very first moment."

She flinched. He saw her hand curl into her skirt, reflexively. He'd struck home, somehow.

"Did you ever think of her, Rhys? Of my mother? Did you think of us? Of the three little girls?"

"I thought of all of you, Sabrina. Sometimes I spent days thinking of all of you. But what I knew was that my mother and sister would have a chance to live, and I admit, I rejoiced in that." His voice was harder now, too.

"But your mother and your sister died, didn't they?"

He was silent.

"Perhaps," she said lightly, "that was the price you paid for sacrificing mine."

He knew he hadn't the right to his rage. And still there it was, tangling with a roiling panic. "Sabrina, damnation, please *listen* to—"

But her own righteous fury had her in its grip, and she wouldn't hear him. She went on, coldly articulate. "With your blood money, you also managed to gain . . . all of this." Her hand sailed out in a gesture, indicating everything about La Montagne. "You don't have your mother, and one of your sisters is dead. And I don't have *my* mother or my sisters. But *you* have all of this. All of these precious, beautiful things."

"Sabrina—"

She lifted up a hand to stop his words. "And now that's all you'll have, Rhys."

She turned so quickly her skirts lashed her legs.

Rhys reflexively lunged across the desk for her, closed his fingers over her slim arm. She froze. Stared down at his arm, looked up into his face.

"Don't go." He said it softly, shocked at how low and even his voice sounded. And yet he'd never felt quite so desperate. There was so much he could say. But it all seemed to be summed up in those words: "Please don't go."

She stared up at him with those clear, direct eyes. He'd seen them dazed and hot with passion, crackling with anger, glowing with pleasure, shy and uncertain.

He'd never seen them so bitterly, bitterly cold.

"Unhand me or I will scream as if I'm being murdered." She said it calmly.

He had enough pride not to cling, and enough sense to believe she would do what she said.

"Sabrina—"

"Unhand me," she repeated calmly.

And so she'd learned to give orders like a countess. There was so much she'd learned from him.

Rhys uncurled his fingers, gently, one by one. Loath to relinquish her, as it might very well be the last time he ever touched her.

Freed, Sabrina turned on her heel and walked away from him.

It wasn't a mad dash, which somehow would have given him hope.

There was only resolve in it.

CHAPTER TWENTY-FOUR

ONCE OUT OF the sight of Rhys, out of his hearing, Sabrina picked up her skirts in her fingers and ran like the devil was on her heels. Down the marble hallway, down the stairway, recklessly out the door into the cold day outside, where the wind tore her bonnet back and whipped her hair loose of its pins.

And like this she ran, like the sturdy country girl she'd always been, to the stables. She was only a little winded when she got there, and Mr. Croy appeared, puzzled.

She drew herself up to her full height, and breathed a moment before she spoke.

"Saddle her again, Mr. Croy, if you will."

She managed to say this calmly, even through her heaving breath, even as Mr. Croy stared at her. She knew her cheeks must be vivid pink; her eyes stung and watered from the wind.

"Saddle her now." She reissued the order, all but snapping it. "A man's saddle. And do it quickly."

And now, she knew, she sounded like a countess, and was glad for the first time of the title. She'd once been glad to be Rhys's wife; the "countess" part had been incidental.

But it was the countess part that would get her to London. For coaching inns would happily extend credit to the Countess Rawden, and she knew she could find the inn because Mary, social Mary, had told her about it. It was the inn that troubled Paul's delicate digestion.

Mr. Croy saddled and bridled the mare, while Sabrina let the fury and pain make her numb.

"And don't you dare follow me," she commanded over her shoulder.

She gripped the saddle and swung herself into it, then kicked the mare into a run.

An hour? Two hours?

For a time, Rhys stared at the space where Sabrina had been, and then he stood in his office like a caged animal, as though an entire vast home didn't surround him.

How long could he leave Sabrina alone with her anger and hurt before he attempted to speak to her again? He refused to accept defeat; he'd never accepted defeat in his entire life. Even when he'd made his ugly, fateful decision so many years ago, he'd done it in part for that reason. He was born to fight, it seemed.

He glanced up to find Mrs. Bailey in the doorway. She curtsied to him. It seemed an inordinately commonplace thing to do, jarring almost, given how his life had changed in a mere two hours.

"I beg your pardon, Lord Rawden, but Lady Rawden hasn't yet told the staff what she'd like to serve for dinner. Will you be taking a light repast in your rooms, then?"

Rhys went still. "When does Lady Rawden typically discuss dinner with you, Mrs. Bailey?"

"By midmorning, Lord Rawden, on a usual day. Even when she dines alone."

He thought he detected a whiff of accusation about the word "alone," but then everything seemed portentous now, somehow. Every word, every tick of the clock.

He glanced at the clock. The small brass hand pointed to four o'clock in the evening. Only an hour or so of daylight remained.

He remembered the resolve in Sabrina's step as she'd turned to leave, the cold determination in her eyes.

She hadn't known about her pride, her temper, her sense of impulse, until she'd met him.

Even as he asked it, he suspected he knew the answer to his next question: "When did you last see the countess, Mrs. Bailey?"

"This morning, sir. In the kitchen. She asked whether two ladies had visited, but she did not discuss dinner, then. And she's so very good about it."

An embellishment from Mrs. Bailey. She didn't want Rhys to think ill of the countess's ability to run a household, clearly. Everyone, even the taciturn housekeeper, had come to care for Sabrina.

His next question was practically a formality, and he was already moving past her, through the door as he asked it: "Will you kindly find her for me, Mrs. Bailey?"

But he suspected he knew the truth. And while the servants would no doubt futilely search the house for the countess, Rhys bolted for the stables.

Mr. Croy blanched, gripping his cap in his hands, and took two steps back from the looming earl. "I'm sorry, sir. She . . . ordered me not to follow her."

"You should know bloody well not to follow a *stupid* order, Mr. Croy, even if it's the countess who gives it."

Rhys knew it was a ridiculous thing to say even as he said it. He inhaled sharply, breathed out to steady himself. "Mr. Croy . . . in which direction did she ride?"

"Toward Buckstead Heath, sir. She . . . fair rode like the devil. Astride. Nivver seen 'er ride like so before. But she seemed very . . ."

"*What* did she seem, Mr. Croy?" Rhys demanded. He reached for Gallegos's saddle himself; Mr. Croy bridled the animal quickly, Gallegos tossing his head a little, sensing Rhys's tension.

"She seemed calm, for all of that. As though she knew what she was about."

Rhys closed his eyes briefly. *She isn't. She doesn't.*

He pictured Sabrina, who rode well enough but was no equestrienne, riding at breakneck speed. He pictured the mare striking an icy patch, tumbling, Sabrina flying from—

He swung himself into the saddle and rode Gallegos at breakneck speed to the vicarage.

No brown horse was tethered outside the churchyard.

Rhys pulled Gallegos's head around hard and nudged him toward the stables, swinging down from the saddle and leaving the reins to dangle. He threw open the door.

But only one horse stood quietly there in a stall, peacefully working a chaw of hay in its jaws and gazing at him with faint surprise. A gray. Geoffrey's horse. Not Sabrina's brown mare.

Where the bloody hell could she have gone?

He swung himself back into Gallegos's saddle and trotted him from the outbuildings to the building that had housed vicars at Buckstead Heath for a century and a half. *1665* were the numbers over the door. The house and the church were built that year; the outbuildings and stables were only a decade or so old.

And all of it belonged again to the Gillrays, thanks to Rhys. And the living here at the vicarage was Geoffrey's, thanks to Rhys.

And Rhys just might kill Geoffrey with his bare hands.

He pounded on the door.

And moments later, Geoffrey flung it open. He was in shirtsleeves and trousers. A faint greasy smell of sausage wafted from the kitchen.

"Where is she?" Rhys demanded.

Geoffrey, accustomed to his cousin's temper, looked a little surprised. "She isn't here."

The bastard hadn't even asked whom he meant. "Let me in." Rhys shoved his leg through the door.

Geoffrey stood aside. "By all means, cousin, come in. It's not precisely La Montagne, so your search shouldn't take long. Crawl under the bed, look under tables. Did you check the stables?"

"I looked in the damn stables."

"Well, if she isn't there, she isn't here. But she's not a reckless sort, typically. Sabrina always has a plan. I assume she left you."

Rhys rounded on Geoffrey. "Don't tell me what *sort* my wife is." His voice was low with threat.

Geoffrey had the good sense to back a few steps away.

There was a silence between them. Rhys stood in the middle of the small vicar's house, heavy with a sense of futility.

He looked at Geoffrey. "Why? Why did you tell her?" He could hear the weariness in his voice.

"I swear I'm sorry. I didn't mean to do it, Rhys. She just—I just—"

"What?" Rhys snapped.

The day was beginning to die beautifully; through the window the lowering sun was staining everything amber. She could be anywhere. Had she taken refuge in a villager's house, Sabrina? Was she lying in a ditch somewhere? He could gallop off into the middle of nowhere, and pound on every door in the village of Buckstead Heath for days, and he still might never find her.

Perhaps she'd gone home to La Montagne. He allowed his mind to toy with the thought, to see if it felt possible, to see if it would turn into hope. He didn't really believe it. Like Geoffrey said: Sabrina usually had a plan.

"She's a country girl, Rhys."

His cousin was trying to tell him that Sabrina was resourceful. It was perhaps the most useful thing Geoffrey had ever said. Rhys knew there was sense in it, and something in him eased just a very little.

"Did your father tell you?"

Geoffrey knew what Rhys meant. "Yes."

"Did you ask him?"

"Yes."

"*Why?*" Rhys made a frustrated gesture. Geoffrey flinched, which pleased Rhys. "Why in God's name did you need to know? Why couldn't you just let it *be?*"

"It was wrong, Rhys. What you did."

Imagine *Geoffrey* sounding righteous.

"Of course it was bloody *wrong*. Your father knew it, I knew it. We did what we needed to do. And it kept you fed, didn't it? And clothed. And it sent you to school. But you squandered it. Your father, whatever he's like now, all but sold his soul for you. And you *bloody squandered it*."

Geoffrey's narrow, handsome face was still and pale. He was too thin, Rhys noticed.

"You've never taken me seriously," Geoffrey said, sounding nearly petulant.

"For God's sake, why should I?" Rhy said this almost reasonably.

Geoffrey went silent again. "You're such a smug bastard, Rhys."

"Is that what sort of bastard I am, Geoffrey? I've always wondered."

Geoffrey gave a short, faint laugh. "You don't see it, do you? I'm not *you*, Rhys. I'm me. But you expect everyone to be a bloody . . . rock. A bloody hero. I haven't your fortitude. I simply don't. You with your contempt, and . . ." Geoffrey's voice broke. "I'm human. And maybe I'm weak, and maybe I'm foolish, but I'm not entirely bad, and yet you . . . even though you did this *thing* so many years ago, you stand in judgment of me."

"You're flat dangerous, Geoffrey. I've never before encountered a curate with no soul."

This made Geoffrey angry; his eyes went hard. And maybe it hadn't been entirely fair, but Rhys was in no mood to be fair.

"You've always had everything you've wanted. Everything was just roses for you yet again, wasn't it, Rhys? And yet you didn't even want her to begin with."

Rhys slowly turned to look at Geoffrey. Then shook his head once, roughly, in pure incredulity. The truth of it cut deep.

"You've no idea, do you?" he said softly.

Geoffrey was fully angry now. "You wouldn't even have known her if not for me. And she was besotted with you. She was so damn . . . *happy*." Geoffrey said it help-lessly. He made it sound like an affront.

"Not anymore. Congratulations, you've accomplished at least one thing you set out to do in your life. And you punished the wrong person."

Geoffrey inhaled and pulled a chair out from the small kitchen table, sat down. Overcome perhaps. "I need money." His voice was faint.

"For your *mission*." Rhys snarled the word ironically.

"No. Honestly, Rhys. I'm in . . ." Geoffrey faltered. "I swear it to you. I'm in trouble. Serious trouble this time."

"I won't argue with that," Rhys said grimly. "This time, get yourself out of it."

"I'm your own blood, Rhys." Geoffrey was pleading now. "Doesn't that mean anything to you? And don't for-get, I happen to know what you did for your own blood seventeen years ago."

Rhys's head snapped toward him. "I'll see your blood if I don't find her, Geoffrey."

"Rhys, I swear to God, if you don't . . ."

"If I don't *what*?"

Geoffrey stared, defiance in his pale face. "You *do* know what your secret is worth, don't you? And you do know who is on trial now in London, don't you?"

There was a silence.

"There's no proof," Rhys said flatly. Although he could never, ever be certain of this.

Geoffrey was silent, eyes blazing. All the fine qualities of the Gillrays were muted in Geoffrey, all the less-fine, that temper, that pride, that sense of entitlement, the excess, had somehow come to the fore, and were all that could contain him. None of it balanced by spine or integrity or true decency. He was amorphous, Geoffrey was. And this, Rhys realized, did make him dangerous.

"Geoffrey—if you destroy the family name—realize you also destroy your every chance at income, because you'll never be able to live on credit again. Every chance at ever making a name for yourself. Any chance of pride for your heirs. The name *means* something."

"What if I said I didn't care?" Geoffrey was wild with desperation. "And I swear to God, Rhys, if you don't give me money now . . ."

Rhys stepped closer to his cousin. "Are you threatening me?" He said it almost curiously. He sounded nearly amused.

Geoffrey swallowed hard. "Eight thousand pounds." The words were almost a whisper. "I swear I need it."

"I don't *have* that kind of money to just hand you, Geoffrey, even if I thought I might. Dear God. It would take a very long time to free it."

"But they're *threatening* me . . . they've hurt me before . . ."

"Who?" The word was a snarl. "Who's threatening you?"

Geoffrey was silent. He lowered his face into his hands. "I swear, Rhys . . . I'll do it. I'll spread the word. I'll tell the secret. Because they're going to kill me, Rhys. My creditors."

Rhys was silent. He realized, finally, he just didn't care. The entire purpose of his life had been to restore the Rawden fortune and name, and now he just didn't care.

"If I don't find Sabrina, Geoffrey . . . you'll be fortunate if they reach you before I do."

Rhys said it almost calmly.

And then he was gone.

Sabrina could scarcely remember the trip. The mad gallop to the coaching inn was a blur now, and there she'd left her horse and requested—demanded—to be taken immediately to the next coaching inn, two towns over, and the inn owner had immediately scrambled to find a carriage to do it in.

Clever of her, she thought. She'd done it in order to stay one step ahead of Rhys, who was just as clever, and would find her soon enough. Still, no sense in making it any easier for him than it needed to be.

Being a countess meant that no one questioned the absence of trunks, or even the absence of a maid: her clothes spoke for her, as did her manners; she merely imitated Rhys, after all, his pride and presence, and her contained anger made her all the more convincing.

Everything—the rooms at the inn, the food she didn't eat, the coach fare—went on the Earl of Rawden's account.

And finally, a day and a half later, she was in London, nearly blind and feeling weightless from fatigue and knowing distantly she was very likely starving but not truly feeling it. She stared up at the town house on Grosvenor Square. She'd merely issued the direction: "Lady Grantham, please"—and the driver had known.

Even the hackney driver knew where her sister lived, while Sabrina might not ever have known her at all.

She used what felt like the last of her strength to raise the knocker and let it fall.

Moments later, a somber, gray-faced man opened the door.

"Lady Grantham, please." Her voice was shredded from fatigue.

"May I tell her who is—"

But there she was, suddenly. A woman had come to the door, and her face blurred before Sabrina's eyes, blending with her memories of long ago, and suddenly Sabrina couldn't tell one from the other. Was she dreaming or awake? Faintly, through her fury, she knew completion and happiness . . . and exhaustion.

And as she'd accomplished her mission, she said one thing to the woman: "I'm Sabrina."

The panic in the woman's expression puzzled her.

"Kit!" the woman shouted, inexplicably.

Sabrina heard even this as if through cotton batting.

And it was the last word she heard before she toppled.

CHAPTER TWENTY-FIVE

SABRINA DIDN'T KNOW she'd been asleep until she opened her eyes to a room softly lit. Impressions seeped in with her slow-dawning awareness: the bed beneath her was soft, the fire low but strong. She turned her head, and discovered a luxuriously plump pillow supporting it, shifting with her as she moved.

"How did I . . . ," she said, almost to herself.

"My husband brought you up." A gentle voice. Concerned. Strange, yet somehow peculiarly, thrillingly familiar. Sabrina turned to the source of it.

She might as well have turned to stare into a mirror. She stared for a long, hungry moment at this woman who must be her sister.

"Don't let him in," were her first words. She'd blurted them. Rude, but somehow it was the first thing her tired mind reached for.

" 'Him'?" said the living, breathing mirror, sounding a bit startled.

But now, fully awake, fully aware, Sabrina couldn't answer. She seemed capable only of staring and staring at the woman.

"Rawden," she finally replied. She could barely get the word out for drinking in her sister. *Her own flesh and blood.* She took in a deep breath, as if she needed extra air to accommodate the magnitude of what she'd done, and who this was.

Susannah returned her regard with the same avid fascination.

And then all at once something like comprehension dawned all over her face.

"*You're* the woman who married The Libertine? The Earl of Rawden? The one he's reportedly besotted with?" She sounded absolutely delighted. "Oh, *well* done."

Sabrina blinked. *Besotted?* How on earth would her sister have heard such a thing?

"That's the rumor, anyhow," Susannah continued happily. "He hasn't been seen about the *ton,* and I've heard it's because he's besotted with his wife, whom no one has ever seen. Now I know for *certain* we're related. We've all managed to make rather extraordinary marriages. For you should *see* Sylvie's husband. But . . . are you well? Are you hungry? I was rather worried."

The only thing in Sabrina's stomach at the moment was a peculiar blend of misery and joy. Very likely she should eat. Collapsing and not recalling her journey up the stairs in the arms of her sister's husband was perhaps an indication that she ought to eat.

"Perhaps some soup." She was practical, after all. She didn't intend to pine away. "I was merely weary and hungry. I didn't faint."

"No. You rather fell asleep." Susannah sounded half amused. "Dropped like a felled tree right there in the entrance. Kit caught you just in time."

"Kit—?" The word Susannah had shouted just before.

"My husband. Viscount Grantham. I could see you were about to fall, so I called for him."

"I came straight from La Montagne, you see," Sabrina said. "Without stopping."

"Or sleeping or eating," her sister guessed. "Sylvie came from France in much the same way."

From France? It was almost too much to take in right now.

"Don't let him in," Sabrina remembered to say, as it seemed urgent. "I don't want to see him."

"Is it a quarrel?" Susannah ventured.

"Not precisely."

Susannah waited for clarification. Sabrina said nothing.

"He hasn't tried to hurt you?" Susannah said with quick ferocity. "Because Kit will—"

"No," Sabrina said quickly. It was true: he hadn't *tried* to hurt her. He simply had hurt her. *And* her sisters. Irrevocably. "He isn't . . . he isn't like that." She decided to test sisterly loyalty. "My husband turned you away from our home. I never knew you'd come to see me."

A stunned silence.

"*Why?*" Susannah demanded. Fierce. Sabrina studied her, strangely pleased with the vehemence. Susannah had longed to find her, too.

"It is between my husband and me," she said firmly. Whatever Rhys had done, she wasn't yet prepared to destroy him by revealing his secret. Now that she had her sisters, she would think about what shape her life would take without him.

"You cannot tell me, or *will* not tell me?" Susannah wondered shrewdly.

Ah, this sounded rather sisterly. Sabrina almost smiled; it was peculiarly exhilarating, this thought. And the newness of this helped offset the loss of her beautiful, false life with Rhys.

"Will not," she said, gently but emphatically.

Susannah smiled a little at that. Then shook her head slowly, to and fro, wonderingly. As though, for some reason, Sabrina had confirmed something for her.

It was quiet now.

"I'm your sister Susannah," Susannah said finally. As though the words were the final ones in a ceremony, a marriage or coronation or christening. The words that made it real and true.

Sabrina reached out her hand, and Susannah took it, held it tightly. Susannah's hand was so smooth and soft. The hands of a lady, for certain, unlike her own, yet the shape of them, long and slender, was familiar. They looked like hers. *My sister.*

"I'm your sister Sabrina."

Susannah smiled a little, but her eyes had begun to shine, and Sabrina knew they were tears.

Once he'd decided to sell the family name in order to save his own skin, Geoffrey began to feel a certain amount of peace. His next decision became very practical: who would be willing to pay the most for it? For there was absolutely no question that *someone* would pay dearly for it. Rhys was already a figurehead of London scandal, reliably notorious, an object of fascination. His ruination would make some fortunate newspaper publisher a fortune a dozen times over.

It could not be helped. He'd seen the look on his cousin's face when he'd left him yesterday. *Get yourself out of it this time*, Rhys had snarled. And this time, Geoffrey intended to.

But Geoffrey knew the scandal sheets would never be able to provide him with the amount of money he needed; they hadn't the budget. Nor would they provide him with the credibility he wanted. He not only needed the money . . . he also wanted the family secret exhumed and examined in a dry, thoroughly credible way, a way that left no room for scoffing, for disbelief. In a way that would make it impossible for Rhys to claw his way back into society's good graces ever again, which would be the final black mark against his reputation, and which might even get him arrested for treason—for assisting a man who was being tried for treason.

Though Geoffrey hadn't the faintest idea of the legality of it all.

The choice became simple then: he settled down to write a letter to Thomas Barnes at the *Times*.

And given the illustrious family name Barnes was to be given an opportunity to destroy, Geoffrey had no doubt the editor would agree to meet him.

And would agree to his price.

Sabrina had nearly reached the bottom of her soup, her sister overseeing every drop she drank of it, when a woman's face peeked into her room.

Green eyes, too. Sabrina could see the flash of them even from this distance. Dark hair. Very pretty.

"I sent for Sylvie while you were sleeping," Susannah explained.

Sylvie came all the way into the room, a little tentatively. She was graceful, nearly regal in her bearing. Pretty, but not quite so soft-looking as Susannah; her very presence crackled. She smiled shyly at Sabrina.

"Sabrina came all the way from La Montagne to London without sleeping or eating," Susannah said to Sylvie, sounding partly amused, partly awed. "Because she is angry with her husband."

"Ah. So she has the family temper." Sylvie said it matter-of-factly. Oddly, Sabrina already felt comfortable with both of these women, more comfortable than ever she had felt sitting with talkative Lady Mary Capstraw, or with her father, or with . . .

She wouldn't think of Rhys.

"Yes!" Sabrina was surprised, half delighted, realizing what Sylvie had just said. "I've a temper!" She hadn't known it until one particularly bloody man had come along. "How did you know?"

"Did you throw something?" Sylvie wanted to know. "I occasionally throw things. *Mon dieu,* it is a curse."

"I once threw a rock out of pique," Susannah confessed. "And I slapped a man."

Sabrina stared at her sisters in awe. *Cor!* Lady Mary might have said.

"I haven't thrown anything," she confessed. "Yet," she said quickly, hating to disappoint them.

"A duel was once fought over Sylvie," Susannah volunteered.

Duels made Sabrina think of Rhys. She pushed the thought away.

"Do you dance?" Susannah asked. "Sylvie is a ballerina."

"A *ballerina*?" Astounding. "I don't dance, but I play the pianoforte very well." She suddenly wanted to confess to a talent, too.

"Ah, she's the family pride as well." Sylvie nodded approvingly.

It was splendid to hear this list of family traits. She might never have known they were within her if it hadn't been for Rhys. He'd challenged her, deliberately cracked her open to reveal pride and poetry and passion.

And if he hadn't, she would never have known how immensely, powerfully, fully she could love, how rich her world could seem. She would have lived a quiet life.

Without him, she would never have known the immensity of this heartbreak, either.

"You'll never guess who she is married to," Susanna said in a hush to Sylvie. "The *Libertine*!"

Sylvie's eyes widened. And then she looked relieved. "We were worried, you see, when we thought you'd been raised by a vicar. We thought you might be *sedate*." She said the last word in a hush, as though it were scandalous.

"Oh, you've naught to worry over," Sabrina said, and it was a trifle bitter. "I was raised by a vicar to be a very good girl, but I'm quite passionate, apparently."

It had been an easy enough thing to track her to London. All the inns of course remembered her, the drivers of coaches remembered her. Rhys was about a half day behind her, and now he stood at the door of the Grantham town house, and he knew she was behind this door.

He was tempted to fling his body at the door, to batter it down, to ascertain she was safe.

He thought, perhaps, he should try knocking first. So he did. Vehemently.

A polite, gray-faced man opened the door.

"I know she's here," Rhys said without preamble.

"I beg your pardon, sir?" Unflappable, the man was.

"Rawden to see my wife, the Countess Rawden," he clarified. He knew he was bloody intimidating when he spoke like that.

"She is not in." Politely said, and as final-sounding as a door closing.

"The bloody hell she's not in."

"Sir," came the even tones of the butler. "I assure you—"

"*Sabrina!*" he bellowed into the house.

"My apologies, sir."

The butler closed the door.

One didn't often hear shouting in Grosvenor Square, but the sound came up to Susannah and Sylvie and Sabrina as they sat in the drawing room.

"What is that sound, Bale?"

"A large, bellowing earl, Lady Grantham."

"Rawden?" she queried.

"Yes, Lady Grantham."

"Sabrina is not at home to him."

"I told him as such. He seems to think otherwise."

"Will you kindly tell him to leave, Bale?"

"As I said, Lady Grantham, he's very large, and he seems quite determined."

Susannah gave it some thought. "Ah, you're quite right, Bale. Sylvie and I best speak to him, then. He doesn't have a prayer against us."

"Perhaps when the viscount or Mr. Shaughnessy is present—"

"The earl shan't harm us, Bale. He's family," Susannah said sweetly.

"*Sabri*—"

The door was flung open. Rhys stopped midbellow.

Two beautiful women stared up at him, and neither was Sabrina. But, oh, they looked enough like her to hurt, with those large clear eyes the Holt women had. These women he'd turned away.

He remembered just in time that he wasn't a brute, and bowed.

"I want to see my wife," he demanded when upright again. He might not be a brute, but fine manners seemed superfluous at the moment.

"Good evening to you, too, Lord Rawden," Susannah said. "I believe Mr. Bale informed you that Sabrina is not at home to you."

"Let me in, and I'll just talk—"

"No." This came from Sylvie, gently but firmly. "You'd best go, Lord Rawden. No amount of bellowing will persuade us to allow you through the door."

Evenly said, but he knew he might as well have been looking at a pair of armed guards. Armed with eyelashes and spines of steel.

"Speak to her for me. You can persuade her to see me."

"Have you only just met your wife, Lord Rawden?"

This was a very good point. No doubt these women had already experienced a taste of how stubborn Sabrina could be.

"But you're her sisters."

"Yes. But if you'd had your way, she would not have known."

He didn't care about these women at the moment, though he knew he should. He knew he was looking at family. He knew he should apologize.

He only wanted to see Sabrina.

He seized upon an idea. "Kit—I want to see Lord Grantham."

"Lord Grantham is not at home, Lord Rawden. Will you kindly leave?"

Rhys drew in a deep breath. The staring among the three of them went on for another tense minute.

"I'll return," he said grimly, making it both a threat and a promise. And he spun on his heel.

Rhys was at the bottom of his fourth whiskey in White's when Kit Whitelaw, Viscount Grantham, appeared next to him.

Rhys glared up at him and said nothing. He merely tossed the whiskey back.

It was so strong it nearly clawed his throat going down, but that was what he wanted. To drink until everything in that damned club blurred and ran together, to forget for a blessed moment that his life was over.

Kit finally spoke. "You look horrible, Rawden."

"You always were quite the diplomat, Grantham."

"So what in God's name did you do to upset your wife?"

And this made Rhys pause in his quest to down the most whiskey ever downed. "Sabrina didn't tell you?"

This was a surprise. For some reason Sabrina hadn't told Kit, which no doubt meant she hadn't told her sisters. He didn't know the reason. Maybe she just hadn't gotten round to it yet, or it might be shame, or it might be loyalty. He would cling to the latter, for it gave him hope. And it penetrated his mind like rays of light through prison bars.

"No. In fact, she won't speak of you at all. I would say she's furious." Kit said this with faint awe. He had nothing but respect for the tempers of the Holt women.

Rhys knew Sabrina. Fury was better than indifference or cold despair, because at the heart of fury was typically passion, and the source of Sabrina's passion was love.

Or so he thought. He didn't truly know. And if it had once been love, he didn't know whether he'd killed it or not.

"So what did you do?" Kit repeated, cozily pulling out a chair, settling in at the table, ignoring the baleful warning glare Rhys treated him to.

"I can't tell you," Rhys said grimly.

"Why not?"

"Because you'd have to shoot me. And I might be irredeemable, but I'm selfish enough not to want to be dead. Yet."

"Oh, spare me the dram—"

Kit was stopped by the flat, grim look in the earl's eyes. "You're serious."

"Oh, yes." Rhys almost sounded bleakly amused.

"It's that bad?" Now Kit looked merely curious.

Rhys stared back at him. Bolted the whiskey and grimaced.

"Worse than Countess Montrose? Worse than Sophia Licari? Worse than all the duels you've fought, combined?"

Rhys waved an impatient arm at the waiter for another glass. "As much as I'm enjoying this recitation of my past misdemeanors, Grantham, I'll have to stop you. It's worse than all combined. It's unforgivable."

The word "unforgivable," unequivocally stated, landed between them, solid as a stone.

And for a moment, Kit had nothing to say to this.

"So you can stop guessing. I won't tell you. Now let me see my wife, damn you."

"She doesn't want to see you," Kit said calmly.

"I bloody well *know* that." Rhys slammed the glass down on the table; heads turned. He lowered his voice. "I know that. *Make* her. It's your home. She's your sister-in-law. You can invite me into your home. Make. Her. See. Me."

And then he heard himself, the rank desperation in his voice. Dear God, he hardly sounded sane. Pride was nowhere.

And he saw the sympathetic look on Kit's face, and despised it and himself.

Rhys held a hand up abruptly, as if to stop anything Kit might say. "I apologize, Grantham. You're right to protect her. Please forgive me."

Kit frowned a little, then leaned back and studied the other man quietly. He was remembering a night when he'd sat across from James Makepeace, another quietly despairing man, in this very club. James had been drinking whiskey, too. Or more specifically, he'd tried to drink whiskey. Kit had finished it for him.

"It might be unforgivable, but perhaps you can make it right, Rawden," he suggested gently.

"No."

"I shot my best friend when I was seventeen years old, and he forgave me."

The faint smile on the earl's mouth was bleak. "Believe it or not, Grantham . . . this is worse."

Kit went quiet. In his experience in the Secret Service, he knew silence was an almost certain way to convince someone to speak. The Earl of Rawden was a formidable man, but he was filled with a secret, and with grief, and whether or not he knew it, with the desperation of love. And so Kit waited.

And even with—one, two, three, four, five glasses of whiskey, Kit counted on the table—Rhys spoke, and spoke clearly.

"All right, Grantham. I owe you this much information. I did a desperate thing many years ago, knowing full well the consequences of what I did. I did it to help me and mine, and it seemed the only thing at the time. But it helped to ruin lives. And *then* . . . ," he added with gallows cheer, "I lied about it to Sabrina. Because that's just the sort of man I am."

Kit studied him with his own sharp blue eyes, looking for clues, for vulnerability, for a way into Rhys's resolve. He found none.

"I know the sort of man you are, Rawden."

"I don't want to hear any 'war hero' nonsense, Grantham. We were all bloody heroes."

"No," Kit said quietly. "That isn't true. And I will tell you something I would never admit to any other man. Do you know what I've learned, in part thanks to Susannah? The kind of man you are in love and war is truly the kind of man you are."

Rhys gave a short bitter laugh. "I hope to God that isn't true. Because if that's the sort of man I am, then I bloody well can't live with myself."

"Tell me this, Rawden: What are you hoping for when you come to my home if what you did was unforgivable? If you know she won't forgive you?"

It was a very good question. "To see her. Just to see her."

And again, the very idea that he might never see Sabrina again seized Rhys by the throat. He squeezed his hand around the whiskey glass, so tempted to hurl it across the room, to hear it shatter the way his life had shattered. It was the sort of thing that would feed the gaping maw of curiosity of all these men in White's who were pretending not to watch his pain.

The *ton* was laughing behind their fans, behind their newspapers. Imagine The Libertine brought low by a woman.

Rhys, as usual, didn't care what anyone said. He began to lift his hand to signal the waiter for more whiskey.

And Kit slapped his hand down. "That's enough," he said quietly.

"What the devil—do you want a fist to the jaw, Grantham?"

Apparently Kit wasn't terribly worried about the fist to the jaw; he closed his hand over Rhys's wrist. "If you truly can't ever make it right for her, maybe you can make it right for *yourself,* so that the rest of us might live with you. Make restitution, do penance, walk on your knees the length of London, wear a hair shirt, flay your skin, for God's sake. And perhaps once you've flagellated yourself enough, you'll find a way to win her back. Or find a way to live without her. You've lived through hell before, Rawden. More than once. You can do it again. You know how to do it."

Rhys jerked his hand away from the other man, and glared at him.

Yes, he'd lived through hell. But then he'd always been able to imagine what the other side of hell would look like, and in imagining it he'd found strength. But now . . . he simply couldn't imagine life without Sabrina. He couldn't imagine life on the other side, if she wasn't in it.

"I want to see her," he demanded. Futilely, he knew.

"Seeing her is not an option," Kit repeated calmly.

And Rhys realized that not seeing her ever again was also not an option. In fact, this Rhys knew more surely than he'd known anything in his life, and he almost laughed. How on earth could something like this have happened, so quickly? How on earth could he so willingly be at the mercy of another human being, when he'd never wanted to need anyone again?

"All right. Then tell me everything you know about Sabrina's past, Grantham. Because I'm going to do what you have so far failed to do."

He saw the flare of competition in Kit's eyes; it satisfied him, somehow. He wanted anger, competition, something to brush up against.

"Really. So how are you going to find Anna Holt, Rawden?"

"Sheer bloody will, Grantham. Watch me."

CHAPTER TWENTY-SIX

H E HADN'T BEEN a spy, like Grantham. He wasn't a gleeful taker of risks, like Shaughnessy, who had been ruined and rebuilt his life, too, into a roaring success. But he was a former soldier, a leader, a strategist, and possessed more determination than nearly any man on the planet.

Still, there was so very little to go by.

I'm going to do what you have so far failed to do.

Quite the boast.

Rhys also knew about art and beauty and collecting beautiful things. *And now they're all you have,* his wife had flung at him. Art, beauty, war. He had those things, at least, in common with the murdered father of his wife.

And yet, as he took the collection of facts and impressions that Kit had given him and sifted through them repeatedly, he still hadn't the faintest idea where to begin looking for Anna, or how any of them might help find her at all.

As Rhys was a poet—or had been once, though the words seemed to have deserted him now—he, like all poets, appreciated Richard's amusement in the name Gorringe, the town named by a duke who had gone mad searching for a rhyme for orange. He knew Richard had left behind cryptic, clever clues to his killer in Gorringe along with the evidence proving his killer's crimes—he'd in fact been more cryptic and clever than anyone would have preferred him to be—but in so doing he'd managed to protect for more than a decade the evidence that had eventually put Thaddeus Morley in the Tower for treason.

He knew that Richard Lockwood and Anna had spoken of going to Italy, because Kit had been told this. He couldn't begin to imagine what that evening must have been like for her: the wrenching fear and loss, the frantic departure. And every time his mind touched on it, his thoughts shied away reflexively. Guilt would only slow his search. It was ballast he could do without.

He needed to think of one thing only: he needed to find Anna for Sabrina.

Kit had already reviewed the rolls of every ship departing in 1803, but of course no one by the name of Anna Holt had boarded a ship to anywhere that winter. And if she'd used an assumed name, it hadn't been Anna Smith, the name she'd used in Gorringe.

Then again, she could have left at any time. She could have hidden *anywhere,* at any time. The hunt for her through England had been thorough and relentless after Lockwood's murder, Rhys recalled, but there were tiny, tucked-away places where London papers might conceivably never have reached, where no one cared about scandals that would never affect them.

Places like Tinbury, for instance.

Running like a current through his thoughts of Anna and Sabrina was the idea that at any moment the scandal sheets might feature a story regarding the Earl of Rawden that, for a change, wouldn't feature a married countess or a duel, but instead contain the seeds of his ruin. Thanks to his cousin Geoffrey.

And if the Rawden name was to be ruined, Rhys wanted to be the one to do it. He would find Anna first, and then confess everything publicly, to exonerate her once and for all.

Two weeks. And then three weeks. His friends had once been accustomed to seeing him nightly; he saw no one. He refused invitations. He vaguely recalled the arrival of Signora Licari at his town house, uninvited. And this was an extraordinary enough event to inspire him to go downstairs to see her. But then he'd found himself muttering something curt and perfunctory to her and turned to go back up the stairs of his town house, entirely unmoved, entirely distracted.

For the very first time in his life he'd seen astonishment on the soprano's face.

He didn't care.

He didn't go to his club. He hardly ate. Instead he pressed Kit again for information, and he visited Daisy Jones, one of the few people who'd known what had happened that night, and pressed her for information. And learned nothing more.

He paid a visit to Mr. Edwin Avery-Finch, who owned a shop of antiquities and had, Kit had delicately told him, been close to Richard. He asked the one question of Mr. Avery-Finch that no one else had asked: Did he know whether Richard had been to Italy?

"Yes," Mr. Finch had told him. He knew that Richard had once visited Italy. But he didn't know *where* in Italy, or why he had gone.

And at last . . . well, perhaps it was the exhaustion. Perhaps fatigue had softened and altered Rhys's mind in the way that strong drink sometimes did, for at last he'd ceased attempting to channel his thoughts because he'd all but lost the ability to do so, and instead let his thoughts have their way with him.

And this is when it occurred to Rhys: Richard had left so many clues to his killer's identity behind, it was as though he was fully aware of the danger he'd been in, and what the outcome might be. He'd left clues to his killer; he'd left clues for his daughters.

And perhaps he would find a clue to the whereabouts of Richard's lover, the wrongly accused Anna Holt, in the very same place Richard had left his other clues: Gorringe.

Two weeks, then three weeks, and Sabrina began to feel like a member of the Grantham household, and her heart, which had once seemed wholly her own, or wholly Rhys's, seemed to have separate chambers for joy and for cold hurt and anger. There was joy in becoming acquainted with her sisters, in the moments both of ease and awkwardness, of laughter and irritation. Of a giddy, glorious sense of belonging she had never known, of being part of a family fabric that was her very own. And since Sabrina, Susannah, and Sylvie had all been so long without it, it would be quite some time before the novelty ebbed. For now, each moment carried the sharp delight of newness.

But neither Susannah nor Sylvie could quite persuade her to go out. They respected her silence on the subject of her husband and didn't press her, though Sabrina suspected it was maddening for both of them. They were both so clearly happy in their own marriages that they suffered on her behalf.

Well, Sabrina supposed they could not have everything in common.

However, when Susannah arrived in her room one afternoon with a glint in her eye and a card in her hand, Sabrina looked up curiously.

"I thought I would bring her card in to you to let you decide what you'd like to say to her," Susannah said solemnly. She extended the card and waited.

Sabrina took the card from her: *Signora Sophia Licari.*

She stared at the name, trying to decide what she felt. She'd managed to cordon off the place in her mind that concerned Rhys, and found it hurt scarcely at all. She'd still a good deal of pride at her disposal. She considered shunning the beautiful, condescending soprano.

But it was pride that made her decision for her.

"I will see her," Sabrina said.

When Sabrina appeared in the drawing room, Signora Sophia Licari rose to greet her and curtsied.

Had Rhys recently sought solace in the opera singer's arms? Looking at Signora Licari, lush and golden in her russet-colored gown, Sabrina didn't know why any sane man would not.

"To what," Sabrina managed with an irony that would do her estranged husband proud, "do I owe the honor of this visit, Signora Licari?"

"He does not eat," the soprano said, every consonant caressed, as usual.

Sabrina frowned. "I beg your pardon?"

"Your husband. He does not eat, he will not speak to anyone. He does not sleep." Every bit of it sounded like accusation.

"And how do you know this?" Sabrina managed calmly. How would any woman know a man did not sleep unless she slept next to him herself? Still, anger made her righteous, and she felt she could hear whatever it was Sophia Licari had to say.

"Here," Signora Licari said, and drew an eloquent mask with her fingers beneath her eyes. "It is purple. He is becoming thin. He does not go out to see his friends. And he is . . ." She made a very illustrative face. "Churlish, when he does speak."

Churlish? My goodness. What a fancy English word from the Italian woman. Though Sabrina knew full well Rhys was *capable* of being churlish.

"Does he see you?" Sabrina's heart was knocking oddly.

There was a silence.

"He only wants one thing, Lady Rawden. And that is why I am here."

It wasn't an answer to her question.

Sabrina looked back at the beautiful woman, met those sable eyes evenly. And she thought she saw a flicker of entreaty in them.

"Why are you here?" Sabrina demanded.

"You should allow him to see you." It sounded more like an order than a suggestion, and it sounded as though Signora Licari had every expectation it would be followed.

"Why?" Sabrina was incredulous. "To make it more pleasant for *you* when you do see him?"

"As I said, he does not see his friends."

It struck Sabrina then: Does Signora Licari consider Rhys her *friend*? And if so, this meant that he would not see Signora Licari, either.

It was clear then that this proud, beautiful, enigmatic woman cared for Rhys, too. And it wasn't pleasant to stand across from another woman who had touched and tasted her husband's body, who might very well be hurting on behalf of the man Sabrina had once thought she loved.

Either that, or it was merely inconvenient for her to see Rhys unhappy, and Rhys had become something of a bore, had ceased to give her gifts, and all of these things had made Signora Licari willing to petition his wife to see him.

Sabrina didn't think so.

Odd to think that this woman might actually care for Rhys, this woman who seemed to possess the allegiance of a cat, and the substance of a ray of light.

Still, Sabrina drew little comfort from the fact that Rhys apparently wouldn't see Signora Licari, either. That he was, quite clearly, suffering so much he was boring the soprano.

And yet he was a man. It was only a matter of time, she suspected, before he saw Sophia Licari again, and perhaps took her to bed.

"Your concern is quite moving, Signora Licari. But no. I will not see him. If you will excuse me?"

She curtsied—she made it shallow and quick, to make her point—and left the room.

* * *

He'd heard of Gorringe, of course. Every poet had, sympathizing with the legend of the duke who had gone mad searching for a rhyme for orange.

Orange made him think of lemon. And Yemen.

And Sabrina gravely pointing out his incorrigible behavior.

She'd stolen his breath, surprised him from the very first moment. It had taken weeks to realize it. And just a few minutes to ruin it.

Rhys made his way up the walk past the yard of tilting stones, pushed open the door, and entered silence.

A medieval church, small and modest, rows of empty pews. Somehow not lonely. There was an air about it that said it was a church well loved and well used, and that people had just left it or would return soon enough. Almost as if the ghost of music once played here lingered in the air.

Rhys settled into the pew and stared up at the chancel, imagining the vicar standing there delivering sermons—drifting, disjointed, if good-hearted sermons, Rhys thought, half smiling, remembering Kit's description of the man. He imagined Vicar Fairleigh standing there when he was a curate so many years ago, never dreaming that the little girl he'd taken in out of goodness—when he could scarcely feed the family he had—was the daughter of a notorious woman, and would grow up to marry an earl.

Rhys didn't think he'd search out the vicar just yet. He wasn't certain he would look for him at all.

He closed his eyes. He didn't precisely pray. He decided he would allow the hush of the church to wash over him, to filter through the tumult in his mind if only for a moment, to find brief relief from everything in quiet. He rested his hands on his knees and leaned against the pew.

Nothing stirred in the church while his eyes remained closed.

When Rhys opened his eyes again moments later, he glanced down at his hand and blinked: for an instant, it looked as though his fingers had gone . . . red and green?

And then he realized the sun was now beaming strongly through the church windows, and the reflection from the stained glass was floating over him. No dust danced in the beam of the light; clearly the church, old as it was, was tended carefully.

Rhys stood, and wandered over to the windows, peering at them closely. Light pushed through them and threw blurred outlines of three words down on the floor, the words Kit had told him about: Faith, Hope, and Charity.

And as he was a lover of beauty and a connoisseur of art, a collector of things, Rhys studied the windows, in the way Richard Lockwood no doubt had. They were lovely and simple, their colors brilliant and pure and distinctive, the design singular.

His breath caught.

Recognizably singular.

And suddenly it was as though his heart had been yanked up from a deep hole into sunlight.

The windows were set deep into the wall, and though he was very tall, he couldn't see the bottom of them from where he stood. He launched himself up onto a pew—it groaned a bit, taking his full weight—and he leaned forward, bracing himself against the wall of the church, prayed . . . and peered.

And there it was, at the bottom right corner of the window, the single word he'd hoped to see, and all the hairs rose on the back of his neck. Very few people in all of England would have known to look. Etched in rough tiny print, it read: *Santoro*.

Santoro lived in Italy, in the village of Tre Sorelle.

In English: Three Sisters.

"I'm not an inconspicuous man, Mr. Gillray. You've requested to speak to me specifically and privately, and in honor of your family name, I have agreed to do so. But I've no patience with subterfuge and games, and I'm a busy man. What is it you cannot share with one of my employees? I imagine you'd like me to pay for it, whatever it is."

Geoffrey had heard that Mr. Barnes was a bit of a poofter. He hadn't expected this brisk man, his face gray and weary but his eyes sharp and clever, his mouth thin with taxed patience. Geoffrey doubted Mr. Barnes would dare speak to Rhys, the Earl of Rawden, quite so very briskly.

But the *Times* was the most respectable of the dozens of newspapers that littered London, which made Barnes a powerful man in his own right. He'd been editor for only three years or so, however, and no newspaper editor lacked ambition, or spent a moment without craving more sales. He would hear him out, regardless.

And once the words were out of his mouth Geoffrey knew he couldn't retract them; he knew what he was about to do was irrevocable. But of course his birthright was of no value to him if his creditors intended to kill him at first opportunity, so it was all the same.

"Very well, Mr. Barnes. I have information linking a wealthy, powerful earl directly to a present-day scandal involving murder and treason."

He said the words calmly. *Murder and treason.* It would have been a pleasure to deliver them with drama, but he thought perhaps Mr. Barnes would be more amenable to a sort of somber directness.

Mr. Barnes's face barely registered the words, but Geoffrey saw the glint in his eyes sharpen immediately.

"Do you have any evidence supporting these allegations?"

"Yes."

"Please continue to talk, Mr. Gillray. I'll buy the brandy."

CHAPTER TWENTY-SEVEN

JOURNEYS ARE ALWAYS made longer by impatience and hope. Desperation made this particular journey seem an eternity. The melting sweetness of a dawning Italian spring scarcely penetrated Rhys's awareness; he acknowledged it only with brief gratitude, knowing the mild weather would make the passage into the hills of Tre Sorelle go more swiftly. A hired carriage took him as far as the town of Fume Bello; he hired a horse to take him the rest of the way into the hills.

Santoro's workshop was built beneath a stand of olive trees for shade, and olives had splattered the roof of it, turning it purple over the years.

Giovanni Santoro was short, round, and rude, and he spoke a fractured blend of Italian and English liberally sprinkled with epithets from other languages. Rhys had met him twice before on trips into the Italian mountains, and the man's language, so matter-of-factly delivered, had all but singed his ears, even as the man's artistry—the genius for color, the delicacy, the originality and purity of line of his designs—had awed him.

Sophia thought he was a cur because Santoro refused to give her a window outright. Santoro appreciated a pretty face—he was a florid and enthusiastic flirt who was on his third wife, having worn out one and driven away another with his excesses—but he was a businessman first. He knew what his work was worth, given that those who could afford the rare and precious and singular came from around the world to see him.

"Signore Rawden!" Forgetting that Rhys was an earl, and a lord. All men, by Santoro's way of thinking, were signores. He did, however, sweep a deep bow.

Rhys hadn't seen the man in two years, and he seemed even rounder now. Santoro noticed the glance at his belly.

"My wife, she feeds me well." Santoro gave a pleased, hearty thump to his stomach, which echoed like a drum. His hands were surprisingly graceful, as if they'd been grafted from another body onto his sturdy one.

"How is she? Any more bambinos, Giovanni?"

"A new bambino, a boy. Enrico. Fat, also," Giovanni said approvingly. "You are here for more windows, signore?"

"I am here on a more important mission, Giovanni. I'm looking for a woman."

"You cannot get a woman in England, signore? What has happened? Have you had them all, then, and need to look abroad, out of boredom?"

Rhys's reputation, and his poetry, had been translated into Italian, of course. The Italians considered it more of a manual of instruction than scandalous, however. "You need to be *più grasso*; the women, they will follow you everywhere," Santoro suggested, and laughed heartily at his own joke.

"Perhaps I *do* need to be fatter," Rhys agreed. "But I cannot eat again until I find one particular woman."

Santoro looked horrified at the thought of not eating again, and then apparently decided Rhys was jesting.

"You think she is in our hills, this woman, Signore Rawden?" He waved a hand at the greenery outside. "A sturdy peasant girl to give you sons?"

"I have a wife," Rhys said shortly.

Santoro almost comically drew his head back, then studied him shrewdly and in silence for a moment. "And she givva you trouble, your wife."

Trouble. That was one way to put it. Trust a man who'd had three wives to recognize wife trouble in the face of another man.

Rhys left the query unanswered.

"My wife resembles this woman. *Assomiglia a questa donna.* And this is the woman I seek."

Rhys extended Sabrina's miniature of Anna Holt. In her haste to flee her husband, Sabrina had left her most precious possession behind.

Santoro took it gently in his fingers, handling it with respect, the way any artist would handle another artist's work.

"*È bella,*" Santoro grunted in approval, after a moment.

"Yes, she is."

"Your wife, she is also . . . ?"

"*Bella?* Of course," Rhys said coolly. "But this image was painted about twenty years ago. The woman you see there might now be forty or so years old."

Santoro cupped the miniature in one hand and stared down at it, rubbing his fingers against his scalp to perhaps help stimulate a memory.

"She is in Tre Sorelle, this woman?"

"She might be. I don't know. I hope so."

Santoro's great furry brows met. He made thinking noises, clucking his tongue against the roof of his mouth.

Santoro squinted up at Rhys thoughtfully. "*È inglese?* Not Italian?"

"She is English," Rhys confirmed. He kept his voice level; with effort, he gripped hope tightly, too, lest it swell beyond his control. It became unwieldy, hope, when it deflated.

"And when did she come to Tre Sorelle, Signore Rawden?"

"I don't know precisely when she might have come, Giovanni. But it might have been as long as seventeen years ago." Rhys knew the dates precisely, of course, of the murder that had set this course of events in motion. But when a ship might have taken Anna Holt here, he could not have said.

And then, all at once, something that looked like inspiration lit Santoro's face, and the craftsman seized Rhys by the arm and drew him out of the workshop.

"There." He pointed up, and, squinting in the sun, Rhys followed the direction of the man's thick woolly arm.

"You take your horse up that road"—the artisan gestured into the hills, where Rhys saw a gold dirt ribbon of a road snaking up, weaving in and out of trees—"a woman, she lives in the villa at the end of the road. *È una vedova.*"

"Is she an *English* widow?"

"*Sì.* She has been here a long time, and she speaks Italian like she was born here, but she is *inglese.* My wife, she has been to her home. I have seen her but a few times. And she is *bella,* this woman."

"But not young?"

"Does it matter, Signore Rawden, as long as they are *bella*?" He grinned at Rhys. "But no, she is not young."

As far as Rhys was concerned: no, it did not matter.

"What is she like, this woman?"

"She is . . ." Santoro rubbed his chin between two fingers. "*È triste e calma.*"

Rhys took in these words: *sad and quiet.* She didn't sound like her daughters, who were proud and passionate. Perhaps time and grief had worn away her pride and passion.

Rhys knew the restlessness he felt at this thought was his own guilt, his own desperation. He needed to go up that road. The past and his future depended upon a sad and quiet English widow.

"What is her name?"

"She is Signora Smith."

Hope flared inside him then, brilliant as the sun; he couldn't stop it. In the church records at Gorringe, Anna Holt had been listed as Anna Smith.

Of course, it could simply be another English widow wishing anonymity. Or the woman living up the mountain in a villa could simply, truly, be an English widow named Smith who had retreated from the English weather to Italian warmth. It was a common enough name, Smith.

And somehow he doubted every English widow retreating from a scandal would have found a home in the tiny town of Three Sisters.

He knew a moment of awe for Sabrina's murdered father, Richard Lockwood, for leaving such a thorough trail of cryptic little clues, obvious to anyone who'd known him, or who'd thought to look.

And Anna, whether she'd done it deliberately or not, had gone to the one place where she could be found.

I'll find her, Lockwood, he promised silently.

For years Rhys had helped protect Richard's murderer. It was time that everyone received justice, even if it included him.

"*Grazi mille,* Santoro. I have no need of a window at present, but allow me to make a gift to you of—" Rhys presented Santoro with a handful of lira.

Santoro was not one to protest the gift of money. He gripped the money in his hand, and bowed shallowly. "*Grazi,* Signore Rawden. Good luck to you."

Italian weather could be unpredictable in this region in spring; snow might still cling to the mountains, the sky might break open and rain plummet ceaselessly down, accompanied by thunder that shook the ground. Rhys counted himself fortunate the skies were clear, and decided not to trust his good fortune. He kneed his hired horse up the steep winding road, coaxing it into a speed it was reluctant to take. It wasn't an easy road, but it looked traveled enough: he saw the droppings of horses and the fresh tracks of carts over older tracks. The small mountain community of Tre Sorelle was isolated but not unsocial; the steep road would pose no deterrent to an Italian hoping to visit another Italian.

He almost missed the villa, so thick were the trees about it, clustered protectively it seemed. Or perhaps this was just how his poet's mind viewed it. He slowed his horse only when a flash of color met his eye: terra-cotta, the wall of a house, peeking through.

He dismounted and looped the reins around a post meant expressly for that, then stood for a moment in the shade, swiping his hand across his brow, smoothing his hair back. He had no way of knowing how disreputable he might look. He only knew his clothing and his accent would speak for him when he opened his mouth to introduce himself.

He stood for a moment, listening. A bird hopped from one branch to another, rattling leaves.

And then he heard a more rhythmic sound: *Snick. Snick. Snick.*

It was coming from behind the house, where no doubt a garden grew. He knew the sound from childhood, in the days before La Montagne had been lost, and his mother had enjoyed the gardens.

It sounded like someone was trimming roses.

"You've another visitor, Sabrina. A Mr. Wyndham." Susannah stood in the doorway, eyes bright. "Handsome. But not a gentleman, I'd warrant."

Sabrina smiled at her sister. Before Susannah had met Kit Whitelaw, the Viscount Grantham, she'd been a London belle; she could assess a lineage or a pedigree within seconds. Sabrina had learned so much about her sisters in her short stay.

And she loved every new thing she learned about her sisters. And every time she considered again the very idea she might have been deprived of them, she knew panic and anger afresh.

"He's not a gentleman," Sabrina confirmed shortly.

It was truly interesting that her husband's friends felt obliged to make the pilgrimage to Grosvenor Square. She considered making Wyndham wait a good long while until he grew bored and went away on his own. She considered imperiously sending him on his way.

She wondered if he had word of Rhys; she wondered if she cared. She held the thought in her mind, but a shell had formed around the place Rhys lived in her. She felt nothing at all.

She looked at herself in the mirror. She was thinner, too, she realized in surprise. The skin beneath her eyes was a pale lavender; her eyes looked enormous. Vanity stirred.

But truthfully, it was boredom that brought her down the stairs and into the parlor.

"You look almost as wonderful as he does," were Wyndham's first words after bowing over her hand.

"I'm not certain that was a compliment, Mr. Wyndham."

"It wasn't, Lady Rawden."

This gave her a bit of pause. "Did you come here to vaguely insult me, Mr. Wyndham, or did you have a mission?"

"I think you should see him." Which was his way of coming bluntly to the point.

"This is becoming a rather dull refrain, I fear."

"I've known him for years, Lady Rawden. We've done—" He looked at Sabrina's face and apparently decided to edit whatever it was he'd been about to say. "We've done rather a lot of things together in that time. I know him very well. But I'd never seen him *happy.*

I frankly didn't think he had the capacity for it. And you made him happy."

Sabrina felt a little surge of anger. Just like that, she should see him, as if she were a carpet, or a painting, or a fanciful stained-glass window. Because it made him *happy.*

"Ah, but you see, he makes me *unhappy*," she explained carefully.

"I don't believe you," Wyndham said flatly.

This brought her up short.

"Mr. Wyndham." She said it coldly, a warning.

"I think he has *made* you unhappy. I do believe there's a difference. One is permanent, Lady Rawden. And the other is a product of incident."

She stared at him. "You are—"

She was about to say "impertinent," but she knew this wouldn't matter in the least to Wyndham.

"Lady Rawden. I swear to you he sees no one at all. Not Sophia. Not anyone at The Velvet Glove—"

The *Velvet Glove*? Good God, but she didn't want to picture what went on there.

But Wyndham had never cared whether or not he was scandalous. "He won't leave the house, except on errands he says nothing about. I haven't seen him in weeks. And when he speaks, he's—"

"Churlish?" Sabrina completed. "What a shame. That cannot be very pleasant for you." She was all mock sympathy. What a different woman she was today from mere months ago.

"I know you're angry. And Rhys is by no means a saint, and he's the last person to claim to be. But you're his wife. You've a duty to him."

"A duty, Mr. Wyndham?" The word made her quietly, ferociously angry. "The earl and I agreed from the outset to live our lives separately. One might say we've been successful in that regard."

"He's an earl, Lady Rawden. He'll want heirs." Wyndham said it flatly.

Sabrina sucked in a breath. "You always did enjoy setting out to shock me, didn't you, Mr. Wyndham?"

"I know so few people capable of being shocked anymore, Lady Rawden. You can hardly deny me the pleasure of shocking you."

She almost smiled. She was quiet instead, turned her head away from him.

"I miss him," Wyndham said simply.

Sabrina looked at Wyndham, his handsome, rakish face, those narrow dark eyes, and she almost knew sympathy. What an odd assortment of visitors Rhys had brought into her sister's drawing room. The disreputable painter who could scarcely paint, and the opera singer who took gifts from other admirers and who had made love to her husband. She ought to have been touched by the outpouring of loyalty.

It changed nothing. They were hardly references for his character. And her husband had killed her trust.

"Did the earl send you here, Mr. Wyndham?"

"No. I swear it on all I hold dear." His face was solemn.

Sabrina was suddenly curious about what Mr. Wyndham held dear.

"You won't see him?" Wyndham asked when she seemed disinclined to interrupt the silence.

"No," she said simply.

Wyndham ducked his head, briefly. Then nodded, as if in acceptance of his defeat.

"Rhys did say you were a good friend." She would tell Wyndham that much.

"Did he?" Wyndham smiled a little. "Tell me, what did Rhys tell you about my artwork?"

"He's an admirer of your painting, too." Sabrina said this gravely.

Wyndham studied her.

And then a faint smile turned up the corners of his mouth. "You're a beautiful liar, Lady Rawden." Surprising her, he swiftly lifted her hand to his lips, lingered over it, relinquished it.

It made her wonder precisely how many hearts Wyndham had broken.

And then he bowed, and was gone.

It wasn't precisely Rhys's intent to creep up on her, but his footfalls were careful and quiet. He followed the *snicking* sound, and peered around the corner.

Gooseflesh washed over his arms.

He knew in an instant, with bone-deep certainty, whom it was he watched.

And an instant later he began to be able to identify the subtle little things that added up to why he knew: the way she moved, graceful, quick and deliberate, so familiar now to him, for it lived in her daughter. The set of her shoulders, and the line of her spine—elegant, straight, as though fashioned out of pride itself. The slender neck—they all had that long, slender neck, the Holt sisters—and her chin: when she turned it a little, he saw it was somehow both stubborn and delicate, even as the skin beneath it had gone a little soft. But there was something indefinable about her essence that spoke so strongly of Sabrina that his heart leaped in fierce recognition, and it hurt.

Her hair, still dark, was coiled at the base of her neck; he could see it beneath the bonnet she wore; it was several years out of fashion and the ribbons were undone, as if she'd been too impatient to get at the roses this morning to tie it. A basket dangling from her arm held four long stems topped with fully blown blooms, brilliant and crimson. No doubt she was cutting them to enjoy in the house before the heat crisped their edges and they nodded on their stems.

She reached for another rose, extended her scissors.

But a shadow, a sense of something, must have alerted her to his presence.

She whirled. Froze and stared.

She didn't drop her scissors, he noticed; she kept them firmly in her grasp. Ah, the resourceful Holt women. Even in a moment of terror, she'd had the presence of mind to hold on to a weapon.

It wasn't until then that Rhys realized he hadn't the faintest idea what he'd intended to say to Anna. He'd been so utterly focused on simply finding her.

So he decided just to speak quickly, in a voice that would reassure nearly any English-born woman.

"My apologies, madam. I am Rhys Gillray, Earl of Rawden."

Belatedly he realized it was a voice that would reassure anyone with the exception, perhaps, of a fugitive from England.

So he bowed low then, which would have given her an opportunity to lunge forward with the scissors should the urge take her. A gesture, he hoped, of trust and, he hoped, not of foolishness.

Once he was upright again, she'd managed to compose herself. Her face was colorless, but she had donned an expression of polite confusion, a mask over her fear. She looked at him more fully then, seeing him. Ah, and despite her trepidation, she had that, too, the Holt women's appreciation for a handsome man: he saw her eyes flare almost imperceptibly.

He smiled a little, reassuringly.

Bella, indeed, he thought. Her eyes were pale, more gold than green, whereas his wife's eyes were decidedly more green. Those delicate bones and soft mouth. Fine lines beneath her eyes evident in the sunlight, as suited a woman her age, a woman who had known grief and fear and loss and love.

She spoke, her voice soft, her hands making a helpless, conciliatory feminine gesture. "*Sono spiacente, signore, ma non capisco l'inglese—*"

"Anna Holt." His voice, soft, gentle as the breeze in the garden, sliced off her sentence as surely as her scissors cut her roses.

She went very still. The hand clutching her scissors began to tremble a little.

Anna had been an opera dancer, perhaps, but she would never have made a convincing actress.

"Anna." Gently, gently said, though he knew nothing could cushion the words he was about to utter. "I am Rhys Gillray, Lord Rawden. And I am married to your daughter Sabrina."

The scissors slipped from her hand, landed with a metallic *thunk* at her feet. She stared a moment, then frowned slightly; her fingers went up to touch her face, a helpless gesture of disbelief.

And Rhys saw her knees begin to buckle.

He was next to her instantly; he caught her folding body in his arms, supporting her while her legs could not. He touched her wrists; her hands were ice cold. He saw a little bench nearby, tucked beneath a tree, and swept her up in his arms and carried her there.

Rhys gently settled her, turning his folded coat into a pillow, lifting her feet onto his lap. He'd been a soldier, after all. He knew a little bit about shock and how to treat it.

For a quiet minute or two, in the garden of a secluded Italian villa, Rhys Gillray, Earl of Rawden, sat quietly with Anna Holt's slippers in his lap.

"I've never fainted," were her first words. Very English, a little surprised, very steady, considering. "Not even when James Makepeace told me about Richard."

She glanced up at him to gauge his reaction to this statement. His silence told her he knew precisely what she meant.

"Are you feeling . . . ," he ventured, gently.

"Better? Yes, thank you, Lord Rawden." She sounded almost wry now. "May I . . . ?" She glanced down at her slippers, tellingly back up at his face.

"In a moment. You're still too pale."

She smiled slightly; her brows went up at his effortless way with an order. But then Richard Lockwood had been a military man, too. He imagined she was familiar with the type.

In the quiet that followed, a bird sang an aria. Rhys began to feel the heat at the back of his neck.

"You say you're Sabrina's husband?" she ventured softly after a moment.

"Yes." He still wasn't certain how to tell her what he'd come to tell her. He suspected he was postponing filling in the years. Postponing the moment when she would begin to hate him.

There was another silence.

"My Sabrina," she whispered. A ghost of a smile. "She was . . ." Anna paused. "How is . . ."

She stopped. And then slowly, before Rhys's eyes, Anna's face crumpled, and her hand fumbled up to her face, as if to ward off the sudden delayed rush of feeling. But she could not. She took in another long ragged breath. And when she exhaled, her body was shaking with racking, near-silent sobs.

Oh, tears. He never knew what to do about tears.

Gently Rhys lowered her feet to the ground. And then he took his wife's mother in his arms, and held her while she wept against his cravat.

"Well?" Geoffrey was impatient.

"We've traced the deed of the house to a Mr. Embry," Mr. Barnes told him evenly.

"And?" Geoffrey said.

"We've been unable to determine whether or not he was an associate of Mr. Morley's. The timing of the sale was as you said it would be, but the proof ends there."

"I'm telling you the truth, Mr. Barnes."

"Perhaps." Barnes looked bored.

"I can sell the story to a scandal sheet."

"For a good deal less than what we'll pay you." Mr. Barnes was entirely unconcerned. "And it's entirely possible no one will believe a word of it. Of course, it all depends upon your motive for selling the story, Mr. Gillray. And it might very well be worth your while to wait."

Geoffrey swiped surreptitiously at his temple. A bead of sweat had begun to form there. The money he'd asked for from Mr. Barnes would allow him to leave the country, abandon his debts here forever. But he was afraid to be in London. He'd had his life threatened. The scandal sheets were looking more and more appealing.

"Why are you so concerned, Mr. Gillray? Is it selling your family name that is making you a bit nervous, or is it something else?"

Geoffrey began to hate Mr. Barnes.

When Geoffrey said nothing, Mr. Barnes spoke again. "If the story is indeed true, I shall publish it and support it, for I enjoy selling newspapers, and intend to sell a good deal more than my predecessor. But my *own* reputation, and that of the *Times*, has no price, Mr. Gillray. So you will wait for corroboration, or you may sell your story to the scandal sheets. It is your decision to make."

Geoffrey knew this smug man, who had no title or family name, who was very close to being common, despised him. Even as he intended to make use of him.

And so they had that in common.

But Morley was on trial now, and who knew when they might decide upon his guilt with the evidence they had at hand, and how sentencing might actually take place? It might be all for naught if they hung the man before the information Geoffrey had to sell reached the public.

But thinking of Morley, Geoffrey suddenly had a brilliant inspiration. And it would deprive this smug man of his story.

"Thank you, Mr. Barnes, but I won't be needing you anymore."

Mr. Barnes merely shrugged.

Rhys and Anna now sat in her tiny villa at a rough wood table. He'd poured a drink of cool water for her; he'd poured water for himself. She'd laid a plate of bread and soft cheese on the table before him. Rhys sipped his water while Anna arranged her cut roses in a vase, a simple one of etched glass. The vivid blooms lit the room almost as surely as lamps.

It was tiny but comfortable, her home. There was a small kitchen, and a stove that burned wood both for heat and for cooking. A sitting room with a settee the color of cognac and two wooden chairs, as though every now and then she'd received company. Nothing like she'd been accustomed to, he was certain, when she was under the protection of a wealthy man like Richard Lockwood. But from what he'd learned about Anna Holt, she was resilient.

He told Anna, as simply as he could, how he'd found her: about Santoro, and the windows in the church. He told Anna that Kit Whitelaw had more or less managed to prove her innocence, and that Mr. Morley was on trial in England, and was expected to be convicted of the crime of treason at the very least.

But then they sat in silence. The history, the questions, the missing years, lay in a great tangle between them.

Neither of them seemed to know where to begin tugging in order to unravel the story. And so haltingly, he told her simple things, the outline of the things that she needed to know: the girls—Susannah, Sylvie, and Sabrina—were alive, and well, and beautiful, and married. And happy.

Well, except for one of them.

"Miss Holt—"

"Anna. Or Mother if you prefer." Her eyes sparked up at him, and in that moment he thought it was both a shame and a relief for the men of the world that there weren't more Holt women in it, for men didn't stand a prayer against any of them.

He smiled a little. "Anna . . . Sabrina was raised by a vicar. I married her this year. And now she won't speak to me."

Her eyes rose up to his in question. "You came to find me to help resolve a quarrel with my daughter?" She quirked her brows.

"I came to find you, Anna, because I'm in part the reason you're here at all."

CHAPTER TWENTY-EIGHT

RHYS TOLD HIS tale without interruption, without embellishment, but with fact and feeling, beginning with his father's death and concluding with Geoffrey's threat to expose the secret to all of England, and it took surprisingly little time given how profoundly the story had colored his entire life. He made himself look at Anna the entire time, watching her eyes. So like his wife's eyes in shape. But she gave him nearly nothing. He once saw a tightening about her jaw; he once heard her draw in a deep breath, bracing herself against some emotion—anger or anguish, perhaps. He, who was so good at assessing everyone, simply couldn't tell.

In the wake of the story, the silence in Anna Holt's little villa was dense.

Anna studied him, her expression unreadable, her eyes as unblinking as Sabrina's could be.

Bravely, he met her gaze. Allowed her to arrive on her own at any conclusions she saw fit. It was one of the harder things he'd ever had to do.

"Did you come here for absolution?" Anna finally asked. Her voice was a little distant. Reflective. She sounded genuinely curious.

"No. I came here to take you back to Sabrina." Un-equivocally said. "And I thought you should know what sort of man intended to take you back to your daughter."

She looked at him a moment, eyes widening.

And then, to his amazement, she smiled, as though something he'd said pleased her.

She leaned forward, absently touched one of the roses, fingered the petals very gently. She seemed to be deciding what to say.

She took a breath before she spoke. "I've my own mea-sure of guilt to bear, Lord Rawden. I wrote letters to James Makepeace years ago inquiring about the welfare of my girls, but I knew it was a selfish thing to do. I knew doing so endangered James and the girls and myself, but there were days I would have happily died for word of them. But I never risked a return to England. I always wondered whether I ought to have tried harder, you see . . . but I was afraid, and I didn't know what else to do. And so the years passed. I did manage to read London papers once or twice, but I didn't actively seek them. I didn't want to call attention to myself. I did sense that the search for me seemed to have subsided. But still I feared. And when I never heard from James, I feared the worst."

She paused for a moment.

"What I'm trying to say, Lord Rawden . . . we all make the decisions we feel we need to make at the time. You didn't kill Richard. In many ways, you were just as much a victim of Thaddeus Morley as Richard or I."

Rhys was stunned. He turned his head away from her briefly to disguise it.

But perhaps he should not have been surprised. The same sort of wisdom and generosity of spirit lived in her daughter. And it wasn't precisely absolution, but it was better. Anna Holt, of all people, understood why he'd done what he'd done.

"Do you love my daughter, Lord Rawden?"

He paused. "Perhaps." When he said the words aloud for the very first time in his life, he wanted to say them to Sabrina alone.

She studied him a moment longer, and then a faint smile appeared on her lips. Again, something about him seemed to satisfy her.

"Well, I find recrimination dull, on the whole, don't you? And now, Lord Rawden, why don't you take me home."

Morley squinted in the light that came through narrow slits.

The king had indeed seized his properties. Mr. Duckworth was informative that way, bringing him little bits of news. But Morley, little did anyone else in the government know, with his instinct for self-preservation, had squirreled evidence of his activities in places the authorities would never find. He might have hung twice over, if they'd found it.

"I've had a fascinating correspondence with a Mr. Geoffrey Gillray, Mr. Morley. He's the cousin of the Earl of Rawden."

The name made Mr. Morley turn to look at Mr. Duckworth for a long moment.

"Is there something we should discuss before the trial? Your day of sentencing approaches, as you know."

"Does it really?" Morley said lightly. "How time flies."

"If there's something you'd like to share with me, this would be an excellent time to do it."

Morley had indeed reviewed his rolls of associates. He did indeed know of one particular earl he could easily hand over to His Majesty. But he very much wanted to hear what Mr. Duckworth had to say first.

The correspondence from Geoffrey Gillray was interesting. Morley had met the lad once years ago. Handsome, dissolute, weak but not in an interesting or particularly useful way. Not worthy of his interest, really . . . until now.

"You may find it interesting that the Earl of Rawden is married to a woman who is rumored to be Anna Holt's daughter. Miss Sabrina Fairleigh." Duckworth sounded mildly bemused by this. He'd encountered stranger coincidences in his profession.

Morley went still. And then a peculiar little smile touched his mouth and quivered there.

What odd, exquisite symmetry there was in the universe, he thought. How had the Earl of Rawden responded when he'd learned his wife was likely Anna Holt's daughter? How on earth had the marriage come about?

Morley believed in symmetry, but not coincidence. He was a strategic sort, and planned his moves accordingly, but he recognized and enjoyed the poetry of proper conclusions, too.

"Do you believe in my innocence, Mr. Duckworth, or do you merely have a professional interest in the outcome?"

"Does it matter, Mr. Morley?"

Morley smiled. Once upon a time, he and Mr. Duckworth might have done business together successfully, he suspected.

"Does Mr. Gillray hope to benefit monetarily from his correspondence with you, Mr. Duckworth?"

Mr. Duckworth said nothing. Which was an answer in and of itself.

The poetry of proper conclusions. And as Morley continued to contemplate this concept, he knew precisely what his next move would be.

"I prefer to do this with a bit of flair, if you don't mind," Morley said almost briskly. "Please inform interested parties, including Mr. Geoffrey Gillray, that I shall make an announcement on Tuesday before sentencing."

As it turned out, Mr. Duckworth, who was not at all averse to publicity as it no doubt would mean more business for him, was amenable.

And when word got out, Westminster chambers would be overflowing with the curious.

"I trust you'll be able to support with evidence whatever it is you intend to announce on Tuesday, Morley?"

"Naturally."

"I shall tell the hangman he needn't come in to fit your noose, then." A dry parting remark from Mr. Duckworth.

Morley simply turned toward the arrow slits and watched the sunlight again, a ghost of a smile at his lips.

Tom handed the scandal sheet to Kit. "Read here."

"Rumor has it that a certain earl has fled the country to avoid being implicated in one of the greatest scandals in English political history. All will be revealed on Tuesday in Westminster chambers."

"Where did you get this, Shaughnessy? You don't normally read this sort of nonsense."

"All manner of things are left lying about The Family Emporium. But since I'm purportedly related to Rawden

through Sylvie, someone saw fit to put it right in my hand.
We'll attend the sentencing tomorrow of course?"

"Of course." Kit wanted to see the judge don a black
cloth for Morley. He'd never take pleasure in the death o
another man; he would, however, derive a certain amoun
of grim satisfaction in justice being done, and justice wa
typically meted out by rope or deportation. No one con
victed of treason would ever breathe free air again, un
less the circumstances were extraordinary. It was simply
the law, and in his own fashion, he had served the law fo
more than a decade. But now . . .

"What the hell do you suppose it means?" Kit rapped
the sheet hard with the back of his hand.

"Possibly it's just a ruse to sell seats in the chambers."
Tom didn't sound confident about this.

Kit suspected otherwise, too. He'd known Morley too
long. The man was resilient; his tentacles were every
where. Kit wasn't naive enough to believe that the shelte
of the Tower had entirely curbed Morley's reach.

And Rawden . . . He wondered what sort of secret Rawden
harbored that his wife still steadfastly refused to divulge, and
whether it was large enough to touch his own family.

Rawden was in Italy, he'd heard, information the
man's taciturn valet had finally divulged. Kit thought he
knew the measure of the man. He hadn't *fled* at all. And
even while Kit had always hoped he'd be the one to do it
he prayed Rawden succeeded in his quest. There was so
much more at stake for him.

Sabrina read the words printed before her on the scanda
sheet, and the ground dropped from beneath her feet.

She took a deep breath, steadying herself. Then realized there was already a steadying arm beneath her elbow.

"Were we wrong to show you this?" Sylvie asked gently.

She began to guide Sabrina toward a chair, but Sabrina, impatient, frowned a little, which made her sisters smile. Stubborn bloody Holts. They suspected Sabrina was the most stubborn of all of them.

"Is he really out of the country?" Sabrina asked it faintly, almost speaking to herself. She thought she would have sensed it if Rhys were gone.

Oddly, she realized she hadn't been afraid when she read those words. Her first reaction was . . . fury. Surely Geoffrey was the source. Geoffrey had betrayed her as surely as Rhys, and for reasons far more craven.

"Rawden's valet told Wyndham that Rawden went to Italy. Wyndham told Tom."

Tom Shaughnessy was another person who associated with all manner of men.

The three sisters exchanged looks, but none of them gave voice to their thoughts, because there was too much pain in the hope.

And Susannah and Sylvie knew by now not to ask Sabrina to share the secret she harbored about her husband. They only knew they should be with Sabrina no matter what occurred.

"Do you still want to come to the sentencing?" Sylvie asked.

She knew, suddenly, that if Morley intended to implicate Rhys, she wanted to be there.

"Of course."

* * *

"Are you certain they want to see me?" Anna asked it, and then felt foolish, because it made her sound so hesitant, fearful. She'd been strong for so long.

But she'd forgotten in her absence what an assault on the senses London could be, the noise and crowds and smells and movement. She'd lived in the country, in Gorringe, and then she'd lived in further isolation in the hills of Italy, and now the clamor made her brace herself. And she'd longed for London for seventeen years, but all the while, London had somehow been the enemy, too, because London had hunted her. She still hardly felt the right to stand where she stood.

This is what I've wanted for seventeen years.

Ah, well: so she was uncertain, but she was no less strong. And it was best to do it all at once, she knew. So much easier to dive in than to wade in slowly.

"I want to see them now," she said. "All of them."

"Very well, then," Rhys said. "I should think they are all in. It's early yet, and I've heard they are seldom apart."

He waited a bit with her, standing at her side next to the hackney as they looked up at the Grantham town house.

"How do I . . ." Anna hesitated, her hand rising up to her hair a moment, fussing with her bonnet.

"Look? Wonderful. Just like your daughter, in fact."

She smiled a little. "Will you come with me?" She made it sound solicitous, but she was embarrassed for asking, mostly because she was partly afraid to do this alone.

"No. I don't want Sabrina to feel obligated to see me just because I've brought you home. And I think you're a big enough surprise on your own, Anna." Wryly said. "Godspeed."

Anna suddenly found it impossible to speak. He was an extraordinary man, her daughter's husband. Strong and flawed. The sort of man every woman needed, because sometimes a man's greatest strengths were merely the inverse of his greatest flaws. She found herself wishing he and Richard might have known each other.

Rhys kissed Anna's hand.

She saw Rhys glance up once at the windows of the town house and inhale, squaring his shoulders. A poignant gesture.

And then he climbed into the hackney and left her to reclaim her life.

On Monday, the day before Morley's sentencing, Susannah heard voices and pushed a curtain aside to peer out into the day. Clouds were moving in to obscure the sun. They might have a spring shower before long.

But it wasn't the sky that riveted her.

"Sabrina, Sylvie . . . a hackney has left a woman at the foot of the stairs."

Susannah's voice was so odd the other girls immediately crowded around the window to see.

Each of them went perfectly still. No one seemed able to speak.

"My God," Sabrina whispered at last, speaking for all of them. Her trembling hand went up to her mouth. "He's done it. It's her."

Rhys had been home for all of five minutes when his valet informed him that Mr. Wyndham was at the door and wished to see him. Urgently.

Rhys had just yanked off his cravat, and was looking forward to yanking off his boots, bolting brandy, and soaking in a bath. But he supposed he could spare a moment for Wyndham, to whom he'd been nothing but rude for weeks.

"Send him up, I suppose."

Moments later, Wyndham swept into the room. "Aside from the fact that you didn't see fit to tell me you were leaving the country, have you seen the scandal sheets, Rawden? I thought you'd better have a look."

"Odd way to greet a man, Wynd."

But the look on Wyndham's face was grim, and Rhys could not recall when he'd ever before seen Wyndham grim. So he looked at the page where Wyndham was pointing, and then seized the paper from him.

"Rumor has it that a certain earl has fled the country to avoid being implicated in one of the greatest scandals in English political history. All will be revealed on Tuesday in Westminster chambers."

Tomorrow, in other words. When Rhys was silent, Wyndham finally spoke.

"Not what they normally say about you, Rawden. At least it's a change of pace." Careful, his words were. Inviting Rhys to speak.

Rhys couldn't speak yet. So Geoffrey, bloody weak Geoffrey, *had* made good on his threat. And this wasn't exactly the *Times,* it was only a scandal sheet, but it had gone as far as to imply that perhaps actual evidence highlighting his guilt would be presented at Morley's trial. Perhaps Morley had kept records after all. Or perhaps he would merely make some sort of allegation aloud, which was damning in itself.

Rhys knew exactly where he would be tomorrow.

CHAPTER TWENTY-NINE

L ATER, NO ONE would remember who spoke first. Or who shed the first tear.

Later, it would all seem of a piece.

They waited, motionless, in silence, for her to come up to the door, and for Bale to bring her in to them. Almost as if she were an apparition, and they feared she would disappear if they moved, or all came at her at once.

Finally, Bale, unflappable Bale, entered the room. But even *he* was pale, and his eyes were lit with bemused wonder.

And when he spoke, his voice shook.

"Anna Holt," he announced.

Some things, the most heartfelt things, can only be communicated with silence. And this was how it was for all of them for a minute or so. A moment of wonder. A moment somehow outside of time.

Someone reached out a hand to touch Anna. No one could remember whom. The hand drew back again. They began to crowd closer to her, then hung back once more, not wanting to overwhelm her.

They paused awkwardly, and once again there was nothing but silence as they all stared.

"My God . . . ," Anna finally faltered. "You're all so *beautiful*."

And for the rest of their lives, they would remember these words. For it was a voice Sabrina, Sylvie, and Susannah knew from a shared memory seventeen years old, of a dark frantic night, of tears, one another . . . and their mother.

And she'd arrived in time to go to court to watch the sentencing of the man who had ruined their lives so many years ago.

All the Holt girls were there, Morley noticed, three lovely, unmistakable, faces, pale and strained and resolute. Hoping to witness justice today. With them were their husbands: Morley's downfall, the Viscount Grantham, no longer a boy, his blue eyes boring into him just as grimly as they had so many years ago. Next to him was his wife, Susannah, one of Anna Holt's daughters, who'd proved impossible for Bob to kill, thanks to Grantham. There was the famous Mr. Tom Shaughhessy, gorgeous devil, former proprietor of The White Lily Theater, sitting with the woman who must be his wife, Sylvie. Lovely girl. Together Richard Lockwood and Anna Holt had created beautiful children.

Every eye in the courtroom that *wasn't* trained on Morley was trained on the Earl of Rawden.

Imposing, handsome, the earl was, and his eyes were on Morley now, unblinking. Brilliant, fierce eyes. He was a formidable man now. He'd been a frightened boy at one time. Morley had seen how to make use of his fear, and it had served him well for seventeen years.

How very dramatic, how very appropriate, that the earl had managed to reappear just in time for Morley's final appearance. And when he'd entered the courtroom boldly, there had been an instant hush and a near-audible swivel of heads. Followed by a rush of murmurs from the crowd, a sound like flame touched to dry branches.

Sabrina had then jerked her head away, and looked into her lap.

Ah, but he'd seen, and everyone had seen, the look in Rawden's eyes. The man just didn't care that everyone knew he was in love with his wife.

How funny fate was.

But now the earl sat apart from his entire family. Interesting. So perhaps they knew Rawden's sordid little secret. What a pity for Rawden.

Morley's eyes moved beyond the earl and then . . .

Well, Morley's vision wasn't what it once had been. But he thought he saw, there in the chambers . . . Anna Holt. He was surprised that his heart didn't clench, causing him to gasp in pain. His heart wasn't what it once had been, either, and the Tower had done nothing at all to bolster his health.

Perhaps she *was* a ghost. Perhaps he ought to spin his head about and look for Richard Lockwood, too. He almost smiled at the fanciful thought. With the dramatic earl present, no one seemed to have noticed her, bundled unobtrusively as she was in widow's weeds. She was older; but she looked so much like her daughters she might simply have been another of them. Or a shadow of one of them.

Morley knew she wasn't a ghost. He realized her presence was merely, again, the exquisite symmetry of the universe at work. It merely confirmed for him the rightness of what he was about to do.

He looked about for the final player and . . . oh, yes, there he was: Geoffrey Gillray. A shadow of his cousin in terms of looks and presence, thin, jumpy. Wealthier, now, perhaps, thanks to the combined efforts of Morley's lawyer and the scandal sheets. It had been an impressive orchestrated effort. Young Gillray looked somehow both defiant and as if he'd like to shrink into his seat so that his cousin the earl wouldn't gobble him alive.

Ah, but Mr. Duckworth was talking now, preparing to ask the final fateful question, and so Morley must listen.

"Mr. Morley, we've a question before we proceed with sentencing. Did you in fact pay anyone, as has been alleged, to lie to authorities in order to implicate Anna Holt in the matter of Richard Lockwood's murder?"

Well, Mr. Duckworth couldn't have put the question any more directly, could he?

Morley waited. He wanted every breath in that courtroom held before he spoke. He wanted every eye fixed upon him. He wanted his words quoted everywhere in London tomorrow, over dinner tables, in salons and clubs, in the papers. He wanted them to be unforgettable, unmistakable.

And then, oddly, he saw the daughter who looked so much like Anna Holt begin to stand. Almost as if she were preparing to speak.

He thought he best relieve the crowd of its anticipation before she *did* speak and ruin his moment.

And so in his best speech-to-the-House-of-Commons voice, Morley said, "No, Mr. Duckworth. I believe you may have been misled by Mr. Geoffrey Gillray, who seeks to taint the good name of his cousin, the Earl of Rawden, and thereby earn notoriety, not to mention a few thousand pounds, from my own unfortunate circumstances."

Good heavens, but Morley enjoyed the gasp that went up.

All was uproar. People on their feet, fighting one another for a look at Morley, at Geoffrey, at the earl.

Mr. Geoffrey Gillray spun this way and that in his seat. Officers of the court moved ominously to guard the exits lest he attempt to flee.

Young Mr. Gillray was unlikely to be a guest in the Tower, thanks to his rank. Newgate or deportation seemed more likely, Morley knew. He smiled a little. He looked at his lawyer, Mr. Duckworth, who was regarding him with an expression of rank betrayal and a little bit of awe, and winked.

Morley didn't like to think it had anything to do with conscience. Or with the late-in-life realization that he did indeed possess a soul, and that he needed to make things right with his Maker—a Maker who, coincidentally, had not precisely come to his rescue so long ago, when he'd lost his entire family in a London fire.

But it was a splendid way to go out, and it had a certain poetry the Earl of Rawden, The Libertine, could not fail to appreciate.

Besides, Morley had no intention of *actually* swinging from a rope.

"Why did you stand up today in the courtroom, Sabrina? When Mr. Morley's lawyer spoke?"

Sabrina gave a start and turned toward her mother. The sisters had finally gone beyond all but gamboling about Anna like puppies, and now they could sit sedately in a room and talk over and around and through one another and still be heard, in the manner of families everywhere.

But Sabrina, for a few glorious moments, had her mother to herself, for Sylvie had gone to attend to the business of the theater and Susannah was speaking to her cook about dinner.

Sabrina came and knelt on the carpet in front of Anna and began to fuss with a basket of wool at her feet, thinking about a scarf she'd knitted. Blue, like his eyes.

But she didn't want to lie, so she stubbornly didn't answer Anna's question.

Her mother raised an eyebrow at the silence. "Are you going to see him?" she asked.

A pause. "No."

She'd left the courtroom with Anna and Sylvie and Susannah and Kit and Tom, steadfastly refusing to meet Rhys's eyes.

"Why not?"

"Mama . . ." How Sabrina loved using that word. "He found you. But it was Rhys who sacrificed you, all of us, in order to save his own family. What Mr. Morley did today doesn't change the truth of that."

"Oh, for *heaven's* sake, Sabrina."

Sabrina whirled around. She'd been home in England for scarcely more than a *day,* and her mother actually sounded both exasperated and a little amused.

"Men are idiots, my dear," Anna said this matter-of-factly. "But so, I fear, are you."

Sabrina gasped. And then her eyes narrowed, her temper rising up. "You've *no* right—"

"Ah, you're absolutely correct, my love. I've no right," Anna agreed almost cheerily. "I might be a veritable stranger to you, but I have loved you all your life, every minute of it, whether you knew it or could feel it or not. And I've something important to tell you. You're young. And you're proud, which is as it should be, and no surprise, given your blood. Your father was proud, and God knows I'm nothing if not proud, and in part it's our strength. But perhaps you're too young to know how rare . . ." Anna's steady tone faltered a little, and she cleared her throat. "How *rare* real love is. How precious, how unlike anything else. And I apologize if I sound maudlin, but you need to hear this, Sabrina."

Sabrina sucked in an impatient breath, bracing herself. These words hurt; they chipped away at the shell she'd built around the very thought of Rhys. She wanted none of this wisdom.

"He has never once told me that he loves me," Sabrina said coldly. "And he never wanted me to begin with."

"Oh, Sabrina." Anna rolled her eyes. "How very dramatic."

Sabrina gaped at her mother. And then she nearly spluttered in outrage. "How can you—"

"Your husband found himself in the remarkably untenable position of being married to a girl he'd betrayed so many years ago. Fate does have a sense of humor, you know. And he was afraid to lose you, and so he did a stupid thing by essentially lying to you, and sending your sisters away the day they came to see you. That was fear, you see. As I said, men are idiots, especially when it comes to love. And he did a desperate thing long ago to save people he loved. Who can say what any of us might have done?"

"*I* would not have—*you* would not have—"

"Hush." Anna was stern now. "You cannot say what you would have done. Enough of the righteousness."

Sabrina was fully furious now with this woman. But despite herself, she was listening, avidly. No one had ever spoken like this to her before, and even as the words stung, she was thirsty for them.

Anna's tone softened, looking into Sabrina's flaming face. "Sabrina . . . I swear this to you: your husband is a brave man. And not just because of the war; war made brave many an ordinary man. But he sat before me and confessed everything, knowing full well I might hate him. For the crime was committed primarily against me, was it not? But he wanted me to know who he was, and why he was there. And he wanted to give me back to you. He did this even while knowing everything he'd worked for his entire life—his title, his properties, the legacy of Rawden heirs for centuries to come—was at risk in his absence from London. I can say this, and I would never say this lightly. He's worthy of you."

Sabrina's heart was either breaking or blooming, she could not be certain. She wrapped her arms around herself tightly to smother the ache.

"But, Mama—" She felt the tears now. Pushing at the back of her eyes, knotting inside her chest. "I can't—"

Anna went on, gentle but relentless. "He brought me to you. He's prepared to live a life without you as long as you have what *you've* always longed for. And that, I tell you, is courage, my love. Because I can tell you what it's like to know that kind of love, and then to have to live without it."

Sabrina dashed her hand against her cheek. The tears were pouring now, hot and furious. "But don't you see, Mama—he was *part* of the reason you needed to leave us. If he'd only confessed the truth at the time—oh, the time we've lost, you and I and Susannah and—"

"My dear, if it hadn't been Rhys, it would have been someone else who lied for pay, for Mr. Morley is just that sort of man. He would have found someone to do it for him, and Richard would be just as dead. But Rhys lied for people he *loved,* Sabrina. It wasn't pretty or right, but he didn't feel he had a choice. This is a man who would do *anything* for someone he truly loves. And remember, Sabrina, everything he now has, everything he worked to acquire, is also yours. And it will all belong to your children, too. And that is nothing to disdain. I've *known* want. It's much better not to want," she said bluntly.

Children. Sabrina closed her eyes. Oh, but she would love to have children.

"And if *I've* forgiven him, then perhaps you can find it in your heart to forgive him, too. I would never wish it upon you, a lifetime of regret. Pride is bloody cold comfort, Sabrina. But if you truly hate him, if you feel nothing at all inside your heart right now, so be it. But I needed to tell you these things, because I couldn't live with myself if I did not."

Suddenly Sabrina was weary, drained. For a time she sat in silence, letting the words, at last, penetrate.

And then, finally, she surrendered to a longing decades old: she tentatively, slowly rested her damp cheek against Anna's knees.

Anna hesitated a moment. And then she laid her hand atop Sabrina's soft head.

And soon it was so easy, so natural, for her to stroke her daughter's hair, soothing her hot forehead.

Sabrina sniffed for a bit. "Mama?"

"Yes?"

"Did he tell you that he loves me?"

"No." Anna said this simply.

Sabrina looked up into her mother's face. "Then how do you *know*—"

"Do you love *him*, Sabrina?"

Sabrina remained stubbornly silent.

Anna sighed. "You're a grown woman now. If you've the courage, do everything you can to find him. And find out from *him* whether or not he loves you. You can decide what to with the rest of your life once you know."

The news arrived the next morning in the person of Kit's father, the Earl of Westphall, who found his son at White's. Westphall, who controlled the movements of His Majesty's Secret Service, was possessed of far more diplomacy than his son could ever hope to lay claim to, but he was a man of few words when the occasion called for it.

"Morley's gone. They found his cell empty this morning. Word just reached me."

Morley had been scheduled to hang in Tower Green in three days' time. A private, discreet death with few witnesses, the sort accorded to dignitaries, in deference to his once-respected position.

Kit's head snapped up. "Gone? *How?*"

"A guard apparently took pity on a condemned man," the Earl of Westphall drawled, "and allowed a woman up to his cell. And that's all I know now. Oh, and that, according to the guard, this woman was 'beautiful as an angel.'" The words sizzled with sarcasm. "I'm off to learn more details. I needn't tell you not to tell a soul. Not the girls. Not anyone."

His father left.

Caroline Allston. Kit knew it in his soul, somehow. Somehow Caroline, a woman who had haunted three men for much of their lives, had helped Morley escape, and no doubt the resourceful Morley had planned it all from the Tower.

Kit then wondered about his friend John Carr, who had thrown his entire life away to be with Caroline.

Gone. So Morley wouldn't die. And Kit sat with the knowledge, stunned, wondering how much it mattered when everyone he loved was safe and together at last, when the girls had one another, and their husbands, and their mother, Anna, once more. Morley had never been a vengeful sort; he was more of a practical and purposeful sort . . . which had made him all the more deadly in his attempts to protect his power. His actions, the violence he had wrought, stemmed from reason, not passion.

And somehow knowing that Morley was free in the world gave everything Kit loved a sharper edge of sweetness, knowing that darkness lurked on its periphery. Knowing that he could never fully ease into complacency somehow suited him, oddly.

And oh, yes: He fully intended to find Morley again.

CHAPTER THIRTY

RHYS WASN'T AT his town house. He wasn't at La Montagne.

Wyndham didn't know where he was. Mrs. Bailey didn't know, his valet didn't know. Nobody knew.

Though this likely wasn't entirely true. Sabrina suspected there was one person who just might know, one person she hadn't yet asked, one person she didn't want to ask, and the one person she very likely needed to ask.

And so Sabrina called upon Signora Sophia Licari.

Sabrina looked about the drawing room of her husband's former mistress. It suited the soprano: tawny shades and gilt, heavy velvets, everything soft and lush. The lair of a tigress, a habitat in which she could lounge and blend. Sabrina wondered how much of it had been paid for by her husband, or other admirers of Signora Licari.

Then again, the soprano's grand talent might pay for more than Sabrina suspected.

"Lady Rawden," Signora Licari said by way of greeting. "Your husband is not here."

"I know," Sabrina said curtly, which made Signora Licari's fair brow hike.

"You are very confident of this." And now the soprano was amused.

Sabrina suspected Sophia Licari would be able to make her feel provincial until the day she died.

"I'm confident because I know my husband."

"Do you? Then why are you here?"

It was a good question. She swallowed her pride to answer it. "Because I know his heart, but I do not know all the details of his life, and I have not known him long. And I don't know where he is. I have looked everywhere I know to look. I wondered if you might know where I should look."

Signora Licari was quiet, and tipped her head to the side. The dim light in the room still gilded her, as if the world understood that Sophia Licari belonged in the light.

"Good. He should be loved," she said at last.

A startling thing to say. "I didn't say anything of the sort," Sabrina said coolly.

Sophia Licari just raised her fair brows again.

The two regarded each other for a moment in silence.

"Do *you* love him?" Sabrina risked the question. She wondered why she wanted to know, and what she would do with the information once she had it. She had asked it more out of curiosity about Sophia Licari than anything else, she realized.

"Ah, my bella Sabrina." The soprano laughed that laugh like silvery bells. She always did laugh at the strangest things. "What does it matter, as long as you do?"

"I didn't say that I did," Sabrina corrected coldly once more. "Once again: Do. You. Know. Where. He. Is?"

Apparently at last weary of milking the moment of drama, Sophia Licari answered, "He likes to fish."

There was a moment's pause.

"Little Orrick," Sabrina breathed. "Damien Russell."

Sophia Licari nodded in approval. "You know your husband better than you think, Lady Rawden."

It struck Sabrina that the moment should contain more drama. As it was, Rhys looked rather peaceful, sitting by himself at the end of a pier, a small blue lake at his feet, blue sky above, fishing pole bobbing in his hands. Perhaps thinking of Damien. Perhaps thinking of her.

"Rhys," she said softly.

She saw his back tense as he straightened. And then he carefully settled his fishing pole on the pier before he very slowly turned around. As though he didn't want to be disappointed if he'd only imagined her voice.

When he saw her, she'd never seen a man rise to his feet so quickly.

His shirt had more open buttons than was gentlemanly, his sleeves were rolled up. His hair was much too long now, she noted, past his collar, and the wind lifted it up out of his eyes. Several days' growth of beard darkened his jaw. Shadows a darker blue than his eyes curved beneath them. She'd never seen him look such a mess.

Dear God, he was beautiful.

He seemed somehow larger, now, framed against all that blue. Or maybe it was just that he would always seem the most important thing on any horizon for her.

He took three swift steps toward her, then stopped. Watched her, those pale eyes rivaling the sky for brilliance. Unguarded now.

So she came the rest of the way to him, slowly. And when she was close enough, she tipped her forehead against his chest. Just to touch him, to breathe him in again.

She heard him exhale a soft laugh. His arms went around her loosely, almost tentatively. Then more decisively, when she didn't pull away from him, he pulled her into his body, wrapping her tightly with his arms.

They held each other for a time, her cheek rising and falling against his chest with his breathing. Almost as though they were too uncertain to look at each other directly, at first.

And then he loosened his arms from her, took her face in his hands. He lowered his head for a kiss, but before he kissed her, he whispered it against her lips:

"I love you."

She wanted to always remember the expression in his eyes when he'd said it. But he kissed her before she could tell him she loved him, too.

Softly, so softly, his mouth against hers. She closed her eyes, and she felt the tears coming again.

"Oh, now . . . ," he murmured. "Tears?"

She laughed a little, then pressed her damp cheek against his chest and rested it there.

"Why did you stand in the courtroom, Sabrina?"

She lifted her head to look at him.

"You saw me stand?"

"I saw almost nothing else but you," he said simply.

She paused. "No matter what Morley said . . . I think I was about to tell the world what manner of man you are. I was so angry that anyone would think they had the right to print things about you. I wanted to tell them why you had done the things he accused you of. Before someone else could say it."

She stopped, and slowly tugged what seemed like miles of his linen shirt from his trousers just so she could press her hands against the warmth of his skin, against the firm muscles of his back. Feel them rise and fall with his breath, and revel in the fact that he was alive, that he was hers.

This was heaven.

"You and your animal nature," he murmured in mock complaint as her hands wandered. He pulled her closer, and then closer still.

"It's your fault," she murmured. "You and your secret to seduction."

A quiet passed, and then he spoke, very softly. And she could feel the words rumbling in his chest, against her cheek, as he spoke.

"No, it was you, Sabrina, who possessed the secret all along."

She remembered to say it then. She tilted her head back to find him looking down at her: "I love you, Rhys."

He was quiet for a moment. "And that's the secret," he said simply.

EPILOGUE

October 1821

RICHARD RHYS WILLIAM James Gillray, heir to the Earl of Rawden, was baptized in the early fall. But not at the church in Buckstead Heath, as one would have supposed. It was at the church in Gorringe, where three windows glowed the words "Faith, Hope, and Charity" onto their small congregation. It was how Sabrina wanted it, when she'd learned the story of the windows. In a way, the three Holt sisters felt closer to their father by being there, their brave, clever, whimsical father who had made it possible from the grave for all of them to be together again.

The little baby, who bellowed quite as manfully as his father could when his own father was in a mood, was named for three brave men: his father, Rhys, his grandfather Richard, and the man who had risked his life to take in the Holt girls and save their mother one cold winter night in 1803. James Makepeace.

And he was given his own name, William, because Rhys and Sabrina rather liked it.

Susannah and Sylvie of course made much of how Sabrina had been the last to marry but had contrived to be the first to have a baby. But since she was married to The Libertine, of all people, everyone said it was to be expected. She didn't even blush anymore when people said things like that.

The pews were full. Sylvie and Tom and little Jamie Shaughnessy, who kept wanting to touch the baby, his cousin. Kit and Susannah. The General and Daisy Jones. Lady Mary Capstraw and the beaming Paul. Wyndham had even come, grousing cheerfully about the need to leave London for the *country*. But as he was going to be Godfather to a future earl, it was the least he could do.

And besides, it was just about the only way he'd see Rhys these days, because Rhys was all but a country squire.

Anna Holt sat in the last pew of the church and gazed at those windows. Unlike Sabrina, Sylvie, and Susannah, she didn't feel Richard in this little church, truly. She and Richard . . . well, spending time in churches wasn't, frankly, how the two of them had managed to have three beautiful, passionate girls one right after the other. Anna smiled to herself, remembering just how they'd managed that. *That* was how she wanted to remember Richard.

She wished, however—she allowed herself one brief indulgent wish, because she found wishing, on the whole, unproductive—he could have seen this very moment, a rare enough moment, where her family was suspended in happiness. Happiness was so transitory, she knew. It had an ebb and flow, and anything could shatter it, alter it, or turn it into something deeper and richer. It helped to have a few purely happy memories to rifle through on long, dark nights.

And yet, in a way, even though he wasn't here today, Richard had all but ensured his girls would find these extraordinary men by leaving a legacy of challenge and intrigue for them to overcome.

Anna closed her eyes for a moment and pictured him and let the warmth coming in through the windows touch her eyelids. *I miss you,* she told Richard in her mind.

When she opened them again, a man was sitting next to her, regarding her with a sort of gently amused interest. She met his gaze for a moment, strangely not startled.

She had the oddest sensation that this man was a gift from Richard.

He looked very much like Kit Whitelaw, only considerably older and—she felt a bit disloyal to think it, but still—considerably more handsome. A mane of gray hair, thick brows, eyes not quite so blue as Kit's. Lines where lines ought to be in the face of a man his age. An elegant face.

Their eyes met for a time, and in moments Anna felt a sweet bemusement she hadn't known in nearly two decades, a curl of anticipation deeper than mere attraction.

She extended her hand finally, remembering that one of them ought to do something, and he very nearly gave a start. He bowed over it. "The Earl of Westphall," he told her.

Ah, naturally. This was Kit's father. The immensely important Earl of Westphall had come to Gorringe to attend the christening of her first grandchild.

And so it seemed she had a weakness for politicians.

"Anna Holt," she told him.

And Anna thought: *Perhaps something of interest can be found in churches, after all.*

ABOUT THE AUTHOR

San Francisco native Julie Anne Long originally set out to be a rock star when she grew up (and she has the guitars in the back of her closet and the gig stories to prove it), but writing was always her first love. She began her academic career as a Journalism major, before realizing Creative Writing was probably a better fit for her freewheeling imagination and overdeveloped sense of whimsy. When playing guitar at midnight in dank sticky clubs finally lost its, ahem, *charm,* Julie realized she could incorporate all the best things about being in a band—namely, drama, passion, and men with unruly hair—into novels, while also indulging her love of history and research. Her first novel, *The Runaway Duke,* was published in 2004, and since then her books have been nominated for numerous awards, including the Romance Writers of America Rita, Romantic Times Reviewer's Choice, Bookseller's Best, the Holt Medallion, and the Quill.

THE DISH

Where authors give you the inside scoop!

♥ ♥ ♥ ♥ ♥ ♥ ♥ ♥ ♥ ♥ ♥ ♥ ♥ ♥ ♥ ♥ ♥

From the desk of Andrea Pickens

After watching all the old James Bond movies more times than I care to count, I began to think . . . why is it that the boys get to have all the fun? They always get to be the spies. Or the pirates. Swashbuckling swagger, daredevil heroics, drop-dead good looks—yes, Johnny Depp and Orlando Bloom cut a fine figure with their flashing swords, but I found myself secretly wanting Keira Knightley to pick up a saber and kick some ass, too. So, I decided to turn tradition on its ear and create a trio of leading ladies capable of beating the men at their own game.

Select Young Ladies, a secret school for Hellion Heroes. I chose to set it in Regency England because that era is so richly romantic. It was a world aswirl in silks, seduction, and the intrigue of the Napoleonic Wars. A time when old ideas were constantly clashing with new radical ones. What better place for an unconventional female to test her mettle?

Siena, the star of THE SPY WORE SILK (on sale now), is given a perilous assignment: unmask a clever traitor lurking among London's wealthiest peers before he strikes again. Her only clue is that the man she seeks belongs to an exclusive club of art collectors. And so, armed with only her wits, her blades, and her body, she journeys to a remote castle where the club's members have gathered for a special auction. However, her prime suspect, the enigmatic Earl of Kirtland, proves a far more dangerous opponent that she ever imagined. Is she a match for his steel?

My research included a good deal of poking around Portobello Road, that delightful stretch of antiques markets in the Notting Hill section of London, where one can spend hours poring over all the wonderful vintage jewelry, engravings, weaponry, and fashions of the time. And for those who wish to get a peek at the wilds of Dartmoor, check my Web site www.andreapickensonline.com for photos of the estate that inspired Marquand Castle.

Enjoy!

Andrea Pickens

♥ ♥ ♥ ♥ ♥ ♥ ♥ ♥ ♥ ♥ ♥ ♥ ♥ ♥ ♥ ♥

From the desk of Candy Halliday

The fun part in writing any series is the opportunity to reunite the characters from the previous book. That was certainly fun for me in the Housewives Fantasy Club series.

Revisiting Woodberry Park and being back together with sassy Fantasy Club members Zada, Tish, Jen, and Alicia was a reunion I didn't want to miss. However, in the second book of the series I wanted to make sure outcast Alicia in YOUR BED OR MINE? finally got her chance at happily ever after.

So . . . THEY'RE BACK!

In the sequel DINNER FIRST, ME LATER? (on sale now) the Housewives Fantasy Club is back in session—turning up the heat and keeping life steamy in Woodberry Park. A little too hot and steamy if you ask Alicia!

How can she possibly tell her best friends and neighbors that the new hunky celebrity who moved into their quaint little cul-de-sac was once her secret fantasy crush?

No way! Alicia vows.

Her Fantasy Club pals would never let her live it down. Besides, that fantasy ended when Jake "The

Rake" Sims went from respected Cubs baseball star to infamous playboy and underwear model—NOT the type of man Alicia wants on her gotta-have-him list!

Or so Alicia didn't think.

But what would you do if your celebrity fantasy crush (and admit it, we all have one) offered you:

A. One night of passion.

B. No strings attached.

And, C. He gave you his promise no one would ever know?

Would you go for it? Or would you chicken out?

I'm not going to tell you what I would do if Matthew McConaughey made me that offer. But I do hope you will visit Woodberry Park again, or choose to meet the Housewives Fantasy Club for the first time in DINNER FIRST, ME LATER? See for yourself if Alicia fulfilled her fantasy with the new bad boy from across the street.

One thing, however, you can be assured—once the Housewives Fantasy Club calls the meeting to order the nights in Woodberry Park are always hot and steamy.

Happy reading!

Candy Halliday

www.candyhalliday.com

Want to know more about romances at
Warner Books and Warner Forever?
Get the scoop online!

WARNER'S ROMANCE HOMEPAGE

Visit us at www.warnerforever.com for all the
latest news, reviews, and chapter excerpts!

NEW AND UPCOMING TITLES

Each month we feature our new titles
and reader favorites.

CONTESTS AND GIVEAWAYS

We give away galleys, autographed copies,
and all kinds of fun stuff.

AUTHOR INFO

You'll find bios, articles, and links to personal
Web sites for all your favorite authors—and
so much more!

THE BUZZ

Sign up for our monthly romance newsletter,
and be the first to read all about it!